SNOW BRIDE

Nancy seems to have found her happily ever after. She is surrounded by family and engaged to marry the man of her dreams. But when her fiancé's father insists they wait a year to prove that their love is true, the young couple's feelings are put to the test.

The path of true love never runs smooth, but as the snow begins to fall, Nancy will need to trust her heart for her Christmas wishes to come true.

SPECIAL MESSAGE TO READERS

DILLY COURT

SNOW BRIDE

Complete and Unabridged

MAGNA
Leicester

First published in Great Britain in 2022 by
HarperCollins*Publishers* Ltd.
London

First Ulverscroft Edition
published 2022
by arrangement with
HarperCollins*Publishers* Ltd.
London

This novel is entirely a work of fiction.
The names, characters and incidents portrayed in it are
the work of the author's imagination. Any resemblance
to actual persons, living or dead, events or localities is
entirely coincidental.

*A catalogue record for this book is available
from the British Library.*

ISBN 978–0–7505–4914–1

Published by
Ulverscroft Limited
Anstey, Leicestershire

Printed and bound in Great Britain by
TJ Books Ltd., Padstow, Cornwall

This book is printed on acid-free paper

For Suzanne Muggeridge

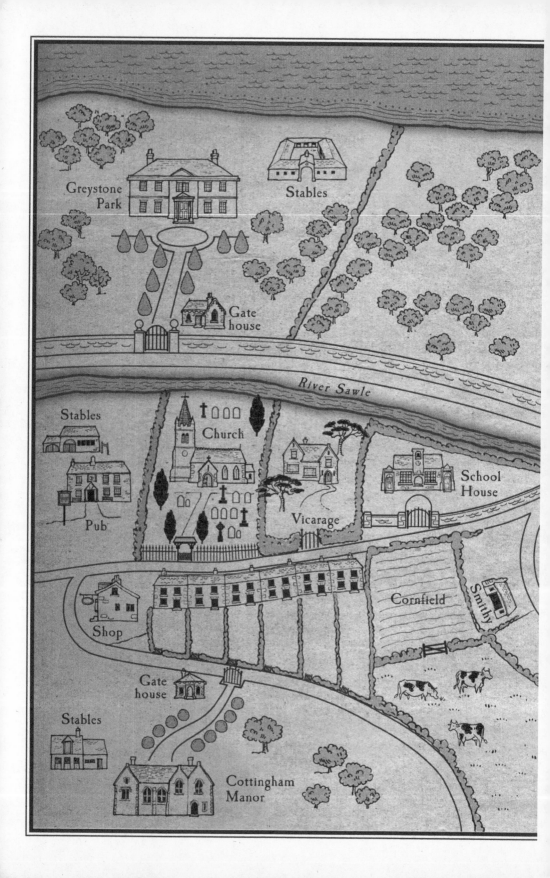

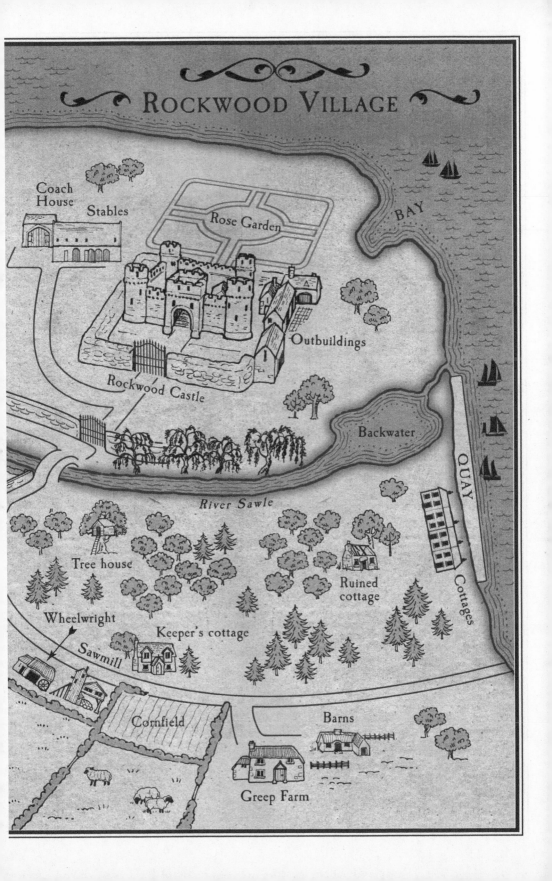

❧ The Carey Family ❧

Lady Hester Carey m Vice-Admiral Sir Lucius Carey m Lady Prudence Carey
(Neé Dodridge) (1776–1853) (deceased)
(b. 1804)

Claude de Marney m Felicia Carey m Wilfred Carey
(b. 1805) (b. 1806) (1800–1851)

Sarah m Bertram (Bertie)   Captain Alexander m Rosalind (Rosie)   Piers Blanchard   Walter m Louise   Patricia (Patsy) m I. Sir Michael
Farthing   Carey   Blanchard   Carey   (b. 1825)   Carey   Shaw   Carey   Greystone
(1829–1847) (b. 1827) (b. 1827) (b. 1830) (b. 1832) (b. 1827) (b. 1834) (b. 1806–1859)
                                                                        m 2. Leo Wilder
                                                                        (b. 1829)

Tommy Carey   Rory   Phoebe   Adela (Dolly)   Charlotte
(b. 1844)   Blanchard   Blanchard   Blanchard   Carey
            (b. 1856) (b. 1858) (b. 1854) (b. 1859)

1

The Orangery, Dorrington Place, April 1863

Nancy gazed in delight at the beautiful emerald and diamond ring on the fourth finger of her left hand. 'It really is beautiful, Freddie.'

'I had it made especially for you, my darling. Nothing is too good for my future wife.'

Nancy clutched his hand and raised it to her cheek. 'I can't believe that your papa agreed to this. He was so set against us marrying.'

Freddie raised her to her feet and kissed her. 'I would marry you no matter what, Nancy. I've loved you since the day we met and I will love you until my dying day.' He kissed her again, releasing her with a reluctant sigh. 'I will remember these moments for ever. But now we really should rejoin the others. I want to announce our betrothal.'

Nancy straightened her ball gown with trembling fingers. Her heart was beating so fast that she was breathless and dizzy with excitement, as well as a certain amount of trepidation. Freddie seemed convinced that there would be no objections to their union, but she was not so sure. Lord and Lady Dorrington had made it clear from the outset that a young woman who had started life as a foundling was no match for their only son. Nancy's newly discovered status as the daughter of the late Sir Oliver Greystone, and her inheritance of the Greystone family estate, seemed to have worked its magic with Freddie's mother, but Lord Dorrington was another matter.

The scent of the hothouse orange blossom filled the air as Nancy took a deep breath.

'All right, Freddie. But perhaps we should wait until you've told your papa.'

A shadow dulled the tender look in his blue eyes for a few seconds but was replaced almost immediately with his charming smile. 'Of course. You're absolutely right. We'll do that now. I can't wait to make our engagement official.'

They walked arm in arm through the elegant, candlelit corridors to the drawing room, which was furnished in the style of Louis Quinze with an eclectic addition of pieces chosen for their comfort as well as their beauty. Lord Dorrington sat in his favourite wingback chair by the fire, resting his feet on a tapestry-covered footstool. Lady Dorrington was seated at a table with a group of people playing cards. The rest of the party had broken away into small groups, leaving Felicia de Marney and her husband, Claude, chatting to the gentleman who had promised to mention that the world-famous opera star might be interested in Mr Chant's next production at the Theatre Royal in Brighton. Nancy was not related to Felicia, but she had been brought up in Rockwood Castle and adopted into the Carey family, of which Felicia was a senior member. Nancy could tell by the flush on Felicia's cheeks and her animated reactions that she had been drinking a little more than was good for her. As always, Claude sat back, smiling indulgently.

'I'll ask Papa to give us a few minutes in private. Then we can make the announcement to everyone here.' Freddie gave Nancy's hand an encouraging squeeze and he strolled over to speak to his father.

Nancy waited anxiously. Her hopes of Lord Dorrington's approval were dashed by the expression on his face, but he rose to his feet and walked purposefully towards her. Freddie followed his father but she could tell by his worried frown that all was not well.

'Come to my study,' Lord Dorrington said abruptly. He left the room, striding through the wide, candlelit corridors.

Freddie grasped Nancy by the hand. 'Don't worry. All will be well, I promise you that.' He led Nancy into his father's study and pulled up a chair for her.

The oak-panelled room was lit only by the glow of the fire, but the shadows seemed to hover menacingly over Nancy's shoulder. The smell of cigar smoke lingered in the air with a hint of fine cognac and wet gundog. Lord Dorrington's faithful black Labrador lay stretched out in front of the fire. Nancy raised her hand to brush a stray curl back from her forehead and the diamonds in her ring blazed in the firelight.

'You don't have to wave that piece of jewellery in my face, young lady.' Lord Dorrington gave her a searching look. 'So this is what you wanted to tell me, Frederick. I had a feeling that you were planning something of the sort.'

Freddie slipped his arm around Nancy's shoulder. 'Mama is on our side.'

'I am the head of the family. You might have convinced your mother that this is a good match, but I am not so easily persuaded.'

'But I love Nancy, Papa. She is all I ever wanted.'

'Sentimental rubbish.' Lord Dorrington moved to the desk and selected a cigar from a humidor. He rolled it in his fingers, holding it to his ear with an appreciative smile. 'The best Havana. There's nothing like it.' He lit the cigar with a spill from the fire.

'I love Freddie,' Nancy said firmly. 'I will make him a good wife, but I want both you and Lady Dorrington to feel happy with the situation.'

Lord Dorrington puffed cigar smoke into the air. 'Do you now? Well, I am not happy *with the situation*, as you put it. Freddie has a duty to marry well and produce heirs to the title and the estate. Lady Letitia Barclay has an impeccable pedigree, to say nothing of a huge fortune. She has been our choice of bride for some time, and continues to be so.'

'I will marry the person I love, P-Papa,' Freddie said heatedly. 'Nancy is every bit as good at Letitia.'

Lord Dorrington pulled the buttoned leather chair from behind his desk and sat down. 'I've no doubt that she is a perfectly amiable young woman, but that is not enough.'

'Mama has undoubtedly told you that Nancy is the heiress to the Greystone estate and she comes from a good family. You can have no objection on those grounds.'

'Have you asked her guardian's permission, Frederick?'

Freddie shot a sideways glance in Nancy's direction. 'Her papa died years ago, sir.'

'I know the circumstances of Sir Oliver's death. It is not something to boast about. His reputation was already damaged by his profligate lifestyle, and his death was ignominious.'

'That has nothing to do with Nancy, sir. She is blameless and I love her.'

'I suppose Bertie — I mean Sir Bertram Carey — is my guardian,' Nancy said slowly. 'I have lived in

Rockwood Castle since I was a child. He thinks a lot of Freddie. I'm sure he won't object.'

'Taken in as a servant.' Lord Dorrington chewed on the end of his cigar. 'I know the circumstances, Miss Sunday, or I suppose I should call you Miss Greystone?'

'Either, if it pleases you, sir. I am not ashamed of my past. All I can tell you is that I love Freddie with all my heart. If you and Lady Dorrington agree to our union I will do my best to make Freddie happy.'

Lord Dorrington frowned. 'Words, miss. Just words. You have no idea how to run a household or manage servants. You've never lived at Greystone Park so how do you think you could eventually be mistress of Dorrington Place?'

'P-Papa, that isn't fair,' Freddie protested. 'You are n-not going to die for a very long time. Nancy and I will have made a life for ourselves long before that happens.'

Lord Dorrington puffed on his cigar for what seemed an interminable amount of time to Nancy. She was beginning to think that whatever either of them said would make very little difference. Lord Dorrington had already made up his mind.

'Please, F-Father.' Freddie reached out to grasp Nancy's hand. 'I'll d-do whatever you wish if you will just give us your blessing.'

Lord Dorrington turned his head slowly to give his son a straight look. 'Have you considered the fact that Miss Sunday is a minor? She cannot marry unless her guardian approves. You will have to gain Sir Bertram's consent as well as my own.'

'Then we'll travel to Rockwood Castle tomorrow, Papa. I'm sure I can convince Sir Bertram that Nancy

5

will be loved and treated with the greatest respect in our family.'

'Bertie won't stand in our way,' Nancy said tentatively.

'But I might.' Lord Dorrington turned to give her a stern look. 'What would you be prepared to do in order to gain my approval of this match?'

Nancy held her head high. 'Anything you ask, my lord.'

'This isn't n-necessary,' Freddie said angrily. 'I-I w-won't have N-Nancy s-subjected to this k-kind of interrogation.'

'I will do as I see fit.' Lord Dorrington flicked ash from his cigar into the fire. 'You say you've inherited Greystone Park, Miss Sunday?'

'Yes, my lord.'

'Then here is my proposition and there is no room for argument. It is either yes or no.'

Nancy exchanged anxious glances with Freddie, but she nodded in assent. 'I'm listening, my lord.'

'You will take up residence in Greystone Park and run the household and the estate for a whole year, with the assistance of a good land agent, of course.'

Nancy eyed him warily. 'I might have some opposition from the late Sir Michael's daughters, particularly Christina. She insists that the land belongs to her and Sylvia because it was left to them in their father's will.'

'That is something the solicitors will fight out between themselves. In the meantime what I suggest still stands. It will just be one of the things you will have to learn how to deal with.'

'I'll help you, my darling,' Freddie said eagerly. 'I'll be there for you always.'

Lord Dorrington shook his head. 'No, you will not. If Nancy is to prove herself worthy enough to become mistress of Dorrington Place, she will do this on her own. You are not to see each other for the full year.'

'That's impossible, Papa.' Freddie faced his father angrily. 'You can't impose those terms upon us. I won't stand for it.'

'I see that you lose the impediment in your speech when you're angry, Frederick. Perhaps this will make a man of you and teach you to stand up for yourself and those you love.' Lord Dorrington turned his attention to Nancy. 'How old are you, Miss Sunday?'

'I am nineteen and my name is Nancy Greystone, Lord Dorrington.'

A glimmer of a smile lit his eyes but was replaced by a stern frown. 'You have spirit, Miss Greystone. Prove to me that you can become the mistress of Greystone Park and I will withdraw my objection to the match.'

Freddie stepped in between them. 'If Sir Bertram gives us his blessing I will marry Nancy whether you agree or not.'

'And you will lose your inheritance. Your cousin Cedric is next in line.'

'That is not fair, my lord,' Nancy cried passionately. 'You can't disown Freddie for such a petty reason.'

'It's all right, Nancy.' Freddie drew her to the protection of his arms. 'If Sir Bertram gives his permission, Father, I will marry Nancy, with or without your blessing.'

'You shouldn't have said that,' Nancy said in a low voice as Freddie ushered her out of the room. 'Your papa might be strict but he wants the best for you. After all, he doesn't know me.'

'But I do.' Freddie closed the door. 'I know my own

7

mind and you are worth more to me than money or position.'

Nancy slipped from his warm grasp. 'I'm not going to allow you to sacrifice everything for me, Freddie.' She took off the ring and placed it in his hand. 'Keep this for me for when I've earned it.'

'Don't take what Papa said to heart, Nancy. I won't allow this to come between us.'

'You mustn't tell anyone about this, Freddie. Tomorrow we'll go and see Bertie. I value his opinion and I'll do whatever he suggests. After all, a year isn't a lifetime. Maybe your papa is right and I do need to prove myself.'

Freddie closed her fingers over the ring. 'I can't believe this is happening, but I won't give you up, Nancy. We'll fight this together.'

She stood on tiptoe to kiss him on the cheek. 'Of course we will. I will make your papa eat his words if it takes a year, so be it.' She tucked her hand in the crook of his arm. 'In the meantime we are still together.'

'If you live at Greystone Park without me I'll go back to the old keeper's cottage in the grounds of Rockwood Castle. Bertie won't object and at least I'll be on hand if you need me.'

'You don't have to do that, Freddie.'

'Oh, yes, I do. I am not going to leave you to go through this alone.'

* * *

April showers followed them all the way to Rockwood Castle, but just as they entered the grounds the sun burst out from its prison of dark clouds. Suddenly everything glittered and shone as if the trees and

8

hedgerows were hung with diamonds. Nancy caught her breath as she gazed out of the coach windows. She might not be a Carey born and bred, but this had been her home for almost ten years of her life and she loved every moss-covered stone.

She turned to Freddie, holding out her hand. 'Bertie will give his permission. I know he will.'

'I'll abide by anything he says,' Freddie said gently. 'I know he's a good man and all the family love you, as they should. I don't want you to go against them in any way, but I will be by your side no matter what. If we have to wait a year or even two, I will be patient.'

She leaned over and kissed him lightly on the lips. 'Thank goodness Felicia and Claude decided to stay on at Dorrington for another day. It was hard enough keeping things secret from her at breakfast this morning. She would have kept on and on at me until I told her everything.'

'If Bertie gives his permission we will go back to Dorrington Place and I'll speak to my father again. I'm sure we can come to a compromise because I don't want you living at Greystone Park on your own.'

'I'll do whatever it takes to make your papa give his consent freely. I love you, Freddie.'

Freddie's reply was drowned by the rumble of the carriage wheels on the cobblestones of the bailey as the coachman drew the horses to a halt at the front entrance. Nancy looked out of the window and smiled to see Jarvis standing in the open doorway, looking as smart and upright as ever despite his seventy-odd years. James, the footman, hurried out to open the carriage door and Nancy alighted, followed by Freddie.

'I need to speak to Sir Bertram, Jarvis,' Nancy said

hurriedly. 'Where will I find him?'

'I believe he is in his study, Miss Nancy.' Jarvis's eyes flickered in Freddie's direction. 'Shall I announce you?'

'No need, thank you, Jarvis.' Nancy beckoned to Freddie. 'The sooner we get this over, the better.' She made her way across the grand entrance hall, automatically patting the visor on the suit of armour reputed to have been worn by Sir Denys Carey in his last battle. As a child she had seen other members of the family treat the ancient artefact with a mixture of respect and affection, and it was a habit she had adopted.

She knocked on the study door and entered when Bertie answered. He looked up with a surprised smile.

'Nancy, what can I do for you?' His gaze travelled to Freddie and his smile widened. 'Good morning, Ashton.'

Freddie went to stand beside Nancy, taking her hand in a firm clasp.

'Good morning, Sir Bertram.'

Bertie raised an eyebrow. 'We are very formal. I take it that this is something serious. Do sit down, both of you.'

Freddie pulled up a chair for Nancy and one for himself.

Nancy sat down. 'Bertie, I won't beat about the bush. Freddie has asked me to marry him and we've come to ask you for your permission to announce our engagement.'

'I love Nancy, sir,' Freddie said earnestly. 'I will do everything in my power to make her happy.'

Bertie leaned back in his seat, looking from one to the other. When he did not answer immediately Nancy felt her heart sink and she tightened her grasp

10

on Freddie's hand.

'I know I'm very young, Bertie, but I love Freddie and I will do my utmost to make him a good wife.'

'You've just come from Dorrington Place,' Bertie said thoughtfully. 'I take it that you've asked Lord Dorrington's permission?'

Nancy and Freddie exchanged worried glances.

'My f-father s-said we should get your p-permission, sir.'

'I thought he had other plans for you, Dorrington.'

Nancy could see that Bertie was going to take some persuading. 'He had, but we managed to convince him that we were serious.'

'And did he agree without reservations?'

'N-not exactly,' Freddie admitted reluctantly.

Nancy leaned forward, fixing Bertie with a pleading look. 'He said that he wants me to take over Greystone Park and manage it on my own for a year. He wants me to prove that I am capable of becoming mistress of Dorrington Place in the future. He also said that Freddie and I were not to have any contact during that time.'

Bertie smiled. 'I thought there might be a proviso. Well, I can see the sense in his proposal, Nancy. You are very young and, to be honest, you haven't been brought up to take on such responsibility.'

'Nancy will always have me by her side, sir,' Freddie said fervently. 'I will n-never allow her to be burdened with anything she cannot manage easily.'

'A year is not such a long time. You have inherited Greystone Park and all that goes with it, Nancy. I think perhaps you should do as Lord Dorrington suggests. An inheritance like that is a huge responsibility and the lives of the tenants depend upon how well you manage the estate. Then there is the matter of dealing with servants.'

'I can learn, Bertie.'

'Of course you can, and to be honest I think Lord Dorrington's idea is eminently sensible.'

'So are you saying you won't give me permission to marry Freddie for a year?'

'For what it's worth, Nancy. After all, I am not your legal guardian, but as far as I am concerned you are part of my family. I care about you and I want only the best for you, and if you love Freddie, as you say you do, you would not want to come between him and his father.'

'But this is my home, Bertie. I won't know what to do with myself all alone at Greystone Park.'

'I think that was Lord Dorrington's point, Nancy. Are you capable of handling such a responsibility?'

'I will abide by your decision, Sir Bertram,' Freddie said slowly. 'It's not something I want, but I will be on hand to help Nancy in any way I can.'

Nancy looked up at him aghast. 'Freddie! Are you saying you agree to waiting for a whole year? I can't believe that you will allow us to be dictated to for no good reason.' Nancy stood up and left the room. She was close to tears of anger and resentment. Of all people, Bertie should have been on her side.

Freddie emerged from the study. 'Don't be upset, Nancy. We can do this together.' He went to put his arm around her shoulders but she pushed him away.

'You didn't stand up to either of them, Freddie. If you really loved me you would have defied your father, no matter what he threatened.'

'It was not an idle threat, Nancy,' Freddie said seriously. 'I am sorry, but I know my father meant what he said. I want to pass Dorrington Place and the estate on to our children when we have them. My cousin Cedric has no interest in Dorrington or the tenants. He will gamble away every penny.'

Nancy gazed at him in horror. 'You care more about your home than you do about me. I release you from your promise to marry me.'

'No, don't say that. I love you more than anything. I'm just being practical. Please take the ring.' He took it from his inside pocket and held it in the palm of his hand.

The jewel sparkled invitingly, but Nancy shook her head. 'No, Freddie. I will take my place at Greystone Park, and if, in a year's time, we both feel the same you may propose to me again.'

'Nancy, please . . .'

'No. I'm going to find Rosalind. She'll understand and she will help me. Go away, please, Freddie. You chose this path, so I must follow it on my own.'

2

Nancy bit back tears as she ignored Freddie's pleas for her to reconsider. She walked away, leaving him standing outside the study, and she did not dare to look back. If she had seen his dejected look she knew she would weaken and run into his arms, but that would be tantamount to admitting that he, his father and Bertie were in the right. Lord Dorrington's ultimatum had shaken and upset her more than she cared to admit. She needed to find Rosalind, who would understand without the need for long explanations.

Rosalind Blanchard, now the mother of three mischievous and adorable children, had taken Nancy under her wing when she was just nine years old. Rosie would always be her best friend and mentor, and Nancy simply had to find her now. She searched the ground floor, but only came across housemaids fulfilling their normal duties. She heard Hester's voice emanating from the blue parlour, but Hester was the last person Nancy wanted to talk to at that moment. Perhaps Hester's overt disapproval of Nancy's unquestioned inclusion in the family was due to the fact that Hester had started out as a servant, graduating to housekeeper, and culminating in marriage to the late Sir Lucien Carey.

Nancy dodged into the music room and was about to escape through the French doors into the rose garden, when she spotted Bertie's son, her childhood friend and companion, Tommy Carey. He was striding

14

towards the door with a swagger in his step. She went to open the door and let him in.

'Tommy, what are you doing skulking around the rose garden?'

'Skulking?' Tommy laughed. 'No such thing. I just wanted to get into the castle without going past Jarvis.'

Momentarily forgetting her own problems, Nancy smiled. 'What have you done now, Tommy? I know that look.'

He seized her round the waist and swung her off her feet. 'You'll never guess.'

'You're probably right. Have you robbed a bank?'

'Not quite. I've joined the army, Nancy. I used the money that Great-grandpapa Lucien left me and bought myself a commission in the cavalry.'

'Tommy, you didn't! What will Bertie say?'

'My papa can hardly complain, considering he was in the army himself.'

'And that is where he received his injuries that left him a cripple, Tommy. Do you think he will want that for you?'

Tommy grasped her by the shoulders. 'Look at me, Nancy. I was sent down from university. I'm not clever and I have no inclination to run the estate. What else will I do with my life?'

'You have a wonderful home and a family who love you. Please don't do this, Tommy.'

He released her with a kiss on the forehead. 'Too late. It's done. I am an ensign now but I will soon earn promotion. If you had loved me instead of Freddie I might have stayed here and learned how to run things, but I have to find my own way.'

'Tommy, don't put the blame on me. I do love you, you know I do.'

15

'Like a brother,' he said with a rueful smile.

'Yes, that's true, but I don't want you to go away and risk your life.'

'Marry me, then, and not Freddie.'

'That's not funny, Tommy. But I do wish you would reconsider you choice.'

'As I said, it's too late. I've signed up and my uniform is being made as we speak. Just wait until you see me in it, Nancy. You might change your mind.' He held her at arm's length, eyeing her curiously. 'What's wrong?'

She shook her head, avoiding his searching look. 'Nothing.'

'Your eyes are red. Who's made you cry? I'll find them and make them put things right.'

'I'm all right, really, Tommy.'

'No, you are not. You can't fool me, Nancy. I know you as well as I know myself.' Tommy led her to a window seat. 'Sit down and tell me.'

Nancy sank down onto the chintz-covered cushions. 'Freddie and I were engaged, but Lord Dorrington said he wouldn't give his consent unless I took over Greystone Park and ran it for a year on my own.'

Tommy frowned. 'That ain't so bad, is it?'

'Freddie and I wouldn't be allowed to see each other during that time. I had to prove that I could be mistress of a great house before Lord Dorrington would accept me into the family. The worst part is that Bertie agrees with him.'

'Does he, by Jupiter? Well, the old man never fails to surprise me. I take it you don't fancy such an arrangement?'

'Greystone Park might belong to me in theory but it's not my home, Tommy. This is the place where I feel most comfortable. I don't know if I could manage the household at Greystone, and then there are the tenants. I don't know anything about running an estate. What if I fail?'

'Marry me and become a soldier's wife. Think of all the adventures we could have if we're sent abroad.'

'Are you ever serious, Tommy?'

'What makes you think I am not? You know I've always loved you, Nancy. We would do well together.'

His eager expression drew a reluctant smile from her. 'You are so sweet, Tommy. I do love you, but not in the way you might want.'

'Well, for a start I wouldn't make you do anything that you didn't want to do. I wouldn't lock you up in dreary old Greystone Park for a whole year. I would take you to balls and picnics.'

'And no doubt I would have to sit on a hill with the generals and officers' wives while you got yourself killed on the battlefield.'

He laughed. 'I didn't have that picture in mind, to be sure.'

Nancy stiffened. 'I can hear Freddie calling me. I don't want to see him yet, Tommy.'

'Your wish is my command, Miss Sunday. Never mind the Greystone name, I will always think of you as my sunny day.' Tommy grinned and pulled a face. 'All right, it wasn't funny — but I am serious. Wait here and I'll go and charm Cook into giving us some food. Talking of picnics has made me hungry.'

'Tommy, it's early April. We can't go for a picnic.'

'Yes, we can. We'll go to the tree house in the woods where we used to hide when we didn't want Hester to find us. You are still wearing your cape, in case you've forgotten.'

17

'I had completely.' Nancy sighed. 'It's been an upsetting morning. I was so happy last evening when Freddie proposed and gave me a beautiful diamond and emerald ring.'

'I hope you threw it at him, Nancy.' Tommy opened the French door. 'I'll go round the back way so that I don't bump into anyone. Come with me and we'll skulk about like criminals. It will take your mind off Freddie and diamond rings.'

Nancy could hear Freddie's footsteps drawing nearer, but she could not face him. She knew that he would do what he considered was right by her and by his father, which was a decision she could not accept. Perhaps she might come round to his way of thinking, but at the moment all she wanted to do was to escape and join Tommy on a picnic, as she had done when they were children. Perhaps if she distanced herself from everyone for an hour or two she might be able to think more logically. She followed Tommy out into the rose garden where signs of burgeoning life were visible in a sudden burst of sunshine. The snowdrops in sheltered places had given way to pools of yellow primroses, and tightly furled buds sprouted on the climbing roses. Ominous rainclouds hung over the horizon, but the sun was warm on her face as she waited for Tommy to work his charm on Mrs Jackson in the kitchen.

An hour later, replete after a meal of cold pie, jam tarts and seed cake, washed down with cider from a flagon that Tommy had purloined from the butler's pantry, Nancy leaned back against the log wall of the tree house. There were patches of damp where the roof leaked and the whole thing swayed ominously in the strong breeze, but Nancy felt relaxed and almost philosophical.

'You're looking happier now,' Tommy said, smiling. 'I knew you would be better if we came here. D'you remember how we used to pretend we were pirates or fugitives from the law?'

'I do. We were children then, Tommy. We're adults now and you are going to fight for Queen and country. I have to take up my responsibilities.'

'So have you decided to comply with Lord Dorrington and my papa's wishes?'

'Freddie seemed to think it was the only way.'

'You are not Freddie. You have a mind and soul of your own, Nancy. What do you say?'

'I love being with you, Tommy. This has been fun, but I know I can't be a child for ever. Perhaps I owe it to everyone to do my best. I will move my belongings to Greystone Park and I'll do my very best to prove myself.'

'You don't have to prove anything to me,' Tommy said stoutly. 'But if that's what you wish I will visit you whenever I can get away from the barracks.'

'That will be wonderful, Tommy. At least no one can criticise us for being together. I'll keep a room ready for you at all times.' Nancy scrambled for her feet. 'It's no use, I must go back to the castle and face everyone.'

Tommy eyed her warily. 'What will you tell them?'

'That I agree to their terms. What else can I do, Tommy? Apart from running away with you, that is?' Nancy managed a smile. 'A year isn't such a long time, after all.'

★ ★ ★

When Nancy arrived at Greystone Park she was surprised to see the servants lined up on the steps outside, headed by Foster, the butler, Mrs Simpson, the housekeeper, Mrs Banks, the cook, and Ivy Lugg, the longest-serving maidservant, as well as three other young girls, who bobbed curtseys as if Nancy was royalty. They stood stiffly to attention while Nancy acknowledged them as she negotiated the steps and entered the house.

'Might I be so bold as to welcome you to your new home, Miss Greystone?' Foster inclined his head.

'Thank you, Foster.' Nancy hesitated. 'I will need your help at times. I hope I might depend upon you and your years of experience.'

'It goes without saying, Miss Greystone. I took the liberty of having the master bedroom made ready for you.'

'Thank you, Foster.' Nancy turned her head at the sound of horses' hoofs and carriage wheels on the gravel outside. She was surprised to see the Carey family crest on the carriage door and equally surprised when James leaped down from his seat beside Jim Gurney to open the door.

Rosalind Blanchard alighted, followed by her three young children, Adela, known as Dolly, Rory and Phoebe. Freddie dismounted from his horse and handed the reins to one of the stable boys from Greystone Park.

'We couldn't allow you to arrive without a proper send-off,' Rosalind said, smiling. 'The children wanted to know where you were going to live, and Freddie explained the rules of engagement to me.'

'It does feel like a bit of a battle,' Freddie acknowledged ruefully. 'But Rosie has been good enough to act as chaperone, and this visit really doesn't count.'

'I suppose we will get used to it,' Nancy said sadly. 'It still feels wrong.'

Rosalind gave her a hug. 'Never mind, dear. It's only for a year. You'll be surprised how quickly it will pass when you get accustomed to the change.'

'I haven't been here before, Nancy.' Eight-year-old Dolly rushed into the great hall, gazing round appreciatively. 'This is very grand. Much more elegant than Rockwood Castle.'

'It's not as old,' Nancy said hurriedly. 'The castle has a long history.'

Seven-year-old Rory rolled his eyes. 'No suits of armour. I like Rockwood better.'

Rosalind laughed and picked up four-year-old Phoebe, who had tripped and fallen. 'It's a very grand house. It was a pity to leave it empty. You will bring your youth and vitality to it, Nancy.'

'This isn't what I wanted,' Freddie said urgently. 'You do know that, don't you?'

She nodded. 'Yes, of course.'

'But you still think I should have stood up to my father, don't you?'

'You had your reasons, Freddie. I suppose a year will soon fly by, but I think Lord Dorrington hopes that we will drift apart.'

Foster had been standing back but he stepped closer, clearing his throat. 'Might I make a suggestion, Miss Greystone? Perhaps Mrs Blanchard and the children would care to take some refreshment in the drawing room.'

'Yes, of course. Thank you, Foster.' Nancy turned to Rosalind with a rueful smile. 'At least I know where the drawing room is situated.'

Rosalind linked arms with her. 'Don't worry, Nancy. You'll get used to being the mistress of the house. I'll do anything I can to help you.'

Freddie glanced out of the window. 'I think that's Christina Cottingham who has just stepped down from her carriage. Are you expecting her, Nancy?'

'No, of course not. How would she know that I was moving in today?'

Rosalind sighed. 'You know how fast news travels in Rockwood. Let's go to the drawing room and leave Foster to deal with her.' She turned to Foster with a persuasive smile. 'I think Mrs Cottingham might need to wait in the morning parlour for a while, Foster. We will be in the drawing room when she has had time to calm down.'

'Precisely so, Mrs Blanchard.' Foster walked off in his slow and stately manner, issuing instructions to the waiting maidservants as he made his way to the front entrance.

Nancy and Rosalind shooed the children towards the wide corridor that led to the drawing room with Freddie bringing up the rear.

'At least you know that Foster is on your side,' Rosalind said in a low voice as Freddie closed the drawing-room door. 'Children, be good and you may have cake and lemonade.'

Dolly eyed the pianoforte in the corner of the large room. 'Shall I do my practice, Mama? That looks like a splendid instrument, not like the one at home.'

'You must ask Nancy. It belongs to her now.'

Dolly sent a pleading look to Nancy, who smiled and nodded. 'Of course you may. You can come here whenever you like, Dolly. I could give you lessons.'

'Really?' Dolly's blue eyes sparkled with excitement. 'I would love that, Nancy.'

Rory scowled. 'I want to be a soldier like Tommy.'

'I suppose you know that he's bought himself a commission?' Rosalind said in a low voice.

'Yes, he told me.' Nancy glanced at Freddie. 'Tommy is like a brother to me.'

'If he was older I might be jealous,' Freddie said, smiling. 'But he's just a boy.'

'He'll be eighteen in November.' Rosalind sent him a meaningful look. 'Boys grow into men, Freddie. You might find you have competition.'

Nancy could see that Freddie was perturbed by Rosalind's answer, but she was saved embarrassment by the arrival of Ivy Lugg with a tray laden with tea, cakes and a jug of lemonade.

'Thank you, Ivy.' Nancy smiled and nodded. 'You may leave the tray. We'll help ourselves.'

Ivy bobbed a curtsey and left the room.

'There, that wasn't so difficult, was it?' Rosalind filled three glasses with lemonade and handed them to her children. 'You are a natural, Nancy. What do you think, Freddie?'

'I never doubted her.' Freddie accepted a cup of tea from Nancy. 'You were born to be a lady, Nancy. My father is too pig-headed to see it.'

Before anyone could answer, the door burst open and Christina Cottingham marched into the room. 'I knew it,' she said angrily. 'I won't be treated like a visitor in my own house.'

Nancy rose to her feet. 'This is my home now, Christina. I don't expect you to be happy about it, but I am the legal heir to the estate.'

'My solicitor has the matter in hand. I will fight this

through the courts if I have to.'

'Christina, there is no need for this animosity,' Rosalind said firmly. 'Nancy didn't ask to inherit everything. She did not know of her parentage until very recently, but there is no doubt that she is Sir Oliver and Lady Helena's daughter, and that makes her the legal heir to the estate. I'm afraid you will have to accept that.'

'Never.' Christina spat the word as if it had a bad taste.

'I've said all along that Sylvia will be welcome to come and live here when she is well again.' Nancy shot a glance in Freddie's direction, hoping that he would remain silent. She could see that he was poised to leap to her defence, but that was the last thing she wanted.

'My sister will never return to Greystone Park. In fact, she might not return to England at all.'

'She isn't worse, is she?' Nancy asked anxiously.

'Not that you would care if she was dying, but as it happens she is engaged to the Swiss specialist who is treating her. He has had some success in curing people with consumption and her condition has improved. They expect to be married in the autumn.'

'That's splendid news, Christina,' Rosalind said, smiling. 'I couldn't be more pleased.'

'Yes, I agree.' Nancy held her hand out to Christina. 'Can't we be friends? I didn't choose this path, but it seems that I am bound to follow it.'

Christina shook her head. 'We can never be friends. As far as I'm concerned you have stolen my birthright and I will never forgive you.' She turned on her heel and marched out of the room, slamming the door behind her.

24

Phoebe ran to her mother and burst into tears. 'Why is the lady cross, Mama?'

Freddie put his cup and saucer down with a thud. 'Christina mustn't be allowed to carry on in such a way. I'll deal with her.' He was about to rise to his feet but Nancy was already at the door.

'No, Freddie. This is my fight and I'm going to tell her so.' She left them before either Freddie or Rosalind could argue.

Christina was at the end of the corridor and about to enter the great hall. Nancy had to run to catch her up.

'Wait a minute, Mrs Cottingham. I did not ask for this position. It was thrust upon me, but that does not alter the fact that Greystone Park and the estate are mine. You may do as you please but do not come to my home uninvited. If you do I will leave instructions with the servants not to admit you under any circumstances.'

Christina spun round, her face contorted with rage. 'How dare you speak to me like that? I was born and raised in this house. It is mine by rights. My father left it to me and my sister in his will.'

'Which was invalid, due to the fact that Sir Oliver and his wife had a child. Sir Oliver's will has gone to probate. You may dispute my claim in court but that will cost a fortune and possibly bankrupt you with nothing to show for it in the end.'

'You are a parvenu and I will make sure everyone knows it. You will lose, Nancy Sunday. I promise you that.' Christina marched across the entrance hall to where Foster stood by the open door. She sailed past him with her nose in the air.

'Foster, on no account is Mrs Cottingham to be

25

allowed entry into the house,' Nancy said firmly.

Foster closed the door. 'Very good, Miss Greystone.'

His stony countenance twitched into a smile, but it was so fleeting that Nancy thought she must have imagined it.

She rejoined Rosalind and Freddie in the drawing room. Freddie had Rory at his side and was recounting a tale that had the boy's full attention, while Dolly practised her scales inexpertly on the pianoforte. Phoebe was seated beside her mother on the sofa, eating a slice of cake with obvious enjoyment.

'I've never seen Christina so angry,' Rosalind said softly. 'She is not someone who likes to be crossed, Nancy. She might try to do you harm, even if it is only by malicious gossip that she spreads around the village.'

'Let her try. I really don't care what she has to say. Everyone in Rockwood knows me and they know the truth. Christina can do little with that.'

'No, dear, but if Christina discovers that Lord Dorrington and Bertie want you to run the estate on your own she will be watching and waiting for you to make the smallest slip. That goes for seeing Freddie, too. She might even pay one of the servants to spy on you.'

'Surely not?' Freddie looked up, startled. 'She wouldn't go that far, would she?'

'The old Christina, the girl I grew up with, wouldn't have stooped so low,' Rosalind said sadly. 'Something has happened to her since she married Ossie. Maybe it was living with Glorina that turned her into the spiteful, vengeful woman she is today. I don't know, but all I can say is: be careful, Nancy.' Rosalind rose to her feet. 'We should go now, Freddie. This must be your last time together for a year, if you keep to your father's rules.'

'I won't be far away, if you need me.' Freddie raised Nancy's hand to his lips. 'I wish there was another way.'

* * *

That evening Nancy dined alone, sitting at the head of the mahogany table that would have seated thirty people in comfort. The flickering light of several dozen candles created moving shadows, as if past guests were hovering in the background. Nancy could almost hear them whispering. Were they calling her an imposter? An upstart who should never have crossed the threshold? Her appetite deserted her and she rose from the table, startling Ivy Lugg, who rushed forward.

'Is anything wrong, Miss Greystone?'

'No, Ivy. I've had enough, thank you.'

'Shall I bring coffee to the drawing room, Miss Greystone?'

'No, thank you, Ivy. I'm tired — I think I'll go to my room.'

'A cup of cocoa might help you sleep, miss.' Ivy smiled apologetically. 'I don't mean to be forward, but my ma always swore by a hot drink at bedtime.'

'No, thank you, Ivy. Maybe tomorrow night.' Nancy left the room and made her way upstairs to the master bedroom. Candles had been lit and a fire burned in the grate, but as she approached the four-poster bed with its ornate tester and heavy curtains, she felt a sudden shiver run down her spine. She had a vision of the mother she had never known giving birth in that very bed. She felt the pain and heard the cries of anguish although the room was in total silence. She was about to ring for Ivy to tell her to prepare another bedchamber, but she hesitated. Lord Dorrington's words came back to her and she knew she must earn the respect of the servants from the start. If she panicked on her first night in Greystone Park, she ran the risk of making herself appear weak and childish.

Nancy picked up a candlestick and held it so that she could see all four corners of the large room. There was a door she had not previously noticed and she assumed it must be a dressing room, or perhaps a very large cupboard. Plucking up all her courage, she crossed the carpeted floor and closed her hands around the doorknob. Her heart was beating twice as fast as usual as she slowly turned the cold brass sphere. The door opened slowly, creaking ominously . . .

3

A waft of cold air greeted Nancy as she opened the door fully. Her hand trembled as she held the candlestick high in order to look round the room, but she sighed with relief when she realised that it was just a dressing room. Dust motes danced in the candlelight and the air smelled oddly of lavender with the faintest hint of stale cigar smoke and expensive pomade. The walls were lined with cupboards and on the opposite wall a truckle bed was piled high with cushions and a patchwork quilt. Nancy made a space so that she could sit down and take off her boots. She had not changed for dinner, although she knew by the look on Foster's face that it was expected of her. She would do better tomorrow, but now she was overcome with exhaustion. She lay down and covered herself with the quilt. Through the open door she could see the comforting glow of the fire in the main bedroom. Moonbeams shimmered on the far wall, lulling her into a deep sleep.

'Miss Greystone.' Ivy's voice interrupted Nancy's dream. 'Are you all right, miss?'

Nancy opened her eyes. 'Ivy?'

'Yes, miss. I've brought you a cup of hot chocolate. Miss Sylvia always enjoyed a cup first thing in the morning.'

'Thank you, Ivy.' Nancy raised herself to a sitting position. She realised that Ivy was trying hard not to stare at her crumpled garments. 'I'm afraid I fell

29

asleep before I had a chance to undress.'

Ivy set the cup and saucer down on a small table. 'You need a personal maid, if you don't mind me saying so, miss.'

Nancy picked up the cup and sipped the delicious warm drink. 'If you are prepared to be my maid that would be wonderful, Ivy. This is all new to me.'

'I understand. It would be my pleasure, Miss Greystone.'

'Then I appoint you as lady's maid. You will pass your work on to one of the more senior housemaids.'

'I will do that right away, but perhaps you would like me to find an outfit for you to change into before I do anything else?'

'My things are still packed.'

'That's easy, miss. I will see to that for you.'

'What time is breakfast, Ivy?'

'Meals will be served when you wish. Perhaps a meeting with Mrs Simpson would be a good idea. Then it's usual to see Cook and discuss the menu for the day, or even the whole week if it's just yourself she has to cater for.'

'I had a lady's maid in London,' Nancy said hastily. 'Do you know Molly Greep, Farmer Greep's daughter?'

'Yes, miss. I know the family.'

'Molly left to get married. Have you got a beau, Ivy?'

'I'm twenty-eight, Miss Greystone. On the shelf, so Ma tells me.'

'Nonsense, Ivy. You would make someone a wonderful wife.'

Ivy laughed. 'You're very kind, miss. I'm happy as I am, and glad to serve you. It will be good to see

30

Greystone Park come alive again. I remember how well you organised things when Miss Sylvia was proper poorly.'

'I did, didn't I?'

'You most certainly did, Miss Greystone.'

'I'd like it if you called me Miss Nancy. Miss Greystone makes me feel like an old woman.'

'I understand, Miss Nancy. Now, if you've finished your chocolate, I'll fetch a pitcher of hot water to fill the wash basin and then I'll find you something to wear.'

Nancy sighed with relief. It was so good to have someone on her side in this huge house. Even though she had stayed here while Sylvia was ill, running things on a daily basis had not been her responsibility. Now, with Ivy's help, she was feeling more positive.

'There's just one thing, Ivy. Who was the last person to sleep in that big bed?'

Ivy frowned. 'It must have been Sir Michael and the second Lady Greystone, Miss Patricia Carey as was. Although they didn't stay here very much, I do recall that Sir Michael often stayed up late and I believe he slept in here so as not to disturb Lady Greystone.'

'Thank you, Ivy.' The knowledge that Rosalind's younger sister, Patricia, was the last Lady Greystone to sleep beneath the heavy tester was a comfort. Yesterday evening Nancy had been tired and fanciful, but this morning she was feeling more positive. She threw off the coverlet and stood up. The answer to her predicament had been there all the time — Patricia was the person to help her become lady of the house. It seemed so simple now.

★ ★ ★

31

Later that morning Nancy sat in Patricia's sunny parlour at the house she shared with her second husband, Leo Wilder. 'So you see, Patsy, you were the last Lady Greystone to sleep in that huge bed. Did you feel it was haunted?'

'Haunted?' Patricia almost choked on her coffee. 'What on earth gives you that idea?'

'My mama must have slept in that bed. I might have been born there. It made me feel very odd.'

Patricia replaced her cup on its saucer. 'You were tired and fanciful. I slept countless times in that old four-poster. I can't say I liked that room because it was so big and filled with old-fashioned furniture, but I never felt nervous.'

'Perhaps because you didn't sleep on your own.'

'That's not exactly true. Greystone often slept in the dressing room, especially if he had been working late at night, or if he had been at a card game with friends. Not that he was a gambler, but he did like to socialise and I think he preferred the company of men to women.'

'I would ask Ivy to make up another room for me, but I don't want to look silly.'

'My darling, you are the mistress of Greystone Park. You can do anything you like, so stop worrying. If you want another room just tell them to prepare the one you like best. You don't have to make excuses. It's your home and your property.'

'Christina doesn't agree. She threatened to take the case to court.'

'Let her, but she won't win. Christina has Cottingham Manor but she is still not satisfied. And, of course dear Sylvia is going to be married in the autumn. I couldn't be happier for her.'

'I was wondering,' Nancy said slowly. 'Would you consider moving back to Greystone Park, just for the year that I have to manage it on my own?'

'You know I would do anything for you, Nancy, but that would be considered to be cheating. Lord Dorrington and Bertie both think you ought to prove yourself capable of handling a large household. I think it's a bit unfair that you are supposed to manage the estate as well, but if I were you I would take it as a challenge.'

'I don't know where to start.'

Patricia smiled. 'But from what you've just told me you have started already. You had a meeting with your housekeeper and your cook. That's excellent. They now know that you are in charge. The rest will follow. Just take things one day at a time.'

'And the estate? What did you do when you were Lady Greystone?'

'Very little, to be honest. I left everything to Greystone, but Gibson is a good land agent, or so I believe. To be honest, I never took any interest in the estate or the tenants. Don't model yourself on me, Nancy.'

'Then perhaps I should send for Gibson and see what he has to say. Where does he live?'

'He has a house on the road to Exeter, about two miles from Greystone Park. If Jones is still employed in the stables he will take a message for you. He was head groom when I lived there, but of course most of the servants were dismissed when the house was closed down.'

'Maybe I should visit Gibson at home?'

Patricia shook her head. 'No, not a good idea. Send Jones with a note asking Gibson to call on you. Give him a set date and time. Be in control, Nancy dear.'

33

'I will do my very best.'

Patricia refilled their cups from a silver coffee pot. 'Freddie was here earlier,' she said casually.

Nancy's hand shook as she picked up her cup and saucer. 'He came here? Why would he do that?'

'The poor fellow is in love with you, Nancy. He came to ask me what he should do, and I told him to be patient. After all, it was his papa who set the rules.'

'Is he staying in the old keeper's cottage?'

'Yes, he said he wanted to see you, even if it was only in church on Sundays.'

Nancy sipped her coffee, giving herself time to think. 'I'm not sure I want to see him like that, Patsy.'

'Why ever not? I thought you loved him.'

'I do, but this is only the beginning of a very long year. Freddie agreed to it, but seeing him constantly isn't going to help me. It might make him feel better, but I think it might be easier if we lived apart completely, as his father wanted.'

'He won't like that very much.'

'Then perhaps he should have stood up to his papa and to Bertie. We could have eloped, but then Freddie would lose his inheritance. I suspect that he loves Dorrington Place and the estate more than he loves me.'

'I don't think that can be true, Nancy.' Patricia frowned. 'I doubted Leo at the start but I came to realise that he was sincere in his feelings for me.'

Nancy sighed. 'I do remember it was a stormy relationship at first.'

'You need to talk to Freddie. He's a good man and he loves you. In my position, as respectable matron and chaperone, I'll bring him to see you this afternoon at three o'clock, and you can have a private conversation.'

'I don't think that's exactly what a chaperone should do,' Nancy said, laughing.

'But I've made you smile again. That means more to me than seeing you miserable. Now drink your coffee and let's talk about something else.'

★ ★ ★

When she arrived back at Greystone Park Nancy sent Jones with a note to summon Cyril Gibson to a meeting next morning. She ate a solitary luncheon in the dining room and at three o'clock she took a seat in the drawing room, waiting for Patricia and Freddie to arrive. Nancy was suddenly nervous, wishing that she had not agreed to what might prove a difficult conversation.

When Freddie walked into the room she knew instantly that he was feeling very much the same. She rose to her feet and went to meet him, holding out her hand. He took it in a firm grasp.

'Nancy, how are you?'

She laughed. 'We only saw each other yesterday, Freddie.'

'I know, but Patricia tells me that you are not happy.'

'I didn't exactly say that,' Patricia protested. 'You two need to talk. I'm going for a stroll in the grounds.' She left the room before either of them had a chance to speak.

'Take a seat, Freddie.' Nancy made an effort to sound casual. 'Would you like some refreshment?'

Freddie sank down on an upright chair. 'You know none of this makes any difference to the way I feel about you. I love you and always will.'

'But you didn't take issue with your papa when

35

he insisted that I live here for a year to prove myself capable of running a household. I feel as if I am on trial. What if I fail? Will you go off and marry the heiress?'

'Of course not. I don't like it any more than you do, which is why I moved into the keeper's cottage. At least we can see each other this way.'

'It's not good enough, Freddie. A whole year of this will tear us apart.'

'Nancy, my darling, I wouldn't have agreed to Papa's plan in the first place had I thought it would be so hard on you. I never intended for you to go through this alone.'

'I don't doubt you, Freddie, but I think you ought to go back to Dorrington Place and concentrate on being the son and heir. I will try to keep my side of the bargain, but if I know that you are living just a mile or so away it will make this harder for me. Perhaps that is what your papa is hoping.'

'If Papa's terms are too harsh we'll elope. I can't lose you, Nancy.'

'But you will lose everything you've been brought up to expect, Freddie. Would you be happy living here? Being master of Greystone Park is not the same as being Viscount Ashton of Dorrington Place.'

Freddie leaned forward, holding out his hands. 'Nancy, you are more important to me than any title. As far as I'm concerned we can elope and damn the consequences. My cousin is welcome to the title and the fortune. If I can't have you I have nothing.'

Nancy was tempted to rush into his arms and agree to anything he suggested that would ensure they remained together, but she had been raised without expectations and she had seen how the poor lived.

Freddie was the love of her life but he had been born and bred to inherit a title and a fortune. He had not been expected to earn his own living, nor had he been prepared for such an eventuality, but that was something she had not the heart to tell him.

'I think we both need to take a step backwards,' Nancy said slowly. 'Perhaps time apart would help us both to learn more about ourselves. Am I capable of becoming Viscountess Ashton? Would I disgrace you in front of your aristocratic friends and relations?'

'Never! We've had conversations like this in the past, when you did not know who your parents were. Now we know that you are Miss Nancy Greystone. The rest will follow.'

'Your papa set me a task and I intend to see it through. After all, we have little choice other than to run away, and I don't think that would work out well.'

'I would be happy living a simple life in the keeper's cottage just to be near you.'

'Freddie, I love you even more for considering it, but you have a duty to your family. Your inheritance doesn't come without responsibilities.'

'What are you saying, Nancy?'

'Just being with you now is unsettling. I think it would be easier if we part now and agree to meet again in a year's time.'

Freddie's blue eyes darkened. 'Do you doubt me, Nancy?'

'No, never. And I know I will love you always.'

'If I agree to this, tell me one thing.'

'Yes, anything.'

'This doesn't have anything to do with Tommy Carey, does it?'

'With Tommy? What has he got to do with it?'

37

'It's obvious that he has a soft spot for you. I'd call it puppy love, but he's a young man, and I believe he's sincere in his regard for you.'

'We love each other like brother and sister. Tommy has enlisted in the army, anyway, and will be living in the barracks unless the regiment is sent abroad. You don't have to worry about him.'

'I hate to think of you struggling on alone.'

'I won't be alone. I will have you in my heart and in my thoughts. A year isn't for ever, Freddie. Maybe your papa will change his mind if he sees that I am doing my very best to comply.' Nancy glanced over her shoulder as the door opened and Patricia walked into the drawing room.

'I hope I'm not too soon, but I almost got caught in a shower. Have you come to any decision, the pair of you?'

Nancy nodded. 'We are going to comply with Lord Dorrington's wishes. Freddie is returning home to Dorrington Place.'

'How do you feel about that, Freddie?' Patricia gave him a searching look.

'I don't like it any more now than I did in the first place, but Nancy thinks this is the right course and I will abide by her decision.'

'I think the pair of you are very brave.' Patricia gave Nancy an encouraging smile. 'Only time will tell if you are taking the right decision, but I will help you in any way I can. Nancy was with me during a difficult period in my life and I will support her, in any way I can.' She wrapped her arms around Nancy, holding her hand out to Freddie, who closed his fingers around it with an attempt at a smile.

'If you need me, Nancy, just send word and I will

come whether it upsets Papa or not. If you need anything just tell Patricia and she will keep me informed. I hate parting like this.'

'We must leave now, before you weaken,' Patricia said firmly. 'I will turn my back so that you can say goodbye properly, but then we should leave, Freddie.'

Freddie took Nancy in his arms and their lips met in a kiss tinged with longing and regret. He drew away quickly, but not before Nancy saw the tears glistening in his eyes. He snatched up his hat and followed Patricia from the room without a backwards glance.

Nancy barely had time to compose herself before Foster entered after a peremptory knock on the door.

'Mr Gibson has arrived, Miss Greystone. He said he received your message and called on the off chance you might see him this afternoon.'

Nancy swallowed hard. If she was to make a success of running the Greystone estate she had better make a start. Maybe taking control of things would ease the ache in her heart.

'Show him in, Foster. Please tell Bertha to bring a tray of tea and maybe some cake or biscuits. That is the done thing, isn't it?'

A shadow of a smile lit Foster's eyes. 'It's not entirely necessary, considering Mr Gibson's station in life, Miss Greystone. However, I'm sure it will be most acceptable.'

'Servants and outside staff were treated almost like family at Rockwood Castle, Foster. But you must tell me if I make a *faux pas*.'

'Of course, Miss Greystone.' Foster left the drawing room at his usual dignified pace.

Nancy glanced at her reflection in one of the many wall mirrors and patted her hair in place. She would

39

have preferred to have some time to compose herself after the emotional parting with Freddie, but perhaps speaking to the land agent would take her mind off her personal problems. She went to sit in a chair by the fire, arranging her skirts neatly around her. She had barely time to settle down when the door opened and Foster ushered Mr Gibson into the room before retreating discreetly.

Nancy rose to her feet, but her smile of welcome froze. She had expected to see a middle-aged man, slightly shabby and earnest-looking, but Gibson was young, probably in his mid-twenties, and impeccably dressed in a hacking jacket, breeches and riding boots. His dark hair was swept back from a high brow and his open countenance was tanned as if he spent much of his time out of doors.

'Mr Gibson?'

'Nicholas Gibson. How do you do, Miss Greystone?' Gibson's brown eyes twinkled and his generous lips curved in an amused smile. 'I can see from your expression that you were expecting my father. He decided to retire when Greystone Park was closed, albeit temporarily, as his health is failing. I have taken his place, subject, of course, to your approval.'

'How do you do, Mr Gibson? You're right, I was expecting someone considerably older.'

'I can assure you that I am a fully qualified land agent.'

'I don't doubt it, Mr Gibson. I expect you know that I only recently inherited Greystone Park.'

He nodded. 'I am aware of the circumstances and I will be only too happy to help you in any way I can.'

'Please take a seat, Mr Gibson.' Nancy sank back onto the chair. 'I know nothing about running a large estate. I wouldn't know where to begin.'

'But you know the area and you are familiar with the village?'

'Yes, of course. I've lived in Rockwood all my life.'

'Then you are probably acquainted with most of your tenants, even if you didn't realise it.'

'I suppose so, although much of the village belongs to Rockwood Castle.'

'Might I suggest we ride around the Greystone estate tomorrow, if that's convenient?'

'Yes, that will be a good start.'

'In fact I hardly know the tenants myself. My father has introduced me to all of them, but I will be getting to know them just as you are. Don't look so worried, Miss Greystone. My father passed on all the information I will need to collect rents and make sure that everything runs smoothly.'

'I have to learn quickly, Mr Gibson. I have a year to prove myself as mistress of Greystone Park. My whole life depends upon how I am judged.' Nancy turned her head at the sound of someone tapping on the door. 'Come in.'

Bertha entered, carrying a tea tray, which she placed on a table at the side of Nancy's chair.

'Thank you. That will be all.' Nancy picked up the teapot as Bertha hurried from the room. 'Do you take tea, Mr Gibson?'

'Yes, please.' Gibson held out his hand to take the cup that Nancy filled with tea and a dash of milk. 'But if I may say so, it's not necessary to entertain me as if I were a guest. I work for you, Miss Greystone.'

Nancy poured tea for herself. 'I am aware of that, Mr Gibson, but I hope to have a good business relationship with you. The servants here know that I am inexperienced so they make allowances for me. I imagine you will, too.'

He raised his cup in a toast. 'I think you are doing very well indeed, Miss Greystone. Shall we make a start by going over the acreage of the farms and the yield we might expect from crops on the home farm?'

Nancy sipped her tea. 'Do you know any gossip, Mr Gibson? I might find that very useful when dealing with tenants' complaints.'

'That is my job, Miss Greystone. However, if I hear any interesting tittle-tattle I promise to pass it on.'

Nancy met his amused look with a smile. 'What made you follow in your father's footsteps, Mr Gibson? Being land agent to a relatively small estate seems an unlikely career for someone like you.'

He laughed. 'Are you always this direct?'

'Yes, if it's an honest question and if I am interested in someone. I didn't mean to cause any offence.'

'I am not offended. You are very astute. It wasn't my first choice, to be honest.'

'What did you want to be?'

'You will laugh if I tell you.'

Nancy was thoroughly intrigued by this time. Curiosity overcame the sadness in her heart and she leaned forward. 'I won't; I promise I will be very serious.'

'I've always wanted to be an actor, but my father thinks that only rogues and charlatans take to the stage. I rebelled, of course, as young men do, and I did achieve a little success in the theatre, but then I was needed at home, so I studied land management, and here I am.'

'An actor,' Nancy gazed at him with renewed interest. 'You have the looks and bearing, if you don't mind me saying so. I imagine you would be a good performer.'

'Well, thank you, Miss Greystone. I appreciate your candour, but I have to support my father. Maybe I will get a chance to pursue a career in the theatre at some time in the future. Who knows?'

'I have performed on stage,' Nancy said proudly. She passed him the plate of small cakes and he took one, eyeing her with interest.

'Really? In what capacity?'

'I accompanied Mrs Wilder on the pianoforte when she sang to audiences in London and in Paris. I've also accompanied her mother, the opera singer Felicia de Marney.'

'I've seen Mrs de Marney on stage. She has a beautiful voice.'

'Are you musical, Mr Gibson?'

'Not really. I can sing if a part calls for it, but acting is my first love.'

Nancy laughed. 'What a pair we are. We are both enacting a part, so to speak. I think we will get along very well. Where shall we start?'

4

Nancy decided to follow Patricia's advice and take control of her domestic situation. She did not move out of the master bedroom, but she had the old furniture removed, including the huge four-poster bed, and she selected pieces from other rooms that appealed to her more. The rather dull Persian rugs were swapped for more colourful carpet squares in shades of pink and blue, and Meggie Brewer, the dressmaker in Exeter, made up curtains in matching colours. Having redone her own room to her satisfaction, Nancy turned her attention to the drawing room. It was elegant although old-fashioned, but with a few changes in the furnishings, the addition of new curtains, and bowls of spring flowers placed on newly polished side tables, the room seemed to come alive.

When Nancy was not occupied indoors she was out riding with Nick Gibson. They had progressed to first-name terms as their friendship grew, even though Nancy knew such familiarity would be frowned upon if anyone found out. However, it was good to have a friend, and Nick made her laugh with anecdotes of his brief stage career. She was able to respond with stories of her experiences in London when she accompanied Patricia during her attempt to make a name for herself as an opera singer. As if sensing her moods, Nick would sometimes break into a comic version of a Shakespearian monologue, which always made her laugh no matter how sad she might have been feeling.

If she arrived at a tenant's farm with tears in her eyes they were tears of laughter, although often misconstrued. Cups of tea would be offered and sympathetic farmers' wives cast warning glances at the innocent Nick.

However, keeping busy was the key to coping with missing Freddie, and Nancy spent as much time as possible with Rosalind and the children at Rockwood Castle. The other person in her life who would have made a difference was Tommy, but his battalion had been sent to Karachi and were stationed at the Napier Barracks. So far Nancy had not heard from him, but it would take a couple of months before any post would get back to England, so she had to be patient. She could only hope that Tommy was enjoying army life; however, she suspected that his naturally buoyant nature and enthusiasm would get him through, no matter what he might face.

There were times when she was tempted to write to Freddie, but she decided it might seem like a request for his company, and she knew that their enforced separation must be as hard on him as it was for her. It was easy enough to keep occupied during the daytime, but evenings alone by the fire with nothing more than a book to keep her company were the hardest. It was a relief when the clock told her it was time for bed and she could sink into the feather mattress and allow sleep to take her to the land of dreams.

Even so, time passed at its usual pace and a showery April soon became a warm May, with the pleasure gardens bursting into huge pools of colour, and the kitchen garden promising to supply the larder with fruit and vegetables for the rest of the year. Ezra Pavey, the aged head gardener, had worked on without pay while the house was closed, helped by his equally aged wife and some of their many grandchildren. Nancy decided to reward them not only with back pay, but with a tea party in the rose arbour, which she organised with the help of Mrs Banks and Bertha. She had taken on several of the former gardeners and groundsmen, who had also been laid off, and they helped to bring trestle tables from one of the outbuildings, which Bertha laid with white cloths.

When the guests arrived on a sunny early June afternoon, Nancy was surprised to see how many grandchildren old Ezra and his wife had, and she wondered if they had brought all the village children with them. It did not present a problem as Mrs Banks had catered for a small army and there were plenty of stools and chairs to go round. The older family members sat in the shade of the pergola, and youngsters perched on wooden benches in full sunlight.

Rosalind had helped Nancy to make paper hats for the children, including Dolly, Rory and Phoebe, who could not be left out of such a celebration, as well as four-year-old Charlotte, the daughter of Walter, Bertie's younger brother, and his wife, Louise. Louise had volunteered to help, as had Patricia, although Patricia was almost eight months pregnant and finding the hot weather tiresome. However, accompanied by a stony-faced Fletcher, Patricia sat on a chair beneath a large parasol next to Bertie in his wheelchair, with the faithful Wolfe in attendance. Nancy's little party for her elderly gardener had turned into something of a village fête, and the food prepared by Mrs Banks was disappearing fast. The shimmering jellies had caused oohs and aahs of appreciation and did not have time to melt as they disappeared down eager throats. Nancy was beginning to think they had not provided enough treats when Nick Gibson arrived with a wooden keg filled with ice cream.

'Where on earth did you get that from?' Nancy looked into the tub. 'It's melting.'

'Then let's serve it immediately.' Nick produced a serving spoon from his pocket and held it in front of the children at the first table. 'Who would like some ice cream?'

The answer was a deafening roar and he laughed as he ladled out the sweet vanilla ice cream onto the plates waved in the air.

'Where did you get the ice?' Nancy asked as the last spoonful was served amidst cries for more.

'Didn't you know about the ice cave on your land?'

Nancy shook her head. 'No, never. Where is it?'

'I was speaking to Ezra and he asked me if we would be storing the ice from the lake this winter. It seems that the cave had been almost forgotten.'

'So you obviously found ice there.'

'Quite a lot, as it happens. I took it to Mrs Greep at the farm and she was only too pleased to use it to make ice cream. She told me how good you'd been to her daughter and she wanted you to know that she is going to be a grandmother later in the year.'

'That's wonderful news. I must call on her, although of course the Greeps' farm is on Rockwood land.'

Nick laughed. 'I don't think that makes you a trespasser, Nancy. Anyway, your party seems to be a great success.'

'I think the barrel of cider has helped Ezra and his sons to make merry,' Nancy said, smiling. 'The ladies are quite happy with tea.'

'I think some of the older boys have been helping

themselves to the cider. I'd better step in before things get out of hand.'

Without waiting for an answer Nick strode over flowerbeds to reach a group of village boys, who were eyeing each other up and hurling insults as they prepared to throw punches. He grabbed the two main protagonists by the ear and dragged them protesting from the rose garden.

'He's a useful man to have on hand,' Rosalind said softly. 'He's very good looking as well.'

Nancy shot her a suspicious glance. 'What are you saying, Rosie?'

'Nothing, dear. It's just that I can see some of the older ladies watching you both and tongues will start to wag. You know how it is.'

'There's nothing between Nick and me, Rosie. You know that.'

'I do, Nancy, but you've been riding round the estate together without a chaperone. If word gets to Lord Dorrington you know what he'll make of that.'

Nancy sighed. 'Why is life so complicated? My relationship with Nick is purely business.'

'And you are young, beautiful and rich. Mr Gibson is young, handsome and comparatively poor. I hear that he was an aspiring actor before his father insisted that he become a land agent.'

'Is there anything the gossips haven't discovered?'

'I dare say not, but obviously you are of great interest.'

'It's all Lord Dorrington's fault. He put me in this position.'

'I have to agree with you, but perhaps you ought to have an older woman living with you. There's always Miss Collins and Miss Moon. After all, Martha is a relation of yours.'

'Please spare me that. I know she helped me to prove my identity but I don't think I could live with her, or her companion.'

Rosalind stooped to pick up a baby who had crawled through the rose beds, unnoticed by its mother or grandmother. 'I'd better return this little one to its mama. Anyway, everything else aside, your party is a great success. At least you have a man to lean on while you learn how to handle the estate. Just don't lean too heavily.' Rosalind strolled off to return the baby to its family.

Nancy sipped a cup of rapidly cooling tea. She watched Nick sorting out another spat between two small boys and she smiled. It was good to have someone around with whom she had much in common. But she could tell by the way the older women had their heads together, casting covert glances at her and Nick, that Rosalind had been right. Perhaps Lord Dorrington had been asking the impossible. If he had allowed Freddie to reside nearby, things might have been easier, although the local gossips would have seized upon that too, so perhaps it would not have made a great deal of difference. The lot of an unmarried woman was not an easy one.

A sudden gasp from Patricia made Nancy turn with a start. Patricia had half-risen from her seat and her face was ashen. Fletcher jumped to attention.

'Wolfe, carry Mrs Wilder into the house.' Fletcher gazed into the crowd. 'Is Mrs Betts here?'

Mrs Betts, the midwife, rose from her seat next to Ezra's wife. 'I'm coming, Miss Fletcher.' She hurried over to Patricia. 'Allow me to help you, Mrs Wilder.'

Patricia leaned on Fletcher, her face contorted with

49

pain. 'I want to go home.'

'I think you had better go into the house, ma'am,' Mrs Betts said firmly. 'Someone send for Mr Wilder at the sawmill.'

Ezra rose to his feet and beckoned to his eldest grandson, who raced off after a brief word from his grandfather.

Nancy hurried to Patricia's side and clutched her hand. 'Come into the house. We'll make you comfortable until Leo gets here.'

'Yes, that's sensible,' Rosalind agreed breathlessly as she joined them. 'I've had three babies, Patsy, so I know how you feel.'

'I want to go home,' Patricia said faintly.

Wolfe scooped her up in his arms. 'Going to walk it, are you? I think not, ma'am. I'm taking you indoors to wait for your man, missis.'

Nancy and Rosalind exchanged amazed glances. Nancy had never heard Wolfe utter such a long sentence, but his words seemed to have had an effect on Patricia, who argued furiously in between gasps of pain as he carried her to the house. Fletcher marched at his side, issuing instructions, although it was obvious to Nancy that Wolfe was not paying any attention to her. Nancy went on ahead with Mrs Betts puffing and panting at her side. They waited for Wolfe in the entrance hall.

'Best take her to the morning parlour,' Nancy said firmly. 'There's a chaise longue where she can be made comfortable until her husband arrives.'

'I just want to go home.' Patricia's voice was faint but insistent.

'You'll stay where I put you,' Wolfe said grimly. 'No nonsense, ma'am.'

Nancy stifled a giggle. Wolfe was normally taciturn and morose, but he seemed to have taken the situation in hand and strode on, carrying Patricia as if she weighed next to nothing. Nancy led the way to the morning parlour and waited while Wolfe made Patricia comfortable.

'Thank you, Wolfe.' Nancy patted him gently on the sleeve. 'You'd better get back to Sir Bertram.'

Wolfe grunted and shambled out of the room, which seemed quite empty without his overpowering presence.

Rosalind hesitated in the doorway. 'Should I send for Dr Bulmer, Mrs Betts?'

Mrs Betts shook her head. 'No, ma'am. Not yet. First babies usually take a long time. You know that yourself. I'll send for him when I think the time is right.'

'Well, Dolly was in quite a hurry to be born, but I know what you mean. How are you feeling, Patsy?'

Patricia lay back against the padded curve of the chaise longue. 'The pain comes and goes. Will it take long, Mrs Betts?'

'I'll need to examine you properly, Mrs Wilder.'

'Will I be able to go home? I don't want to give birth at Greystone Park. That would be too ironic. If I'd had a child with Greystone I would be mistress here now.'

'Yes, ma'am. Now lie back, please.' Mrs Betts turned to Rosalind. 'Maybe you'd like to stay with us, Mrs Blanchard, but I suggest that you return to your guests, Miss Greystone.'

'But I want to be with Patsy.'

'No, it's all right,' Patricia said faintly. 'Please do as Mrs Betts says. Perhaps you could tell Leo that I'm

51

all right when you see him. You know how he worries.'

'Of course, I will.' Nancy left the room and found Fletcher standing guard outside the door. 'I'll send Mr Wilder in as soon as he arrives, Fletcher.'

Fletcher grunted. 'Men have it easy. I'm glad I never succumbed to flattery and sweet talk. I can't be doing with them.'

'I'll try to intercept Mr Wilder when he arrives.' Nancy hurried off. She had no intention of entering into a discussion about the failings of men with Fletcher, whose views on the opposite sex were well known.

Nancy stepped outside into the sunshine and was met by an anxious Nick Gibson.

'Is everything all right?'

'Mrs Wilder is having her baby.'

'Ezra said he had sent his grandson to fetch her husband. I could saddle up and be there quicker than anyone on foot.'

Nancy smiled. 'Thank you, but that boy knows the short cuts across the fields. He's probably at the sawmill by now. Anyway, Mrs Betts said it could be a long time before the birth is imminent.'

'Of course, but if there is anything I can do, just ask.'

'Thank you, Nick. I will.'

He gave her a steady look. 'Is anything wrong?'

'No, not really. It's just living in a village community. Rosalind thinks people are gossiping because we are seen riding out together without a chaperone. It's ridiculous, but there it is.'

'I'm sorry, Nancy. I hadn't thought of that.'

'I suppose it would be different if your father was still the land agent.'

'I could wear a false beard and moustache, and powder my hair so that it's grey. I've played older men when I was on stage.'

Nancy laughed and some of the tension left her. 'Maybe so. It is quite ridiculous, of course.'

He gave her a wry smile. 'Yes, as you say — quite ridiculous. However, if there's nothing we can do here perhaps we should return to the party. At least I can be useful in separating the village boys when they decide to knock seven bells out of each other.'

'You go on, Nick. I'm going to wait until Leo arrives. I promised Patsy that I would calm him down. He's sure to be anxious.'

'As I would be in similar circumstances.' Nick laughed. 'That's if any woman would have me as a husband.' He strolled off before Nancy had a chance to respond.

She waited on the carriage sweep, pacing up and down until she heard the sound of hoofbeats on the gravel and Leo rode into view. He flung himself off his horse and threw the reins at a stable boy who had run to meet him.

'Where is she, Nancy?'

'Patsy is being well cared for by Mrs Betts. They're in the morning parlour at the moment and Fletcher is standing outside the door like that dog I learned about in school — the one guarding the gates of hell.'

Leo shrugged. 'I'm no scholar, Nancy. All I want is to see my wife and take her home.'

Nancy glanced at his horse. 'On horseback?'

'I didn't stop to think about having the carriage made ready. I just wanted to get here as quickly as possible.'

'Don't worry. If Mrs Betts says that Patsy is all right

to travel home I'll have my carriage at the ready. Go in, but please keep calm.'

Leo brushed a damp strand of hair back from his forehead. 'Thank you, Nancy. Always the practical one.' He dashed into the entrance hall, leaving Foster to close the door.

Nancy sighed. She would have liked to stay with Patricia to help her through the hours of labour but she knew she was not needed. She went to rejoin the party, which was still in full swing, but after an hour or so, when all the food had been demolished and the cider barrel was empty, Nancy decided it was time for the festivities to end. With Nick's help she managed to convince the family to return home, leaving the servants to clear up after them.

'I'd better go, too,' Nick said quietly. 'I don't want to give the gossips more to talk about by staying on.'

'I'm going back to the house to find out how Patsy is doing, but thank you, Nick. Your help has been invaluable and the ice cream was a touch of genius.'

'I'm sorry if my presence has made it awkward for you in any way.'

'Don't be. We will continue as before — let people say what they like.'

He smiled. 'I'm glad. I enjoy our work together.'

'But the false beard and moustache sound very appealing. I would like to see you do your rounds dressed like that.'

'Maybe you will.' Nick strolled off to help two of the maids as they tried to dismantle a trestle table.

Nancy turned away and walked swiftly back to the house. She felt an undeniable attraction to Nick, which made her feel guilty. Freddie was the love of her life and the present situation was not of her

54

choosing. However, her thoughts were more occupied with Patsy and her baby than her own problems, and she quickened her pace.

When she entered the house she found Wolfe standing behind Bertie's chair while Fletcher paced the floor. Alex and Rosalind were trying to calm the excited children, while Louise waited patiently with Charlotte, who watched her lively cousins wide-eyed. As usual, Walter had opted to remain in the library at Rockwood Castle, working on his next novel. Nancy felt quite sorry for Louise, who was often left to deal with family matters on her own. Walter spent so much time poring over manuscripts that he was only seen at mealtimes.

'What's happening?' Nancy asked Alex as he swung Phoebe into his arms.

'I'm taking Louise and the children home. Rosie is going to stay here until Dr Bulmer decides whether Patsy can go home or whether she ought to remain here for the birth. He's with her now, as is Mrs Betts.'

'It could be a long wait,' Nancy said slowly. 'I can have a room made ready for her if necessary.'

Alex reached out to grab Rory by the sleeve as he was about to race off. 'We should get the children home. There's nothing we can do here.'

'No, of course you must.' Nancy nodded in agreement. The children were over-tired and Rory was getting fractious.

'Gurney will be here with the carriage in a few minutes and Hudson is bringing the wagonette to take Bertie's chair. I suggest we wait outside, Louise.' Alex sent a warning glance to Rory, who was trying to wriggle free from his father's grasp.

'I want to ride on the wagonette, Papa.' Rory

stopped struggling and smiled angelically.

'Me, too. Oh, please, Papa.' Dolly gazed up at her father with appealing blue eyes.

'Perhaps,' Alex said, smiling. 'We'll see.'

'There's nothing I can do here.' Bertie turned to Wolfe. 'We'll wait outside.'

'I will keep you informed,' Nancy said hastily. 'Let's hope it doesn't take too long, for Patsy's sake.'

Wolfe wheeled Bertie in his chair towards the main entrance. 'I suppose someone ought to send a telegram to Mama when the infant arrives,' Bertie said over his shoulder. 'Can I leave that to you, Alex?'

'Yes, of course, although I'm not entirely sure where she is.'

'Mrs de Marney was hoping to appear in a production at the new Theatre Royal in Brighton. They were talking about it when I was at Dorrington Place,' Nancy added apologetically.

'Trust Mama to use a social gathering to further her career,' Bertie said resignedly. 'She never misses an opportunity to put herself in the spotlight. Let's go home, Wolfe. I've had enough excitement for today.'

Wolfe grunted in answer and manoeuvred the chair out of the front entrance with the help of Foster.

Rosalind sighed. 'I don't suppose Mama will be any more interested in Patsy's child than she was in ours, Alex.'

He slipped his arm around her shoulders. 'You should be used to her by now, my love. Felicia will never change.' Alex frowned at his young son, who had broken free and was racing up and down the entrance hall.

'Rory, stop running around. You're making my head spin,' Rosalind said wearily. 'Where is the carriage?

56

The children are over-excited and it's time they had supper and bed.'

Louise glanced out of the window. 'It's coming up the drive, Rosie. Shall I take the children home? You and Alex can follow on later.'

Alex glanced outside. 'That's not our carriage, Louise.'

Rosalind hurried to his side. 'Isn't that Corbin, Lady Pentelow's coachman?'

'I believe it is. Why would my great-aunt come here to Greystone Park? We weren't expecting her, were we, Rosie?'

Rosalind shook her head. 'No. I haven't heard from her for ages.' She peered out of the window as the carriage drew up outside and the footman leaped down to open the door. 'Good heavens! It's Aurelia with Rupert Charnley. What on earth are they doing here?'

Nancy remembered her duties as lady of the house and she hurried to greet the unexpected guests. 'Aurelia, this is a pleasant surprise.'

Aurelia brushed past her. 'I'm sorry to intrude, Nancy. We went to Rockwood but Jarvis told us that you were all here. I want to see Rosie.'

Rosalind detached herself from Phoebe's clinging hand. 'I'm here. Is anything wrong? We weren't expecting you.'

'Why are you all here, anyway?' Aurelia demanded crossly. 'Are you working here now, Nancy?'

'No, she is not,' Rosalind snapped. 'For goodness' sake, Aurelia, you can't turn up and demand attention like this. We are here at Nancy's invitation. She is the owner of Greystone Park, which I'll explain later. Moreover, Patsy has gone into labour and we are waiting to find out if Dr Bulmer will give her permission

57

to go home for the confinement. You could not have arrived at a more inopportune moment.'

'You must forgive us for the intrusion.' Rupert Charnley took Rosalind's hand and raised it to his lips. 'We have very little choice in the matter.'

Alex picked up Phoebe, who had started to cry. 'I don't know what this is all about, Aurelia, but as it's you I imagine it will be some kind of drama.'

'That's not fair, Alex.' Aurelia pouted. 'We've been nearly three days on the road and I'm exhausted. Can you imagine how I felt when we reached Rockwood Castle, only to be turned away?'

Rosalind shook her head. 'That can't be so, Aurelia. Jarvis would never do such a thing.'

'Here is our carriage,' Louise said urgently. 'Bertie and Wolfe have gone in the wagonette. I'd be happy to take the children.'

Alex held Phoebe in one arm while he reached out to grab Rory. 'I wouldn't impose, Louise. We'll take the little ones home. You can tell me all about it later, Aurelia.' He followed Louise, who had Charlotte and Dolly by the hand.

'Shall we go to the drawing room?' Nancy suggested tentatively. She could see that Rosalind was angry and Aurelia was ready for an argument. Rupert Charnley appeared to be calm, but Nancy sensed an underlying tension.

'Yes. I'll tell you everything if you will stop glaring at me, Rosalind.' Aurelia reached for Rupert's hand. 'We are in love, and everyone is against us. We need your help, Rosie. Please don't turn us away.'

5

Half an hour later, Nancy, Rosalind, Aurelia and Rupert were seated around a small tea table in the drawing room. Alex and Louise had taken the children back to Rockwood Castle and Leo was pacing the floor outside the morning parlour, despite Nancy's pleas for him to join them.

Rosalind passed a cup and saucer to Aurelia. 'Now, slow down and tell us exactly what brought you here.'

'Rupert and I are in love,' Aurelia said, reaching out to hold his hand. 'But Grandmama refuses to give her permission for us to marry.'

'Just a moment,' Nancy said, frowning. 'You are over twenty-one, Aurelia, and a widow. Why do you need your grandmother's permission?'

Rosalind nodded. 'Yes, by my reckoning you must be nearly twenty-eight. You are not a child, Aurelia.'

'I know, but she has threatened to disown me and cut me out of her will if I marry Rupert, and Piers is no better.'

'But surely — and forgive me if I'm being too inquisitive — you a̶r̶e̶ ̶v̶e̶r̶y wealthy, Rupert.' Nancy gave him a searching look. 'I visited your home when Hester and I went to Barbados to find out what had happened to Alex and Leo. It was very grand.'

Rupert nodded. 'You're right, but it isn't just about money. Aurelia loves her grandmother and her brother. The truth is that Lady Pentelow does not want Aurelia to leave Cornwall, let alone live in another country far across the sea.'

'She is an old lady.' Rosalind laid her hand on Aurelia's arm. 'Perhaps you could still marry but agree to stay near her, at least for her lifetime.'

'She will live to be a hundred just to spite me. Piers has used Rupert's business knowledge to restart the mine, which is showing promising results. They don't need me. This is my last chance at happiness, Rosie. You must understand that.'

'I have to return to Barbados,' Rupert said apologetically. 'My money is tied up in the plantation. My elder brother is the heir, but I have shares in the business and I have to work for my living. I can't just stay in Cornwall to suit Aurelia's family.'

'So you've run away.' Nancy replaced her cup on its saucer. 'Why didn't you simply book a passage home?'

Aurelia's bottom lip trembled and her eyes filled with tears. 'We need to be married before we set sail for Barbados.'

'It's a small island,' Rupert added seriously. 'It would cause a scandal if we arrived unmarried, and my father is very old-fashioned. He would have nothing to do with me or Aurelia.'

'I see,' Rosalind said slowly. 'So you went to Rockwood Castle hoping to get married from there.'

'Yes, we need to be married as quickly as possible. We don't need a huge reception or a formal wedding breakfast.'

'You could have done this in Cornwall with a special licence, Aurelia.'

'Grandmama lost her temper and she told Rupert to leave. I couldn't allow that to happen, so we packed our bags and I persuaded Corbin to drive us to

Rockwood.' Aurelia sipped her tea, holding the cup with two hands in order not to spill the hot beverage. Her eyes filled with tears and she blinked them away.

'You are welcome to stay here,' Nancy said gently. 'I have plenty of room.'

'Thank you, Nancy.' Aurelia's voice broke on a sob.

Rosalind rose to her feet. 'I can see you have matters in hand, Nancy. At the moment all I can think about is Patsy. I have to go home, but I want you to let me know the moment the baby arrives and I'll return. There's nothing useful I can do here for the time being.'

'Yes, of course. I keep forgetting about poor Patsy. How selfish of me.' Aurelia took a hanky from her reticule and mopped her eyes. 'Would you really have us here until we can be married, Nancy?'

'Most definitely.' Nancy shot a sideways glance at Rosalind. 'After all, you did say I should have someone older living with me, Rosie. Aurelia's presence will make me respectable.'

'In that case I suggest that Rupert comes to Rockwood and remains with us until after the wedding.' Rosalind walked purposefully to the door and opened it. 'Do you agree, Aurelia? You want to do everything properly, I assume.'

Rupert stood up. 'I agree, Mrs Blanchard. I'm most grateful to you for the very' He raised Aurelia's hand to his lips. 'Leave it all to me, my love. I will make the necessary arrangements. We will be married as soon as possible and I will book our passage to Barbados.'

'I can't wait to be Mrs Rupert Charnley,' Aurelia said, smiling.

'Perhaps you would like to accompany me now, Rupert.' Rosalind held the door open. 'We could use

61

your carriage and Corbin can spend the night at the castle before driving back to Trevenor. I assume you won't be keeping Lady Pentelow's carriage here.'

'No, she will want its return as quickly as possible. Thank you, Mrs Blanchard.'

'It's Rosalind. You are practically one of the family now, Rupert.' Rosalind gave him a beaming smile as she left the room and he followed her, turning briefly to blow a kiss to Aurelia as he closed the door.

'Isn't he amazing?' Aurelia said dreamily.

'He's very charming and good looking,' Nancy agreed. 'But isn't all this rather sudden, Aurelia? I mean you haven't known him for long.'

'It was instant, Nancy. The moment I saw him I knew.'

'Well, if you're certain, I will help you to make the necessary arrangement for your wedding. It would give me great pleasure to have something to do other than worry about household accounts or how well the estate farms are doing.'

'I need new clothes, Nancy. I'm afraid mine are drab and out of date. It didn't seem to matter, living at Trevenor, but that was before I met Rupert. I'm sure you understand.'

Nancy had a fleeting vision of how she took extra care of her toilette when she knew that Nick would be calling at the house, and she was instantly ashamed. She was virtually engaged to Freddie, the most lovable man she had ever met, but now she found herself attracted to someone else. Suddenly the whole situation seemed utterly ridiculous. She and Freddie had allowed his father and Bertie to dictate the terms with which they must both comply for no better reason than her youthfulness and inexperience in managing a great house. The situation in which she found herself now was even more difficult, and she needed to be very careful.

Nancy stood up and rang the bell. 'I'm sure you would like to go to your room to change out of your travelling costume, Aurelia. I need to see if there is anything I can do for Patsy.'

'Yes, of course. I'm being very selfish. Not having had any babies of my own I really don't know much about such things, but I would like to go and rest before dinner. Perhaps Patsy will have been delivered of the child by then.'

'We can only hope so, for her sake.' Nancy waited until a knock on the door preceded Bertha's slightly flustered appearance.

'You rang, ma'am?'

'Yes, Bertha. Will you take Mrs Gibbs to the Rose Room and help her to unpack?'

'Yes, Miss Nancy. Please come this way, ma'am.'

Aurelia drank the last drop of tea and rose to her feet. 'I'm exhausted after travelling so far, added to all the emotional upheaval.'

'Yes, you must be.' Nancy followed them out of the drawing room. She was beginning to lose patience with Aurelia, who seemed to think of nobody other than herself. Nancy made her way swiftly to the morning parlour and found Leo still pacing the floor outside.

'How is she?' Nancy asked eagerly.

'I wish I knew. They won't let me into the room, but I can hear her cries and it breaks my heart to know she is suffering. I wish I could take her home.'

Nancy laid her hand on his arm. 'But it will be worth it when you meet your son or daughter. She will have forgotten the pain, or so everyone tells me.'

'I'm not sure I believe that,' Leo said grimly. 'It's been hours already.'

'Perhaps they will let me in.' Nancy knocked on the door and Mrs Betts opened it just a fraction.

'Yes? What is it?'

'May I come in?'

'You may, but not Mr Wilder. This is no place for gentlemen.' Mrs Betts opened the door wide enough for Nancy to slip inside.

'How is she, Mrs Betts?'

'It's going to be a long labour.'

'Mr Wilder still wants to take her home. Would that be possible?'

Mrs Betts shook her head. 'I think it would be better if a room could be made ready for her here. I don't think a journey in a carriage would be a good idea.'

'I'll have a bed brought down here. It won't take more than a few minutes for the servants to dismantle a single bed and put it up in here.'

'Nancy, is that you?' Patricia's voice was edged with pain as she attempted to sit up. 'Is Leo here?'

'Yes, he's outside. He wants to take you home.'

'I would advise strongly against it.' Dr Bulmer washed his hands in a bowl on a washstand that seemed to have appeared from nowhere.

'I've just told Mrs Betts that I can get the servants to bring a bed down here, Doctor. Would that be suitable?'

'Excellent, Miss Greystone. Please arrange it quickly, although I think it might be a few hours yet before Mrs Wilder holds her infant in her arms.'

'I want to see Leo,' Patricia said plaintively.

'The birthing room is no place for husbands, Mrs Wilder.' Dr Bulmer dried his hands meticulously on

64

a clean white towel.

'I want to see him now.' Patricia made as if to rise from the chaise longue.

'No, Mrs Wilder. Please remain where you are.'

'No, I won't. I will walk home if you don't allow my husband to be with me.'

Dr Bulmer and Mrs Betts exchanged worried glances.

'What harm can it do?' Nancy demanded crossly. 'I'm sending Mr Wilder in and I'll have a bed brought down immediately.' She hurried to Patricia's side and pressed her gently onto the chaise longue. 'Don't worry, Patsy. I won't allow them to keep Leo away when you need him.' She marched out of the room without giving anyone a chance to protest.

'Well?' Leo pounced on her, grabbing her by the wrist. 'What's going on? How is Patsy?'

'She's been asking for you, Leo. Go in and comfort her. It looks as if it's going to be a long time before the baby arrives.'

He barged past her and let himself into the morning parlour. Nancy heard Patricia's cry of delight and the low rumble of Dr Bulmer's voice as the door closed. Nancy smiled as she went in search of Foster to make arrangements for a bed to be brought down to the morning parlour as quickly as possible. If Lord Dorrington could see her now maybe he would change his mind about making her and Freddie wait a whole year before they could get married. She was managing very well — in difficult circumstances.

Nancy found Foster in his office below stairs and he set about having a bed brought down from one of the little-used rooms on the second floor. She could tell by his raised eyebrows that he did not approve of babies being delivered in the morning parlour, but he maintained a stony silence.

* * *

Patricia's son was delivered at two minutes past midnight. Nancy had been unable to sleep and she joined Leo, who had been banished from the room when the birth was imminent. Mrs Betts opened the door, her face white with fatigue but a happy smile on her lips.

'Congratulations, Mr Wilder. You have a son.'

'May I see them both, Mrs Betts?'

'You may.' Mrs Betts stood aside to allow him to enter the room.

'How is Patsy?' Nancy asked urgently.

'She's very tired but she's strong and she'll recover well. He's a fine boy, Miss Greystone.' Mrs Betts smiled tiredly. 'To think it was nineteen years ago that I attended your mama during her confinement in this house.'

Nancy sighed. 'I wish I'd known her, Mrs Betts.'

'She was a delightful lady, but very delicate, God rest her soul.' Mrs Betts retreated into the morning parlour, closing the door behind her.

Left alone in the dark corridor, there was nothing Nancy could do other than to make her way to her own room. She lay down on the bed and closed her eyes.

* * *

Fletcher arrived before breakfast next morning. She marched past Nancy, who had just emerged from the

66

morning parlour, having met Patsy's newborn son and, despite having made suitably admiring comments, Nancy could not imagine how any parent could see beauty in a wrinkled, snub-nosed, red-faced scrap of humanity; but it was obvious that both Patsy and Leo were already besotted with the tiny boy, whom they had named Charles Leo.

Nancy realised that she was really hungry, as with all the excitement of the previous day she had eaten very little. She went straight to the dining room and was surprised to find Aurelia seated at the table.

'You are up early, Aurelia.' Nancy helped herself to buttered eggs, bacon and grilled tomatoes. She took her plate to the table and sat down.

'I barely slept a wink, Nancy.'

'You shouldn't have worried about Patsy. She had her baby at just after midnight — a lovely little boy.'

'Really? That's nice for her. No, it wasn't that. I was worried about my wedding outfit and trousseau. I have to go to London to get something suitable for my new life as the wife of a plantation owner.'

Nancy opened her mouth to say that Rupert was only second in line for inheriting the plantation, but she stopped herself in time. Let Aurelia have her dreams. She might be disappointed with the reality, but dashing her hopes now would be like pulling the wings off a butterfly.

'Yes, of course. Although we have a good dressmaker who lives in Exeter.'

'She may be good enough for provincial places and country residences, but I want to be a leader of fashion in my new life. I want to go to London today, Nancy. Will you accompany me?'

'It will cost quite a lot of money, Aurelia.'

67

'Rupert will pay. We'll take your carriage to Rock-wood Castle and he'll give me the money, and then we'll go on to Exeter and catch the London train.'

'But I can't leave Patsy and the baby, not yet.'

'Why ever not? Leo is here, and no doubt Rosie will come over as soon as she can. They won't even notice you've gone.'

Nancy took a deep breath. It would be wonderful to abandon her responsibilities, if only for a day. She loved London, in spite of some of the hard times she had experienced there, and the lure of exciting shops was too tempting.

'All right. As soon as I've finished my breakfast I'll send for the carriage, but I must change into something more suitable for a day in town.'

'You see — you're excited already.'

'Well, it will make a nice change.' Nancy tried to sound casual, but she could not quite keep a note of excitement from her voice.

★ ★ ★

Rupert was not in favour of his fiancée spending a day in London with only Nancy as company and he insisted on going with them. Alex backed him up, leaving Aurelia and Nancy no alternative but to give in and allow Rupert to accompany them.

All went well until they reached London, when Rupert decided that he could do some business in the City. Aurelia insisted that she needed plenty of time to choose her most important gown, which entailed a visit to Oxford Street. Nancy could hardly inter-fere, and there was a long argument, which Aurelia won by bursting into tears and declaring that Rupert

68

did not love her. In the end Rupert agreed to meet them back at the railway station at six o'clock in the evening to catch the train back to Exeter. He gave Aurelia a substantial amount of money, which made her smile happily as she tucked the leather pouch into her reticule. She parted with him on affectionate terms and left for Oxford Street in a hansom cab with Nancy.

Shopping with Aurelia proved to be an experience that Nancy would not care to repeat. It was exhausting, frustrating, and the shop assistants were pushed to the limits of patience by their demanding customer. Eventually, when she was running out of money, Aurelia decided that she was happy with her purchases and she and Nancy celebrated by treating themselves to ice cream and cake at Gunter's. It was a fine summer evening as they emerged from the warm atmosphere of the celebrated teashop. Berkeley Square was congested with horse-drawn vehicles, and both Nancy and Aurelia were laden with bandboxes and packages wrapped in brown paper. Finally, after several failed attempts to attract the attention of a cabby, Nancy managed to hail a hansom cab. However, by the time Aurelia was settled with all her purchases around her there was no room for Nancy.

'We're terribly late,' Aurelia grumbled. 'For goodness' sake, get in, Nancy.'

'I can't, there's no room. You've bought half of Oxford Street, by the looks of things. Go ahead and I'll follow in another cab. You can explain to Rupert. I'll meet you on the platform.'

'You better hurry then. Cabby, Waterloo Bridge Station.'

The cabby flicked his whip and the horse edged its way into the stream of traffic. Nancy stood on the kerb, waving frantically to each cab as it passed her. She opened her reticule to examine the small pocket watch that she had borrowed from Rosie, but to her dismay she realised that she had spent the last of her money settling the bill at Gunter's. She backed into the crowd, wondering what to do. She could hardly expect a cabby to wait for her to rush into the station while she went looking for Aurelia, and worst still, Aurelia had the railway tickets in her reticule.

For a moment Nancy was overcome with a feeling of panic and she gasped for air, feeling the ground moving beneath her feet, but she took a deep breath and forced herself to be calm. She was penniless and alone in London, but she had friends. There was Tamara's aunt in Doughty Street; Molly and Reuben, who now lived in a cottage close to the market garden in Highgate; and there were Tamara and William, who now had a pretty house in Chelsea. Eleanora, who was now Lady Marshall, lived in Highgate. It was simply a question of which one was the nearest. It would be a risk if she took a cab to any of the addresses and found no one at home who could pay what she owed, and it was a long walk to any of them. Nancy decided that Chelsea was the nearest and she knew the way, although she had never walked that far. She had little choice and she set off heading, as far as she remembered, in the right direction.

Nancy was not really dressed for a long walk but it was a fine evening and still quite hot. Her feet were sore and she could feel her clothes sticking to her back. However, she had little alternative other than to keep going. She had been full of confidence when she set off, but when she reached the mean streets close to the newly built Victoria Station, she was feeling tired and slightly nervous. The East End had become familiar to her but this area was new and she was not quite sure how to proceed. She headed towards the river but she soon realised that she was lost in the maze of back streets. Worse still, she knew she was being followed. She stopped and turned quickly but whoever was behind her was too quick and had vanished into one of the narrow alleyways.

Nancy quickened her pace but the footsteps behind her grew closer and she began to run. Her breath was ragged and her heart pounding. For a moment she thought she had shaken off her pursuers but suddenly she was surrounded by a group of ragged, rough-looking boys. They ranged in age from eight or nine years old to thirteen or fourteen. All of them were pale, dirty and half-starved, if their skinny limbs and gaunt cheeks were anything to go by.

'What do you want?' Nancy demanded boldly. 'I haven't got any money or jewellery.'

The tallest boy, seemingly the leader of the pack, stepped forward. 'Your duds cost more than a penny or two, miss. You ain't poor.'

'No, I am not, but I have nothing on me of value to you. Now please allow me to pass.'

'You got spunk, lady. I'll give you that. But you must be worth something to someone.'

'No, I assure you . . .' Nancy began, but two of the bigger boys grabbed her by the arms, holding her with surprising strength considering their emaciated appearance.

'What shall us do with her, Gus?'

'Take her to the den. The rest of you scatter. The

cops are never far away. Meet up later.' The older boy marched on ahead, but Nancy was not going to go easily. She struggled and kicked out at her captors, receiving a clout around the head that made her ears ring. Dazed and in pain, there was nothing she could do other than try to keep on her feet as the boys broke into a run. To be dragged over cobblestones would be even more painful than trying to match their strides, and soon Nancy was breathless as well as dazed and disorientated.

It was a nightmare and she could not believe that this was happening to her in broad daylight, but the gang knew all the back alleys and the only clue as to their whereabouts was the occasional toot of a boat on the river. Apart from that, Nancy was quite lost. She tried calling out for help when they passed a group of men who were loitering on a street corner, smoking clay pipes. They laughed and turned their backs on them, leaving Nancy in no doubt that she was in a place worse than Clare Market. Eventually she was pushed down a steep flight of stone steps and manhandled into a cellar below a tall building. The rest of the gang appeared to have arrived before them and she was thrown onto a pile of stinking sacks.

'What you got there, Gus?'

Nancy blinked as her eyes grew accustomed to the dim light of a single tallow candle. She struggled to her feet, facing the boy who had just spoken.

'I don't know who you are but please tell your gang to let me go. I have no money and no jewellery, as I've told them already.'

'She's a cheeky one, Todd,' Gus said crossly. 'Say the word and I'll knock some sense into her.'

'What did you bring her here for?' Todd demanded. 'She's a lady and someone will be looking for her. Are you off your head?'

Gus stepped forward, lowering his voice. 'Look at them duds, Todd. We're broke and we're starving. My aunt has a stall in Rosemary Market. She could sell them for enough to feed the lot of us for a couple of days.'

'You're a fool, Gus. That would take days, and your old aunt would sell her grandmother for a couple of pence. We'd die of hunger waiting for her to cough up.' Todd turned to Nancy, his hazel eyes gleaming in the candlelight. 'What shall us do with you, lady? I suppose if we turns you loose you'll go straight to the cops.'

Nancy looked him in the eye and saw a lonely boy, bearing the weight of responsibility for the younger children, who were crowding through the door. She felt a sudden wave of pity for them all.

'Why are you here, Todd? Haven't any of you got a home to go to, or parents who care?'

A gurgle of childish laughter rippled around the cellar.

'You don't know nothing, lady,' Todd said scornfully. 'You comes from a different world. We only got each other, but we get by.'

'I'm hungry, Todd.' One of the smaller boys tugged at Todd's jacket. 'My tummy hurts.'

'Shut up,' Gus hissed. 'We're all blooming starving, so shut your gob.'

'We ain't had nothing to eat since yesterday.' One of the other boys spoke up boldly. 'What you going to do about it, Todd?'

Nancy could see that the situation was getting serious. She drew Todd aside. 'I can see your problem

73

and if I had money I would gladly give it to you to feed those poor boys.'

Todd stiffened. 'We don't need charity, lady.'

'But you do need some help or you'll have a mutiny on your hands at the very least. Those children need food.'

'I don't need a toff to tell me that.'

'No, but you do need help, and quickly.' Nancy thought rapidly, recalling her days with Patsy in the East End when money ran out. 'Is there a pub nearby where they have a piano in the bar?'

Todd gazed at her in stunned amazement. 'What are you on about?'

'There's money to be made entertaining drinkers in a bar. Answer my question.'

Gus moved closer. 'There's the White Swan — it's not far from here.'

'Have they got a piano in the bar?' Nancy asked eagerly.

'I dunno, but I think I heard music when I was nearby.'

'When I lived in London a few years ago I used to play the piano for a lady who sang to the men in the taproom. I can't sing as beautifully as she did, but I can play well enough. They'll give me tips and I will give them to you.'

'Why would you do that, lady?' Todd asked suspiciously. 'Is this a plot to make your escape? If it is, you can forget it. I'm sure someone will pay to have you returned to them. You must have got family back at home.'

Nancy glanced at one of the smallest boys, who had slumped down on a pile of sacks, clutching his empty belly and sobbing quietly.

'My family are in Devonshire. Can you afford to wait for days until they get the message? That child will have died of starvation by then. Are you willing to take a chance?'

6

Nancy had no clear idea of what her strategy for escape would be. Aurelia and Rupert might have waited for a while, and no doubt they were worried about her, but they would almost certainly have left for Devonshire by now. Faced with the inevitable, Nancy's main priority at this moment was to get money to feed the starving boys. She had no real plan as she entered the taproom of the White Swan, although she could tell by the look on the landlord's face that she was not welcome and was about to be escorted from the premises. There were a few women in the bar, but they were obviously plying their trade and were not eager for competition. Nancy considered asking one of them for help, but the look she received from the flamboyantly dressed woman with painted lips and cheeks was far from encouraging. Todd and Gus had accompanied her but she sensed that they were as nervous as she was, and as they had no money they too would be evicted from the pub if the landlord had his way.

The vision of the dank cellar room and the ragged, ill-nourished children made Nancy bold. Without waiting to announce her intention she walked purposefully to the piano, pulled out the stool and sat down. She struck a chord and played the introduction to 'Polly Perkins of Paddington Green', or 'The Broken-Hearted Milkman'. There was a surprised silence and then an appreciative murmur as Nancy

76

sang in a clear soprano. She knew her voice did not have the range or the power that Patsy's did, but the song seemed to be going down well. There were sympathetic noises for the poor lovelorn milkman and a sigh of satisfaction when hard-hearted Polly met her fate. When the song came to an end there was a round of applause and cries for more, and Nancy launched into 'Come into the Garden, Maud'. When she played the last note Gus seized Todd's cap and went round the taproom waving it in front of the drinkers until they made a contribution. At that point, Todd grabbed Nancy by the hand and led her out into the street.

'Don't get no ideas of asking for help.'

Nancy shrugged. 'I don't think they would be very sympathetic, but I've done what I said, so now let me go.' She almost added that she could walk to Tamara's residence in Chelsea but she stopped herself just in time. That would be a fatal mistake. Anyway, she was determined to see that the money was spent on food and that the youngest boys had their fair share. She was not scared of Gus, for all his bravado and posturing as the tough leader of the gang, and Todd was even less of a threat.

Todd waited for Gus to catch up with them. 'How much did we get?'

Gus counted out the coins, grinning from ear to ear. 'There's enough for a jug of ale and a pie each.'

Nancy seized the cap and emptied the contents into her reticule. 'No. We'll go to that dairy on the corner and I'll get food for you all. No beer.'

'Hey, you can't do that,' Gus protested, taking his hat from her and ramming it on his head. 'I'm the boss.'

'You can tell the boys what to do but I say they all

need proper food. You won't have a gang if you don't look after them.'

'But we're hard men,' Gus said lamely. 'We don't do what women tell us to do.'

'More's the pity.' Nancy walked off in the direction of the dairy she had noticed on the way to the White Swan. 'I'm going to buy the food and I'm going to make sure that the little ones get their fair share.'

'She'll be making us wash our hands next,' Gus said in an undertone. 'Can't we give her back to her family quick, Todd?'

'Maybe she's right, Gus. Young Alfie ain't too well and I dunno what to do for him. Teddy don't look too good either. Perhaps a bit of food in their bellies will make them perk up.'

'I've run out of baccy for me pipe,' Gus said grumpily. 'It's me only pleasure in life.'

Nancy turned on them. 'You sound like a pair of old men, not the leaders of a tough gang. And you are too young to smoke, Gus. You'll stunt your growth.'

'It stops me belly aching when I'm hungry.'

'All the more reason to eat properly.' Nancy stalked into the dairy, leaving the boys outside on the pavement. She purchased milk, cheese, butter, eggs and bread, which the shopkeeper explained he took in from the bakery after it closed for the evening. Satisfied that she could at least feed the boys something nourishing, Nancy left the shop. Todd and Gus were waiting for her.

Todd glanced at the large package she was clutching. 'I suppose you spent it all?'

'Yes, I did. I suppose you have some way of heating water in your cellar room.' Nancy fell into step beside them.

'You ain't going to make us wash,' Gus said firmly.

'No, I am not. But I bought some eggs and if you have a kettle or some sort of pan we could boil them, or even fry them in a little butter.'

Todd shook his head. 'No fireplace. But they got one upstairs in Masher's room.'

'Who is Masher?'

'You don't want to meet him,' Todd said grimly. 'He's a nasty piece of work, but he has a kettle. I know because I seen it one day when I was taking a peek into the room where he takes in dossers. It's a penny for sit-ups and tuppence to hang over a rope.'

'You don't mean that's how people sleep, do you?'

Gus snorted. 'That's all you know, lady.'

'Maybe he would let me use his kettle, if I ask nicely.'

Todd and Gus dissolved in fits of laughter, leaving Nancy in no doubt that Masher was not a person who would be eager to oblige. 'There's no harm in asking,' she said mildly.

★ ★ ★

When they arrived back at the squalid cellar that the boys inhabited, Nancy was upset to find Alfie lying on the pile of sacks in a semi-conscious state. She felt his brow, but he was cool, almost too cool, and this was more frightening than if he had a slight fever. Teddy was sitting cross-legged by his side.

'He won't talk, miss,' Teddy muttered. 'Is he dead?'

'No, he is very much alive, but he needs looking after and so do you.'

'I'm in Gus's gang,' Teddy said boldly. 'We are tough boys.'

79

Nancy smiled. 'Even tough boys have to eat, Teddy.' She glanced round at the dirty faces of the rest of the gang. They were sitting on the cold, damp floor, and without exception they looked hollow-eyed and deathly pale. Nancy set the package on a small table in the corner of the room and unpacked the food. Instantly, sniffing the air like starving hounds, the boys surrounded her. She held up her hand. 'No, wait. I'm going to cut the bread if someone has a knife.'

Gus swaggered over to her, taking a vicious-looking knife from a sheath on his belt. 'I'm the only one allowed to have a weapon inside.' He handed it to Nancy. 'I want it back when you've finished.'

Nancy did not answer. She busied herself cutting slices from the loaf, buttering them and laying them with thinly sliced cheese. The boys could hardly contain themselves and she was faced with clawed hands reaching out to her in a plea for something to eat. She left them to help themselves while she took a slice of buttered bread and a cup of milk to where Alfie lay on his bed of sacks. She kneeled down beside him and raised him to a sitting position. She held the tin mug to his lips and was rewarded when he managed to swallow a little of the cold milk. After a few minutes he seemed to revive considerably and was able to eat the bread and butter. Instantly a little colour warmed his cheeks and he became more alert.

The level of noise in the dark room had grown considerably now that the boys had been fed. There was still the matter of the eggs, and Nancy was wondering whether to brave the fearsome Masher. She was sure that no reasonable human being would deny her the right to use his kettle in which to boil the eggs, but then she heard the tramp of booted feet on bare boards coming from above. Todd told her that it was the dossers arriving for their night's sleep, and she decided that this was not the best time to approach Masher.

Todd nudged her with his elbow.

'Yes, Todd, what is it?'

He thrust a crust of buttered bread with a sliver of cheese into her hand. 'Seems only fair, miss. You sang your heart out to get this for us.'

She smiled. 'Thank you, Todd. You are a gentleman.'

'You are welcome, miss.'

Nancy bit into the crust, realising suddenly how hungry she was. 'What do you do for food normally, Todd?' She glanced at Teddy, who was staring at the bread and licking his lips. Filled with guilt, she gave her slice to him and he stuffed the whole of it in his mouth.

'We gets bits here and there,' Todd said casually. 'If we have a good day selling wipes and wallets to the Old Man we gets pies and tea from the stall down the road.'

'So you pick pockets for a living.' Nancy eyed the boys, who were seated in a circle on the floor, savouring the last crumbs of bread and cheese. 'Who is this old man?'

'Can't say, miss. He'd have my guts for garters.'

'That sounds truly frightening. Why do you live like this, Todd? You're a bright boy, I'm sure you could do something better with your life.'

'You was born rich, miss. You dunno what it's like to be left on the street to fend for yourself. We got no families so we make our own.'

Nancy nodded. 'As a matter of fact I do understand,

at least a little, Todd.' She sat back on her haunches. 'I admire the way you've tried to look after these boys, but living like this won't end well for any of you.'

'You ain't going to preach at us, are you, miss?'

'No, Todd, but I want you to release me. I know people who live not far from here. They will help me and then I will do something for you.'

'Do I look green?' Todd stepped away, gazing at her with his brows knitted into the frown. 'If I lets you go that'll be the last we see of you. If you want to help, you can stay and earn money to feed us, like you did tonight.'

'I can't live here, Todd.' Nancy looked round the darkening room with a shudder. 'It's a dreadful place and if you aren't caught and put in prison some of you will die of disease or lack of proper nourishment.'

'We ain't letting you go.'

'Think about it, Todd. I can't even cook the eggs I bought for you. Let me go to my friend's house and I will boil them and bring them back to you tomorrow.'

'Yes, with the cops. I know your sort. You pretend to be kind and helpful and then you call the cops.'

'That may be true of some people, but not me. Come with me now if you don't believe me. You'll see where I'll be staying for the night. I won't desert you, I promise.'

Todd eyed her suspiciously. 'Why should I believe you? Why would you care about us?'

'I don't honestly know, Todd, but I do care. Let me go to my friends tonight and I will think of a plan to get you out of here, but I can't do that if you keep me prisoner.'

'I need to talk to Gus.'

Nancy shook her head. 'No, you don't. You are the

real leader of the gang. The boys look up to you and the decision must come from you.'

'Yes, you're right. I am the boss, not Gus.' Todd strode off, pacing the floor with his hands clasped behind his back. He returned moments later. 'All right. I'll take you to your friend's house, but if I suspect anything I'll drag you back here double quick.'

'You have my word that I won't betray you, Todd. That should be enough. You'll have to start trusting people one day, so you'd better start with me.'

The younger boys were huddling together on the bare brick floor. The food had made them sleepy and although the older boys tried to appear wide awake their heads were nodding. Todd took Gus aside, whispering in his ear before returning to Nancy's side.

'All right. I'm going to trust you. Gus is going to stay on watch until I get back.'

Nancy rose to her feet. 'You won't regret this, Todd. I meant what I said. I won't abandon you. I'll be back in the morning.'

'With the boiled eggs,' Todd said with a wry grin.

'Yes, Todd. With the boiled eggs.'

★ ★ ★

Todd waited on the other side of the road while Nancy knocked on the door of the pretty three-storey house in Chelsea. Nancy prayed silently that Tamara and William were at home. The maid who opened the door stared at her wide-eyed before remembering her manners.

'If you'll wait there, please, miss, I'll see if the mistress is at home.'

'Yes, of course.' Nancy waited for a few minutes

and was rewarded when the door opened again and this time it was Tamara who stood silhouetted against the gaslight in the entrance hall.

'Nancy, it really is you? I thought someone was playing a trick on me. Come in, please.'

Nancy followed her into the parlour at the front of the house. 'Thank goodness you are at home, Tamara. I don't know what I'd have done had you been out.'

'William is at a business meeting, but he should be home soon.' Tamara gave her a searching look. 'What's happened, Nancy? Why are you out alone in London at this time of night?'

Exhaustion combined with lack of food made Nancy dizzy and she sank down on a chair. 'I'm sorry. I've had a difficult day.'

'You're very pale. When did you last eat?'

'I had a cream cake and ice cream at Gunter's.'

Tamara beckoned to the maid who was hovering in the doorway. 'Fetch some food for Miss Sunday, Nell. There might be some soup left over from dinner. Ask Cook to make up a tray.'

'Yes, ma'am.' Nell bobbed a curtsey and left the room.

'Now then, Nancy. Start at the beginning and tell me everything. What brings you here all on your own?'

Nancy explained the situation as briefly as possible. Tamara was an appreciative audience but she insisted on asking questions just when Nancy was in the middle of her tale. It was a relief to Nancy when Nell returned with a tray laden with a bowl of soup, hot bread rolls, butter and a large slice of apple pie. Pushing all thoughts of the starving boys out of her mind, Nancy ate heartily. If she was to help them she needed all her strength.

'Well, you were certainly very hungry,' Tamara said, smiling. 'Now tell me more about these boys who kidnapped you. Surely you can't be serious in wanting to help them?'

'Yes, I am. They are the unfortunates whom no one seems to want. Some of them are very young and they are living in appalling conditions. I've never seen the like.'

'Yes, but surely there are charities who deal with cases like these. Haven't you got enough on your hands with attempting to run Greystone Park on your own?'

'I'm not entirely on my own, Tamara. I have Nick Gibson to assist me when it comes to running the estate. The household practically manages itself now that Mrs Simpson and I have come to an understanding.'

'Well, I admire you for doing all these things, Nancy. I can manage here in my small house but I would be lost if I had to be mistress of a mansion and a huge estate.' Tamara put her head on one side. 'What about Freddie? You haven't really mentioned him.'

Nancy sighed. 'I don't know. I love him dearly but I wonder if he really needs me. Surely he would fight harder to be with me if he truly loved me?'

Tamara's eyes glistened with tears. 'I do feel for you, Nancy. I think it was a cruel thing for Lord Dorrington to do. You are trapped in that great house, proving just what? If you were married to Freddie you would learn how to manage Dorrington Place. I know I've had to start from the beginning.'

'But you are happy with William?'

'Oh, yes. I adore him, and he's so kind and he makes me laugh. I think Papa has forgiven me for marrying

85

the man I love instead of the man he chose, especially now.' Tamara patted her belly.

'When is the baby due?'

'In August. Isn't it wonderful?'

Nancy leaped to her feet and gave Tamara a hug. 'I am so happy for you. I can just imagine you with a little girl who is an exact copy of you.'

'Or a boy, who would be just like William.' The laughter faded from Tamara's blue eyes. 'But what will you do now, Nancy? You promised to return to the boys. Was that wise?'

'Wise or not, they need my help.'

'I don't really see what you can do.'

'I need money, for a start. You should see the dreadful circumstances where they live. The youngest ones are sickly and malnourished. It's a terrible situation.'

'But they let you go free.'

'Todd is very intelligent and he's a good boy at heart, but they don't stand a chance on their own.'

'What are you thinking? I know that look.'

'I want to take them all back to Greystone Park. That old house has been virtually empty since Sir Michael died. It's mine now and I intend to do something useful.'

'But, Nancy, what will Lord Dorrington say? You can't just take a gang of street urchins into your home. They'll steal all the valuables and run away.'

Nancy shook her head. 'I think they are all young enough to change their ways and become useful citizens. Look at me, Tamara. I was ten years old, in service, when Rosie found me. Heaven knows where I might have ended up had she not taken me under her wing.'

Tamara sat back in her chair, eyeing Nancy with a

worried frown. 'That's all very laudable, but what will Freddie say?' She turned her head as the door opened and her husband entered the room. 'William, you're home early.'

'The meeting ended sooner than I thought it would.' William Russell gazed at Nancy in surprise. 'Nancy, it's good to see you. Freddie didn't say you were in London.'

Nancy almost choked on a piece of bread roll. She swallowed convulsively. 'Freddie! You've seen him recently?'

William bent down to kiss Tamara on the cheek. 'Freddie called the meeting. He was standing in for his father. Lord Dorrington is a major shareholder in one of the shipping companies I represent. He is unwell and Freddie took his place.'

'Is Freddie staying in London? I need to see him.'

'I believe he's staying at the family home in Piccadilly — for tonight, anyway.'

'Then I must see him immediately.' Nancy placed her empty plate on the tray and was about to stand when Tamara motioned her to remain seated.

'You're exhausted and you need to rest. Also a change of clothes and a wash would be wise before you go looking for Freddie.'

William went to a side table and poured himself a drink. 'What's this all about, Tamara?'

'I'll explain later. You are going nowhere tonight, Nancy. After a good sleep and a decent breakfast we will take a cab to Piccadilly. I don't think Freddie would approve of you jaunting around London on your own.'

'You're talking about Freddie,' Nancy said tiredly. 'He was always willing to help me in anything I did.

Why would he disapprove?'

William sipped his brandy. 'Tamara is right, Nancy. Freddie has taken on a lot of the responsibility from his father since Lord Dorrington's illness.'

'No one told me that he was unwell.'

'Freddie probably didn't want to worry you, dear.' Tamara exchanged meaningful glances with William. 'I'll ring for Nell and have a bed made up for you in the guest room. I assume you've eaten, Will?'

'Yes, we dined royally at Freddie's expense. Are you telling me that Freddie knows nothing of your visit to London?'

'Please sit down, darling,' Tamara said gently. 'We'll tell you everything and then you'll understand the situation.' She stood up and tugged at the bell pull.

'You might as well tell me what's going on.' William settled himself on the sofa next to his wife. 'Maybe I can help.'

Once again Nancy launched into an explanation as to why she had turned up on their doorstep so late in the evening and unattended. Thoughts of Todd returning to that dreadful hideout were at the back of her mind. Would little Alfie survive the night? She had heard a rattle in his chest and she suspected that he might have contracted lung fever or pneumonia in those damp conditions. Teddy was only a little stronger, and both were very young to commit to a life of crime.

William listened in silence until she finished speaking.

'What do you think, Will?' Tamara asked anxiously. 'I told Nancy I thought she was taking a terrible chance if she had them to live with her at Greystone Park.'

'The sentiment is excellent, although I'm not sure that it would work out in practice. Who knows what these boys have undergone in their short lives? Could you turn them around? I'm not sure. And should you be doing such a job? I don't know. What Freddie will say is another matter.'

'Then tomorrow I will find out,' Nancy said firmly. 'I'll go to Piccadilly first thing and tell him everything.'

★ ★ ★

Next morning Tamara was confined to her room with a return of the nausea she had suffered earlier in her pregnancy, but she insisted that Nell should accompany Nancy to Piccadilly. Nancy laughed and accused her friend of making sure she returned to Chelsea with all the latest news. However, when Nancy arrived at Dorrington House she was pleased to have the company of a maid. She knew that the servants were judging her silently and unobtrusively, but she held her head high. Tamara had loaned her a smart travelling costume, which she insisted no longer fitted, due to her condition, and a perky little straw bonnet completed the outfit.

Nancy was shown into a small, elegantly furnished parlour on the ground floor, where she waited for several minutes. She was unaccountably nervous of meeting Freddie in such an unexpected fashion. She knew this was ridiculous, but their enforced separation had created a barrier between them despite their vows of eternal love. She walked around the room examining the priceless ornaments and artefacts from all over the world, no doubt the results of the grand tour that Lord Dorrington had undertaken when he was young. Nell had been whisked away to the servants' hall and no doubt was being cross-examined by those who wished to know everything about the future Lady Dorrington. Nancy tried to imagine herself as mistress of this imposing edifice and failed miserably. Perhaps this had been Lord Dorrington's intention all along. She was beginning to wish she had not come when the door opened and Freddie strode into the parlour.

'Nancy. They told me you were here, but I thought it was a mistake. Why aren't you at Greystone Park?'

Nancy was shocked by this abrupt version of a welcome. 'Is that all you can say, Freddie? Aren't you pleased to see me?'

He came to a halt, frowning. 'Of course I am, you know that. B-but why are y-you here? Y-you know what the conditions were.'

'Conditions? You make it sound like a formal business arrangement. We were supposed to be engaged, Freddie.'

He grasped both her hands, raising one to his lips. 'Yes, forgive me. I have had to take on a lot of my father's responsibilities due to his recent illness. I am not in the b-best mood to be romantic.'

Nancy withdrew her hands, allowing them to fall to her sides. 'I came here for help, Freddie.'

'I'm sorry. Sit down, please. Tell me what you need, but I have an important meeting in half an hour.'

Nancy remained standing. 'Surely Viscount Ashton does not have to be punctual to the second. There must be some allowances for an important person.'

A wry smile twisted Freddie's generous lips. 'You make me sound like a p-pompous idiot.'

'I'm sorry, Freddie, but that's how you sounded.'

'Then I apologise wholeheartedly. Tell me why you are in London.'

'I came with Aurelia to help her choose a gown for her wedding to Rupert Charnley. It's a long story, but I want to take some poor children home to Greystone Park and I need money for our fares.'

Freddie stared at her in amazement. 'You are teasing me, surely?'

'I've never been more serious.'

'Who are these children?'

Before Nancy could answer, Freddie's attention was diverted by a rap on the door and the appearance of the butler.

'You'll excuse me, my lord, but the carriage is outside and you are already late for your appointment with the Lord Chancellor.'

'All right, Briggs. I'm coming now.' Freddie turned to Nancy with an apologetic smile. 'I have to go, my love. Just wait here for me. I'll be gone all morning but perhaps we can have luncheon together and you can tell me everything.' He leaned over to brush her cheek with a kiss before hurrying from the room.

Nancy snatched up her reticule and ran after him, but he had stepped out onto the pavement before she had crossed the entrance hall.

'Is there anything I can do, miss?' Briggs eyed her sympathetically.

'Please send for my maid and find me a cab.'

Briggs nodded and signalled to the first footman. He sent the second footman to find a cab and within minutes Nancy and Nell were on the return journey to Chelsea. Nancy was simmering with anger and disappointment. Freddie had put duty before love and had treated her as a person of lesser importance. She entered the house even more determined to help the boys than before.

Nell took Nancy's bonnet, shawl and gloves before ushering her into the morning parlour. Tamara was looking a great deal better than she had done first thing and she rose from her seat by the window with a wide smile.

'Nancy, you have a visitor.'

7

'Nancy, you're all right. Thank goodness.' Nick Gibson rose from his seat. 'You had us all worried.'

'Nick. What are you doing here?'

He gave her a searching look. 'Sit down, please. You look exhausted.'

'I'm quite all right. There was no need to worry. But how did you know where to find me?'

'I'll send for some tea, or coffee if you would prefer it.' Tamara gave the bell pull a tug. 'You seem to have your family worried sick, Nancy.'

'It was not by choice. But you haven't answered my question, Nick.'

'Mrs Wilder sent me. She was furious with Mrs Gibbs for abandoning you in London. I was called on to meet every train that arrived in Exeter that evening, and when you didn't turn up I offered to come to London to find you. Mrs Wilder agreed wholeheartedly and she suggested I might start here.'

Tamara resumed her seat by the empty grate. 'What did Freddie say, Nancy?'

'He was too busy to listen to me. He suggested I wait for him to finish his meeting with the Lord Chancellor and then we could have luncheon together.'

'But you didn't stay.'

'I have a group of starving children waiting for me to return with a basket of boiled eggs, which will be the only food they have had since yesterday. How could I sit at Lord Dorrington's table and be waited on by a fleet of servants when those boys are dying from slow starvation?'

Nick sat down beside her. 'Tamara told me about your experience with the young villains, and that you want to take them back to Greystone Park.'

'They haven't had a good start in life, Nick. They are just boys and I believe they could do well if they were given half a chance. I need to take them food, and then I will do my best to persuade them to accompany me to Greystone Park. The old house needs new life in it and all those empty rooms will serve a good purpose.'

'You really are intent on saving them, aren't you?'

'Yes, but I need money. Those boys are dressed in filthy rags. They need half-decent clothes, a good meal and the train fare to Exeter.'

'If you go now you could see that they have something to eat,' Tamara said thoughtfully. 'You might still be in time to have luncheon with Freddie. I'm sure he will help you financially.'

'He was too busy to even sit down and listen to what I had to say. I can do this on my own, Tamara.'

'I have money,' Nick said hastily. 'I brought a reasonable amount with me because I didn't know what to expect or if I would have to stay in London for a while.'

'Thank you so much, Nick. I can repay you when we get home.' Nancy jumped to her feet. 'I'll collect the eggs from Cook. I'll go now and try to persuade them that life in Devonshire is preferable to their existence in London.'

'I'll come with you.' Nick rose to his feet. 'You're not going back there on your own, Nancy.'

Tamara looked from one to the other. 'Very well.

94

Come back and let me know how you get on, but please don't bring a dozen street urchins to Chelsea. I don't think William would like it.'

Nancy laughed. 'Don't worry, I wouldn't foist them on you. Fate seems to have thrown me in their path and I'm going to handle this on my own, but with a little help from you, if you don't mind, Nick.'

★ ★ ★

Nancy hesitated at the top of the area steps in Vauxhall. Everything looked different from this perspective and she was not sure if she had brought Nick to the right house. Then she saw Todd peering out of the narrow window that let a little daylight into the basement. He stepped outside, but at that moment the front door opened and a tall brawny man emerged from the house. His matted brown hair fell in a mane to his shoulders and his face was half-covered in an equally unkempt beard and moustache. He was in his shirtsleeves and he lumbered down the steps with a dog-like growl.

'Get away with you. Don't want no toffs pretending to be charitable while nosing round. This is my drum and what goes on here is my business.'

'We are not going to interfere with you, Mr Masher,' Nancy said politely.

'Who are you, lady?' Masher fisted his hands. 'What d'you want?'

'This has nothing to do with you, sir,' Nick said calmly. 'Stand aside, please.'

Todd stopped halfway up the basement steps. 'You'd best go away, miss. He's nasty even when he hasn't been drinking.'

95

'Stand aside, please.' Nick placed himself between Masher and Nancy. 'I'm asking nicely. I won't be so polite if you don't get out of our way.'

Masher took a swing at Nick, who parried the blow and caught Masher with an upper cut to the jaw that felled the big man.

'Like a blooming tree in a gale,' Todd said, chuckling. 'Well, blow me tight! I never thought no one could get the better of Masher. You'd best come inside afore he comes to.'

Todd raced down the steep steps and opened the basement door. He let them in and closed it behind them, bolting it top and bottom. 'Masher might come after you.'

Nancy set the basket of eggs on the table. 'Here are your eggs, and there's bread, cheese and some pork pies in there, too.' She looked round. 'Where's Alfie?'

'Over there, miss.' Todd pointed to what looked like a bundle of rags in the corner of the room.

Nancy went over to the child, taking a cup of milk with her. She raised him and held the cup to his lips. 'You're all right now, Alfie. I'm going to take care of you.'

Nick moved to her side. 'Is the boy sick?'

'I'm not sure, but he's undernourished and very thin. He certainly needs to see a doctor, but now you see them you can understand why I need to get them away from this place.'

Nick glanced round at the boys, who were stuffing food into their mouths like starving animals. He nodded. 'Yes, I see the problem.'

'I need to get them clean enough to travel on the train, and they'll need new clothes, even if I have to go to a second-hand shop or the market.'

'I'll send a telegram to Mrs Wilder to tell her that you're safe and well. We'll go on from there.'

'Thank you, Nick. I don't know what I would have done if you hadn't come to find me.'

He smiled. 'I think you would have found a way. You are a very resourceful woman and Ashton doesn't know what a lucky man he is. Will you return to Piccadilly to see him later today?'

'No. He was too busy to talk so he can come looking for me if he wishes. I intend to take these boys to the public baths and then I'll get clothes for them.'

'I can take them into the baths, although they might need a little persuasion.'

'I'm sure they will do as you say. I saw the expression on Todd's face when you knocked Masher down. You will be their hero.'

Alfie seemed to revive a little and Nancy gave him some bread and butter. She was not sure at first whether he would be able to go to the public baths, but the food gave him energy and Nick carried him on his shoulders, which made the other boys giggle. Nancy smiled to see them behaving like normal children. The night before they had been like little old men, bent and frail from lack of good food. This morning they were still ragged and filthy, but that could be remedied. They were all in good spirits as they walked to the public wash house in Marshall Street. It was a long way and the younger boys tired easily, but Nick kept them in good spirits with tales of his life on the stage and recitations of comic poetry, which had them in fits of laughter. Nancy walked at the rear, holding young Teddy's hand as he was struggling to keep up.

She left them at the baths and went to a second-hand shop she had seen on the way there. Armed with money from Nick, she purchased enough shirts, trousers and jackets to clothe them all. She saw several pairs of boots that were in reasonable condition and she added these to the large bundle. The garments might not be the best fit but they were clean and infinitely better than those the boys were currently wearing. She took the clothes to the wash house and left them with an attendant, who promised to give them to Nick.

An hour later the boys were almost unrecognisable. Beneath the layers of dirt were clean, shiny-faced children with freshly washed hair and outfits that were a surprisingly good fit. Not that any of them seemed to worry about such details. They paraded and pranced about, mimicking gentlemen promenading in the park. This made Nancy and Nick laugh with pleasure at the sight. Nancy breathed a sigh of relief. She had thought they might rebel, but instead all, including Todd and Gus, appeared to be delighted with their new looks. On the way back to Vauxhall Nick stopped at a coffee stall and bought them all baked potatoes swimming with butter, and mugs of tea, which they drank on the spot, saving their food until they got to their pathetic home. Nick volunteered to stay with them while Nancy took a cab to Tamara's house to tell her that they had managed to persuade the boys to visit Greystone Park.

'I didn't tell them that it was going to be a permanent arrangement.' Nancy took a seat beside Tamara on the sofa. 'They think it's going to be a nice holiday before they return to London, but I'm hoping I can prove to them that life in the country can be wonderful.'

Tamara nodded. 'I hope for your sake that they

settle down, but what will you do with them, Nancy? You can't adopt twelve boys. Will they work for you? How will they support themselves when they get older?'

'I'll think about that when we get home,' Nancy said evasively. 'The main thing is to get them away from a life of crime. You would die if you saw the conditions under which they've been living, Tamara. It was really dreadful.'

'I'm sure you're doing a fine thing, but what about Freddie? If he comes here looking for you what shall I say?'

Nancy shrugged. 'Tell him I've gone home. His papa said I was to spend a whole year at Greystone Park and that's what I intend to do. Perhaps we should stick to the rules set down by Lord Dorrington and Bertie. They said that Freddie and I should keep apart, so maybe they were right.'

'I'm sure you don't believe that, Nancy.'

'Maybe not, but what else can I do? For the moment I'm concentrating on Todd and the boys. I was given a second chance in life, and that's what I hope to do for them.'

'Are you leaving for Devonshire today?'

'Yes, we are. I just came to say thank you.' Nancy gave Tamara a hug. 'You must look after yourself and you will let me know as soon as he or she is born, won't you?'

'Of course, Nancy. I'd like you and Freddie to be godparents, if you would.'

'I will with pleasure, but I can't speak for Freddie.'

'You sound unsure of him now, Nancy.'

'To tell you the truth I've never seen him this way before. He was more interested in business affairs than in me or even in us. He wasn't my Freddie, he seemed more like his papa. It was as if I was speaking to a stranger.'

Tamara kissed her on the cheek. 'I'm sure things will work out in the end. Good luck with the boys. I'll be dying to know how they get on in the country.'

★ ★ ★

The train journey to Exeter was hectic and Nancy was very glad that Nick had accompanied them. The boys, none of whom had ever travelled by rail in their whole lives, were understandably excited. It was almost impossible to make them sit down for any length of time and they kept jumping up and rushing from side to side of the carriage as they spotted something new out of opposite windows. The only thing that kept them quiet for a while was the picnic lunch that Nancy had the forethought to purchase on the way to the station. They ate voraciously and washed the food down with bottles of fizzy lemonade, another unheard of luxury in their short lives. Nancy found herself looking after Alfie, Teddy and Stanley, the three youngest boys, while Nick exerted his influence over the older boys, resorting to stern words when they did not behave.

It was hard work keeping the young ones occupied but it helped to keep Nancy's mind from straying back to her last meeting with Freddie. His casual attitude had hurt more than she was prepared to admit even to herself, and it left her wondering whether the Freddie she knew and loved was the real person, or if he had changed almost overnight and become a replica of his father . . .

A cry of alarm from Teddy alerted Nancy to the fact that Stanley had climbed onto the seat and stuck his head out of the open part of the window. She dragged him back to safety.

When they reached Exeter it was late afternoon but Nick managed to find a farmer who had just unloaded milk churns at the station and was returning to Rockwood with an empty cart. It was not the most comfortable way to travel, but again it was a novelty to the boys. Nancy perched on the driver's seat next to the farmer while Nick sat in the cart, keeping order.

By the time they arrived at the gates of Greystone Park the younger boys were sound asleep and even Todd and Gus had quietened down and were looking around, wide-eyed as they took in their new surroundings.

They had to walk along the avenue of trees to the house, although Alfie was so exhausted that Nick had to carry him. Todd gave Teddy a piggyback and Nancy held Stanley's hand. The other boys seemed to get a new lease of life and they raced on ahead, coming to a sudden halt when Foster opened the front door. They seemed to have turned to stone as they gazed up at him open-mouthed, but Nancy was not far behind.

'Good evening, Foster. As you see, we have some young guests. Will you send Mrs Simpson to me in the drawing room, and ask Mrs Banks to prepare supper for twelve hungry boys?'

'Will they be staying the night, Miss Greystone?' Foster's impassive expression remained intact but there was a slight break in his voice.

'Yes, Foster. That's what I want to discuss with Mrs Simpson. The boys can eat in the kitchen this evening, but from tomorrow they will take their places

101

at the dining table.'

'Yes, Miss Greystone.' Foster's eyes bulged and a vein in his forehead throbbed visibly.

Nancy smiled to herself as she led the boys into the entrance hall. They were suddenly very quiet and subdued as they followed her to the drawing room. They sat in a circle on the floor, suddenly looking very small and insignificant when faced with the opulence and grandeur of the room, which Nancy now took for granted.

The door opened and Nancy looked round, expecting to see Mrs Simpson, but it was Aurelia who entered the room, coming to a sudden standstill.

'My goodness, Nancy. What have you done? Where did all these children come from?'

'Perhaps I'd better go now,' Nick said hastily. 'I'll come first thing tomorrow morning, Nancy. You might need a hand.'

'Thank you for everything, Nick. I don't know what I would have done without your help.'

Aurelia looked from one to the other, saying nothing until Nick had left the room. 'Well you two are on very familiar terms. What's going on, Nancy?'

At that point Mrs Simpson entered the room, barely waiting for her gentle rap on the door to be answered. 'You wanted to see me, Miss Greystone?' She came to a halt, staring open-mouthed at the boys.

'I see that Foster did not warn you.' Nancy kept a straight face with difficulty. 'That was thoughtless, but, as you can see, we have visitors. Twelve of them, to be exact. Which rooms would you find the easiest to have made up for them, Mrs Simpson?'

'I — I'll have to give it some thought, Miss Greystone. Will they be staying for long?'

'I don't know yet. That depends.'

Mrs Simpson pursed her lips. 'I will need to know so that I can order more supplies. In my experience, young boys have large appetites.'

'I suggest you cater for a month and we will assess the situation then. The boys will need a meal as soon as Cook can manage it. Something simple will suffice for tonight, and I will dine at the usual time with Mrs Gibbs.'

'Very well. Is there anything else, Miss Greystone?'

'I think I've given you quite enough to do, Mrs Simpson. Thank you for all your efforts. I'm sure the boys will be very grateful.'

Mrs Simpson backed towards the doorway, eyeing the unusually silent boys as if expecting them to leap up and start demolishing the room with their bare hands.

Nancy sighed as the door closed. Bringing the boys here had been the easy part. She had a feeling that life was going to be far more complicated from now on.

'Please, miss,' Stanley's high-pitched voice broke into her thoughts. 'I need to piss. Shall I use one of them pots on the table?' He pointed to a Meissen vase on a side table.

'No, certainly not.' Nancy sprang to her feet. She rang the bell and almost as if she had been waiting outside, Ivy entered the room.

'You rang, Miss Greystone?' Ivy said innocently.

'You weren't listening outside the door, I hope.'

'Heaven forbid. I was just passing.'

'Will you show all the boys where the privy is outside, and explain to them about using commodes and where to find them. I'm afraid they are unused to our country ways.'

Ivy shot a disapproving look at the boys. 'Come with me, young gents. I'll show you where everything is, and by then Cook should have your food ready.'

'It ain't going to be gruel, is it?' Gus demanded, scowling. 'That's all us had to eat in the boys' home.'

'Certainly not.' Ivy shook her head. 'Cook is going to a lot of trouble frying sausages and bacon. There might be fried bread if you're very lucky, and apple pie to follow.'

There was a stunned silence and then a murmur of appreciation.

'I knew that.' Gus squared his thin shoulders. 'I was just testing you, miss.'

'I'm Ivy, and you can call me that, but only if you are polite and do as I say. Now come with me, all of you. That little fellow looks as if he needs the privy urgently.' Ivy shooed them all out of the room and closed the door.

Nancy sighed, wondering for the first time if she had taken on too much. Looking after so many small boys was a huge responsibility. In London it had seemed like the natural thing to do, but now she was not so sure. However, she had to take charge and show the servants that she was capable of running things, no matter what. She made her way to the third floor, just below where the servants had their rooms. The sound of windows being flung open and the chatter of two new housemaids who were making up the beds led her to the rooms that Mrs Simpson had allocated for the boys' use.

Nancy entered the largest of the rooms where two single beds and a truckle bed were already made up. The room was bare of any kind of decoration to soften the stark white walls and beige linen curtains, but it was spotlessly clean and at least each child would have his own bed. The rest of the rooms were similar and in different stages of readiness, but Nancy was satisfied that the boys would be comfortable and get a good night's sleep, probably for the first time in their short lives.

She returned to the drawing room and found Aurelia there, seated in a chair by the hearth with an embroidery hoop in her hands, although she did not seem to be working on the intricate pattern of leaves and flowers.

'What on earth were you thinking of?' Aurelia discarded the hoop and rose to her feet. 'You've turned the house into a bear garden. I'm glad I don't have to wait too long before the wedding and I can escape to Barbados with Rupert.'

'You could stay with Patsy if you don't like it here, Aurelia. Remember it was you who abandoned me in London. I didn't have a penny piece in my purse so I couldn't follow you in another cab.'

'That was your fault. You insisted on settling the bill at Gunter's. I didn't know that was all you had.'

'You could have stopped the cab and turned back to get me. I was kidnapped by those boys.'

'Then they should be punished instead of bringing them here to a respectable house. What were you thinking of?'

'I was trying to do something for someone else, unlike you, who think only of yourself.'

'Well, if anything of mine goes missing I will not hesitate to send for the constable. Those little urchins might murder us in our beds.'

'Nonsense, Aurelia. They are just children — poor little orphans who have no one to care for them. No wonder they resorted to petty crime in order to feed themselves. I intend to make sure they flourish while they are in my care. You won't be here for long so please don't make things more difficult than they already are.'

Aurelia shot her a knowing look. 'I take it that Freddie doesn't agree with what you are doing.'

'He doesn't know that I've brought them here.'

'I wonder what he'll say when he finds out. I can't imagine that Lord Dorrington would approve, nor Bertie, if it comes to that. How are you going to persuade them that turning Greystone Park into a home for young villains is a good idea, Nancy?'

★ ★ ★

Nancy's first task next day was to placate Cook, who had been pestered for food by several of the boys from early that morning. She was on the point of handing in her notice and Nancy spent half an hour calming her down with promises that the boys would be made aware of what was and was not acceptable. Having left Cook in a happier state of mind, although not entirely convinced, Nancy went to round up the boys. She assembled them in the drawing room and tried hard to explain how things were run in a great house such as Greystone Park. Alfie and Stanley began to cry and she had to comfort them before she could continue. It was something of a relief when Nick arrived, bringing with him Miss Martha Collins and Miss Moon.

Nancy rose from her chair, trying not to look too relieved. 'Miss Collins, Miss Moon, this is an unexpected pleasure.' Nancy sent a questioning look in Nick's direction.

106

'I thought you might need some expert help,' he said, smiling. 'It came to me last evening. I know that these two ladies have been teachers in the past, and one thing the boys need is some schooling.'

'Of course. I'd quite forgotten.' Nancy held her hand out to Miss Martha. 'I am in dire need of expert help. The boys have had little or no education.'

'I don't need to go to school,' Todd said angrily. 'I can read and count the change what people gives me. I ain't a kid.'

Martha Collins stepped forward, fixing him with a stony expression. 'You, young man, are in no position to argue. Besides which, I need someone to keep the youngsters in order. That will be your job.' She turned to Nancy with raised brows. 'That's if you agree, Miss Greystone. I am so bored with living like a hermit. I would welcome the challenge to return to teaching.'

'And I would, too,' Miss Moon said shyly. 'I haven't got Martha's experience, but I would love to teach the little ones.' She took a hanky from her pocket and wiped Teddy's runny nose.

Gus snorted. 'You ain't going to fall for that one, are you, Todd? We're men and we have a gang. We ain't schoolboys.'

'Suit yourselves,' Nick said casually. 'But if you don't live by the rules that Miss Greystone puts down, you are free to leave. I'll give you the fare back to London and you can ask Masher to let you have your cellar room back.'

Todd and Gus exchanged wary glances.

'You wouldn't do that, mister,' Gus said boldly. 'You'd be afraid the lads would come with us.'

Nancy stepped in between them. 'You are all free to go if you wish. You aren't prisoners here. You may leave now, but I believe Cook is roasting a couple of chickens for luncheon, followed by a treacle pudding. It would be a pity to miss out on that.'

Todd squared his thin shoulders. 'Maybe I'll think about it after we've eaten.'

Martha slipped off her shawl and peeled off her gloves. 'I know where the schoolroom is situated, but we might need more seats and desks, Nick. Perhaps you would take a look in the attic? Anything will do for the time being. Best foot forward, boys. We'll begin right away.' She spun round at the sound of a giggle. 'Silence. Line up and follow me. Anyone misbehaving will forfeit their portion of treacle pudding.'

To Nancy's surprise, the boys lined up behind Todd and Gus. They followed Martha with Miss Moon at the rear, holding Teddy and Alfie by the hand while Stanley trotted obediently at her side.

'Don't worry, Nancy,' Nick said, smiling. 'I was once one of Miss Martha's pupils at the village school. I didn't turn out too badly.'

Nancy stared at him in surprise. 'I know so little about you.'

He laughed. 'When I've helped the ladies sort out the schoolroom, I'll have to tell you my life story until the time we first met.'

'I can't wait.' Nancy smiled. 'Thank you, Nick. Bringing Miss Martha and Miss Moon here was a stroke of genius. I was beginning to feel I'd made a terrible mistake.'

'We'll do our best by the boys, but I think you might have a difficult time convincing your relations and the Dorringtons that this is a good idea.'

'You're right, but it's really none of their business. Greystone Park belongs to me and I can do what I like in my own home.'

Nick gave her a quizzical glance. 'That's the first time I've heard you call this place home.'

He left the drawing room, closing the door behind him.

Nancy stared after him. Perhaps this was what Lord Dorrington had planned from the start. Maybe he thought she would grow to love her ancestral home and not wish to live in the palatial Dorrington Place. She shook her head. Nick was right about one thing: she needed to tell her family what she was doing before Aurelia descended upon them and gave them an exaggerated version of what was happening at Greystone Park.

8

It seemed to Nancy that everyone at Rockwood Castle was against her taking in a group of young criminals, even though their law-breaking way of life had been thrust upon them. Rosalind worried that they might turn on Nancy and steal all the valuables in Greystone Park before rushing back to London. Bertie, Alex and Leo said they thought Nancy was making a huge mistake and she was too young for such responsibilities. Walter agreed with them, although he did say it had given him an idea for his next novel. He had stopped writing poetry, finding it unprofitable, and was concentrating entirely on the popular market, which was financially more rewarding. Louise was clearly disturbed by the idea of Nancy caring for so many young hooligans, and Hester was frankly sceptical. She made no secret of the fact that she thought the whole idea was doomed to failure.

The only person who gave Nancy encouragement was Patricia, although she was so enraptured of baby Charlie that she had little time for anything or anyone else.

Eventually, the boys settled in with the help of Nick, Miss Martha Collins and Miss Moon, and arrangements for Aurelia and Rupert's wedding were finalised. The reception was to be held at the castle, although Aurelia had originally wanted to have the wedding breakfast at Greystone Park. However, she had changed her mind when she discovered that the boys would be present. Nancy laughingly suggested Aurelia might have twelve pageboys, but Aurelia's sense of humour did not stretch that far. It was, after all, to be a quiet family affair.

Piers and Lady Pentelow arrived at the castle the day before the wedding and Nancy was invited to the dinner arranged to welcome them back to Devonshire. Hester and Lady Pentelow were old adversaries and Rosalind made sure that they were kept as far apart as possible. That was even more necessary at mealtimes, and they were put at opposite ends of the long dining table. Nancy, on the other hand, found herself seated next to Piers, who not so long ago she had met in Barbados and attempted to persuade to return to Cornwall. He was in his late thirties but still a handsome man, his body honed to a fine muscular physique after years in the penal colony in Australia, and his skin still tanned from his time spent running the blockade to the Southern States of America. Nancy knew that he had made Rosalind's life miserable during their brief marriage, but it would seem that he had never found anyone else with whom he wished to spend the rest of his life. Nancy found herself oddly attracted to him, or maybe it was the effect of the wine that Bertie served so generously with their meal.

Rupert and Piers seemed to be getting along reasonably well, which made Aurelia happy, as her brother was going to give her away. Lady Pentelow did not bother to hide her displeasure at the match. She lost no time in reminding Aurelia of her failed marriage to Martin Gibbs, who had run the mine at Trevenor quite literally into the ground. At dinner that evening she had just made a sarcastic remark aimed at Aurelia's choice in men when Piers stood up to propose a toast.

'My grandmother is not in favour of the match, as we all know, but I am happy for Aurelia and Rupert. I think they are well suited and I wish them a long and happy marriage. Something I was not able to achieve for myself,' he added, raising his glass to Rosalind.

'That's enough, Piers,' Alex said sharply. 'Keep your smart remarks to yourself. Your loss was my gain.'

'Undoubtedly, old chap. I was a fool in those days. Anyway, here's to Aurelia and Rupert.' He raised his glass and everyone joined in. The feeling of tension was momentarily lifted.

'I suggest we ladies retire to the drawing room,' Hester said hastily.

Lady Pentelow glowered at her. 'You might have the title, Hester Carey, but you are not the lady of the house. I take priority over you.'

Hester glared at her. 'You might rule the roost in that godforsaken part of Cornwall, but here I am the dowager Lady Carey, and what I say is of great importance in Rockwood.'

Rosalind rose to her feet. 'Ladies, please. We are a family, and there is no need for anyone to feel less important than another. I think coffee in the drawing room is an excellent idea. There are fine details we need to discuss before the ceremony tomorrow.'

Patricia turned to Tilly, who had been waiting on table. 'It's time for Charlie's feed. Will you ask Jennet to bring him to the drawing room?'

Lady Pentelow had been about to leave the room but she came to a sudden halt. 'Surely you are not feeding the child yourself?'

Leo grinned. 'Well, I'm afraid I am not equipped to help out in that instance.'

'Vulgar man.' Lady Pentelow cast him a deprecating glance. 'Surely a wet nurse is called for?'

Patricia laughed. 'Why? I enjoy feeding my son. I'm sorry if it offends your sensibilities, my lady.'

'Insolent girl. You always were a problem.' Lady Pentelow sailed out of the room in front of Hester, who pulled a face behind her ladyship's back.

'I will swing for that woman one day, mark my words.' Hester marched out of the dining room, followed by Rosalind and Nancy, who could not stop giggling.

'And I thought it was going to be so dull here tonight,' Nancy whispered.

'Hush, they'll hear you.' Rosalind could not quite keep the laughter from her voice.

'It's my wedding,' Aurelia said plaintively. 'I don't know why Grandmama has taken against my marriage to Rupert.'

Nancy slipped her arm through Aurelia's as they walked to the drawing room. 'She doesn't want to lose you, Aurelia. Barbados is a long way away and she's an old lady.'

'Well, she doesn't have to spoil everything.'

'Never mind. Tomorrow you will be Mrs Rupert Charnley and in a couple of days' time you'll be on board ship headed for your new life.'

Hester reached the drawing room first and made a grand entrance, much to the obvious annoyance of Lady Pentelow, who had no alternative but to follow her rival into the room. Hester chose the largest wingback chair and lowered herself onto it as if she were sitting on a throne, leaving Lady Pentelow to find somewhere less prominent.

Patricia sat on the sofa next to Rosalind, leaving

113

Nancy, Aurelia and Louise to find seats for themselves. However, Patricia leaped to her feet when Jennet entered with baby Charlie.

'My beautiful boy,' Patricia crooned as she took the baby in her arms. 'Thank you, Jennet. Has he been good?'

'He's a perfect angel, ma'am.' Jennet bobbed a curtsey and left the room, giving mother and baby an affectionate glance over her shoulder as she closed the door.

Patricia settled herself on the sofa and began undoing the buttons of her elegant dinner gown.

'No! You are not going to feed the child here, in front of us all?' Lady Pentelow stared at her aghast.

'He's hungry. It's a perfectly natural thing to do, Lady Pentelow,' Patricia smiled, and guided the greedy little mouth to her breast, where he latched onto the nipple, making appreciative noises.

'I wish I'd had the courage to do that,' Louise said ruefully.

Hester rolled her eyes. 'It would not have been done in my day.'

'Indeed no. The younger generation never fail to shock me,' Lady Pentelow said, nodding.

Rosalind sighed. 'That's the first time you ladies have agreed on anything. Now may we call a truce until after the wedding tomorrow?'

'Yes, indeed, that would be such a relief.' Aurelia sent a pleading look to her grandmother. 'I will come home and visit you often, Grandmama. You might even brave the ocean and come to Barbados. You always complain about the cold winters in Cornwall.'

'She's always complaining,' Hester said in a low voice.

'I heard that, Hester Carey,' Lady Pentelow sniffed, and turned her back on Hester. 'I expect comments like that from a person risen from the servants' quarters.'

Patricia laughed and Louise covered her mouth with her hand, but Rosalind frowned and shook her head. 'Please stop bickering. This is meant to be a joyous occasion.'

'You should be telling Nancy off, not me,' Aurelia said loudly. She was prevented from elaborating on the subject by the arrival of Tilly with the coffee tray, which she set on a table at the side of the sofa.

'I'll pour, thank you, Tilly.' Rosalind stood up and began filling cups with coffee from a silver coffee pot. She waited until Tilly had left the room. 'Was that really necessary, Aurelia?'

Aurelia pouted. 'Well, everyone seems intent on giving me good advice. What about Nancy? She's taken in a gang of street urchins, attempting to turn them into little gentlemen.'

'They are decent boys at heart.' Nancy rose from her seat to help distribute the coffee. 'You'll see.'

'What's this? Has the world gone completely mad? You have adopted a street gang, Nancy?' Lady Pentelow stared at her aghast.

'Not exactly, Lady Pentelow. I have given them shelter, and Miss Collins and Miss Moon are giving them lessons.'

'I think it's a very laudable project,' Rosalind said firmly. 'Well intentioned, although I'm not convinced that it will work in the long run.'

'We'll see.' Nancy handed a cup of coffee to Hester. 'They are just children. I have plenty of people to help me.' She looked up as the door opened and Piers strolled in ahead of Alex, Walter and Bertie, who was as usual in his Bath chair, being pushed by Wolfe.

Piers gazed at Patricia and the baby and raised his eyebrows. 'I've never seen that done at a dinner party.'

'Dinner is over, Piers,' Patricia said sharply. 'Don't look if it offends you.'

'I'll thank you to stop staring at my wife.' Leo took a step towards Piers, who merely laughed and held up his hands.

'No offence meant, old chap. Patricia always was a law unto herself. I could tell you tales about her exploits when younger.'

'There is nothing I have done that is a secret from my husband.' Patricia moved the baby to her other breast, covering herself modestly with a lace shawl. 'You always were a despicable person beneath an outward display of charm.'

'Rosie didn't think so, and neither did you before you grew up to be a hypocrite, Patsy.'

Leo made as if to grab Piers by the collar but Wolfe, at a signal from Bertie, stepped in between them. No one in their right senses argued with Wolfe. Nancy eyed him thoughtfully. If the boys gave her trouble, she knew the very person to sort them out. She dragged her thoughts back to the present and she could see that Leo was furious.

Alex took him by the arm. 'Ignore my cousin, Leo. I grew up thinking Piers was my brother until the truth came out. He's an expert in causing trouble, as the law decreed. It seems that five years in the penal colony did nothing to improve your social skills, Piers.'

Piers shrugged and smiled. 'Nobody likes hearing the truth about themselves.' He turned to Nancy. 'Is there a spare cup of coffee? I would appreciate something to take the nasty taste from my mouth.'

Bertie half rose from his chair. 'That's enough, Piers. If you can't control your tongue you'd better leave us now. I won't have anyone upset in my house.' He shot an angry look at Lady Pentelow. 'And that goes for you, too, my lady. I know you are unused to being remonstrated with, but I would remind you that my stepmother deserves respect as much as you do.' He sank back on his seat. 'Where's the brandy? Pour me a glass, Wolfe. Pass the decanter round to anyone who feels the need for sustenance.'

Piers took a seat next to Nancy. 'Now what's all this about you starting a school for bad boys? It sounds like something close to my heart.'

'Leave her alone, Piers,' Rosalind said hastily. 'Nancy is only nineteen but she's unofficially engaged to Viscount Ashton, so don't think you can charm your way into her good books.'

'Ashton?' Piers leaned back in his seat, eyeing Nancy curiously. 'I believe I met him once. A little old for you, isn't he?'

'Freddie is more Nancy's age than yours, Piers,' Rosalind said with a wry smile. 'I'm sure that they will be the next happy couple to be married from here.'

'Is that true, Nancy? You really are a lucky young lady. And you inherited Greystone Park, too.' Piers winked at Patricia, who was holding Charlie over her shoulder to burp him. 'That must rankle, my dear. It should have come to you as the grieving widow.'

'I was fond of Greystone, despite the disparity in our ages,' Patricia said icily.

Nancy filled a spare cup with coffee. 'You are a mean man. I was prepared to give you the benefit of

117

the doubt, but I can see that everyone told the truth about you.'

'I am much maligned. If you give me a chance I will prove to you that I am a changed man.'

Nancy passed the cup to him, but the look in his eyes made her hand shake and she tipped the rapidly cooling liquid onto his lap.

Piers leaped to his feet. 'You did that on purpose.'

'My hand slipped. But I don't think anyone would blame me if I did tip coffee over you. We have standards here, and manners, too. You seem to have forgotten how to treat people, if you ever knew in the first place.'

Piers made a quick recovery. He stretched his lips into a wide smile. 'I like a woman of spirit. I hope Ashton can handle someone like you, Nancy.'

Lady Pentelow smiled indulgently. 'You are a perfect gentleman, Piers. I am so glad to have you back at Trevenor. The old house wasn't the same without you.'

Rupert, who had said very little all evening, went to stand behind Aurelia's chair. 'This time tomorrow, you and I will be man and wife, my love. We'll be on the boat heading for Barbados and home.'

'I know. It's so exciting. I'll be mistress of a great plantation.'

'I thought you were the younger brother, Rupert,' Piers said slyly. 'My sister loves to exaggerate.'

'If Dolph doesn't marry I suppose my wife will have that honour, but my brother has an eye for a pretty woman and I doubt if he will remain celibate for much longer.'

'How disappointing for you, Aurelia,' Piers said, laughing.

'Don't tease her, Piers.' Alex frowned. 'This is her

special time. Don't spoil it.'

'I agree.' Bertie signalled to Wolfe. 'Pass the brandy round, please. We don't want any arguments to spoil the evening.'

'Actually I am a little tired.' Aurelia rose to her feet. 'I want to look radiant tomorrow so I really would like to go back to Greystone Park with Nancy.'

Nancy stood up. If she were to be honest, it was a relief to be able to leave without appearing rude. 'Of course, Aurelia. If someone would kindly ring for a servant I'll order my carriage.'

'I think you are nearest, Lady Pentelow,' Hester said sweetly. 'Would you care to oblige?'

Lady Pentelow's bosom seemed to grow in size as she took a deep breath, but Rosalind was on her feet in seconds and she tugged at the bell pull.

'It's all right, ma'am. Please don't trouble yourself.' She cast a warning look in Hester's direction. 'Lady Pentelow is our guest, Hester.'

'As she keeps reminding us.' Hester beckoned to Wolfe and took a glass of brandy from him. 'Here's to the happy couple. Let us hope that all goes well tomorrow.'

Nancy gave her a suspicious glance but Hester was smiling innocently.

An apprehensive shudder ran down Nancy's spine. She had a sudden vision of Greystone Park burning to the ground, Todd and the boys dancing round the flaming ruins. 'Are you ready, Aurelia?'

★ ★ ★

Fortunately for everyone, the house was still standing when Nancy and Aurelia reached Greystone Park.

To Nancy's surprise, the boys were all asleep in their beds when she went upstairs to check on them. Foster informed her that Miss Collins had made all the boys work so hard that they could hardly keep their eyes open. Miss Moon had taken them for a long walk after supper, and that had added to their state of exhaustion. Nancy was able to help Aurelia to bed without any fuss and she sent Ivy upstairs to Aurelia's room with a cup of warm milk to aid her sleep. As she made her own way to bed Nancy could not help wondering what it would have been like had this been the evening before her wedding to Freddie. He seemed very remote and far away at this moment.

* * *

Next morning Nancy was up early. Ivy was sent to Aurelia's room with a tray of breakfast and a jug of hot chocolate, although most of the food remained untouched. Aurelia was so nervous it did not seem possible that she had been married before and knew exactly what to expect. Nancy managed to calm her down, but Aurelia kept relapsing into fits of the jitters that would have been amusing in any other situation. It took both Nancy and Ivy to get Aurelia into the cream silk gown that had been purchased in London. It fitted perfectly, emphasising Aurelia's slender figure and tiny waist, although her stays had been pulled so tight that she complained she could hardly breathe. The matching silk bonnet was trimmed with pink roses and tied with pink ribbon. The whole outfit was delightful and Aurelia looked beautiful. The thin, tired-looking woman had vanished, leaving a blushing bride who would make any man's heart leap at the mere sight of her.

Nancy dressed hurriedly in a turquoise-blue gown, which was her favourite, even though it was not new. Anyway, the bride would be the centre of attention and she was simply the bridesmaid. Rosalind's two girls, Dolly and Phoebe, were flower girls, as was little Charlotte, Louise's daughter. Rory, however, had refused point-blank to be a pageboy, and had created such a fuss that his mother gave up her efforts to persuade him.

Todd and the boys were not invited to the church, although Nancy had promised that they would be allowed to join the servants at Rockwood Castle. A tent had been set up in the grounds and a separate feast spread out for the servants' enjoyment. There would be music and dancing, although none of the boys, not even Todd, was interested in that. However, they looked forward to the party and had promised faithfully to be on their best behaviour. They were to walk to the castle, escorted by Nick, who arrived punctually.

'I don't want any trouble,' Nancy said in an undertone as he marshalled the boys into a line two by two. 'If the village lads cause trouble I want you to bring Todd and the others home at once.'

Nick smiled. 'Don't worry, Nancy. I have it all under control.' He lowered his voice. 'By the way, you look beautiful. The bride appears pale and uninteresting when standing next to you.'

'You are a flatterer, but don't let Aurelia hear you say things like that. For some reason she is terribly nervous. I don't know why, but I'll be glad when she's safely married to Rupert.'

'I saw crowds outside the church when I came past.

121

It's going to be quite a spectacle.'

Nancy pulled a face. 'It was supposed to be a quiet affair, but word must have got round. Anyway, the carriage is waiting. I'd better get Aurelia to the church.'

Nick had spoken the truth. It seemed as though most of the village had turned out to see the bride arrive. Aurelia pulled the veil over her face as the coachman drew the horses to a halt and he climbed down to open the carriage door and help her alight. Rosalind was waiting in the porch with Dolly, Phoebe and Charlotte all wearing frilly white dresses and carrying small wicker baskets filled with rose petals.

'I'm so nervous,' Aurelia said in a low voice as Rosalind led the girls into the church.

'Rupert looks very handsome,' Nancy said encouragingly. 'He's waiting for you at the altar. This is your moment, Aurelia.'

Piers approached them from inside the church door and proffered his arm to Aurelia. 'You look wonderful, little sister. I am proud of you.'

Aurelia took a deep breath. 'Thank you, Piers. I'm glad you are here to give me away.'

He grinned. 'For the second time. Let's hope this is the last one, Aurelia.'

'In a short while I'll be Mrs Rupert Charnley, with a whole new life ahead of me.' Aurelia stepped forward, treading on the path of petals strewn on the aisle by the little flower girls.

Nancy followed behind, clutching a posy of pink roses, similar to the one that Aurelia was carrying. When they reached the altar, Rosalind took the flower girls to sit with her in the front pew and, having taken the bride's bouquet, Nancy sat down next to Alex.

Louise's father, the Reverend George Shaw, welcomed the congregation in a short speech and then the organist struck up the introduction to a hymn. The service began in earnest, with the vicar rambling on a bit, which was hardly a surprise. George Shaw was notorious for lengthy sermons, and members of the congregation had been known to nod off. Most of those present were very familiar with the wedding ceremony and there was a momentary lull when the vicar asked if anyone knew of a reason why the couple should not be married.

'I know a reason.' A voice from the back of the nave brought a gasp of surprise from everyone present, and all heads turned to see who had spoken.

Nancy gazed in horror at the man who was supporting the veiled young woman who had cried out with such passion.

Hester clutched her hand to her bosom. 'Tobias. Is that you?' She rose to her feet and was about to rush down the aisle to greet her son, but Walter held her back.

Tobias nodded to his mother as he helped the distraught woman towards the couple at the altar.

'What have you to say for yourself, young woman?' George Shaw demanded angrily. 'Who are you?'

'I am Clara Charnley, Rupert's wife.' The woman's voice broke on a heart-rending sob. 'We were married secretly in Bridgetown two years ago.'

'That's not true,' Rupert said in a low voice. 'It was not a real marriage.'

Clara threw back her veil to reveal a face ravaged by grief. Nancy was struck by the beauty of the girl with bronze skin and jet-black hair. She looked like an exotic flower in a field of daisies. A ripple of amazement ran through the assembled family and villagers.

'Come into the vestry,' George Shaw said hurriedly.

'I don't understand.' Aurelia gazed up at Rupert with tears pouring down her cheeks.

'It wasn't a real wedding, my love,' Rupert said nervously. 'Clara is lying.'

Clara wriggled free from Tobias and lunged at Rupert, fingers clawed. She caught his cheek leaving long red scratches.

'You lied to me. What about our child? Did you tell her you have a son?'

'Into the vestry, please.' The vicar shooed them towards the vestry, Tobias restraining Clara, although she was struggling violently.

Hester broke free from Walter's grasp and hurried after them. 'Tobias, how did you become involved in this?'

His answer was lost and there was an uncomfortable silence in the church. Then Piers stepped forward, but Nancy caught hold of his sleeve.

'Leave them to sort it out by themselves.'

'She's my sister,' Piers said angrily. 'I'll thrash the fellow.'

'Sit down, Piers.' Alex leaned across to grab Piers by the arm. 'Leave them to talk it through.'

Piers subsided onto the pew next to Nancy. 'He won't get away with this.'

'Someone should be with Aurelia.' Nancy rose to her feet. 'I'll go.' She made her way to the vestry without giving anyone a chance to argue.

Aurelia had collapsed onto a chair, and was sobbing as if her heart would break. Rupert was trying to quieten Clara, who was quite hysterical, with Tobias

124

attempting to stop her from attacking her alleged husband.

George Shaw and the verger stood together, looking helpless.

Nancy placed her arm around Aurelia's shoulders. 'I'm so sorry.'

'How could he do this to me?' Aurelia shot a sideways glance at Rupert. 'This was supposed to be a wonderful day. Now it's a nightmare.'

The vicar seemed to shake off his lethargy. He laid his hand on Clara's shoulder.

'My dear lady, this is not helping anyone. Tobias, I suggest you take her out through the side door.'

'But my wedding,' Aurelia sobbed. 'Everyone will be waiting in the church.'

'My dear, I cannot marry you to this man who appears to have a wife already.'

'Is it true, Rupert?' Aurelia gazed up at him, her eyes magnified by tears.

Clara struggled with Tobias as he tried to manhandle her from the vestry.

'I have a certificate,' Clara cried furiously. 'I have it here, if this man will let me go.'

Tobias released her. 'I only brought her here because she was a passenger on my ship. She pleaded with me to bring her to Rockwood Castle, but I wish I'd left her on board.'

Clara pulled a crumpled piece of paper from her bodice and thrust it into the vicar's hands. 'There, that proves we are man and wife.'

George Shaw examined it carefully. 'What do you have to say, Mr Charnley?'

Nancy gave Aurelia a gentle hug. 'Be brave. This isn't your fault.'

'I thought I was in love,' Rupert said lamely. 'She said she was with child.'

'We have a little boy.' Clara grabbed Rupert by the lapels. 'You are the father of my child. We are legally married, but you didn't want your father to discover that you'd married the daughter of a slave. Now the whole world will know.'

'But how did you find out that I was getting married?' Rupert demanded.

'You're a fool. You wrote to your brother and he told everyone. Did you think you could keep it a secret?'

'What will I do?' Aurelia cried.

'I am truly sorry, Aurelia,' Rupert said sadly. 'I really did love you.'

'You've made a fool of me, Rupert Charnley. I hate you.'

Nancy sent a pleading look to the vicar. 'What do we do now, Mr Shaw? What will you tell the congregation?'

'The ceremony cannot proceed. There is nothing for it but to send everyone home.'

Nancy wrapped her arms around Aurelia as she collapsed in a fresh bout of sobbing.

'You are a spiteful woman, Clara,' Rupert said in a low voice. 'How could you follow me to England and humiliate me like this?'

Clara would have flown at him if Tobias had not caught hold of her.

'I'll take her outside to cool off.' He half carried, half dragged the protesting Clara from the vestry.

'I'll go and announce the unhappy news,' the vicar said mildly. He was about to open the door when Piers burst into the small room.

'What's going on? Is this true, Charnley? Have you

126

been leading my sister on?'

Rupert backed away, eyeing Piers' fisted hands nervously. 'It's not what it looks like, Piers. I do love Aurelia. I intended to divorce Clara when I returned to Barbados, but I didn't know I would meet and fall in love with your sister.'

'But you knew you had a wife.' Piers grabbed Rupert by the throat and they struggled, knocking over a chair.

Nancy opened the door and beckoned frantically to Leo and Alex. They pushed past George Shaw as he was about to make the announcement to the bemused wedding guests and they rushed into the vestry. Nancy stepped aside as the scuffle ended as quickly as it had begun. Alex restrained Piers with difficulty, and Leo manhandled Rupert out into the churchyard to join Tobias and Clara.

'Let me go,' Piers said furiously. 'That swine deserves a good thrashing.'

'I agree.' Alex released him. 'But now is not the time.' He leaned over Aurelia, proffering his handkerchief. 'I'm so sorry. That was a rotten thing to happen.'

Nancy moved aside as Rosalind hurried into the vestry, followed by Hester, Lady Pentelow and Patricia.

Louise hesitated in the doorway. 'What can I do? Papa has told everyone the ceremony is cancelled.'

'Take the children home, please.' Rosalind slipped her arm around Aurelia's shoulders. 'I'm so sorry. This is a terrible situation.'

'What about the wedding breakfast and the party in the grounds?' Nancy hardly dare ask the question, but someone had to be practical.

Aurelia held up her hand. 'Let it all go ahead. We will celebrate my lucky escape. How could I have imagined that man was in love with me? He would have married me bigamously and taken me to a strange country where I knew no one.' She rose shakily to her feet. 'I am all right, or I will be very soon. Grandmama, I want to return to Trevenor as soon as possible.'

Piers patted his sister on the shoulder. 'Well said, but I'm going to make sure that Charnley sails for home with his wife.' He strode out into the churchyard, calling Rupert's name.

'I hope he's not going to resort to violence,' Rosalind said anxiously.

'A black eye is the least of what Charnley deserves.' Alex took Aurelia by the hand. 'You're being very brave. We could take you back to Greystone Park, if you'd rather.'

'No, thank you. I have to face everyone sooner or later.' Aurelia wiped her eyes. 'I won't allow Rupert to humiliate me. I have my pride.'

Nancy kissed her on the cheek. 'Well said, Aurelia. I'll go outside and make sure Charnley and Clara have gone, so that you don't have to see either of them again.'

9

Hester was standing beneath one of the ancient yew trees, berating Tobias for bringing Clara to the wedding, although somewhat half-heartedly. She then turned on Rupert, who was standing a few feet away from Piers, with Leo and Alex ready to spring into action and prevent any further altercation between them.

'You, young man, ought to be ashamed of yourself,' Hester said, wagging her finger in Rupert's face. 'How did you think you would get away with such a heinous crime? Or is it common where you come from?'

Rupert hung his head and Nancy felt almost sorry for him. He was surrounded by unfriendly faces and one word out of place would find him in even greater difficulties.

'I am truly sorry, ma'am,' he said humbly. 'I suppose I thought my lawyer could sort it out when I returned to Barbados. I wasn't thinking clearly.'

'You cast me aside.' Clara eyed him malevolently. 'You have a son and you disowned him. Shame on you, Rupert Charnley. I hate the sight of you.'

'Take her back to the ship, Tobias,' Hester said firmly. 'I feel for the poor girl, but she is doing herself no good here. And you should go with her, Mr Charnley. You are not welcome here either.'

'I know that, ma'am. Again I am so very sorry.' Rupert turned to Tobias. 'I will pay well for a cabin on your ship, Mr Harding.'

'You will have to share with your wife,' Tobias said, grinning. 'That will be punishment enough, I think.'

'I will make you pay for the way you've treated me and that woman in the church.' Clara's vengeful smile did not bode well for Rupert. It was obvious that he was going to spend a few weeks tortured verbally by the woman he had wronged.

'I don't envy him, Hester,' Nancy said in low voice. 'Anyway, I think I'd better go to the castle and warn them what's happened. If we are to have the wedding breakfast I assume it will be without the bridegroom.'

'Definitely.' Piers moved to her side. 'I'll accompany you, if you have no objections, Nancy. It's up to me to make things run as smoothly as possible. I was about to give my sister away to that bastard — excuse the language, ladies, but I have no other word to describe Mr Charnley.' He proffered his arm to Nancy. 'You were a child when I last met you. I can't believe how much you've changed over the years.'

Nancy smiled. 'I'm old enough to know a ne'er-do-well when I meet one, Piers.'

'I can see I will have difficulty in charming you, Nancy Sunday.'

'Nancy Greystone, sir.' Nancy laid her hand on his arm. 'My carriage is waiting in the lane.' She turned to Hester. 'We'll go on ahead, unless you wish to come with us, of course.'

Hester shook her head. 'I'll stay here with Tobias.'

'We came in a hired vehicle, Ma,' Tobias said hastily. 'I'll take Mrs Charnley back to the ship, but you'd better go with Miss Nancy. You'll be more comfortable.'

'Just a minute.' Rupert looked from one to the other. 'I need to collect my things from Rockwood Castle.'

'I'll have them packed and taken to the docks, Mr Charnley,' Hester said firmly. 'I think it best if you go straight to the ship. My son will take you.'

'I suppose I have no alternative.'

'That's settled then,' Tobias said, nodding. 'I'll come and visit you when we're next in dock, Ma.'

Hester kissed him on the cheek. 'Very well, son. I hope to see you again very soon.'

'It's a regular run so I should be back in a few weeks. Come along, Mrs Charnley. I think it's time we left.'

'Tell her she's had a lucky escape,' Clara said angrily as Tobias led her away, followed reluctantly by Rupert.

'We'll take you back to Rockwood, Hester.' Piers proffered his arm but Hester backed away.

'It's Lady Carey to you, Piers Blanchard. You might have forgotten what you did to my family but I haven't. I think you and your grandmama should take Aurelia back to Trevenor.'

Nancy shook her head. 'Aurelia can stay at Greystone Park until she feels up to making the journey home.'

'Don't fall out, ladies,' Piers said, laughing. 'I'm sure Grandmama will be only too glad to return to Trevenor. As for myself, I'm not so sure.' He gave Nancy a charming smile. 'I rather like it here. After all, Rockwood was my home for the two years when I was married to Rosie, or have you forgotten?'

'That's something I will never forget, Piers. Don't include Nancy in your plans. She's spoken for.' Hester walked back into the vestry and slammed the door.

Nancy sighed. 'Come with me, Piers. My carriage is in the lane. I want to get back to the castle quickly.

I'm sure my boys will be on their best behaviour, but it seems that anything can happen on a day like this.'

★ ★ ★

Nancy and Piers were the first to arrive back at the castle. They were greeted excitedly by the servants, who had remained there to finish the preparations for the wedding breakfast and the party in the grounds. Two large tents had been erected and tables laid with pasties, pies, cooked meats, salads and an array of cakes. Nancy left Piers to break the upsetting news to the servants while she went in search of Nick and the boys. She followed the sounds of merriment and found them down by the river, paddling and splashing each other with water.

'Well?' Nick eyed her closely. 'How did it go?'

'The marriage was called off. It turns out that Rupert is married. His wife came all the way from Barbados to put a stop to the wedding. It seems that they have a child, but Rupert's family disapprove because Clara is the daughter of a slave. She is very beautiful — I can see the attraction — but I can't forgive Rupert for what he's done to Aurelia.'

'That's tragic for both women. Where is he now?'

'Hester's son, Tobias, has taken both of them to the ship. They sail tonight, which reminds me, I must get Tilly to pack Rupert's cases and have them sent to the docks.'

'Should I take the boys back to Greystone Park?'

'No need. Aurelia wants the party to go ahead as it would have done had she and Rupert gone through with the ceremony. It seems a little odd, but it would be a shame to let all that food go to waste.'

Nancy made her way back to the castle and made arrangements for Rupert's luggage to be sent to the docks. She found Piers in the great dining hall, eyeing the splendid banquet set out on the long mahogany table. He had a glass of wine in his hand and he raised it in a silent toast.

'Here's to what might have been. Poor Aurelia, she doesn't have much luck when it comes to men. Or rather, she has poor taste.'

'She wasn't to know that Rupert had a wife.'

'No, but she saw the way they live out in Barbados. Dolph Charnley is a notorious womaniser, and it seems that his brother is little better.' Piers drank thirstily. 'Have a glass of wine, Nancy. You look as though you need it.'

'No, thank you. I'm just finding it all a bit overwhelming at the moment. It was supposed to be Aurelia's lovely day.'

'She married Martin Gibbs, who was a common fellow from the village. Not her class at all, so naturally after a while it became untenable. Gibbs nearly bankrupted the mine, then died during a riot there. Fortunately for the family I came to the rescue.'

'Fortunate indeed.' Nancy backed away from him. Piers was too full of self-importance for her liking. Handsome he might be, but there was a cynical twist to his lips when he smiled, and a calculating look in his eyes. 'If you'll excuse me I'll go and see what the boys are doing.'

'Oh, yes, your protégés. I'd better send one of the servants to count the silver spoons.'

'Don't worry about that. My boys don't need to steal now. They are just children and they were desperate in London.' Nancy walked away before she

133

said anything more. People were so judgemental. Her boys deserved better.

As she left the dining room she could hear the sound of voices from the great hall as the family returned from the church. She went out through the music room, through the rose garden to the grounds where the party for the servants was to be held. At least the boys and the servants would have a good time.

But the sounds that reached her ears, even before she emerged from the stand of trees, did not bode well. Todd and Gus had seemingly taken on a group of the village boys, who were out for a fight and had found easy prey. The smaller boys had joined in, except for Alfie and Teddy, but Stanley was rushing about attempting to land punches on anyone who was threatening his friends.

There was no sign of Nick, and Nancy ran towards them shouting for them to stop. Then a sudden loud scream from Aurelia, who was leaning dangerously over the side of the open carriage, brought the boys to a sudden halt. The sight of the bride in her beautiful cream silk gown leaping from the vehicle was enough to make anyone stop and stare.

Aurelia raced down the grassy slope, brandishing her bouquet, the breeze whipping her veil into a frenzy. 'Stop that at once or go home. I won't have anything else to ruin my day.' She sank to her knees and sobbed.

10

Nancy ran towards her but it was Todd who reached Aurelia first. He kneeled at her side, placing his arm around her shoulders.

'I'm sorry, missis. We was just standing up for ourselves. We never meant to spoil your wedding day.'

Aurelia laid her head on his shoulder. 'It's too late. It's ruined already.'

Nancy rushed up to them. 'I'm so sorry, Aurelia. My boys didn't start it, I'm sure.'

'No,' Todd said firmly. 'We didn't. It was them.' He jerked his head in the direction of Nat Wills, the son of notorious ex-smuggler, Seth Wills, and his cousin Jan.

The rest of the boys hung back, eyeing them warily.

Nancy helped Aurelia to her feet. 'Well, boys, you should all be ashamed of yourselves.' She looked round to see Nick hurrying towards them. 'Where were you, Nick? Poor Aurelia had to witness a scrap. It's the last straw.'

Aurelia shook her head. 'No. I'm all right now, Nancy. Let's go inside.' She reached out to pat Todd on the shoulder. 'Thank you, boy. You are the only one who came to my aid.'

'It weren't nothing, missis.' Todd's pale skin reddened. 'I don't like to see ladies cry. My ma was always sobbing because the old man laid into her when he was drunk.'

Aurelia's eyes widened. 'You poor boy. I suppose I

135

should count myself lucky that I haven't married the wrong man.'

'Come with me,' Nancy said gently. 'We'll go into the castle. If you don't feel like talking to anyone I'll find somewhere quiet for you to sit and recover.'

'No. I have to face them all sooner or later. I want to get it over and done with.'

'I'm sorry about the fight, Nancy. I was only gone five minutes or so.' Nick followed them as they headed towards the castle gates.

'It's over now. No real harm done, except for Aurelia's wedding dress.' Nancy looked down at the grass stains where Aurelia had fallen to her knees.

'I will never wear this gown again,' Aurelia said angrily. 'I don't want to be reminded of my folly.'

'I heard what happened, Nancy.' Nick lowered his voice. 'That's why I wasn't here when the fight started. Pip Hudson brought the news when he came to harness up the horses for Lady Pentelow's carriage.'

'So everyone in the village will know by now.' Aurelia braced herself. 'I'll join the party, Nancy. I refuse to skulk around as if it were my fault.'

'Quite right. You are very brave.' Nancy tucked Aurelia's hand in the crook of her arm. 'Come on. We'll walk in as if nothing has happened.'

★ ★ ★

Despite her brave attempt to appear unconcerned, Aurelia tired quickly. She decided to return to Greystone Park with Nancy, leaving the family to enjoy the evening without her. She had stood up to several hours of being comforted and pitied, and she agreed to travel home to Trevenor with her grandmother the next day. Piers was undecided whether to go, but Lady Pentelow insisted that he should accompany them, and he was no match for his grandmother when she had made up her mind.

Nancy was relieved. She was aware that Piers was attracted to her, or perhaps he fancied being the master of Greystone Park as well as Trevenor. She decided that for the rest of the year she would concentrate on her boys. Romance would have to wait until she was allowed to see Freddie or until he decided to flout his father's orders. She could only hope that he would see sense, but she was not going to run after him. His apparent indifference to her problems had hurt more than she cared to admit.

Nick took the boys back to Greystone Park and Nancy followed on in the carriage with Aurelia, who was now exhausted and ready to collapse into bed. As Ivy and the other servants were still at Rockwood Castle, Nancy helped Aurelia to undress and put her to bed. Mrs Banks was the only member of staff who had remained at the house and she listened eagerly when Nancy told her what had happened in the church. Mrs Banks was moved to make hot chocolate for all of them, as well as the boys, who were now in their rooms. Nancy could hear their excited chatter coming from the floor above, but Aurelia did not seem to mind.

'I'll be asleep very soon. It's nice to hear children's laughter, and Todd was such a dear. I think you did the right thing in bringing them here, Nancy. They are just children and they deserve a second chance.'

Nancy left Aurelia to settle down and she went to the room that Todd and Gus shared. She knocked and entered to find Gus smoking a clay pipe and Todd

137

lying on his bed eating a pasty.

'Don't let Mrs Simpson catch you eating in your room,' Nancy said, laughing. 'If you get crumbs in your bed you'll be in trouble.'

Todd snapped into an upright position. 'I'm sorry, Miss Nancy. I didn't think you'd mind. The food we had was too good to leave any for the birds to peck at.'

'Of course. And, Gus, you shouldn't smoke up here. Be careful when you put your pipe out.'

'Yes, miss.' Gus grinned guiltily. 'I tap it out on the windowsill.'

'I didn't come here to tell you off. I wanted to thank you, Todd, for rushing to Mrs Gibbs' side when you saw that she was distressed. It was a kind thing to do.'

'I didn't stop to think, miss. She was so upset.'

'I've been thinking about your future, Todd.' Nancy perched on the edge of his bed. 'You are old enough to be apprenticed to someone, if you wanted to learn a trade. What would you like to do when you are grown up?'

'I'd like to be a doctor, but I know that's not possible for the likes of me.'

Nancy eyed him thoughtfully. She had not considered anything other than a trade for Todd, but he was a bright boy. 'Miss Collins says you are good at lessons. You would have to go away to school, but would you be prepared to do that and study so that you could go to a big hospital to train?'

'Yes, miss. I ain't afraid of hard work.'

'I think I'd like to work in the sawmill,' Gus said seriously. 'I ain't much good at book-learning.'

'Maybe Mr Wilder has a place for an apprentice, Gus. I'll ask him, if you are serious.'

'Would I get paid?'

'I don't suppose you'd get much to start with, but you could earn a good wage when you were qualified. It depends if you work hard and if Mr Wilder takes a liking to you. Put that pipe out before I go. I don't want the house to burn to the ground in the night.'

Gus grinned, took a last puff on the pipe, and tapped the bowl on the windowsill sending a shower of bright sparks into the night air.

'Good night, boys.' Nancy left the room to a chorus wishing her a good night, too. She made her way to her bedroom and sat on the window seat, gazing out into the gathering gloom of a summer night as she sipped her rapidly cooling chocolate. She had spoken to Todd with confidence, but to send him to a good boys' school would cost money she did not possess. However, she was not going to let that put her off. There must be a way.

★ ★ ★

Next morning Aurelia was up early. Ivy helped her to pack her things and she was ready to depart for Cornwall when the carriage arrived. Lady Pentelow and Piers came to collect her and they left a little after mid-morning. Nancy was sorry to see Aurelia go. She had been company, if rather difficult at times, but she was not sorry to see the back of Piers. Even saying goodbye, he managed to give her the impression that he was undressing her with his eyes. She was barely polite to him, but that only seemed to encourage him. He was obviously unused to women gainsaying him, and it made him even more determined to win her good opinion. Even so, she had a feeling it was all a game to Piers Blanchard. The chase was all, and

139

when won he would lose interest in his quarry. Nancy waved to Aurelia as the carriage set off again, but she pretended not to see when Piers blew her a kiss.

Martha Collins and Miss Moon had already begun lessons in the schoolroom, leaving Nancy with nothing to do. Nick had gone to the outlying farms to collect rent and she was free to do as she pleased. She decided to pay a visit to Patsy, who always lent a sympathetic ear to her problems. Perhaps Leo might be able to help Gus with an apprenticeship, which would certainly be good for the boy. He was too old to sit in the classroom with the younger ones and he was frankly bored with schoolwork.

Nancy took her bonnet and shawl from her bedroom, snatched a parasol from the umbrella stand in the porch, and set off to walk to the sawmill.

* * *

Fletcher let her in, holding her finger to her lips. 'Master Charlie is asleep,' she said in a stage whisper. 'Wake him at your peril.'

Nancy handed her bonnet and parasol to Fletcher. 'Don't babies sleep most of the time?'

'Not Master Charlie. He doesn't want to miss anything, the little monkey.' Fletcher smiled benevolently and Nancy stared at her in amazement. She had never seen Fletcher in such a good mood and her smile was quite disturbing.

'I'd like to see Mrs Wilder.'

'Of course. She's in the drawing room. You don't need me to announce you.' Fletcher bustled off with Nancy's outdoor things.

Nancy entered the drawing room to find Patricia

140

dozing off on the sofa. She opened her eyes with a start. 'Good heavens, Nancy, you startled me.'

'I'm sorry, but Fletcher told me to walk in. She's in such a good mood I hardly recognised her. She actually smiled at me — which made a shiver run down my spine.'

'Fletcher is in love,' Patricia said, laughing.

'With a man?'

'Well, he will be a man one day. No, she's fallen in love with Charlie. She dotes on him and fusses over him all the time. I can hardly get a look in.'

'Who would have thought it?' Nancy took a seat in a chair by the fireplace.

'How is Aurelia this morning?' Patricia asked anxiously. 'I don't particularly like her, but she didn't deserve what happened yesterday.'

'As a matter of fact she's been very brave about the whole thing. She was very upset at first, of course, but she was sensible enough to be relieved that she discovered Rupert's duplicity before they were actually married. She left for Trevenor with Lady Pentelow and Piers less than an hour ago. She's better off without Rupert Charnley, for all his wealth and charm.'

'Oh, I agree entirely. I was heartbroken when Alex didn't get home in time for our wedding, but now I see that it was the best thing that could have happened. We would have been miserable had we married each other, but Rosie is just right for Alex, and Leo is a wonderful man. I love him desperately.'

'Yes, he is, and it's lovely to see you both so happy.'

'Happier than I deserve, probably. I was a very selfish woman before I fell in love with Leo. I thought only of myself in those days, as you probably remember, but now I'm a different person — well, almost,'

141

Patricia added, laughing.

'You are an amazing wife and mother, and you haven't lost your sense of humour.'

'No, we all need that, especially when things are difficult as they have been for the past day or so. Anyway, what brings you here this morning, Nancy? Not that it isn't always a pleasure to see you, but you've been so occupied with Greystone business and your boys recently that we haven't had much time to chat.'

'Don't put all the blame on me, Patsy. You've been equally busy with young Charlie.'

'Yes, that's true. I had no idea that motherhood would be so all absorbing. I have to admit I adore my baby boy, but I'll always have time for you, Nancy.'

'Actually, I did have an ulterior motive in coming here today. I was wondering if Leo might be in a position to take on an apprentice in the sawmill.'

'Were you thinking of one of your boys?'

'Yes, Gus is thirteen, almost fourteen, as far as he knows. He's a good, strong lad and very eager to start work. He's not much good at lessons, unlike Todd, who is very bright. Todd wants to be a doctor. Can you believe that?'

Patricia frowned. 'That would mean going to a boarding school, which costs money. I hope you haven't committed yourself to paying his fees.'

'I don't think I could afford it, but he's worth encouraging, Patsy. You should have seen how he leaped in to comfort Aurelia yesterday.'

'That doesn't make him a suitable candidate for the medical profession.'

'I know, but he has ambition and he's a really nice boy. I would love to see him fulfilling his ambition and having a good life away from the sordid city streets.'

142

'You are a dreamer, Nancy. But you stood by me when I was on my own and trying so hard to have a career in opera. If you believe in this boy maybe there is a way. As to the apprenticeship, you'll have to ask Leo. Why don't you go to the mill now? I'd come with you but Charlie will wake up for a feed soon.'

'All right, I will.' Nancy rose to her feet. 'I suppose you know that Hester thinks you should have a nanny for your baby, and a wet nurse.'

'Nonsense. I don't want him to grow up not knowing his mama, as my brothers and sister and I did. I will be here always for Charlie — and any other children we might be lucky enough to have.'

Nancy smiled. 'You could not be less like your mama. I suppose she's still singing to audiences in Brighton, unless she's gone abroad again.'

'You know my mother almost as well as I do. She will turn up in between engagements and then she'll disappear again for weeks or months, even a year or two. She hasn't seen Charlie yet, although we sent her a telegram announcing his birth.'

'Did she reply?'

'She sent flowers with a messenger and a note of congratulations. That's all.'

'Maybe she'll turn up for the christening.'

'Who knows? I really don't care.' Patricia stood up and went to the door, holding it open. 'Fletcher, Master Charlie is crying.'

'I'm halfway there already, missis.' Fletcher's voice from somewhere upstairs made Nancy chuckle.

'She's worse than you, Patsy. Charlie has both of you wound around his little finger.'

'Wait until you and Freddie have a baby, Nancy. See how you feel then.'

143

Nancy shrugged. 'I'm beginning to forget what he looks like. Even when I saw him not long ago he seemed quite different.'

'What about Nick? You've been seen in his company rather a lot lately.'

'He's my estate manager, that's all. We get along very well but there's no romance, whatever people might say. I like him, and that's as far as it goes.'

'People do talk. What if it gets back to Freddie that you are seeing too much of your agent?'

'Maybe Freddie will come and see me and we can talk. Being separated like this is not good.'

'I'm sure that's what Lord Dorrington intended. Don't let the old man win.' Patricia hurried out of the drawing room as Fletcher came down the wide staircase, holding a sobbing baby Charlie in her arms. He stopped crying the moment she placed him in his mother's arms.

'You see, Nancy. It's like magic,' Patricia said tenderly. 'Come along, my little poppet, let Mama take care of you.' She disappeared into the drawing room, taking Charlie with her.

'I'm just going,' Nancy said hastily.

Fletcher went to a cupboard and took out Nancy's bonnet, shawl and parasol. 'I don't want them hooligans rushing around the sawmill. I know what street urchins are like.'

'You were listening outside the door.'

'It's the only way to find out what's going on. Mark my words, them boys is trouble.' Fletcher stomped off in the direction of the kitchen.

Nancy put on her bonnet and shawl before leaving the house. Fletcher might have grown up in the mean streets of the East End of London, but she did not know the boys. Given the opportunity, they would become respectable citizens and lead good lives, of that Nancy was certain — almost.

She left the pretty house with its garden surrounded by a picket fence and walked the hundred yards or so to the sawmill. As it happened, Leo had just dismounted from his horse and handed the reins to Robbins, who did odd jobs around the mill.

'Good morning, Nancy. This is a pleasant surprise.'

'I've just been to see Patsy and young Charlie. He's a fine boy, Leo.'

'Of course he is — he's my son. But you didn't come to the mill to tell me that.'

'No, I wanted to speak to you — in private,' Nancy added as she could see Robbins straining his ears to listen.

'Come into my office and tell me what's on your mind. You know I'll do anything I can to help you.' Leo led the way into the dusty mill. The aroma of fresh sawdust mingled with the smell of oil and burning coal. The great steam engine that powered the mill belched smoke and roared like an angry beast. Nancy was glad she did not have to work in such a noisy and dangerous environment, but she had no doubt that it would be heaven to someone like Gus.

Leo's office was small, untidy and the floor was strewn with sawdust. Nancy took a seat opposite Leo's desk. He cleared a space with a sweep of his hand and perched on the edge, eyeing her curiously.

'Well, what is it? Are you having trouble with those boys?'

She shook her head. 'On the contrary, they are doing really well. In fact, there is one of them, Gus, who is nearly fourteen, who is eager to train with you

145

in the mill. I was wondering if you could take him on as an apprentice.'

'I'd have to meet this fellow and have a chat with him, but to tell the truth I have been thinking of getting extra help. However, having said that, I don't know how much assistance a fourteen-year-old lad would give.'

'Isn't that the point of having an apprentice? I mean, you could teach him how to do things your way. Gus is a bright boy and full of energy. He needs a firm hand, though.'

'I had Jan Wills in mind, but I could interview both of them.'

'It was Jan who started the fight at the party.'

'He comes from a well-known family of ne'er-do-wells, but I believe in giving youngsters a chance.'

'So do I. I don't think you'll be disappointed in Gus.'

'Tell him to come and see me this afternoon. I'll be here for the rest of the day.' Leo gave her a searching look. 'There's something else on your mind. What is it, Nancy? You can tell me.'

'I know I can, Leo, but I don't think you could do anything for Todd. He told me he would like to be a doctor. He's a bright boy and Miss Collins says he's really good at lessons, and diligent, too. He really needs to go to a good school, but I can't afford the fees.'

'You have a good heart, Nancy. However, you can't do miracles for these street children. Working in the mill is one thing, but becoming a physician is another.'

'So you think I should discourage him?'

'Not at all, but he isn't your responsibility. Why not take the boy to see Dr Bulmer? Ask his opinion and see if he has any ideas that wouldn't cost you a fortune.'

'I hadn't thought of that. I'll do it, Leo.' Nancy rose to her feet. 'I won't waste any more of your time, but thank you for your help. I knew I could count on you.' She left the office feeling buoyed up with the news she was about to give Gus, and then it was a matter of taking Todd to see Dr Bulmer, who might not be able to help, but it was worth a try. They had to start somewhere. She hurried home.

* * *

After luncheon that afternoon, Nancy left the younger boys in the care of Miss Moon, who delighted in putting them through their paces outdoors. They played her version of cricket with five a side, and she had them doing relay races to wear off their excess energy.

Nancy took Gus to the mill and introduced him to Leo, and then she went on to Dr Bulmer's house with Todd. Luckily the doctor was at home and his housekeeper showed Nancy and Todd into the small front parlour, where they were joined minutes later by the doctor himself. He sat in his chair by the table, which was strewn with books and papers, and he listened intently. Nancy explained what she knew of Todd's background and then Todd spoke for himself with such sincerity that Nancy was impressed. She could see that the doctor, who had looked sceptical at first, was beginning to take interest in the boy.

'Well, then,' Dr Bulmer said slowly, 'you seem like a bright young fellow. I'm prepared to give you a chance. I need someone to help me by running errands and taking medicine to my patients. You could lodge here with me and Mrs Lloyd, and you could come with me on some of my visits. That way you will be able to decide if this is the career you want. If not, I might be able to apprentice you to the apothecary in Dawlish.'

'I'd rather learn from you, sir.'

Dr Bulmer turned to Nancy. 'You seem to be the boy's unofficial guardian. What do you say?'

'I think it's a wonderful opportunity for Todd to decide what he wishes to do.'

'He will have to study in his spare time,' Dr Bulmer said sternly. 'I will work you hard, young man.'

Todd beamed at him. 'That's all I want, sir. I can prove myself and become a man like you, who does something good for people. I don't want to go back to thieving for a living.'

Dr Bulmer cleared his throat. 'The least said about that the better.'

'When can I start, sir?' Todd asked eagerly.

'Well, now, you are keen.' Dr Bulmer smiled.

Nancy was struck by the twinkle in the doctor's blue eyes and for a brief moment she could see him as a young man before life had etched his face with furrows of pain and worry.

'Don't pester the doctor, Todd,' Nancy said warily.

'It's quite all right, Miss Greystone. I like a boy who is enthusiastic. You may start tomorrow, Todd. I'll speak to Mrs Lloyd, and if she can get a room ready in time you can move in.'

'Thank you, Dr Bulmer.' Nancy rose to her feet. 'I'm sure that Todd will work very hard.'

'I will, sir. Thank you.'

'Tomorrow morning at half past seven sharp. I hate unpunctuality.'

'Yes, sir. I'll be here.' Todd followed Nancy from the

148

doctor's parlour and out into the village high street.

Nancy set off towards Greystone Park with Todd at her side.

'I wish the people in the workhouse could see me now.' Todd threw his cap into the air and caught it deftly. 'They said I'd never amount to nothing. I'll show 'em.'

'You probably find it hard to believe, but I was a foundling and I spent my first years in an orphanage. It was the vicar's wife who found me there and took me on as a servant when I was only eight years old.'

Todd stared at her in amazement. 'But you're a lady now, miss. How did that happen?'

'It's a long story and I'll tell you one day, but it just shows that you don't have to take what life deals out to you in the first place. You've got a chance to become a professional man, Todd. Take it with both hands.'

'I will, miss. I certainly will.'

'And Gus can start tomorrow at the sawmill. Mr Wilder is going to give him a chance to prove himself before he signs him up as an apprentice. I am so proud of both of you.'

They walked on, acknowledging the greetings from the villagers, most of whom knew Todd and the rest of the boys by sight, if not by name. Nancy introduced him to everyone, telling them that this was Dr Bulmer's new assistant. This caused quite a stir as well as a lot of interest. Todd handled it very well, considering that this was all new to him. Nancy was as proud of him as if he were her younger brother.

When they reached home Todd rushed off to tell his friends the good news and Nancy went to find Miss Collins and Miss Moon, who were tidying the schoolroom after the morning session.

'That's excellent,' Martha said, nodding. 'Those two are definitely the brightest, although some of the other boys are doing well, but there's only so much I can teach them.'

'What are you saying?' Nancy pulled up a chair and sat down. This sounded serious.

Martha handed her a list. 'The little fellows are fine. Alfie, Stanley and Teddy, together with Rob, Joe and Mick, are all capable of learning a lot from me. Moon helps them if they have difficulty reading, and she teaches them how to play cricket after a fashion. She sees that they get plenty of fresh air and exercise.'

Nancy consulted the list. 'That leaves Ben, Frankie, Jonah and Moses. They are all about ten years old, according to what they can remember of their past, maybe a year older.'

'Yes, precisely, and none of them is particularly academic. They can all read and they can write their names and simple text. They can add up enough to get by in daily life, but teaching them further is, in my opinion, a waste of time. They need to learn a trade or be put to work on the estate. They'd be fine with farm work or gardening, or even in the stables.'

'I understand. May I keep this list? I'll give it to Mr Gibson. He's sure to know who would be willing to take them on.'

'I'll miss them,' Miss Moon said sadly. 'They're good boys at heart.'

'I see no reason why they should have to move out until they are ready to do so. As far as I'm concerned they can live here in the house. I'm not about to turn anyone out.'

Martha nodded approvingly. 'I was hoping you'd

150

say that. It would be a shame to send them back to a life on the street when they've achieved so much in such a short space of time.'

'That I will never do. Those boys got together to form a family of sorts. They must make their way in the world, but they still need help and I'll do whatever I can for them.'

'That's all any of us can do.' Martha smiled. 'I've discovered a new purpose in life, thanks to you, Nancy.'

Nancy laughed. 'I wouldn't own Greystone Park if you hadn't made it possible for me to prove who I am. As far as I'm concerned, you and Miss Moon are welcome to move into the big house, if you so wish. Unless you want to remain in your cottage.'

Martha and Miss Moon exchanged meaningful glances. 'Thank you, Nancy,' Martha said slowly. 'It's a generous offer, but what would Christina say? You know how she feels about this place.'

'Christina has Cottingham Manor all to herself now that Glorina has moved into the dower house there. Christina just enjoys making things difficult for me. Greystone Park is mine to do with as I wish.'

'I think we'll stay where we are, but thank you for the thought,' Martha said firmly. 'You will try to find work for the older boys, won't you?'

'Of course. I'm seeing Mr Gibson this afternoon. I'll ask him then.'

Nancy saw the knowing look that Miss Moon gave Martha, but she chose to ignore it. Nick Gibson was her land agent. Why did everyone try to make more of it than that?

11

Nancy and Nick spent the next two weeks exploring the possibilities of sending the older boys to work locally where they would learn to support themselves when they were adults. However, it seemed that most of the farmers had sons who worked for them for very little pay, apart from their keep, and very few of them were interested in taking on city boys unused to country life. Ben spent most of his spare time in the stables, and the head groom was pleased to take him on as a stable boy with a view to becoming a groom should he prove to be useful. Frankie was interested in gardening and Nancy persuaded Ezra Pavey, the head gardener at Greystone Park, to take him on temporarily to see if he was suited to the work. That left Moses and Jonah, and Nancy decided to visit Rockwood Castle in an effort to settle them. Bertie was always keen to help young people find employment. The only other large house in the area was Cottingham Manor, but Nancy did not think Christina would be interested and very unlikely to want to help, despite her position as the wife of a clergyman.

* * *

Bertie listened with interest. 'Two boys, you say. How old are they?'

'We think they are ten or even eleven. Neither of

the boys knows his date of birth and they are quite small, having been poorly fed for most of their young lives. But they are keen to work, Bertie. They deserve a chance to make good.'

Bertie nodded. 'Yes, I agree. I'll have a word with Hudson and see if he needs a stable boy. His son, Pip, is under groom now, so they might be glad of a youngster. Maybe Abe Coaker will take one of the boys on to work in the gardens. He's due to retire soon and his grandson, Noah, will take over. He's a decent young fellow and he will probably be glad of an extra pair of hands.'

'Thank you, Bertie. I knew you would be keen to help.'

'The younger generation will take over soon enough. I just wish that I was able-bodied. I get so tired and frustrated being stuck in this damned chair.'

Nancy stared at him in surprise. 'Bertie, I've never heard you complain before.'

'I know. I try to keep my feelings hidden. I'm sorry to burden you, Nancy.'

She leaned over to clasp his hand as it rested on the arm of the Bath chair. 'You aren't burdening me. I'm glad you feel you can speak openly. It's hard to imagine what you must have gone through.'

'Thank you, Nancy. The worst part is that I've had a telegram from the powers that be telling me that Tommy has been badly injured in a skirmish of some sort. He's been sent home, but apparently they took him off the troop ship when they landed in Gibraltar and he's in the military hospital.'

Nancy's hand flew to cover her mouth. 'Oh, no! Poor Tommy. Do you know how bad he is?'

153

'No, I don't. The telegrams are terse, to say the least, but they might not send him home for weeks, maybe months, depending on how he progresses. I'm going to travel to Gibraltar to bring him home.'

'I'm sorry, but surely someone else should go?'

'Why? Because I'm a cripple?'

'No, well, yes. I suppose so.'

'I've been stuck in this chair for longer than I care to remember. I'm still Tommy's father, even though I did nothing for him in his early childhood because I didn't know he existed. You must know the story.'

'A little,' Nancy said hesitantly.

'I won't go into all that now, but Rosie will tell you anything you want to know. Anyway, I'm going to take Wolfe with me and we'll bring Tommy home. I don't care how much it costs, but I'm going to do my duty as his father for the first time in his young life.'

Nancy squeezed his fingers. 'You've been a wonderful father to him. He loves you, Bertie. We all do. No one thinks any the less of you because of your disability.'

He withdrew his hand gently. 'Maybe not, but this is something I must and will do.'

'Then I'm coming with you. Tommy was my friend from the first day I arrived here as a terrified ten-year-old. We practically grew up together so I love him as much as you do. I might be able to help look after him.'

'But, Nancy, you have a life of your own now. You are mistress of Greystone Park, and you have the responsibility for all those boys. Wolfe and I can manage on our own.'

'The boys are settled and being well cared for by Miss Collins and Miss Moon, not to mention Nick

Gibson. I rely on him to help me with estate matters and he gets on well with the boys. A few weeks away from Greystone Park will do me the world of good and I can repay a little of the kindness you've always shown me. Besides which, I can't bear the thought of Tommy ill and alone in a military hospital.'

Bertie gazed at her, frowning. 'It might be a good thing to have you with us. I can't look after him on the sea voyage home, and Wolfe is not exactly a ministering angel.'

'Then that's settled, Bertie. When are you planning on leaving?'

'As soon as we can book a passage. Wolfe is going down to the harbour to see if there are any ships due that might take us to Gibraltar.'

'Then I'll go and find Rosie and tell her that I'm going with you. Perhaps she could arrange for my boys to work here in some capacity.'

'I can see there's no way to convince you that this is a mad idea.'

'No. None at all. We're going together whether you like it or not.'

'And what about Freddie?'

'I'm not allowed to see him for another few months. He won't even know I've gone. You and Lord Dorrington wanted it this way, Bertie. I'm supposed to become a responsible person, and that's exactly what I'm doing now.'

Bertie gave her a wry smile. 'You certainly know your own mind, Nancy.'

'Yes, I do. I'm going home now to pack a bag and make the necessary arrangements with the servants and Miss Collins. Let me know when Wolfe has booked a passage.' Nancy made to leave the room, but she hesitated in the doorway. 'Please make sure he books a cabin for me, too.'

* * *

It was the beginning of August when their ship docked in Gibraltar Harbour after a reasonably smooth passage. Oddly enough, it was Wolfe who had suffered from seasickness, to the extent that he was laid up for days on end, unable to move from his bunk. Nancy had managed to get Bertie up and dressed, with the help of several members of the crew, who had been more than willing to be of assistance. Nancy suspected that Bertie gave them generous tips, but she said nothing that would embarrass him. She understood his reluctance to appear helpless, and she did her best to help him surreptitiously.

Wolfe appeared to recover miraculously the moment he stepped ashore, and the colour gradually returned to his ashen cheeks. It was incredibly hot and the sun beat down mercilessly as they sat in an open carriage on the way to the garrison. The town was crowded with small dwellings, and the smell of sewage hung in a pall over the maze of narrow streets. Nancy was relieved when they reached the army headquarters, although it was disappointing to discover that it was little better than the rest of the island. They had been told that accommodation in the town was very basic, but as it happened Bertie knew the commanding officer, Colonel Fielding, having served with him in the Crimea, and they were welcomed into his home.

However, when Bertie asked to see his son the colonel hesitated. 'I'm afraid that's not possible at the moment, Bertie.'

156

'Why not? We've come all this way to take him home where he will receive the best of treatment.'

Colonel Fielding raised an eyebrow. 'Are you suggesting that he isn't being looked after properly here?'

'No, of course not, but he will recover faster at home.'

'When can we visit him?' Nancy asked anxiously. She could see that Bertie was growing impatient and Wolfe was scowling. It would not do to unleash Wolfe on the colonel if he lost his temper. Nancy could visualise them all ending up in the island prison.

'It isn't my choice, Miss Greystone,' Colonel Fielding said equably. 'But I understand that Tommy is being treated for cholera as well as the bullet wound he sustained.' Colonel Fielding reached for a cut-glass decanter and topped up Bertie's glass with brandy.

'Have you any more details of his wounds?' Bertie demanded, ignoring the proffered glass. 'I have so little information.'

Colonel Fielding took a sip of his drink. 'Your son received a gunshot wound while stationed in India. The bullet missed all his vital organs and was successfully removed, but it was deemed wise to send him back to England to recuperate. He was brought ashore here to await a ship, but unfortunately he contracted cholera.'

'Oh, no!' Nancy choked on a sob. 'Poor Tommy.'

'He must have the best treatment possible,' Bertie said anxiously. 'I'm not a wealthy man but I would sell Rockwood Castle if necessary.'

'I understand, Bertie. In your particular circumstances I can see how difficult this is for you, but I'm just telling you what the doctors told me. I think Tommy has passed the crisis, but you will need to

157

speak to his physician.'

'I do want to talk to him urgently, and I want to see my son.'

'Sir Bertram wishes to see Master Tommy,' Wolfe growled. 'He wants to see him now.'

Colonel Field shot a nervous glance in Wolfe's direction. 'Bertie, kindly tell your man not to interfere. Cholera is endemic here and the fewer people who visit the wards the better.'

'It's all right, Wolfe,' Bertie said hurriedly. 'Leave this to me.' He turned to Fielding. 'How would you feel if it were your son, Elliot?'

'The same as you, Bertie. But if you or the young lady or your manservant go down with cholera you will be no help to Tommy. We've had many deaths from the disease, so you can't be too careful.'

Nancy could see that Bertie was not about to accept this. She laid her hand on his arm. 'We won't help Tommy by contracting the sickness ourselves.'

'Miss Greystone is quite correct.' Colonel Fielding downed the last of his brandy and stood up. 'I suggest you go to your rooms and rest until luncheon. I have duties to perform but we can have a chat this evening.' He signalled to a servant who had been standing to attention by the door. 'Show our guests to their rooms and make sure that they have everything they require to make them comfortable.'

Bertie opened his mouth as if to argue but Nancy stepped in between him and the colonel. 'Thank you, Colonel. It's very good of you to have us here at all. Isn't it, Bertie?' She turned to him, willing him to agree.

'Yes, of course it is.' Bertie shook the colonel's hand. 'But I would like to see Tommy as soon as possible.

158

Perhaps someone could tell him that we're here.'

'Of course,' Colonel Fielding said with obvious relief. 'We are doing everything we can for him. I really must leave you now, but we'll discuss this further at luncheon.' He left the room quickly, as if afraid that to linger might involve further questioning about Tommy's condition.

The servant cleared his throat. 'If you would follow me, please.'

Wolfe picked Bertie up as if he were an infant and carried him from the room with Nancy following.

Their rooms were next to each other on the second floor of the tall, narrow house. Nancy's was little bigger than the cabin she had used on board ship, but it contained a single bed, a chest of drawers and a washstand. It was all she would need for a short stay.

'We need a wheeled chair for the master,' Wolfe said gruffly as the servant ushered them into the next room. Nancy stood in the doorway, waiting until she was sure that Bertie had everything he wanted.

The servant bowed. 'I'm sure there must be one somewhere in the hospital, sir.' He backed away and Nancy heard his feet pounding on the stairs as he went to investigate, or perhaps he merely wanted to get away from Wolfe, who had that effect on most people. Wolfe closed the bedroom door with rather more force than was necessary and Nancy found herself alone on the landing. She went into her room, but it was gloomy with a small window high in the stone wall. She could only look out if she stood on the chest, and that was risky. She sat on the bed for a while, but the thought of being stuck in such a small room for several hours until luncheon was too much for her. She decided to explore. Colonel Fielding had

159

not forbidden them to walk around the garrison; he had merely wanted them to keep away from the fever wards.

Nancy went downstairs quietly. She felt quite nervous in the strange house with the sound of marching feet on the parade ground, and the loud voices of the drill sergeant as he shouted orders to the soldiers. No one seemed to notice her, and she found a shady spot where she could sit on a wooden bench and observe the comings and goings.

She gradually pieced together the different parts of the garrison buildings. The smell of cooking wafted from the kitchens, and the officers' mess seemed to be in the building adjacent to the colonel's residence. What she wanted to find out was where the wards were situated, and she watched for medical orderlies, following them visually until they disappeared into what she gathered must be the hospital. She spotted several women carrying large wicker baskets of washing, and the smell of lye soap wafted from what must be the wash house furthest away from the main buildings. They were either soldiers' wives, or perhaps they were local women. Nancy made up her mind to try to speak to one of them if the opportunity arose.

It was very hot in the sun and suddenly she was tired. They had risen early to disembark and, lulled by the heat, Nancy closed her eyes. She had not intended to fall asleep but suddenly she was awakened by someone tapping her on the shoulder.

'Are you all right, my duck?'

Nancy opened her eyes and found herself looking into a friendly face. The snub nose and freckles were those of a young woman, not much older than herself. Her flame-coloured hair was scraped back into a tight knot, only partially covered by a slightly grubby mob-cap. Her blouse and skirt were equally soiled, as was her apron. She dumped a wicker basket filled with cleaning cloths and tins of polish onto the cobblestones.

'I felt a bit faint,' Nancy said weakly. 'It must be the heat.'

'I ain't seen you afore.'

'No. We only arrived this morning. My brother is sick in the hospital here. Well, he's not my brother really, but we were brought up together.'

'You got no chance of visiting. They don't like civilians on the wards.'

'Do you live here?'

The young woman grinned and wiped her hand on her apron. 'Ettie Mayes. My old man is a private. I follows the drum, if you know what I mean.'

Nancy shook her hand. 'I'm Nancy Greystone. How do you do?'

'Nice to meet you, miss.'

'Nice to meet you, too, Ettie.' Nancy eyed her speculatively. 'Do you know the hospital wards?'

'I should. That's what I does. I cleans the wards, scrubs the floors and I takes the soiled sheets to the laundry. Now that's where I'd like to work — it's clean and smells nice there.' Ettie lowered herself onto the bench. 'I shouldn't sit down but me feet are killing me.'

'I'm sorry. Surely no one would mind you taking a short rest?'

'You don't know about military regulations. They applies to such as I as well as the men.'

'So you are a sort of soldier.'

'If you like. We do get paid a pittance for working,

161

but it's better than nothing.'

'I don't suppose you know the names of the patients?'

'Not all of them, but I gets to know some of the men who's in for a long time.'

'Do you know Tommy Carey?'

Ettie laughed. 'Tommy is my pet. He's so poorly, bless him. I prays for him every night.'

'Could you smuggle me in to see him?'

'I dunno about that, miss. I'd be in trouble if we was found out.'

'I just want to see him and let him know that I'm here.'

Ettie glanced round nervously. 'Well, I suppose I could do with a hand to carry the laundry basket tonight, but you'd have to wear something less fancy. I mean, you look like an officer's wife and they don't go nowhere near the hospital wards.'

'Of course. Maybe you could lend me an apron and a headscarf.'

'Like dressing up for a play.' Ettie giggled. 'Lord have mercy on me. I'll do it. Meet you here at ten o'clock. It's me last round and most of the guards are half asleep or dead drunk. Don't say nothing to no one.'

'I won't, I promise.'

'Now I got to get on.' Ettie rose to her feet. 'Best not tell anyone we had this chat, miss. I'm not supposed to speak to officers' womenfolk.'

'That seems very unfair, but I wouldn't want to get you into trouble.' Nancy stood up and gave Ettie a hug. 'Thank you. I'll be here at ten o'clock on the dot.'

Ettie picked up her basket and walked away. Nancy returned to the colonel's house and was greeted by a young woman, who was probably the same age as Ettie but her youth and beauty had not been dimmed by a hard life. Her abundant dark curls were glossy and her skin had the freshness of youth. Her green eyes sparkled with interest.

'I'm Cordelia Fielding. My papa is the colonel. How do you do?'

'How do you do, Cordelia? I'm Nancy Greystone.'

'Yes, I know. Papa told me. Do come and sit down.'

'Thank you.' Nancy took a seat by the window where she had a view of the parade ground.

'I'd offer you tea or coffee, but luncheon will be served very soon.'

'That's quite all right.'

'You look rather flushed. It isn't advisable to go out in the heat of midday.'

Nancy smiled ruefully. 'Yes, I realise that now.'

'It's so exciting to have visitors, especially from home. Papa tells me you come from Devonshire.'

'Yes, we're very close to the sea, as you are here.'

'I can't say I enjoy living on the Rock. I wish we could return to London. I miss the city and the theatres, not to mention the restaurants, but we have to go wherever Papa is posted.'

'Your mama is here, too?'

'No, sadly she died five years ago. I have to act as hostess when Papa entertains, which isn't very often here. If we were back home in England it would be different. However, now I have you to tell me everything. Have you been to London recently?'

'As a matter of fact I have, and I had quite an adventure there.'

Cordelia sat on the edge of her seat. 'Oh, please tell.'

Nancy related the events that had led her to be

abducted by the boys, and the way they had become her friends and her responsibility. Cordelia was a good audience and she bombarded Nancy with questions, so much so that it was a relief when Colonel Fielding entered the room, followed by Wolfe pushing Bertie in a Bath chair borrowed from the hospital.

'I've just been informed that luncheon is ready, Cordelia. But first I must introduce you to Sir Bertram Carey.'

Cordelia bobbed a curtsey. 'How do you do, Sir Bertram?'

'How do you do, Miss Fielding?'

Cordelia laughed. 'Cordelia, please. It's so lovely having guests from home. Nancy has been telling me a little about Rockwood Castle and Greystone Park.'

'Perhaps you and your papa would be able to visit us one day,' Bertie said eagerly.

Nancy was struck by the way his serious expression changed into one of admiration when he looked at Cordelia. 'That would be lovely,' Nancy said, smiling. 'I'm sure you have many interesting stories about the events you've witnessed here. Our lives would seem very dull in comparison.'

Colonel Fielding glanced at the grandfather clock in the corner of the room. 'I suggest we go to the dining room for luncheon. I'm afraid I have duties to perform in less than an hour, but Cordelia will look after you both.'

'That will be an absolute pleasure.' Bertie smiled at Cordelia, who lowered her eyes and blushed prettily.

Nancy was amused and slightly shocked. She had grown up accepting Bertie in his present disabled state. The notion that he was still an attractive and relatively young man had never occurred to her.

164

Cordelia walked beside Bertie as Wolfe wheeled him into the dining room and Cordelia sat next to Bertie at table. By the time the meal ended Nancy was beginning to feel annoyed. They had come to rescue Tommy, but his name had not come up since they first arrived and Bertie had asked after his son. Now it seemed as if Bertie had forgotten all about Tommy and he was basking in the sunny attentions of Cordelia Fielding.

The colonel left them when coffee was served, explaining that he had papers to sign and a meeting with the local mayor to discuss the present water shortage. Bertie dismissed Wolfe, telling him to go to the servants' quarters where he would have his meal, and Nancy sat silently, listening to the chit-chat between Bertie and Cordelia. It was not until Cordelia seemed to realise that she had been monopolising the conversation that she turned to Nancy with an apologetic smile.

'I'm so sorry, Nancy. We've been ignoring you, but I find Sir Bertram such a fascinating man. Our shared experiences of army life must sound terribly boring to you.'

'Nancy doesn't mind,' Bertie said airily. 'She's a real trouper, aren't you, my dear? We've been through a lot at Rockwood Castle and Nancy has always been stalwart in her support of the family.'

'I wouldn't say that exactly,' Nancy began, but was interrupted by Cordelia, who laughed and shook her head.

'I can see how staunch a companion you are, Nancy. If I can persuade Papa to bring me to Rockwood, you and I will have a wonderful time together.'

'Yes, I'm sure.' Nancy struggled to think of an excuse to leave the room without appearing rude, but

165

Cordelia was already on her feet.

'It's a lovely day. I don't want to be trapped indoors a moment longer. I suggest we go for a walk in the garrison gardens. Papa makes sure that the plants are well tended even in the hottest weather.'

'You'd better ring for my manservant,' Bertie said eagerly. 'I would love to see your garden.'

'We don't need that scary man with us.' Cordelia seized the handle of the wheelchair. 'I can push you, Sir Bertram. Nancy can help if we get stuck.'

Bertie's brows snapped into a frown. 'No. I don't think that's a good idea.'

Cordelia merely laughed and manoeuvred the chair out of the dining room with Nancy hurrying after them.

'Really, it's quite dangerous,' Nancy said anxiously. 'Wolfe is very strong and the chair tilts easily.'

'I can manage very well. See how easy it is.' Cordelia pushed the chair along the narrow passage to the entrance hall. 'Open the door, please, Nancy. And you'd better take a parasol; the sun is very hot at this time of day.' Cordelia whipped a bonnet from a peg on the wall and balanced it on her head, laughing merrily.

She seemed to be enjoying herself and Bertie began to laugh, too. Nancy opened the door with a feeling of misgiving, but neither Bertie nor Cordelia seemed to share her worries. They were giggling like children as Cordelia gave the chair a mighty shove that sent it down the steps to the cobbled yard, which unfortunately for Bertie was on a steep slope. The chair rolled off, Cordelia and Nancy racing after it.

'Help,' Nancy cried in desperation. 'Somebody stop the chair before there's a terrible accident.'

12

Cordelia screamed and Nancy uttered a cry of despair as Bertie's chair bounced down the steep incline, heading towards a brick wall. A group of officers had been standing outside the door to the mess when one of them saw the danger and in two long strides intercepted the runaway Bath chair. With a sweep of his hand he grabbed the steering mechanism from Bertie and turned the chair so that it ground to a halt.

Nancy was the first to reach them. 'Thank you, officer. You saved Sir Bertram from a terrible accident.'

Bertie laughed. 'That was excellent. I haven't enjoyed myself so much for years.'

'You might have been killed,' Nancy protested.

'Not with this gallant fellow around.' Bertie proffered his hand. 'Bertram Carey. Thank you, sir.'

'Lieutenant Downton. I'm glad to have been of service, Sir Bertram.'

'Timothy, thank goodness you were there.' Cordelia rushed up to them. She grasped Lieutenant Downton's hand. 'You were splendid.'

He gazed at her unsmiling. 'What were you thinking of, Cordelia? Sir Bertram might have been killed.'

She shrugged. 'It was just bad luck. I was taking him to the garrison gardens. You will help, won't you, Timothy?'

'I'm on duty, Cordelia.' Lieutenant Downton saluted and walked away.

'He's so conceited,' Cordelia said crossly. 'He thinks he knows everything.'

'Well, you were silly to think you could handle a wheeled chair on such a slope.' Nancy's hands were shaking. 'I'll get Wolfe. He'll be furious.'

'He's just a servant,' Cordelia said crossly. 'He has no right to have an opinion. I was just doing what I thought Bertie would enjoy.'

Bertie raised his hand. 'Don't argue over me, ladies. Yes, Nancy, please fetch Wolfe. I enjoyed the moment of excitement, but it's probably not a good idea to repeat the exercise. However, I would still like to see the gardens, Cordelia. When Wolfe arrives perhaps you would lead the way?'

'Of course.' Cordelia gave him a brilliant smile. 'I am sorry if I did the wrong thing.'

'You weren't to know, my dear. I could have stopped you had I wanted to.'

Nancy walked away, unable to watch Cordelia simpering and fluttering her long dark eyelashes at Bertie for a moment longer. She found Wolfe in the kitchen, finishing off a large plateful of steak pie, with the cook standing over him. Nancy could tell from the woman's expression that Wolfe had made a favourable impression on her, which boded well for Wolfe's large appetite. She broke the news of Sir Bertram's close encounter with disaster and, as she had expected, Wolfe was furious, but what was even more worrying was the fact that he said nothing. His heavy brows knitted in a glowering frown and white lines etched the creases from his nose to his mouth. He rose from the table like a giant about to crush an enemy kingdom, much to the amazement of the cook, who gaped at him in a mixture of fear and admiration.

'I'll take you to him,' Nancy said hastily. She spent the time it took to reach Bertie attempting to convince Wolfe that no harm had been done.

Cordelia took one look at Wolfe's face and the colour drained from her cheeks. 'It was an accident,' she said tearfully.

Bertie shook his head. 'It's all right, Wolfe. As you can see, I am unharmed. Miss Fielding meant well, and to be honest I thoroughly enjoyed the experience. Now, if you would kindly push me to the garrison gardens I will be even more content.'

Wolfe's only answer was a low growl, but he did as Bertie asked.

Nancy fell into step beside Cordelia. 'The lieutenant is very good looking,' she said mischievously. 'Is he your beau, Cordelia?'

'Timothy? Heavens, no. He's arrogant and bossy, and he's always telling me what to do, just because I allowed him to kiss me after the ball at Christmas. Although I have to admit it was rather exciting.'

'I thought so,' Nancy said, laughing. 'There was something in the way he looked at you that was anything but indifferent.'

'He can look all he likes, but I have my sights set higher than a mere lieutenant. I am a colonel's daughter, after all.'

Nancy nodded. 'Yes, there is that, I suppose. Who have you in mind, exactly?'

'I haven't quite made up my mind.' Cordelia turned her head to give Nancy a searching glance. 'Are you spoken for, Nancy? I mean, is there a special person in your life?'

'Yes, I am unofficially engaged to Freddie Ashton. At least I accepted his proposal but Lord Dorrington,

169

his papa, insisted that we must wait for a whole year because I am not yet twenty-one. We aren't allowed to have any contact and I have to prove myself capable of running the country house and estate I inherited. It's not very interesting.'

Cordelia clasped her hands together. 'I think it sounds so romantic. What is Freddie like? Is he rich? Do tell.'

Wolfe came to a halt, turning his head to glare at Cordelia. 'Where now, miss?'

'I'd better go on ahead,' Cordelia said reluctantly. 'Follow me, please.'

Nancy walked behind them. It would be easy to get lost in such unfamiliar surroundings and she kept close to Wolfe. The gardens were small, but made a beautiful green oasis in the scorching heat. Cordelia was obviously more interested in Bertie than she was in horticulture and when it came to naming the plants she was at a loss, covering her lack of knowledge with blushes and giggles that seemed to act like a charm. Nancy did not know whether to be amused or irritated by Bertie's eagerness to fall under Cordelia's spell. As they walked back to the colonel's house Nancy began to wonder if any female had bothered to treat Bertie like an attractive man since the wounds he received in the Crimea had crippled him. Everyone at home loved him and turned to him in times of trouble, but she doubted if anyone ever thought of Bertie Carey as a person in his own right. She made up her mind to speak to Rosie and Patsy about their elder brother. Although at the moment it looked as if Cordelia had her sights set on becoming Bertie's second wife. The poor girl he had married in secret when he was very young had died when Tommy was a very small child, and their union had remained a secret for many years after her death. If anyone deserved happiness it was Bertie, although Nancy had the feeling that Cordelia was more interested in marrying a title and living in a castle than being the dutiful and loving wife of a man who would never walk again.

However, it appeared that Cordelia was oblivious to anything other than her own wants and desires, and she kept Bertie entertained all the way back to the house. She ordered tea and cake, and they sat in the front parlour sipping the tea and eating small custard tarts. Apart from the shouts of the drill sergeant and the thud of marching feet, they could have been anywhere in England. Cordelia bombarded Bertie with questions about Rockwood Castle and the size of the estate, to which he replied equably and without exaggeration. It was clear that Cordelia was very impressed and equally clear that Wolfe had seen through her tactics. He stood behind Bertie's chair, glowering at her in a way that would have put most people off their stride. Nancy waited for Cordelia to falter and become embarrassed, but that did not happen. Cordelia apparently was made of stronger stuff and it looked to Nancy as if Wolfe had met his match. She sat back to enjoy the spectacle of Wolfe being outmatched by a pretty young woman.

Eventually they were joined by the colonel, who was delighted to hear that they had visited the garden, which was his pet project. Then it was time to dress for dinner. Nancy had travelled light and the only other gown she had with her was pink and white sprigged muslin. It was cool and pretty, although rather girlish when compared to Cordelia's low-cut gown in emerald-green satin, which emphasised her tiny waist and billowed out over a crinoline hoop. Her dark hair had been coiffed by her maid into a glorious tumble of curls that framed her perfect oval face and hung down her back in a cascade. Bertie stared at her open-mouthed and ate his meal as if hypnotised by her undeniable beauty. Nancy had witnessed the girls at Miss Maughfling's Academy for Young Ladies in London when they were out to impress their gentlemen friends, but Cordelia could have outshone them all. Colonel Fielding sat at the head of the table, smiling benignly while his daughter took over the conversation, and Wolfe stood silently by the door. Nancy recalled the saying 'If looks could kill', and she had to stifle a giggle.

Dinner went on much longer than was considered usual and Nancy began to worry about the time. She had promised Ettie Mayes that she would meet her at ten o'clock, and when the hands on the wall clock reached half past nine Nancy decided it was time to plead a headache and retire to her room.

'Are you unwell, Nancy? I'm so sorry. Perhaps we kept you outside in the sun for too long this afternoon.' Bertie gazed at her with a worried frown.

'No, Bertie. I'm just a little tired after all the excitement. My headache will go if I can lie down and close my eyes.'

Colonel Fielding rose to his feet. 'If there is anything you need, just ring for a servant, Miss Greystone. I do hope you will feel better in the morning.'

'I can stand any amount of heat,' Cordelia said pleasantly. 'I am used to living in hot countries. I'm sure you will recover after a good night's sleep.'

Nancy rose from the table. 'Yes, I'm sure you are right. Good night, everyone.' Nancy caught Wolfe looking at her as she left the dining room. She knew by the look in his eyes that he had seen through her deception, but she trusted him not to say anything. She let herself out into the corridor and hurried to her room to change out of her elegant gown.

At the stroke of ten Ettie emerged from the shadows carrying a large basket over her arm. She came to a halt beside Nancy.

'I got a pinafore and a scarf to wrap round your head, miss. Are you sure you want to go into the ward? Cholera is a nasty sickness.'

'Yes, I'm absolutely certain. I want to see Tommy and let him know that I'm here and that we're going to try to take him home.'

Ettie nodded. 'Can't hang about, miss.' She took the apron and scarf from the basket and a grubby shawl. 'Put these on, please, and follow me. Don't say nothing. If anyone sees us, just keep your head down and act like you're dumb. I'll tell them you're one of them workers from Spain. But let's hope we can get in and out without being spotted.'

Ettie walked up to the guard, saying something in a low voice that Nancy could not quite catch. The guard, who seemed to know Ettie well, made a coarse joke and waved them both inside the hospital building. They went from ward to ward collecting the soiled sheets and placing them in large wicker laundry baskets, which Ettie explained would be picked up later by male orderlies as they were too heavy for the women to carry. Ettie produced small items from her basket and gave them to the male patients who were recuperating from injuries, but they were not permitted to visit the patients in the cholera ward. The nauseating smell that emanated from the long dark room was barely masked by copious amounts of the sickly-sweet-smelling carbolic acid used to clean the floors.

'Where is Tommy?' Nancy whispered as they walked past the closed ward.

'There's a small side room just along the way.' Ettie marched on purposefully. She stopped by the door. 'I'll go in first to make sure there aren't any orderlies in there. Wait here.'

Nancy stood there, gazing around nervously in case anyone came into sight, but almost immediately Ettie opened the door and beckoned to her. Nancy slipped into the side ward, covering her face with her hand. The stench of the disease was truly dreadful but she was not going to be put off by anything. She approached the bed slowly, barely daring to breathe.

Tommy lay there as if dead. His skin was grey and his cheeks hollow. She shuddered in horror to see her beloved friend in such a state, but then he opened his eyes and smiled.

'I must be dreaming.'

Nancy reached out to clasp his thin hand. She could feel all his bones and the skin was clammy, but she grasped it to her cheek.

'It's me, Tommy. I've come with your father. We're going to take you home.'

'Nancy.' His voice broke on a sob. 'I can't believe you're really here.'

'I am here, Tommy. I'm not going to leave you in this place.'

'I'm in the army, Nancy. I can't just get up and go home.'

'Your papa will see to everything. You mustn't worry. Just get well enough to travel. We'll do the rest.'

174

'Come on, miss.' Ettie tugged at Nancy's sleeve. 'We got to go now.'

Nancy blew Tommy a kiss. 'I'll be back. I promise.'

Nancy waited until they were out of the hospital to thank Ettie. 'I could cry, seeing him like that, but it's wonderful to know that he's alive and on the road to recovery.'

'You'd best get back to the colonel's house, miss.' Ettie glanced round, sighing. 'I'll be in dead trouble if this gets around.'

'I promise I won't tell anyone that you helped me. I am truly grateful, Ettie.' Nancy took off the scarf and apron and handed them back to her. 'If there's anything I can do for you while I'm here, please tell me.'

Ettie grinned. 'There's no need, honest. But I got to get on me way. Good night, miss.' She disappeared into the shadows, leaving Nancy to make her own way back to the colonel's house.

There was no one about and Nancy managed to get in without being seen and went straight to her bedroom. She longed to speak to Bertie and tell him that she had spoken to Tommy, but she would have to wait until morning. It was important that no one in the household knew of her visit to the hospital, and the last thing she wanted was to get Ettie into trouble.

★ ★ ★

Next morning at breakfast Nancy was dying to talk to Bertie alone, but everyone arrived at the table within minutes of each other and there was no opportunity to speak privately. However, Bertie seemed to be in a very good mood and Wolfe's normally grim expression had lightened slightly, or was that her imagination? Nancy glanced from one to the other, but as usual Cordelia had turned the conversation to her own advantage and was openly flirting with Bertie, apparently with her father's complete approval. The colonel buttered his toast and drank his coffee, smiling benevolently at his daughter, and agreeing with everything she said.

'What do you think, Nancy?' Cordelia turned to her with a questioning look.

'I'm sorry. I was miles away,' Nancy said hastily. 'What were you saying?'

'Oh dear, I'm afraid I'm boring you with my chatter.' Cordelia shot a sideways glance at Bertie, who smiled and shook his head.

'You are the least boring person I have ever met,' Bertie said gallantly. 'I expect Nancy was thinking of Tommy, who is the reason we are here, after all.'

'As a matter of fact I was wondering when we will be able to see him.'

'That is the good news, Nancy, my dear. Colonel Fielding has agreed to speak to the doctor in charge of the fever wards. If he says I may visit Tommy I will be eternally grateful.'

'Yes, I don't see why you should be kept from him. I gather that Lieutenant Carey is in a side ward and is thought to be on the road to recovery.' Colonel Fielding smiled benignly. 'You know you are very welcome to stay here until Lieutenant Carey is well enough to rejoin his troop.'

Bertie frowned. 'Surely he deserves time at home to convalesce? I was planning on taking him back to Devonshire with me.'

'He is still an army officer, Sir Bertram. He might choose to sell his commission, but he has barely

176

begun his career.'

'As you say, Colonel, my son is still very young. He joined up on impulse and I need to know whether he still feels that he wishes to follow in my footsteps. It's not an easy life, and Tommy has other responsibilities.'

Cordelia leaned forward, fixing Bertie with an intense stare. 'Do you mean that Tommy will inherit the castle, Sir Bertram?'

Nancy laughed. 'I think Bertie has a good few years left, Cordelia. Of course Tommy will inherit eventually, but hopefully not for a long time.'

'I suppose you could marry again, Sir Bertram,' Cordelia said with a coquettish toss of her head. 'Is there a lucky lady waiting for you in Devonshire?'

'I'm afraid not, Miss Fielding.' Bertie reached for his coffee cup. 'Anyway, enough about me. Might I see my son today, Colonel?'

'I don't see why not, but I was going to suggest that Miss Greystone might like to visit the upper rock to see the Barbary macaques.' He turned to Nancy, smiling. 'They are monkeys, who live on the island.'

'How exciting,' Nancy said eagerly. 'I would really love to see more of the island before we go home.'

'I hate monkeys,' Cordelia said sulkily. 'But perhaps Sir Bertram would accompany us. I would feel safer with a strong man at my side.'

Wolfe cleared his throat noisily, then looked away when Nancy sent him a curious glance. She was sure she saw his lips quiver but he had his emotions under control.

Bertie smiled. 'Perhaps another time, Miss Fielding. I really need to see my son.'

★ ★ ★

Cordelia sulked all the way to the top of the island where the Barbary macaques were to be found. However, the sudden appearance of Lieutenant Downton brought the smile back to her face and she clung to his arm, feigning terror every time a monkey drew near. Nancy ignored her and went with their driver, who happened to be Private Mayes, Ettie's husband.

They were a good distance from Cordelia when one of the macaques took a fancy to Cordelia's straw bonnet. The ribbons had come undone, or maybe she had untied them herself due to the intense heat, but the cheeky monkey tore the bonnet from Cordelia's head and with amazing agility leaped over the rocks and out of reach. Cordelia sobbed hysterically, begging the lieutenant to rescue her favourite hat.

Nancy could see that Cordelia's tears were genuine and she hurried to her side. 'I'm so sorry, but maybe the monkey will tire of it quickly.'

'It will be ruined,' Cordelia cried. 'Timothy, please save my bonnet.'

'It would take a mountain goat to follow that little fellow,' Lieutenant Downton said, smiling. 'I will buy you another bonnet, but I will not clamber over the rocks and risk breaking my neck for a straw hat.'

Cordelia sniffed. 'I'm disappointed in you, Timothy. As to purchasing anything so personal for me, I will have to decline your offer.' She tossed her head and snapped her parasol open. 'I think it's time we returned to the barracks.'

'But Nancy has only seen a little of the island, Cordelia.'

'I have a headache,' Cordelia said crossly. 'I didn't

178

want to come in the first place, but Papa insisted.'

Private Mayes looked from one to the other. 'Is it the barracks, sir?'

'Yes, if Miss Greystone doesn't mind.'

'I think we'd better get Cordelia out of the hot sun, Lieutenant. I've seen the monkeys. They really are as mischievous as Colonel Fielding said.'

'They are horrid,' Cordelia snapped. 'Come, Timothy. Let's go before the evil monkeys return to steal my reticule. I hate the gibbering little things.'

As if to return the compliment, another of the macaques leaped over the rocks and landed at her feet, grinning up at her and chattering.

Cordelia swooned into the lieutenant's arms and he carried her to the waiting carriage with Private Mayes hurrying ahead to open the door. Nancy suspected that Cordelia used this tactic every time she was in a situation that she could not control and she followed on, climbing into the carriage to sit beside Cordelia.

'Don't worry, Lieutenant Downton, I'll look after her until we get to the colonel's house.'

'Yes, thank you, Miss Greystone. I rode here or I would come with you.'

'I'm all right, Timothy,' Cordelia said faintly.

'I'll call on you later today, but I have an errand to perform for your papa and I'm already late.'

'Military business must come first,' Cordelia said automatically. 'I'm sure Nancy will take care of me.'

'Yes, of course.' Nancy nodded. 'Don't worry.'

'Thank you.' Lieutenant Downton slapped his hand on the carriage door. 'Drive on, Private.'

★ ★ ★

179

Cordelia went straight to her room when they reached the colonel's house, leaving Nancy free to do as she pleased. She did not have long to wait until Bertie and Wolfe arrived from the hospital. Bertie looked pale and drawn, but he was smiling as Wolfe wheeled him into the parlour.

'How is Tommy?' Nancy asked eagerly.

'He's on the mend, or so the doctor told me. Poor boy, he looks dreadful, but then he's lucky to have survived both the bullet and cholera. We're a tough breed, us Careys.'

'Will he be able to come home with us?'

'Well, that's for the authorities to decide. He should remain here until he's strong enough to rejoin his unit, but I want to take him back to Rockwood. I think he's had enough of the army and I'm more than happy for him to sell his commission.'

'That would be wonderful. I don't want Tommy to risk his life again.'

Bertie gave her a straight look. 'You're very fond of him, aren't you, Nancy?'

'I love him like a brother.'

Wolfe cleared his throat. 'Shall I fetch you a cup of coffee, sir? Or maybe something stronger?'

'After being in that dreadful place I think a brandy would be beneficial, Wolfe.'

'Yes, sir.' Wolfe left the parlour, closing the door behind him.

Nancy perched on the edge of the nearest chair. 'You know, don't you, Bertie?'

'Know what, my dear?'

'That I visited Tommy last night.'

Bertie smiled. 'He told me. You're a brave but foolish girl, Nancy Sunday. I'm sorry, I can never think about you as a Greystone. To me you will always be that little girl Rosie found slaving away for Tabitha Shaw, who is not, to my mind, what a clergyman's wife ought to be.'

'I owe everything to Rosie, and to you and Patsy. I would still be in service if Rosie hadn't taken pity on me.'

'I'm sorry I sided with Lord Dorrington about keeping you and Freddie apart for a whole year, Nancy. I see now that it was wrong and even rather cruel. I should have allowed you two to sort it out between you. As it is I've put you through unnecessary hardship.'

'No, not really, Bertie. I have grown up a lot since I took over Greystone Park.'

'But there seems to be a shadow over your relationship with Freddie. I never meant to keep you apart permanently.'

'I don't know how Freddie feels now. He was very distant when I saw him last, and he hasn't made any attempt to see me again. Perhaps Lord Dorrington was right and we were both too young to know our own minds.'

'Are you having second thoughts, Nancy?'

'No, of course not. Well,' Nancy eyed him warily, 'perhaps a little. If I could see him again and talk to him I'm sure things would be as they were.'

'Everything you say makes me more determined to get us all back to Rockwood as soon as possible. Leave it to me, Nancy. I'll persuade the colonel to pull a few strings so that we can take Tommy home as soon as possible.'

'The colonel seems to think that you are falling for his daughter, Bertie. I'm certain she would love to be

Lady Carey of Rockwood Castle.'

Bertie laughed. 'I imagine Lieutenant Downton might have something to say about that. Don't tell Cordelia, but I believe Timothy Downton is due for promotion very soon. Maybe that will make her change her mind.'

13

Cordelia might have wanted the title of Lady Carey, but the colonel was candid in his wish to keep his daughter close to him. Lieutenant Timothy Downton received promotion to captain within weeks and this seemed to coincide with Tommy's recovery. Permission was granted for Bertie to take his son home to Devonshire, and Tommy's commission was sold equally quickly, freeing him from the army. Nancy had enjoyed her time in Gibraltar but she was eager to return to her old life.

It was the end of September when they finally arrived home. The whole family was waiting to greet Tommy, but Nancy stood back, not quite knowing what to do. The castle was no longer her home and Tommy was the centre of attention. She had cared for him on board ship and they had enjoyed their time together, but it was time to say goodbye and return to Greystone Park. The trouble was that it did not feel like home to her. She had never admitted it to herself, preferring to keep up the pretence that she was delighted to be someone of note, but being with the family made her realise what a lonely existence she had suffered since moving to Greystone Park. Patsy would understand, but she was too busy making a fuss of Tommy to notice that Nancy kept herself apart. In the end, Nancy asked Jarvis to send for a carriage. It was only Hester who realised that she was leaving.

'Going so soon, Nancy? Won't you stay for dinner?'

'Thank you, Hester, but I really should return to Greystone Park. Heaven knows what state I'll find it in.'

Hester smiled. 'Well, you took on all those London lads. I haven't heard of any problems, and Miss Collins isn't the sort of woman to allow them to run riot.'

'You're right, but I'm not needed here. I'll come and visit Tommy when he's had time to settle in.'

'Yes, you do that, Nancy. You two were always together when you were on holiday from school. You might as well be brother and sister.'

Nancy nodded. 'Yes, that's how I think about Tommy.'

'Goodbye. I'll tell the others you had to leave.'

'Thank you, Hester.'

'Oh, by the way, I heard a rumour you might want to know about,' Hester said vaguely. 'But perhaps it had better wait. I'm sure there's nothing in it.'

Nancy caught sight of Jarvis standing at the front entrance. 'I think the carriage is here, Hester. You can tell me another time. I really must go.'

Somewhat reluctantly Nancy walked away from the happy family group. It had always been this way. She was welcome but she was not a Carey and never would be. She belonged at Greystone Park, even though it felt alien to her.

* * *

The house and grounds looked peaceful as the Careys' carriage tooled up the drive and deposited Nancy at the front entrance. She rang the bell and after a few moments Foster opened the door.

184

'Good afternoon, Miss Greystone.'

His look of surprise, although wiped away almost instantly, registered with Nancy. It was not the welcome she might have hoped for. 'You were expecting me, weren't you, Foster?'

'We were told you would arrive tomorrow morning, Miss Greystone. But it doesn't matter; I'm sure we are all delighted to have you at home again.'

'Thank you, Foster. My luggage is on the step.'

'I'll have it seen to right away.'

'Is something wrong, Foster?'

'It's not for me to say, Miss Greystone, but you might want to go to the drawing room before you do anything else. Mrs Cottingham is in residence.'

Nancy stared at him aghast. 'Do you mean that she's staying here?'

'Mrs Cottingham moved in a couple of weeks ago, Miss Greystone. She said it was to keep the house from falling into disrepute with the boys running riot.'

'That can't be, Foster.'

'There was nothing I could do to prevent Mrs Cottingham from doing as she pleased, Miss Greystone.'

'I'll sort this out once and for all.' Nancy was not in the mood to be generous. She strode off in the direction of the drawing room. She flung the door open and stood, arms akimbo, gazing round the once familiar room, which had undergone subtle changes. The furniture had been moved round, with the addition of various ornaments and knick-knacks that she did not recognise.

'Christina!'

Christina Cottingham rose from the sofa, her face composed into a stony mask. 'You took this house from us under false pretences. I have taken it back.'

'You can't do that, Christina. Greystone Park is legally my home, not yours.'

'You are a nobody and this is where Sylvia and I grew up. You will have to move your things out. Go to Dorrington Place and live with your lover.'

'Freddie is not my lover. How dare you suggest such a thing? And as to me moving out, that is for you to do. I am the rightful heir to Greystone Park. You have Cottingham Manor — why can't you be satisfied with that?'

'Because this is my birthright. You were happy enough to rush off to Gibraltar to rescue Tommy Carey — perhaps that's where you belong. It most certainly isn't here.'

'Where are the boys?' Nancy demanded. 'I left them in the care of Martha Collins and Miss Moon.'

'Martha and her friend have returned to their cottage. As to your street boys, I turned those ruffians out. I believe they have found themselves homes in the village. I don't care where they are, personally.'

'You had no right to do that. I want you out of my house now.'

'How are you going to achieve that, Nancy? Are you going to throw me out bodily?'

Nancy clenched and unclenched her fists. Christina was right. She could not resort to physical force and she knew Christina well enough to realise that she was a determined woman and would not be easily persuaded that this course of action was both foolish and illegal.

'What does your husband say to all this, Christina? He is supposed to be a man of God. Does he condone such actions as yours?'

'Oscar says and does what I tell him to do. Cottingham Manor is nothing when compared to Greystone Park. This house is mine. You are the usurper.'

'I am not going to stand here and argue with you, Christina. I'm going to my room to unpack.'

'It is no longer your room, Nancy. I have had all your belongings packed up and sent to the stables to await your instructions. You may have them back when you decide where you are going to live.'

Nancy strode over to the bell pull and tugged at it. 'I'll send Foster to collect my things. You are not doing this to me, Christina.'

'Foster is in my pay now. He watched me grow to womanhood. He won't go against me, not if he knows what is good for him.'

'You really are an evil person, Christina Cottingham. Perhaps Glorina has cast a spell on you to make you so greedy and grasping.'

'It doesn't matter what you say. I am mistress of Greystone Park. You are a parvenu. You need to leave now, or do I send for the footman to throw you out? Think how humiliating that would be.'

Nancy hesitated. She knew that Christina was capable of anything when she wanted to get her own way, but this was like walking into a nightmare.

'Tell me one thing, Christina. How did you keep this from my family at Rockwood? No one mentioned you when I was there earlier.'

'Even loyal servants will keep silent when their jobs are at risk. Cousin Martha would lose her home if she went against me, and she knows it. As for your land agent, Mr Gibson, I'm afraid I had to let him go. It's a shame because he's a very presentable fellow and quite intelligent for someone who was once an actor.'

'I can't believe you did that. But what about my boys? Where are they?'

'Heaven knows. I really don't care. Now go. You are beginning to bore me.'

'I will leave now, but I will be back, Christina. I'll take you to court to settle this, if necessary.'

'Just try, my dear. Oh, and by the way, I intend to bring my daughters here tomorrow. Oscar may come if he so desires, or he can stay at the manor house with his mama. I'm sure that Glorina will be only too pleased to move back from the dower house.'

Nancy could see that she was getting nowhere. She turned away and walked out of the room with Christina's laughter ringing in her ears. Anger, frustration and helplessness raged in her breast as she left the house. She came to a halt, wondering where to go next. No doubt Christina had given orders that she was not allowed to take her horse from the stables and Nancy was in no mood for a protracted argument with the head groom. She set off for Miss Collins' cottage.

Martha opened the door and her face fell when she saw Nancy. 'You've found out.' She enveloped Nancy in a hug that almost knocked the breath out of her. 'I am so sorry. There was nothing that Moon and I could do to stop her. Christina was a little minx as a child, and she's twice as bad now.'

'Where are my boys, Miss Collins? I can't bear to think of them thrown out on the streets. Why did no one try to help them?'

'You need to speak to Mr Gibson. He took the younger ones under his wing. Some of the older boys had been apprenticed locally, so they are all right.'

'I thought he had moved in here, but that obviously

hasn't happened since you and Miss Moon are back in residence.'

'I can't say for certain, but I think Gibson took them to the cottage on the Rockwood estate, the one where Viscount Ashton stayed for a while. When Christina threw us out she sacked Gibson and he went to see Captain Blanchard, who gave him permission to use the cottage until you returned.'

'So Alex knew what happened. I wonder why he didn't warn me.'

'I can't say, but maybe he didn't have a chance to speak to you in private. None of us could do anything until you returned from Gibraltar.'

'I am here now,' Nancy said firmly. 'And I intend to sort this out once and for all. Christina is not going to get away with such behaviour.'

'Come inside, my dear. You've had a shock. Moon will make us a pot of tea.'

'No, thank you. I am going to find Nick. I want to make sure that the boys are taken care of, and then I'll return to the castle. It's more my home than Greystone Park ever was.'

'You shouldn't be wandering around on foot, Nancy. Come inside and I'll saddle up our old pony. You can send him back with a groom when you're safely at home with the Careys.'

★ ★ ★

It was late afternoon by the time Nancy dismounted from the tired old pony outside the cottage in the woods. She knew by the sound of childish voices that this was where Nick must have brought at least some of the boys and she sighed with relief. She had barely

189

tethered the animal to a tree when Alfie and Stanley came running to meet her, followed closely by Teddy, who was eating a slice of bread and jam. Nancy scooped them up in her arms and hugged each one in turn.

'So you know the worst.' Nick Gibson stood in the doorway gazing at her with a worried frown.

'I wish someone had warned me,' Nancy said crossly. 'Apparently Alex was aware of the situation at Greystone Park. I don't know if anyone else knew what Christina had done.'

'Probably just Captain Blanchard. We decided to keep it quiet, hoping perhaps that Mrs Cottingham's husband might step in and make her see sense.'

'If you believe that, you don't know Christina. I've only had a few dealings with her, but she isn't the sort of woman to see reason when she has her mind set upon something. She actually packed up all my things and they're stored in the stables until I can collect them.'

'Come inside and sit down. You look as though you could do with a tot of brandy.'

Nancy gave the boys one last hug. 'No, thank you. I am just delighted to see that you've been taking care of my boys. Where are the others?'

'Rob, Joe and Mick are inside, finishing their lessons. I wouldn't let them come out until they'd completed the last paragraph of the work Miss Collins set for them. Ben and Frankie are living in at the Black Dog. Ben is working in the stables there and Frankie is helping the potman. Jonah and Moses are both living in at the Greeps' farm, learning the work, and Farmer Greep is very pleased with them so far.'

'What about Todd and Gus?'

'Todd seems to be doing well with Dr Bulmer, but Gus is a bit of a problem. He didn't do well working for Leo, so he's been doing odd jobs. He comes with me when I visit the farms, but he's eaten up with anger at the way you've been treated. You are his family, as far as he is concerned, and he's furious with Mrs Cottingham. Anyway, come inside and share our supper. It's only bread and cheese but Mrs Greep baked the bread this morning, and it's her best cheese, so no one has complained about my cooking.'

Nancy laid her hand on his arm. 'Thank you, but I'm not hungry.'

'I've just made a pot of tea. Perhaps that will whet your appetite.'

'Thank you. That would be nice. It seems I have so much to thank you for, Nick. You've done more than anyone could ask of you. I'm truly grateful. But why didn't you go and live with your father?'

'He passed away just after you left for Gibraltar. The cottage was rented so it didn't belong to either of us. I stayed at Greystone Park for a while, but then Mrs Cottingham decided to move in and I came here. It's quite cosy.' He smiled and led her into the cottage kitchen, which took up the whole of the ground floor. The three boys who were supposed to be working jumped up from the table and came to greet Nancy with more hugs. It was so unusual for them to show any emotion that she had a lump in her throat and tears in her eyes.

'I've really missed all of you,' she said, choking back a sob. 'Thank you, Nick, for looking after them.'

Alfie, Stanley and Teddy followed them into the kitchen and they squashed onto a bench at the pine table.

'How have you managed for money, Nick?' Nancy asked in a low voice. 'It's been nearly two months since you were last paid, and I certainly didn't expect this to happen. Has Mrs Cottingham been giving you your wages?'

He shook his head. 'I'm no longer employed by the estate, which is why we are here. We've been living on what little savings I have and . . .'

'We've been entertaining the crowds on market days,' Alfie said proudly. 'Nick has taught us the words and we acts them out.'

'I takes round the hat at the end.' Teddy puffed out his chest. 'Because I'm small people think I'm a little kid, not a big boy of seven.'

Nancy sat down on the only chair in the room. 'My goodness. So you've gone back to acting, Nick?'

'In a small way, yes. We perform one-act plays, which seem to amuse the crowds. It has brought in enough to feed us and purchase candles and oddments we might need. There's plenty of firewood free for the taking, thanks to Captain Blanchard's generosity.'

'I'm amazed,' Nancy said with a sigh. 'You've done magnificently in spite of everything. It's hard to believe that Christina has acted as she has, but perhaps I should have expected something of the sort. She never accepted the fact that I was their cousin.'

Nick took a Brown Betty teapot from the range and filled two mugs, handing one to Nancy. 'What are you going to do now?'

She laughed. 'Perhaps I should go on tour with you and your young troupe of actors. I am an accomplished pianist, even if I say so myself.'

'What would Lord Dorrington say about that?'

'I'm sure that Freddie would be on my side, but his

papa might think differently. I was supposed to prove myself capable of running a large household. It seems I have failed miserably, since I find myself quite literally out on the street.'

'I doubt if either of them would think that way, but most pressing is where are you going to stay tonight? There are only two small rooms upstairs and the boys sleep there. I have a straw-filled palliasse, which I place by the range. It might not be the most comfortable bed but at least I am warm all night.'

'I'll return to Rockwood. There's no question about that. Perhaps in the morning I'll have a better idea of how to go about evicting Christina from my property.' Nancy turned her head as the door opened and Gus burst into the room.

'Gus, this is a nice surprise.' Nancy rose to her feet, holding out her hand.

'You should be at the big house,' Gus said, scowling. 'Has that old besom thrown you out?'

'Come and sit down, Gus.' Nick filled another mug with tea and placed it on the table. 'Have something to eat.'

'Yes, please do. I appreciate your concern, but I will handle things in my way, Gus.' Nancy moved to his side and placed her arm around his skinny shoulders. 'I'm just glad you boys are safe here.'

'But she's in your house, miss. That ain't right.'

'No, it isn't, Gus. But the law will take its course. I plan to visit my solicitor in Exeter tomorrow and see what he says. Now, please eat your supper and tell me what you've been doing since I went away.' Nancy guided him to the table and the younger boys made a space for him on the bench. It was a squash but none of them was big and Gus could perch on the end even if it did not look too comfortable. Nancy had a sudden recollection of them as they were when she had first entered the cellar room in Vauxhall. They were different children then; now they had colour in their cheeks and their faces had filled out. They no longer looked like a band of ragamuffins, but were normal, happy and spirited children.

Gus attacked a plate of bread and cheese as if he had not eaten all day, interspersing mouthfuls with an account of what he had been doing, which consisted of odd jobs and running errands, for which he had earned the princely sum of threepence.

'It's blooming hard work,' Gus said, swallowing the last morsel of food. 'I cleaned windows and swept the street clean of horse muck. Then an old man wanted it to put on his garden and I had to fill pails with the smelly stuff and cart it across the village to his cottage. He give me a halfpenny for all that work.'

'You've done very well, Gus,' Nancy said earnestly. 'I'm proud of you.' She glanced at the eager faces around the table and smiled. 'I'm proud of you all. You make everything worthwhile.'

A murmur of appreciation mixed with embarrassed grins rippled around the table.

'They have all worked hard since you went away.' Nick ruffled Stanley's hair. 'We've made quite a name for ourselves locally. Mr Shaw has asked us to perform at the harvest supper.'

'That's wonderful,' Nancy said eagerly. 'I could play the piano if you need someone to accompany you. We are part of the village community, no matter what Christina Cottingham thinks.'

'She's an evil witch.' Gus thumped his fist on the table. 'She called us all manner of names and threw

194

us out. She made poor Alfie cry.'

'I'm so sorry, boys.' Nancy was close to tears as she thought of how scared they must have been. Their young lives had been blighted enough already, without someone like Christina Cottingham adding to their misfortunes. 'We will get our home back, but now I really should be going. It will be dark soon enough and I have to ride the poor old pony to Rockwood Castle.'

Nick reached for his jacket. 'I'll come with you and see you safely home, Nancy. Gus — you're the eldest — I'll leave you in charge. The young ones can go to bed when they've washed their dishes. We run a tight ship here, don't we, lads?'

Nancy blew the boys a kiss as she left the cottage. Nick was about to follow her, but she turned to him with a smile. 'You don't have to leave them. I'll be quite all right. It's hardly any distance to the castle.'

'I wouldn't sleep tonight if I didn't see you to the door.' Nick untethered the pony and helped Nancy to mount. 'Are you really going to involve your solicitor? Wouldn't it be better to speak to Mrs Cottingham's husband first? After all, he's legally responsible for everything she does.'

'I hadn't thought of it like that, but I could go to Cottingham Manor in the morning. I'll speak to Patsy and Rosie about it. They know Oscar much better than I do. I hope we can settle this without too much fuss.'

Nick fell into step beside the pony as it walked slowly towards the castle. Dusk was swallowing up the surrounding countryside and candlelight glimmered in cottage windows as they left the village and crossed the bridge leading to Rockwood Castle.

Nancy breathed a sigh of relief as she dismounted outside the front entrance. 'I always feel I've come home when I arrive here, which is something I never experienced at Greystone Park. Maybe it should belong to Christina and Sylvia.' She rang the doorbell and its peal echoed throughout the great hall.

'Nonsense. It's yours by rights. You're just tired and upset.' Nick took the reins from her. 'Shall I take this old chap back to the cottage for the night? I'll return him to Miss Collins in the morning.'

'Thank you, Nick. You've been marvellous. I don't know what would have happened if you hadn't been there to take the boys in.'

'They're a good bunch. Some of them need a bit more discipline than others, but by and large they do you proud, Nancy.'

The heavy oak door opened and Jarvis held up a lantern. 'Miss Nancy.' He ushered her inside.

'I'm just leaving,' Nick said affably. 'Good night, Nancy.'

She turned to give him a warm smile. 'Good night, Nick, and thank you once again.' Nancy had barely stepped over the threshold when Rosie came hurrying to greet her.

'Nancy, my dear, Alex has just told us what Christina has done. I'm so sorry you were left to find out the hard way. He didn't have a chance to warn you.' Rosie threw her arms around Nancy in a warm embrace. 'Jarvis, will you send one of the maids to make up Miss Nancy's room immediately? She's come home.'

Jarvis nodded and walked off in his slow and stately manner.

'Now I know I'm home,' Nancy said, smiling. 'Foster

196

is very efficient but he is not like Jarvis.'

'No one is like Jarvis.' Rosie tucked Nancy's hand in the crook of her arm. 'We're in the drawing room waiting for dinner to be served. Patsy and Leo are here, too. We're all on your side, Nancy.'

'Christina threw me out, Rosie.'

'We knew that she had evicted the boys and that Mr Gibson was taking care of the younger ones, but none of us knew she had moved into the house. Alex thought she was just making threatening noises and going there in the day to prove a point.'

'No, she's definitely moved in and has no intention of allowing me back, at least not without a legal battle, which she is sure she will win.'

'We'll talk it over with the others. I'm sure Mr Mounce, our solicitor in Exeter, will be able to help.'

Nancy nodded tiredly. 'To be honest, I feel like giving in and letting her have the place. I would never have lived there had it not been for Lord Dorrington being difficult.'

Rosie hesitated outside the drawing room. 'We must let Freddie know what's happened.'

'No!' Nancy shook her head. 'His papa would find some way to blame me for losing my estate to Christina. I have to get it back without their help.'

Rosie opened the door and ushered Nancy into the room, where she was welcomed by a sea of sympathetic family faces.

★ ★ ★

Nancy went to bed in her old room that night, lulled to sleep by the sound of the waves beating against the rocks at the bottom of the cliff. She put all thoughts of Greystone Park and Christina Cottingham out of her head and was sound asleep when she was awakened by someone shaking her.

'Nancy, wake up.' Rosie's voice seemed to come from afar. 'Nancy, for goodness' sake, wake up.'

'What's the matter?' Nancy raised herself on her elbow. 'It's the middle of the night.'

'Greystone Park is on fire. You can see the flames from the front windows.'

14

There was nothing anyone could have done better. The estate staff and villagers had formed a human chain, filling buckets in the River Sawle, and passing them from hand to hand in their attempts to douse the flames. But the old timbers of Greystone Park were beyond saving.

Next morning Nancy stood alone on the carriage sweep surveying what remained of her inheritance. The smouldering ruin filled the air with acrid smoke, and small pockets of fire hissed as they met with puddles of river water. The stables were far enough away from the main building to have escaped the conflagration, but the horses, grooms and stable boys had been evacuated as a precaution. An eerie silence hung over the smoking ruin.

Everyone had gone home to change out of their wet and soot-covered garments ready to begin a normal day's work. Bertie and Wolfe had been with Nancy in the small hours of the morning as they watched helplessly, while Alex, Walter and Leo joined in the effort to save the old building. But the fire was a voracious feeder and refused to give up its hold. Now, oddly enough, the only part of the building standing was the stone arch around the front entrance and the solid oak door, banded and studded with iron. It swung open suddenly as if by an unseen hand and the hinges groaned, wresting a hysterical giggle from Nancy's lips. She turned her head at the sound of someone calling her name and saw Miss Collins hurrying towards her, followed, as always, by Miss Moon.

'My dear Nancy,' Miss Collins said breathlessly. 'You should not be here now. Your gown is soaked and you've had a terrible shock.'

'You poor thing,' Miss Moon added anxiously. 'Come to the cottage and I'll make you a nice hot cup of tea.'

'Thank you both, but I'd better return to Rockwood. There's nothing I can do here.'

'Look who's coming.' Miss Moon pointed to a gig being driven by the Cottinghams' coachman, Christina seated behind him.

The vehicle drew to a halt beside them and Christina leaned over the side, her face contorted with rage. 'You couldn't stand to lose to me, could you, Nancy Sunday?'

Nancy stared at her in disbelief. 'What are you saying?'

'That you sent your pack of wolf cubs to set my home on fire. You would rather see Greystone razed to the ground than allow me to live there. I might have been burned alive if the servants had not wakened me.'

'You're talking nonsense,' Nancy said hotly. 'Why would I want to burn down my home?'

'Because you know you would lose if I took you to court. My papa left the land and property to me and my sister. You are the usurper.'

'Don't be silly, Christina,' Miss Collins said sharply. 'Nancy is right, you are talking nonsense. I'll put it down to the shock of the fire, but you cannot go round making wild accusations.'

'Wild, are they? One of her boys was seen skulking round the property shortly before the fire started.

200

Foster spotted him and told him to go away or he would send for the constable.'

A sudden memory of Gus's angry words made Nancy shiver. 'That doesn't mean he was guilty, whoever it was. This was the boys' home before you threw them out, Christina. They have more right to be here than you.'

'You haven't heard the last of this matter,' Christina said angrily. 'I am on my way to speak to Constable Burton, and I will accuse that boy who smokes a pipe. The surly young fellow.'

'Calm down, Christina.' Miss Collins shook her finger at her cousin. 'Come to the cottage. We'll all have a cup of tea. There's little enough anyone can do now, and you still have a home. Nancy has just lost hers.'

'It wasn't hers to begin with. As for you, Cousin Martha, you had better mind what you say or you and Moon will be looking for another home. Drive on, Curtis.'

'The cheek of the woman,' Moon said sharply. 'I'm sorry, Martha. I don't usually speak out of turn but Christina is being objectionable.'

Nancy watched Christina's smart gig being driven off at speed. She sighed and shook her head. 'This is an outcome that no one could have foreseen.'

Miss Collins frowned. 'The trouble is that Gus is quite capable of doing something like that. He's devoted to you, Nancy. I know Christina treated them badly but I wouldn't put it past him to retaliate in any way he saw fit.'

'Do come to the cottage, Nancy,' Miss Moon said gently. 'You've had a terrible shock.'

'Thank you both for being so kind, but I need to see Nick Gibson. If Gus has done something stupid

I want to know. He's not a bad boy at heart, but if Christina accuses him of arson he won't stand a chance, guilty or not guilty.'

'I agree,' Miss Collins nodded. 'Christina can be very vindictive.'

'Nick was here all night fighting the fire, as far as I remember,' Nancy said thoughtfully. 'But he might know if Gus was missing for any length of time before that. I'll go to the cottage and ask him.'

'You should rest, Nancy.' Miss Collins eyed her anxiously. 'You've been here for hours. I'm surprised that Sir Bertram allowed you to stay here on your own.'

Nancy smiled. 'It was so chaotic no one knew what anyone was doing. We are all bone weary, but I must make sure that Gus is all right. Those boys had a hard enough time in London. It's a wonder they are as good as they are now.'

Nancy walked away but halfway down the avenue of trees she felt her knees give way beneath her and she sank down onto the damp grass. The sound of a horse's hoofs on the gravel made her look up and she saw Nick riding the old pony. He leaped off and hurried to her side.

'Are you all right? What are you doing here now? I thought they would have taken you home.' He helped Nancy to her feet.

'I'm just a bit tired. I was fine until I started walking, but then the enormity of it all hit me.'

He lifted her onto the saddle despite her protests. 'I'll take you back to Rockwood. I'm sure Miss Collins won't mind if we keep the old nag a few hours longer.'

Nancy looked at him and began to laugh. 'Your face is blackened with soot. You look quite a sight.'

He grinned. 'So do you, if you don't mind me saying so. Practically every able-bodied person in the village looks the same.'

'I was coming to see you about Gus. Christina was here and she's going to tell Constable Burton that Gus set fire to the property.'

'I know he was furious with Mrs Cottingham, but I don't think he'd go that far, Nancy. He's not stupid.'

'Far from it, but as you say, he was very angry. Christina's word will carry more weight than anything Gus could say in his defence. Did he remain in the cottage after I left?'

'To tell the truth I haven't seen him since I got back there last evening.'

'We need to find him before Constable Burton starts looking for him. I want to hear his side of the story.'

'Agreed, but you need to go home first, if only to change out of those damp clothes and wash the soot off your face.'

'Yes, all right. But I can walk now.'

'You'll ride home in relative comfort, and I'll go back to the cottage. I'll question the boys and see if they know where Gus might be found.'

'You're right, Nick. I'll come to the cottage as soon as I can.' Nancy urged the pony into a trot. It might be shocking but she was more concerned about Gus than she was about losing the home she had inherited and all that went with it.

* * *

Everyone was sympathetic at Rockwood. Rosie wanted Nancy to catch up on some sleep, but Nancy

203

wanted to speak to Bertie in private. She had to get past Wolfe, but a quick word in his ear made him back away and he left them alone in the wainscoted study.

'You really should be resting, Nancy,' Bertie said gently. 'I am so sorry about the house, but it can be rebuilt.'

'It's not the bricks and mortar that worry me, Bertie. Christina is accusing young Gus — you know, one of the older boys I brought back from London. He was very angry with her for evicting me from the house, and even more so when she threw all the boys out.'

'Understandably.' Bertie nodded. 'Go on.'

'She's going to tell Constable Burton that it was arson and Gus is the culprit. She has no proof, but with the boy's reputation it won't be hard to convince him.'

Bertie steepled his fingers, a furrow creasing his brow. 'Yes, I see the problem. Do you think the boy capable of such a crime?'

'Yes. In the circumstances I wouldn't be surprised if he set a small fire or something to teach her a lesson. I don't for one minute imagine he wanted to raze the house to the ground, or to endanger life.'

'And you think he's a good boy at heart?'

'I'm sure of it, Bertie. Just as Tommy is, only Tommy has all the advantages of being your son. Gus has no one to defend him.'

'How old is he?'

'I'm not exactly sure, but I think he's thirteen or fourteen.'

'Old enough to join the army. I still have some influence in that direction. I could put a good word in for him.' Bertie's expression lightened. 'By the way,

Tommy wants to see you. He knows what happened last night and it was all I could do to make him stay in his room. He's not a very good patient now he's on the road to recovery.'

'I'll wash and change and I'll go and see him before I do anything else.'

'That would be good. He's been asking for you.'

'I'm sorry, but this business with Christina has put everything else out of my mind. I will apologise to Tommy, and it looks as if you'll have me living here again.'

'My dear girl, this will always be your home. We all love you.'

★ ★ ★

Nancy left the study and made her way to the tower where Tommy had his room. Bertie's words had comforted her and cheered her, despite the desperate situation. She knocked and entered to find Tommy seated in a chair by the window. He had a rug wrapped around his legs and another around his shoulders. His scowl melted into a welcoming smile.

'Nancy, how are you? Rosie came and told me what happened last night.'

She went to sit on the edge of the bed. 'It's terrible, but in a way I'm relieved. I couldn't say that to anyone but you, Tommy.'

He threw off the warm blanket and grasped her hand. 'I understand. You never wanted to live there in the first place. I blame Lord Dorrington, and my pa, too. They should not have interfered.'

'Bertie has always been so kind to me. I know he thought he was doing it for my benefit, but if they hadn't made us wait, Freddie and I would have been married by now, and Christina could have had Greystone Park with my blessing.'

'Well, I'm glad you are still single,' Tommy said with a mischievous twinkle in his golden-brown eyes. 'I might still have a chance to win you.'

She leaned over and kissed him on the cheek. 'You are such a tease, but I do love you.'

'Like a brother — I know.'

'I haven't any brothers of my own so I can't say, but all I do know is that I couldn't bear the thought of you sick and alone in the military hospital.'

'Hardly alone, Nancy. I had orderlies and nurses buzzing around me until I wanted to tell them to go away and leave me in peace. I can't tell you how wonderful it was that night to open my eyes and see your beautiful face. I thought I'd died and gone to heaven.'

Nancy laughed. 'So you think you'll go to heaven? After all the pranks you played when you were younger, I doubt it. However, I didn't come here to tell you off. I wanted to know how you are feeling now. Forget Greystone Park — it's gone for ever unless someone rebuilds the house.'

Tommy sighed. 'I feel so much better, but I'm still shaky on my legs. Really, Hester is worse than a sergeant major when it comes to bossing me about. She insists that I sit here for a couple of hours and then I have to lie down and rest. I have to drink hot milk, which I hate, and she doses me up with some horrible concoction she's brewed from herbs and honey.'

'You poor boy. But you must admit she means well. Everyone wants you to recover and be the old Tommy we love.'

'Do you really love me, Nancy?'

She squeezed his fingers. 'More than anyone in the world.'

'More than Freddie, for instance?'

'I haven't seen Freddie for weeks, months even. He is doing what his papa wanted and leaving me on my own, but it doesn't feel right, Tommy. When I saw him last he wasn't the same Freddie I fell in love with.'

'I'm sorry, Nancy. My own feelings aside, I am genuinely sorry that he's treating you like this.'

'I don't want to talk about Freddie just now. I really wanted to ask your advice. You know all about my boys. I told you about them on the voyage back from Gibraltar.'

'Yes, of course I remember. I can't wait to meet them all.'

'Well, Gus is in trouble. Christina has accused him of setting fire to Greystone Park and she says that Foster, the butler, saw him skulking around last evening. It's true that Gus was furious with her for the way she's treated me and the fact that she evicted him and all the boys from the house.'

Tommy leaned forward, giving her a searching look. 'Do you think the boy was responsible?'

'I think it's possible because he was so angry, but with his background and the fact that he was always in trouble in London, I don't think he stands a chance of a fair hearing. Your papa suggested that Gus would be better off in the army, and I must say I think he's right.'

'It would certainly make him grow up very quickly.'

'The trouble is, I don't know where to find him. What would you do, Tommy? If you were in his shoes where would you go?'

Tommy was silent for a moment. 'You said he was

207

friendly with the boy who led the gang. What was his name?'

'Todd. Yes, they were inseparable until Todd was taken on by Dr Bulmer. Todd is a bright boy and he desperately wants to become a doctor. He's living in the doctor's house now.'

'Then that's where I'd go first. If Gus is in trouble I think he'd make for the one person he trusts above all others.'

'Of course. Why didn't I think of that?' Nancy leaped to her feet and gave Tommy a gentle hug. 'You are right. I'll go there now. I need to find Gus before Constable Burton gets his hands on him.'

Tommy rose unsteadily to his feet. 'Let me come with you, Nancy. I am sick and tired of being cooped up in this room like a prisoner.'

Nancy hesitated. 'I don't know about that, Tommy. What would Bertie say? More importantly, what would Hester say?'

'I don't give a fig for what either of them says, Nancy. I want to help. If we go in the carriage no one will think it odd. The whole village knows that I've been ill, and a visit to the doctor won't look suspicious.'

'You haven't been outside since we returned.'

'All the more reason to go now. I need fresh air and sunshine.' Tommy indicated his garments. 'Look, I'm dressed ready to go out. All I need is a jacket. Go downstairs and send for the carriage and I'll join you.'

'No, that won't do. I'll help you down the narrow staircase to the first landing. A tumble on the stone steps will set you back weeks or even months.'

'Yes, ma'am,' Tommy said, grinning. 'Anything you say, ma'am.'

She threw a pillow at him, but seeing that he was in earnest she went to the clothes press and selected a tweed jacket. 'Here, put this on. We'd best go as fast as we can, Tommy. Once Christina has made up her mind she won't allow anything or anyone to get in her way.'

★ ★ ★

Tommy was weaker than he had admitted, but eventually they made it to the grand entrance hall and Nancy sent James to the stables to have the carriage brought to the front entrance. Fortunately for their plans it seemed that the rest of the family were otherwise occupied and they were able to leave the castle unseen.

When they reached the doctor's house, Jim Gurney climbed down a little creakily from the driver's seat and opened the carriage door. He helped Tommy to alight and then he held out his hand to assist Nancy.

She went to knock on the front door, acknowledging the sympathetic smile of Maud Causley, who ran the Black Dog with her husband. Nancy hoped that Maud would walk by, but she stopped, ready for a chat.

'Such a terrible thing to happen, Miss Sunday. I mean, Miss Greystone. It's just lucky that no one was killed.'

'Yes, indeed, Mrs Causley.'

'I suppose everything has gone,' Maud continued eagerly. 'All your prized possessions gone up in smoke.'

'The fire did a lot of damage.' Nancy held her hand out to Tommy. 'If you'll excuse us, ma'am, Tommy needs to see Dr Bulmer.'

'Yes, we all heard of your injuries and your illness, Master Tommy. I do hope you feel better soon.' Maud waited for a reply but just then Mrs Lloyd opened the door.

'Yes, Miss Nancy. Can I help you?'

'Mr Carey would like to see Dr Bulmer. It's just for some more of the tonic that the doctor prescribed,' Nancy added hastily. She knew that whatever she said would be bar gossip when Maud Causley reached home.

'Come inside. You don't look as though you ought to be out and about yet, Master Tommy.'

'Good day, Mrs Causley,' Nancy said firmly as she helped Tommy over the threshold.

Once inside Nancy closed the front door in case Maud Causley was still loitering outside.

'We need to speak to Todd, Mrs Lloyd,' Nancy said in a low voice. 'Is he at home?'

'No, miss. He went out with Dr Bulmer. He's been a great help, running errands and delivering medicines. He's a good boy.'

'Yes, he is. I was wondering if you'd seen his friend Gus, recently.'

Mrs Lloyd stiffened. 'I don't know the boy,' she said through pursed lips.

'He might be in a lot of trouble, Mrs Lloyd.' Tommy staggered and sat down on a chair outside the front parlour where Dr Bulmer held his consultations. 'I'm sorry, I'm still a bit weak.'

'You really shouldn't be out and about, sir.' Mrs Lloyd eyed him warily.

'We need to speak to Gus, Mrs Lloyd,' Nancy said urgently. 'I believe that he might have come to Todd for help, and he certainly needs it. Mrs Cottingham has accused him of setting fire to Greystone Park and Constable Burton will be looking for him even as we speak.'

Mrs Lloyd recoiled, biting her lip. 'I promised not to say anything. I felt sorry for the lad when he turned up on the doorstep. He was obviously very distressed.'

'Where is he, Mrs Lloyd?' Nancy caught her by the hand. 'We can help him, but we have to speak to him urgently.'

Mrs Lloyd opened the parlour door. 'Wait in there, if you please. I'll send him to you.'

Nancy helped Tommy to his feet and they stepped into the small parlour where Tommy collapsed again on the nearest chair. He held up his hand.

'Don't fuss, Nancy. I am all right, it's just that spending so much time in bed has made my legs weak. I need to exercise in order to make them work properly again.'

'Of course. I understand, but you mustn't overdo it, Tommy. You have to be sensible.'

'When was I ever sensible, Nancy?'

'Never, but now would be a good time to start.' Nancy's laughter was cut short when the door opened and Gus sidled into the room.

'I never done it, miss. At least I never set the whole blooming house on fire.'

Nancy placed her arm around his shoulders. 'Tell us what happened, Gus. We're here to help you.'

'I was mad as fire, miss. I hates that woman, but I didn't want to kill her.'

'She isn't dead,' Nancy said hastily. 'No one was hurt, luckily.'

'I wanted to scare the old besom out of your house

211

so I made a small fire under her bedroom window. I threw stones at the glass panes until she poked her head out and I slipped into the shadows. She couldn't have seen me. It was too dark.'

'Foster spotted you — I don't know how. But if you didn't set the house on fire, who did?'

'It could have started accidently in the kitchens or maybe a candle caught the curtains on fire in one of the rooms,' Tommy said thoughtfully.

'But you believe me, don't you?' Gus said tearfully. 'I could get me head chopped off if the law caught me.'

'I don't think they'd hang you, Gus, but it would mean a lengthy prison sentence if you couldn't prove your innocence.' Nancy took Gus by the hand. 'Now listen to me. We're going to smuggle you back to Rockwood Castle. Then we'll make plans to get you to safety.'

'How do you feel about becoming a soldier, Gus?' Tommy rose to his feet. 'I had to sell my commission, but it would be a good life for a chap like you.'

'I dunno. I never thought about it.'

'We'll sort something out.' Nancy opened the door. 'Mrs Lloyd, we're going to take Gus to Rockwood Castle. Our carriage is outside. If you would be kind enough to keep watch I'll take him to the carriage.' Nancy took off her bonnet and rammed it on Gus's head, ignoring his protests. She wrapped her shawl around him. 'Now keep quiet and when I tell you to move, jump into the carriage and make yourself as small as possible. Tommy and I will follow.'

'I'd rather be a soldier than dress up like a blooming girl.'

'Or perhaps you'd like to go to prison for ten years,' Tommy suggested, giving Gus a shove towards the door. 'Do as you're told, young man. Constable Burton is looking for you.'

★ ★ ★

Nancy took Gus straight to Bertie's study. Tommy insisted on accompanying them, although he moved slowly and with obvious effort. However, he was determined to conquer his physical weakness, and Nancy was not about to make a fuss. At this moment her main concern was for Gus, who seemed suddenly very young and defenceless. She laid her hands on his shoulders as they faced Bertie across his desk.

'Gus, tell Sir Bertram what you told me.'

Gus shivered but he held his head high. 'I did light a fire, guv. I meant to scare the old besom. I never intended to burn the place down.'

'Is it possible that your fire could have spread to the main building?' Bertie eyed him severely.

'No, sir. The ground was damp and it was more smoke than flames.'

'You do realise that Mrs Cottingham can have you arrested for trespass and for damaging the house she considers to be her property?'

Gus hung his head. 'Yes, sir.'

Bertie leaned forward, concentrating on Gus. 'As I see it, you have two options, Gus. The first is to hand yourself in to Constable Burton and tell him the truth. The second is to allow me to take you to the recruiting office for you to join the army as a drummer boy or a bugler.'

Gus nodded. 'It ain't much of a choice, guv.'

'Perhaps you should have thought of that before you acted so stupidly,' Bertie said coldly. 'We're trying

213

to help you, boy.'

'Don't be too hard on him, Bertie.' Nancy tightened her grasp on Gus's thin shoulders.

'Life is tough — the boy knows that — but I'm giving him a chance of a better existence than returning to the city streets.' Bertie turned his attention back to Gus. 'What do you say?'

Gus nodded. 'The army has it, guv. I don't stand a chance as far as the law is concerned, and I would guess that the army is better than prison.'

Tommy had sunk down onto a chair but he rose to his feet. 'I'll come with you, Gus.'

Nancy was about to protest that Tommy was not well enough to travel but a look from Bertie silenced her. She knew instinctively that this was their business and she must not interfere. At least Gus would be safe from falling into the hands of the criminal gangs in London.

Bertie's stern expression softened. 'Good boy, Gus. Who knows, you might rise through the ranks and become a leader of men.'

'When do we leave?' Tommy leaned against the back of the chair.

'I think we should keep young Gus hidden, even from the servants. We'll go early tomorrow morning, which gives us all time to rest and recover from last night's disaster.'

'Gus can sleep in my dressing room,' Tommy said, grinning. 'He can tell me about his life before he came to Devonshire, and I'll give him some pointers about getting on in the army.'

'Can I go and see Todd?' Gus asked anxiously. 'I don't want to go without saying goodbye to him and the boys.'

Nancy could see that this was going to be met with a firm rebuttal, but she knew how much Todd meant to Gus. They had been closer than most brothers. 'I tell you what, Gus. I'll send Pip Hudson to the doctor's house to request some more medicine for Tommy. That means Todd will deliver it later today and you can explain everything to him then. I'll tell Jarvis to let me know when Todd arrives.'

'Ta, miss. You're the best person I ever met.'

'She most certainly is,' Tommy said, smiling. 'Now if you'd like to give me a hand, young Gus, I think I'd better go to my room and rest a while.'

'I'll bring up extra food at mealtimes.' Nancy opened the door and looked both ways to make sure the coast was clear. She hesitated. 'Wait a minute, Jarvis is coming this way. Stay where you are, Gus.'

There was a sense of urgency in Jarvis's step. 'I'm sorry to bother you, Miss Nancy, but Constable Burton is here. He insists on seeing you and Sir Bertram.'

15

Constable Burton seemed more embarrassed than suspicious when he was shown into Bertie's study, and he left soon after, apparently satisfied with Bertie's assurance that if Gus put in an appearance at Rockwood Castle he would be dealt with in an appropriate manner. Nancy went to bed that night comforted by the knowledge that Bertie was on their side and determined to get Gus to safety. She did not like keeping his presence in the castle a secret from Rosie and Alex, but they were more concerned with the children, who had developed rashes and mild fevers and were confined to the nursery. However, this made it easier for Gus to slip out of the building in Tommy's wake early next morning, and they were joined by Bertie and a disapproving Wolfe. Nancy suspected that Wolfe's grumpy attitude was due to the fact that he had not been involved in the plan to get Gus to the relative safety of the army recruitment office. However, he said little and Bertie did not encourage him to speak his mind. Nancy waved them goodbye, dashing tears from her eyes. She could only hope that Gus would find army life acceptable and would thrive. He was a good boy at heart and she would miss him.

It had occurred to Nancy in the early hours of the morning, when she had awakened from a nightmare seeing the old house enveloped in flames, that the servants would now be homeless. She wondered if Christina had taken them in at Cottingham Manor and had come to the conclusion that it was unlikely. As there was nothing she could do in the castle, Nancy put on her riding habit and walked to the stables to have a horse saddled. If the truth were told, she preferred riding astride, but custom dictated a side saddle and she was not about to cause comment in the village.

'Do you want me to accompany you, Miss Nancy?' Pip, the under groom, asked shyly.

'No, thank you. I'm only going to Greystone Park.'

'Terrible business, miss. It's a mercy you wasn't there when the place went up in flames.'

'Yes, indeed. If anyone asks, I won't be long, Pip.' Nancy climbed onto the mounting block and settled herself in the saddle. She flicked the reins and gently urged the horse into motion. It was a fine autumn morning but the air still carried the acrid smell of burning even as far as Rockwood. When she reached Greystone Park she saw that the ruins were still smoking although the flames had been extinguished. It was a sad sight. Nancy dismounted outside the front entrance where Foster was standing very still, gazing at the smoke-damaged but intact front door as it swung gently on its hinges.

'Foster, I am so sorry.'

He turned his head and Nancy was shocked to see tears running down his thin cheeks. 'I've spent more than half my life serving the family, Miss Greystone. I know no other home than this.'

'Where are you staying, Foster?'

'The Causleys at the Black Dog took me in, and Mrs Banks as well. Mrs Simpson has a daughter in Dawlish and she went to stay with her. Ivy is back at home with her ma, and Bertha was taken on by Mrs

Blanchard at the castle. The housemaids are staying wherever they can.'

'Has Mrs Cottingham been in contact with you, Foster?'

'No, miss. Not a word.'

'Then you are virtually homeless. I was wondering how the servants were faring.'

'Not very well, miss. We haven't been paid this quarter either.'

'This won't do, Foster. I'm going to ride over to Cottingham Manor and have a word with Mrs Cottingham. She threw me out of my home and she took on the responsibility for the staff. I'll find a way to make this better.'

'I'm afraid it might be the workhouse for some of us if we can't find other positions. I'm not a young man, Miss Greystone. I doubt if anyone would take me on.'

Nancy shook her head. 'You won't suffer for this act of arson, whoever did it. I'll make sure of that.'

'It wasn't the boy, miss. I did see him skulking around, but there was a man, too. I wouldn't swear to it because it was dark, but it looked like Jeremiah Stewer. He used to work at the manor house until Mrs Cottingham sent him packing. He had to put his wife and children in the workhouse while he looked for another position, but his wife died of a fever and the young ones are left to cope on their own.'

'That's a sad story. I'm so sorry. Leave everything to me, Foster. I'll do whatever I can to make this right.'

Nancy kept her tone even but inwardly she was fuming. Christina had no feelings for her fellow human beings, but she was about to hear a few home

218

truths. The loyal servants who had been with her since childhood must not suffer on her account. Nancy's horse was still fresh and ready to be off again. The animal needed only a little encouragement to race through the lanes to Cottingham Manor. The house, which had once impressed Nancy with its size and imposing half-timbered façade, now seemed small in comparison to Greystone Park and Dorrington Place. However, she was not in a mood to bother about architecture or the size of a dwelling and she hammered on the front door until a servant opened it. The girl eyed Nancy warily.

'Can I help you, miss?'

Nancy pushed past her. 'I want to see Mrs Cottingham. Where is she?'

'You can't come in like that, miss. I have to go and ask my lady if she will see you.'

'Don't bother. She will see me whether she likes it or not.'

The girl, who could not have been much older than twelve, backed away nervously. 'Madam is in the morning parlour, miss. But please don't go there.'

Nancy followed the direction of the maid's scared glance. The morning parlour, she guessed correctly, was on the opposite side of the entrance hall. Nancy barged in without knocking.

Christina was seated at the table drinking coffee, but she jumped to her feet, spilling liquid on her voluminous skirts. 'How dare you enter my home uninvited?'

'I dare because that's exactly what you did to me. Greystone Park was mine legally until you took it into your head to claim it for yourself. And look where that got you. I've just spoken to Foster and he tells me that you didn't pay the servants, nor did you offer to take them in until they had found accommodation or another position in service.'

'That is none of your business.'

'Oh, but it is, Christina. Whether you like it or not, I inherited Greystone Park and you took it from me. Not only that, but it appears that a disgruntled servant whom you sacked was the one who started the fire — deliberately. You tried to blame it on one of my boys because it suited you, but the man you treated so heartlessly is the arsonist.'

'You are lying. You just want to get that brat from London out of trouble.'

'Gus has gone where you can't touch him. But the servants are another matter. We owe it to them to give them somewhere to live until they find new jobs.'

'I can't take them in here. You'd better have them at the castle. The Careys never have enough servants.'

'You are a vindictive, nasty woman, Christina. I'm ashamed to call you cousin.'

'At least we agree on something. Now get out of my house, or do I have to send for the servants to throw you out?'

'I'm going, but don't you dare set your foot on Greystone soil again.' Nancy left the room, slamming the door behind her. 'I'll see myself out,' she told the frightened young maid. 'And you should keep out of your mistress's way for a while, if you know what's good for you.'

Nancy left the house, taking the reins of her horse from the stable boy who had been holding them patiently. She tossed him a penny as she rode off. She felt better for putting Christina in her place, but she had not done anything to help the homeless staff. As she rode at a much slower pace she remembered the old Dower House at the edge of the Greystone estate. It had fallen into disrepair long ago and she had intended to have it made habitable, but there had been more pressing needs at the time. Quite what state it was in was uncertain, but it was a large house, fit for a dowager and her servants. It was possible that the keys had been destroyed in the fire at the main house, but if anyone knew where they were it was Foster. Nancy rode to the Black Dog and dismounted outside.

Ben raced towards her, grinning broadly. 'Everyone is talking about the fire at Greystone. The boys was lucky to get out.'

'Mr Gibson saw them to safety, Ben.'

'How are you, miss?'

'I'm well thank you, Ben.' Nancy handed him the reins. 'And Gus is safe. Don't tell anyone other than the boys that I said so, but you don't need to worry about him.'

'He never done it, miss. We know he didn't.'

'I agree, but I can't stop and chat. Have you seen Mr Foster recently?'

'Yes, miss. He went into the taproom. I expect he's having a pint of ale with Mr Causley.'

'Very likely. Hold my horse, please, Ben. I won't be long.'

Nancy strode into the taproom but this time there were no disapproving looks and one man actually cheered. She gave him her most brilliant smile. 'Has anyone seen Mr Foster?'

'I'm here, Miss Greystone.' Foster rose from a seat in the inglenook. 'What can I do for you?'

Nancy wove her way between the tables, acknowledging the approving smiles from the men. 'Foster,

221

do you know what happened to the keys to the Dower House?'

'I have them in my room, Miss Greystone. When I escaped the fire I made certain I had the big bunch of house keys with me.'

'Will you give it to me, please? I have had an idea that might suit all of us, depending upon the state of the old house.'

'It isn't so very bad, miss. I used to check on it regularly, in case someone broke in and set up home there. The structure is sound, although there might be a few tiles missing off the roof. It's very dilapidated, but a bit of hard work and a lot of cleaning should make it reasonably habitable.'

'If you have the keys I want to see it for myself.'

'I'll come with you, miss. You never know who might be lurking around these days.'

'Very well. I'll wait for you outside.'

★ ★ ★

The Dower House was almost hidden by trees with a small stream gurgling past the outbuildings as it raced to join the River Sawle. Nancy had only ever seen the house from the outside, and even then she had not really paid much attention to the building, but the trees parted suddenly to reveal a large house of elegant proportions. However, the shutters were closed, making it look as if the building was sleeping, and ivy clambered over the portico as if intent on swallowing up the house with its clutching green tendrils.

'It looks sad and unloved,' Nancy said, sighing. 'I wouldn't mind living here myself.'

Foster dismounted from the aged pony loaned to

him by Ned Causley and he pulled a large bunch of keys from his coat pocket. 'I think I know which one it is.' He handled the jangling bunch of metal deftly and within seconds had found the right key. It grated in the lock but the door opened with the minimum of force. Nancy had dismounted and tethered her horse to the fence that kept the wild deer from roaming into what must once have been a pretty garden.

'After you, Miss Greystone.' Foster stood back to allow Nancy to pass.

She stepped over the threshold, holding her hand to her nose as dust flew up in small clouds with each footstep. A large square entrance hall with a staircase sweeping up to the gallery on the first floor must once have been the height of elegance, but the plaster was flaking off the walls and the paintwork was peeling. Shreds of wallpaper hung in tassels on the walls and the floor was covered with dead leaves. It was too dark to see everything and Nancy flung the wooden shutters open, allowing a trickle of autumn sunshine to illuminate the scene. She went from room to room, letting in the light with Foster following her. He shook his head at the dilapidated state and the years of neglect.

'Who was the last person to live here, Foster?' Nancy ran her finger along the mantelshelf, leaving a deep furrow in the dust.

'I believe it was Sir Michael's late mother. She was a very particular lady, as I recall, although she had her own servants. They will have had the top floor. I believe the kitchens and servants' quarters are at the back of the house. When this was built they liked to keep the kitchens as far from the main property as possible in case of fire.'

'It's ironic that this house is still standing and the main building has burned to the ground. Let's explore the rest of the house, Foster. From what I've seen I think it could be made habitable quite quickly. There will be room for any of the servants who wish to return to Greystone Park.'

'That's wonderful news, Miss Greystone. I would be more than happy to live and work here.'

'When we've seen everything I'll see if I can find Mr Gibson. I need him back in his old job quickly if we're to keep the estate going. It seems to me that Mrs Cottingham only wanted the house. She has no interest in the land or the tenants.'

'I can arrange for cleaners to come and give the house a good going over, Miss Greystone.'

'Thank you, Foster. I will ask Mr Gibson to find tradesmen to repair the plasterwork and repaper the walls. I want to check everything from the cellar to the attics before I take on such a big project.'

It did not take Nancy long to decide that this house could be perfect for her and the younger boys. Winter was coming and she wanted a home of her own again. Living back at Rockwood was lovely, but after having a taste of managing her own household Nancy knew it would be difficult to return to a more subservient role. Rosie would understand and so would Patsy. As for Lord Dorrington, he would see that she was a resourceful woman quite equal to running a stately home and dealing with the difficulties that now faced her. She longed to tell Freddie what she planned, but she was not about to run after him. He could come to her if he still felt as he had done when they were forced to part.

An hour and a half later, Nancy was seated at the

kitchen table in the cottage on the Rockwood estate where Nick was taking care of the boys. The young ones were at Miss Martha's cottage, doing their lessons, but Nick was eager to hear her plans. He let her speak, listening intently until she had finished telling him about the Dower House.

'Of course I can come back to my land agent work right away. It's time to visit the farms to collect the rent anyway. I just didn't know if Mrs Cottingham had engaged a man to do it for her.'

'Christina has washed her hands of the estate. She only wanted the house and the glory that she thought went with it. She really isn't a businesswoman at heart or she would never have sacked you.'

Nick grinned appreciatively. 'Thank you. I'm flattered, but I'm eager to get back to work. I know where the Dower House is, of course, but I have never been inside.'

'We can soon remedy that. It must have been quite splendid many years ago, but it has suffered badly from neglect. Foster is arranging for cleaners to go in but we'll need plasterers and painters to start with. We might find other problems as we go along.'

'I can help there. My father kept lists of reliable tradesmen. I kept all his papers so it's just a question of going through them.'

'The sooner we can get this old house habitable, the better, Nick. I want a home of my own again. Although I love being with the family at the castle, it's not quite the same as being mistress of my own property.'

'I'm sure they are happy to have you, Nancy.'

'I know and I don't want to sound ungrateful. Anyway, I really should get back to Rockwood or they will

225

be worried about me, but perhaps later this afternoon you could meet me at the Dower House.'

'I'm so glad you've found somewhere that inspires you. I thought we had lost you when you moved back to the castle.'

'Never. I love my boys and I'm intent on making a home for them. I won't allow them to go to the workhouse.'

'Don't worry, Nancy. There's no question of that. I'll adopt them myself if the worst comes to the worst.'

She stared at him in amazement. 'Would you really?'

'Yes, I've grown fond of the little devils. They deserve a good home and someone who cares what happens to them. They all show promise in one way or another.'

Nancy laughed. 'You don't intend to start a theatrical troupe with them, do you?'

'No, it was simple necessity that forced us to take that course, although I must admit I enjoyed being back on the boards, so to speak. We have the harvest supper coming up and we'll entertain the village, but that's the end of it as far as I'm concerned.'

'You never know, you might have inspired one or two of the boys to follow in your footsteps — as an actor, I mean. I had a lot to do with the theatrical world when Patricia was trying her hand at being an operatic star like her mother. I even accompanied Mrs de Marney at Dorrington Place one Christmas. How long ago that seems.'

'Still no word from the viscount?'

Nancy shook her head. 'No, and I'm not going to chase after him. If Freddie wants to find me he knows where to look.' She rose to her feet. 'I must go. I'll see you later at the Dower House.'

Nick stood up, frowning. 'I'm sorry, Nancy. I didn't mean to upset you.'

She paused in the doorway. 'You didn't. I've come to terms with the fact that Freddie might have changed his mind about marrying me. I am not going to mope around like a lovesick young girl.'

'You are an amazing woman, Nancy.'

'I'll see you later.' Nancy left the cottage and was suddenly hit by a multitude of emotions. Nick's mention of Freddie had unsettled her and his open admiration had stirred something inside her that she had been deliberately ignoring. She mounted her horse and rode off in the direction of the castle. It was her safe place where she felt protected and loved. She wondered if Tommy and Bertie had returned. She crossed her fingers superstitiously, hoping that the army had taken Gus on and he would be safe from Christina's spiteful desire for revenge, no matter who it affected.

She arrived back at the castle to find the stable boys and grooms busy with a pair of matched bays and a sturdy cart horse. There was a new carriage of the latest design in the coach house, as well as a less glamorous cart standing on the cobblestones outside, which was being unloaded of trunks and baggage of all kinds.

Nancy's heart was beating twice as fast as usual as she left her horse with Pip and hurried towards the castle. The only people she knew who were wealthy enough to own such a vehicle must be the Dorringtons. She could hardly breathe when Jarvis opened the door to let her in.

16

Nancy's heart sank when she spotted Felicia's maid, Violet Tinker, who was standing by a pile of valises and bandboxes, arguing with James.

'I'm sorry, miss,' James said stiffly. 'I can't take these to your mistress's room until I know where she will be sleeping. Mrs Blanchard hasn't given us any instructions yet. You weren't expected.'

Nancy could see that James was getting annoyed and she stepped in between them. 'Miss Tinker, this is a pleasant surprise.'

Violet's dark eyes filled with tears of frustration. 'Please tell this fellow that Mrs de Marney is a very rich and famous operatic star, and she is used to being treated as such.'

'I think we are all aware of Mrs de Marney's fame, Violet. But she can't expect to turn up as if this is a hotel in London or Paris and have a room immediately to hand. James can't oblige until Mrs Blanchard issues instructions as to where the guests will sleep. Have you travelled far today?'

'We've been on the road for three days. Mrs de Marney insisted on bringing everything apart from the furniture, which is being brought by Pickfords.'

'You must be tired, Violet. Why don't you go to the servants' quarters with James and have a nice cup of tea? There will be plenty of time to arrange rooms and unpack later.'

James nodded. 'Yes, come with me, Miss Tinker.'

228

Nancy left them to take the servants' stairs to the kitchen. Her curiosity was piqued by Violet's assertion that Mrs de Marney was now a woman of means. Last Christmas Felicia and Claude had been glad to be invited to Dorrington Place because Felicia was temporarily resting. Had she made a spectacular comeback? Nancy was eager to find out. She headed for the drawing room.

She walked in without knocking and found Felicia and Claude seated on the sofa, Rosie and Alex standing together with their backs to the fire. There was a definite *frisson* in the air, and it was not one of excitement.

'Bertie isn't here at the moment, Mama,' Rosalind said calmly. 'But of course we are delighted to see you and Claude.'

Alex curled his fingers around his wife's hand. 'That is a very smart carriage you have now. Is it hired?'

Felicia shot him a scornful glance. 'Certainly not. It was custom-made for us, wasn't it, Claude?'

'Yes, my love, it was.' Claude beamed at Nancy. 'It's good to see you, Nancy. Or should I call you Miss Greystone?'

'Nancy will do nicely. It's good to see you, too, Mr de Marney, and Mrs de Marney, of course.'

'We might have to stay with you at Greystone Park if my daughter cannot find room for us,' Felicia said crossly. 'Really, Rosie, is it asking too much for a more wholehearted welcome? I feel as though I'm not wanted in my own home.'

'You cannot really call this home, Mama. You were hardly ever here even when we were growing up.' Rosalind turned to Alex. 'Darling, will you go and find Walter? I'm sure he would like to welcome Mama,

229

and Louisa, too, if she has finished at the school. It looks as if it's going to be a long visit.'

'I don't know why you say that, Rosie. You make it sound as if we are sponging off you.' Felicia tossed her head. 'I can assure you that money is no object, is it, Claude?'

'I can honestly say that we are better off now than we have ever been,' Claude said proudly. 'My dear wife has met a very wealthy gentleman who is intent on backing her with almost unlimited means.'

Felicia smiled modestly. 'It was pure luck. He was in the audience at my first performance in Brighton and he came backstage to meet me. He said he intends to build a theatre outside London. He thinks opera and good music should be available to people throughout the country. I am to choose where it will be built and I will put on my own productions.'

'Which is wonderful,' Claude added. 'My dearest wife is not as young as she was and her voice will not last for ever.'

'Claude! That's insulting. Are you saying that my voice is going?'

'No, my love. Of course not. I was merely pointing out that this will be our future. No one knows the opera circuit like you do, my dear.'

'It sounds marvellous,' Rosalind said hastily. 'Please fetch Walter, Alex. He will want to greet Mama and Claude.'

Alex eyed Felicia warily. 'Yes, of course. He will be as delighted as we were to discover that you plan to stay with us, Felicia.'

'It all sounds very exciting, Mrs de Marney.' Nancy sank down on a chair by the door. 'Where do you plan to build this theatre?'

'I'm glad that someone is interested. Although I suppose you are too grand to wish to appear on stage now, Nancy?'

'I think you should know that Nancy has had some very bad luck, Mama.' Rosie took a seat by the fire. 'Greystone Park was razed to the ground by a terrible fire. Fortunately no one was hurt.'

'Goodness gracious, how awful.' Felicia turned to Nancy, giving her a calculating look. 'Are you planning to rebuild the house?'

'Not at the moment, ma'am. It only happened a day or two ago. I've quite lost the track of time, and I'm still trying to come to terms with the loss of everything I owned, even if I was mistress of a great house for such a short time.'

'You poor girl.' Claude shook his head. 'How did it happen?'

'It was arson, Mr de Marney. It's a complicated story and the police are looking into it.'

'So there is nothing left of the old house?' Felicia exchanged meaningful glances with her husband.

'Just the front door, oddly enough, and that looks ready to fall down at any moment.'

'Maybe, Claude, just maybe . . .' Felicia smiled roguishly. 'Perhaps my instinct for returning to my old home was correct.'

'What plot are you hatching now, Mama?' Rosalind demanded suspiciously. 'I know that look of old. It usually meant that you were planning a trip abroad.'

'Not this time, Rosie. I think my travelling days are coming to an end. Anyway, I'm assuming it will be all right if Claude and I stay here for a while? And Tinker, of course.'

'You know that you are always welcome, Mama. I'll

231

have your rooms made ready.'

'Thank you, my darling girl. You were always my favourite, Rosie. I love your sister, of course, but she was always so wild and wayward. I can't think where she got those traits from.'

Nancy and Rosalind exchanged wry smiles.

'Are we in time for luncheon, my dear?' Claude asked anxiously. 'I realise it is rather late but we wanted to get here as soon as possible and we haven't made a stop since breakfast.'

'I'll ask Mrs Jackson to make something for you and Mama, Claude.' Rosalind turned to give Nancy a questioning look. 'Have you eaten today?'

'I don't think so. I was so busy I forgot.'

'Neither have I, come to that. I've been up with the children. They are getting over a slight fever and a rash, but Dr Bulmer assures me it isn't serious,' Rosalind added hastily. 'It's nothing catching, Mama.'

'I hope not. I have to protect my voice. Perhaps I won't see my grandchildren until they are completely better.'

Rosalind stood up and rang the bell. 'We'll have a light meal in the dining room. Dinner will be at the usual time.' She looked up as the door opened and Alex ushered Walter into the room.

'Mama, Claude. What a nice surprise.' Walter rushed over to his mother and gave her a peck on the cheek. 'You both look very well. Are you planning to stay with us for a while?'

'I'm looking for a site to build a new theatre,' Felicia said grandly. 'I have a wealthy backer and the theatre is to be named after me.'

'Isn't it rather out of the way? I mean Rockwood is

hardly the centre of activity, Mama.' Walter sat down beside her on the sofa. 'Mind you, I could give poetry readings.'

'We are quite close to Exeter,' Felicia said vaguely. 'I agree with Sir Bentley that culture should be shared equally throughout the country. He made his money in the manufacturing of cotton. He owns several mills in the North.'

'But he likes opera.' Rosalind shrugged. 'It sounds rather odd when you put it that way, Mama.'

'Why should it? Plenty of self-made men invest in art and music. Just because he isn't old school doesn't mean he is a Philistine.'

Rosalind hurried to the door to answer a timid knock. 'Yes, I rang, Bertha. Will you ask Cook to make a light luncheon for four?'

'Make that five,' Alex added. 'I haven't eaten yet.'

'Six,' corrected Walter. 'Neither have I. Louise is teaching at the village school but she'll be here for dinner.'

'For six,' Rosalind said gently. 'In the dining room, Bertha.'

'Yes'm.' Bertha backed away.

Rosalind closed the door. 'I took Bertha Tuckett on after the fire at Greystone. Her poor mother has so many children to care for, and Bertha's father is away at sea for anything up to two years at a time.'

'You are too soft, Rosie,' Felicia said, yawning. 'You will never be rich because you take on all the waifs and strays.'

'I'd rather do that than be like Christina Cotting-ham.' Rosalind shrugged. 'Money isn't everything, Mama. Although you seem to be doing very well since you met Sir Bentley . . . what is his full name?'

233

'Sir Bentley Crooke,' Claude said hastily. 'An unfortunate name, but an honest man for all that, and a true supporter of the arts. He has founded theatres in the North as well as in the South-East. It is his mission in life to bring culture to the masses.'

Walter smiled eagerly. 'It sounds like a wonderful thing to do. Where were you thinking of building this theatre, Mama? Maybe I ought to write a play or two.'

'I was thinking there might be a spare plot of land on the Rockwood estate, Walter, darling. But now I learn that Greystone Park has been razed to the ground by fire, I think that would be an ideal spot.'

'There's only one problem, Felicia,' Alex said firmly. 'The land belongs to Nancy.'

Felicia turned to give Nancy a beaming smile. 'My dear girl, it could be the answer to all your problems. I don't suppose you have funds available to clear the site and rebuild, but thanks to Sir Bentley, I do. You would still own the land and lease it to the theatre. That way you would get rent for the land.'

'But she will still be homeless, Mama.' Rosalind went to stand behind Nancy. 'It isn't as simple as that.'

'Actually, I do have somewhere to live,' Nancy said slowly. 'I've just been to look over the Dower House. It's quite large enough for me and my boys, and if Sir Bentley is willing to pay rent for the land that will cover the cost of renovation and redecorating the house.'

'Your boys?' Felicia stared at her, frowning.

'The children are Nancy's protégés, Mama.' Rosalind laid her hands on Nancy's shoulders, giving them a gentle squeeze. 'Nancy has saved them from a life of crime in London. She brought them to Devonshire and she took them into her own home.'

'You always were an odd child,' Felicia said dismissively. 'That's just the sort of wild project I would expect of you.'

'But very laudable.' Claude smiled at Nancy. 'Good for you, my dear. If only there were more people in the world like you.'

'I am doing my bit for humanity, Claude,' Felicia said sharply. 'My work satisfies the soul.'

Walter turned to his mother. 'Do you think you might put on plays or poetry readings, Mama? I am keen to try my hand at something like a drama. I've just finished reading a book called *East Lynne*, by Mrs Henry Wood. I could write something of the sort as a play. What do you think?'

'Maybe, Walter. I rule nothing out. Maybe you could collaborate with a composer of music and write an opera just for me.'

'That's a ripping idea, Mama.'

Felicia's bright smile faded as she turned back to Nancy. 'Of course, this all depends upon you, Nancy. I'm not saying that the family fortunes will be made by my efforts but it will be a legacy for my darling grandchildren, who are sadly indisposed at the moment. Maybe we should stay with Patricia until your children recover, Rosie.'

'It's your choice, Mama, but according to Dr Bulmer they are well enough to socialise without passing on the infection.'

'Nevertheless, one cannot be too careful. I'll see them at a distance, but in any case I am going to be extremely busy. Oh, did I mention the fact that Sir Bentley will be arriving tomorrow?'

'Mama, you haven't invited a complete stranger to stay with us?' Rosalind stared at her in horror.

'He isn't a stranger, darling. Sir Bentley is going to be the founder of our financial success. Rockwood Castle will benefit, and he might even suggest using the grounds for outdoor productions in the summer. You could earn money to pay for the crumbling stonework or the leaking roof.'

Alex opened his mouth to speak but a rap on the door preceded Bertha's entrance. She took a deep breath. 'Luncheon is ready. Come and get it.'

Felicia fanned herself vigorously. 'If this is an example of how someone repays your kindness, Rosalind, I suggest you put her to work in the laundry room.'

'Thank you, Bertha. We're coming now.' Rosalind held her hand out to Alex. 'Shall we lead the way?' She lowered her voice. 'Or I might say something to Mama for which I will be very sorry.'

Nancy overheard the last remark and she stifled a giggle. 'Before we go to the dining room, may I say that I will consider your offer, Mrs de Marney? I will give it a lot of thought, but perhaps you ought to visit the site with Sir Bentley before you come to a final decision.'

Felicia rose to her feet in a swirl of lace and expensive perfume. 'Of course. That's exactly what I plan to do.'

* * *

Nancy left the castle as soon after luncheon as it was polite to do so, although Felicia still had centre stage and Nancy doubted if anyone would notice her absence. She decided to walk to the cottage, where she hoped to find Nick and the younger boys. As luck would have it, the children had just returned from

Miss Collins' cottage where they had spent the morning doing lessons.

'I've found a painter and decorator,' Nick said proudly. 'I remembered the name of a fellow after you had gone and I was lucky enough to catch him at home. He's in between jobs at the moment so he's available right away. He knows other tradesmen, so I think we can trust him to assess what needs doing and we can go on from there.'

'That's excellent.' Nancy breathed a sigh of relief. 'I'd like to move to the Dower House as soon as possible.'

Nick eyed her suspiciously. 'What's changed since earlier today? You were quite happy to wait until everything was done.'

'Mrs de Marney and her husband have virtually moved in at the castle. She wants to build a theatre in the ruins of Greystone Park.'

'A theatre?' Nick's eyes lit with an intense glow. 'Really?'

'Well, an opera house, to be exact, but Walter was babbling on about writing plays and performing poetry readings.'

'I think it's a wonderful idea, but what about you? That house was your home, if only briefly. Wouldn't you like to rebuild it for yourself?'

'You know the amount of money the estate brings in, Nick. There wouldn't be enough to build a cottage, let alone another fine house. Greystone Park never seems to have been a particularly happy home. Perhaps it's better this way.'

'Your year of separation from Freddie is already half over. Will you wait and see if he comes for you?'

'If Freddie comes to find me I will see how I feel

237

then. Perhaps his father was right to make us wait, although I refuse to be judged on my ability to run a household. If that is all there is to marriage I might just as well apply for a position of housekeeper at Dorrington Place. I've grown up a lot since Lord Dorrington forced us to keep apart. Freddie might not like the person I've become.'

'I'm sorry, Nancy. You deserve the best of everything.'

She smiled. 'Yes, I agree. Now let's go to the Dower House. The boys can come too, because it will be their home as well as mine.'

'I haven't told them of your plan yet.' Nick glanced out of the cottage window. 'They're outside kicking a ball around. Miss Moon gave it to them. She's very much into training their bodies as well as their minds and they enjoy the exercise.'

'We won't tell them until we've shown them the house and noted their reactions. I can't wait to see their faces when they realise they have a permanent home.'

Nick caught her by the sleeve as she was about to walk out of the door. 'What happens to them if Freddie turns up and you agree to marry him? Who will look after the boys then? Have you thought of that?'

'I haven't until now, but whatever happens I won't abandon them, Nick. They have all suffered enough in their short lives.'

Nancy stepped outside into the autumn sunshine. 'We're going for a walk, boys. Would you like to come with us?'

★ ★ ★

The boys were delighted with the Dower House and would have moved in right away without even a mop or a duster being lifted. However, Nancy managed to calm them down and she promised that they could help get the rooms ready for occupation, although the majority of the work would be done by skilled tradesmen.

She left them at the cottage with Nick and made her way back to the castle. She had a lot on her mind and most of all she needed to talk to someone about Felicia's offer. It was a difficult situation. Whatever Rosie and Patsy might say about Felicia, she was still their mother and family loyalties were strong. Nancy was relieved to find that Tommy had returned and he was taking a rest in his room before dinner.

He looked up and smiled delightedly as she walked into the bedchamber. 'We did it, Nancy. Gus was signed up on the spot and Papa persuaded the sergeant to take him in straight away. He'll be whisked off to a training camp by morning and no one will be any the wiser.'

'That's wonderful, Tommy. I'm sad to see him go but I know it's for the best.'

'It will be the making of him, Nancy. I know people always say that, but Gus needs discipline and training. He'll be a fine soldier.'

Nancy perched on the edge of the bed. 'Are you sorry to have left the army, Tommy?'

'No, not at all. Sometimes you need to go away to really appreciate what you have at home. I know now that my future is here, at Rockwood. I'll take over from Papa when he no longer feels he can run the estate.'

Nancy giggled. 'You'll inherit Wolfe.'

'That's a thought. Maybe he will retire with Pa. They could spend their days fishing or reading Walter's poetry.'

This made Nancy laugh outright. 'My imagination won't stretch that far. But seriously, Tommy, have you heard what Mrs de Marney intends to do with Greystone Park — if I agree, that is?'

'No. I came straight to my room when I saw that they were here. Grandmama is all right in small doses, but I find her a bit overpowering.'

'Well, she has found a rich backer who wants to bring culture to the ignorant people in the countryside. Or rather she didn't put it that way, but that is what she meant. Sir Bentley Crooke is a man with more money than sense, it seems to me. He has given her the funds to build a theatre and she wants to put it on the site of my old house.'

Tommy's eyes widened. 'Really? That sounds quite a good idea, although I don't know where the audience will come from.'

'That won't be my problem. I get rent from the site and the land still belongs to me. I'm going to renovate the Dower House and move in there with the boys.'

Tommy leaned forward to lay his hand on hers. 'You talk as if Freddie doesn't matter anymore, Nancy. Doesn't he come into your plans?'

'I don't know, Tommy. I really don't know how Freddie feels. I haven't heard from him for so long that I'm beginning to think I imagined what happened between us. I feel as if Lord Dorrington has won. He never approved of me.'

'Then Lord Dorrington is a fool, and if Freddie has changed his mind about you he is an even bigger fool.'

Nancy gave him a watery smile. 'You always say the

240

nicest things, Tommy.'

'Only because they're true. I've known you most of my life, Nancy. I love you more than anybody in the world and I know your worth.'

'We are more like brother and sister, Tommy.'

He pulled a face. 'That's not what I meant, but I'll settle for that. Just stay in my life, Nancy. Never leave me.'

'You must concentrate on getting better and I'll take you to the Dower House. I want your opinion on what I should do with some of the rooms.'

'I'd like that. How about tomorrow morning?'

★ ★ ★

Next morning, as Dolly, Rory and Phoebe were on the mend after their illness and Rosalind felt able to leave them for an hour or two, Nancy decided she would take her to see the Dower House, too. They set off in the landau with Gurney driving, but when they arrived at the Dower House, Felicia and Claude were already there, peering in at the windows.

Felicia waved excitedly. 'Rosie, over here. I've discovered this darling house that looks like something out of a fairy tale. I wouldn't be surprised if there was a sleeping princess inside.'

Nancy leaped from the carriage without waiting for Gurney to assist her. She marched up to the front door and unlocked it with a flourish. 'This darling house belongs to me, Mrs de Marney.'

'Even better,' Felicia said, smiling. 'It will make a wonderful hotel. The theatregoers from out of the area will need somewhere to stay. I'm sure it can be made habitable with a little hard work.'

Rosalind joined them, slightly breathless. 'Mama, I don't think you were listening. This is Nancy's property. She intends to live here.'

Felicia raised her delicate eyebrows. 'Oh, no. That won't do, my dear. This will fit in so well with my plans. Sir Bentley will be thrilled.'

Nancy beckoned to Tommy. 'Come in, Tommy. It's too chilly to stand outside when you are still recuperating from your illness.'

'I'm not an invalid now, Nancy.' Tommy made his way slowly up the path to the front door. 'I just need to find my legs, so to speak. But this house is charming. I can't wait to see the rest.'

Rosalind followed them into the entrance hall but she held her hands up to bar her mother's way. 'No, Mama. I'm sure Nancy will welcome you and Claude as visitors, but not as prospective owners. It's your decision.'

Felicia shrugged. 'All right, Rosie. I understand — but she might feel differently if Sir Bentley agrees with me. He is incredibly wealthy and if he says that a hotel would be absolutely necessary, he will spare no expense in order to get what he wants.'

'My love, you should listen to Rosie,' Claude said anxiously. 'This is going to be Nancy's home. You can't take that away from her.'

'If Sir Bentley agrees with me Nancy will have enough money to build herself the house of her dreams. Beside which, I thought she was going to marry Freddie Ashton and become a viscountess. What happened to him, I wonder.'

Nancy had been about to show Tommy and Rosalind into the morning parlour but she came to a halt in the doorway. 'I will choose whom I marry,

Mrs de Marney, and I'll thank you to remember that this is my house on my land. You are here under sufferance because you are Tommy's grandmother. Now please leave before I say something I will regret.'

Felicia stormed off, uttering dire warnings that she would find another site for her theatre, but Nancy was not in a mood to placate her. Claude murmured excuses for his wife as he followed her down the path to the waiting carriage.

'I'm sorry if I've upset your grandmother, Tommy,' Nancy said reluctantly, 'but she is an impossible woman.'

'Don't worry about it.' Tommy followed Nancy into the entrance hall. 'From the little I know of Grandmama, she will recover quickly when she realises that she has the most to lose. Claude will soothe her ruffled feelings, but I'm more interested in seeing the rest of this house.' Tommy tugged at the strip of peeling wallpaper and it came away in his hand. 'It needs a lot of work, but it's a fine house beneath all the dust and grime.'

'That's what I think. I'll feel a lot more at home in the Dower House, even in this state, than I did at Greystone Park.'

Rosie appeared at the top of the staircase. 'Come up and see what must have been the drawing room. It's delightful, Nancy. I can just see you living here.'

'I know,' Nancy said as she mounted the stairs. 'I've already furnished it in my head, Rosie. I've even chosen my bedroom and decided on the colour scheme. The trouble is, it's going to cost money I haven't got.'

Tommy caught her up. 'But you will if Sir Bentley approves of Grandmama's plan. He will pay you rent for the land. Make sure you get a good deal.'

243

17

Sir Bentley Crooke arrived at Rockwood Castle with an entourage in three separate carriages. His amanuensis, Cyrus Wegg, a small man with a bald head and an anxious expression, travelled in the second carriage with Sir Bentley's valet, Dixon, and in the third carriage was Sir Bentley's personal chef with his kitchen assistant.

Nancy watched from a distance as Felicia rushed out to meet the wealthy business magnate, but Nancy found herself excluded from the meeting that followed in the castle drawing room. Sir Bentley left afterwards, taking Felicia and Claude in his carriage, with his retinue following them, presumably to view the site of the proposed theatre.

'So much for gaining your permission, Nancy.' Tommy shook his head. 'I think Grandmama has taken over yet again.'

'I've had a lot of experience with Mrs de Marney,' Nancy said ruefully. 'I worked for her for a while in London. She was not an easy person to satisfy.'

'Let's follow them,' Tommy said with a mischievous grin. 'We'll make sure that Sir Bentley knows just who owns the property.'

Nancy shot him a wary glance. She did not want Tommy to overexert himself, but she could tell by the excited gleam in his eyes that he was ready to do combat on her behalf.

'Yes, I agree. Shall we walk or ride?'

'I'll drive the chaise. It's so long since I held the reins; I shall feel like my old self.'

Hester appeared from the morning parlour. 'What are you two up to now?'

'Don't worry, Hester,' Tommy said, laughing. 'I'm taking Nancy to Greystone Park. We're going to make sure that Sir Bentley knows that Nancy is the owner, not Grandmama.'

For a moment Nancy thought that Hester was going to intervene, but a slow smile spread across her plump cheeks. 'Good. It's time someone spiked Mrs de Marney's guns, so to speak. But don't overdo things, young man. You might have been an army officer but when you're at home you are still Tommy, and we don't want you falling ill again.'

Tommy laughed. 'You'll never change, Hester. Don't worry about me, I have Nancy to take care of me.'

Nancy snatched up her bonnet and shawl that she had carelessly draped over a chair and hurried after Tommy. His enthusiasm was infectious and she was beginning to enjoy herself. Whatever the outcome, it would give her a certain amount of satisfaction to be in a superior position to Mrs de Marney. After all the years of being a nobody, she was now a woman of property, and both Felicia and Sir Bentley needed her agreement to fulfil their plans.

They arrived at the site of the burned-out building to find it being investigated by Sir Bentley and his followers while Felicia and Claude stood by watching.

Nancy went to stand beside Felicia. 'Don't you think you ought to have consulted me before bringing Sir Bentley here?' she said in a low voice. 'This is my

245

property, Mrs de Marney.'

'Yes, yes, we all know about your rise from the gutter to the minor gentry,' Felicia sighed impatiently.

'Grandmama!' Tommy lifted Nancy out of the way with surprising strength for someone who was supposed to be convalescent. 'You will not speak to Nancy like that. She is part of our family whether you like it or not.'

Felicia rolled her eyes. 'You would say that, Tommy. Your parentage was in doubt for some time, as I recall. However, we won't speak of that. If Sir Bentley agrees to finance a theatre here it will be the making of Greystone Park, and it will be impossible for Christina Cottingham to interfere.'

'How did you know about that?' Nancy demanded.

'I am not stupid, Nancy. I went into the matter with Bertie, who told me of the problems you have had with Mrs Cottingham. This will put an end to her antics once and for all. You should be grateful to me for giving you an easy way out rather than a lengthy court case.'

Before Nancy had a chance to think of a suitable reply, the sound of childish voices drowned out Sir Bentley's booming voice as he shouted instructions to Wegg. Nancy looked round and saw Alfie leading the boys as they ran towards her, Nick attempting to catch up with them.

'We wanted to see the rich toff,' Alfie said, staring at Sir Bentley. 'If I was back in London I'd have his wallet in a flash.'

'Take those street urchins away from here.' Felicia made shooing movements with her hands as if to ward off a horde of annoying insects.

'The boy meant no harm, madam.' Nick hurried

246

up to them, frowning ominously.

'Take them away, please,' Claude said firmly. 'This is a business meeting. No place for children.'

'It's all right.' Nancy stepped in between them. 'These boys are in my care.'

'Then look after them and keep them away from me.' Felicia shuddered as if there was a nasty smell lingering beneath her nose.

Sir Bentley turned round, scowling. 'What is all this noise?' He stared at Nick with a slow smile spreading across his ruddy features. 'Nick Gibson?'

Nick stepped forward. 'It is indeed, sir. I'm amazed that you recognised me.'

Sir Bentley strode towards him, holding out his hand. 'You were the best Hamlet I've ever seen.'

'Thank you, sir. I'm very flattered.'

'Sir Bentley?' Felicia stared at him, her eyes round with surprise. 'You know this person?'

Sir Bentley turned to her with a wide smile. 'Indeed I do. This young man was a very promising actor, but he disappeared from the stage. What happened, Nick?'

'My father was unwell, sir. I had to return home to look after him, but sadly he has since passed away.'

'A good son,' Sir Bentley said appreciatively. 'So what are you doing with these boys? Are you teaching now?'

Nick laughed. 'No, sir. That's beyond me, although we have done a few short plays when we needed the money.'

'And the harvest supper, Nick,' Stanley tugged at his sleeve. 'We got that tonight if you remembers.'

'And you are all invited,' Nick said grandly. 'Although it's probably not what you are used to, Sir Bentley.'

'Nonsense, my boy. I grew up in a small Lanca-shire town and I remember the productions the local theatre group used to put on, especially at Easter and Christmas. It's what got me interested in all things theatrical and fuelled my ambition to own a play-house. Now I have several dotted all over the country, bringing education and pleasure to the masses.'

Nancy moved to Nick's side. 'What an amazing coincidence.'

'It is, isn't it? I should have put two and two together when you told me that someone wanted to lease the land, but I didn't think of Sir Bentley.'

'We'll talk later, my boy,' Sir Bentley called out. 'I've taken all the available rooms at the village inn. We'll chat over a bowl of rum punch. What d'you say to that?'

'I'll look forward to it, sir.' Nick gathered up the boys. 'They wanted to see the Dower House again. Would that be all right, Nancy?'

She smiled. 'Yes, of course.' She took the key from her reticule. 'Let me have it back as soon as possible. I've only one key at the moment, but I'll get more cut.'

'I'll bring it to the castle when I've settled the boys with Miss Moon. She's going to take them for a long walk on the beach.'

Sir Bentley slapped him on the back. 'You're a good chap, Gibson. I may have use for you in my new thea-tre. That's if Miss Greystone is willing to talk business.'

'Yes, indeed.' Nancy tried to keep a note of excite-ment from her voice. 'Would you like to come back to the castle for luncheon, Sir Bentley? We can discuss details then.'

'Thank you, that sounds excellent.' Sir Bentley

beckoned to Wegg. 'You'd better come with me, Wegg, but send the others back to the inn. The sooner this deal is completed, the better I will like it.'

Felicia clasped her hands together, smiling. 'Then you are going to go ahead with the plans we discussed, Sir Bentley?'

'Yes. I can't think of any reason not to, ma'am. This seems like a beautiful spot, and if we add a reasonably sized guest house to the site I think we will do very well.'

'Let's get back to the castle,' Tommy said in a low voice. 'We'd better warn Cook that Sir Bentley's chef might descend upon her kitchen in the near future.'

Nancy giggled. 'There would be knives thrown if that happened. But you're right. Let's get there before the others arrive.'

* * *

Nancy and Tommy went straight to Bertie's study. After a quick discussion Bertie agreed with Nancy. The old house would never be rebuilt as a dwelling, but a theatre and a guest house would bring prosperity not only to Greystone Park, but to the whole area.

'It's your property, Nancy,' Bertie said judiciously. 'So you must take the initiative. Don't allow Sir Bentley to beat you down in price when it comes to renting the land, and you'll need to see Mr Mounce, our solicitor in Exeter, to draw up a lease. But don't do any of this unless you are absolutely certain it is the right way for you. This will change the landscape for ever.'

'Yes, I agree. I have thought it through, Bertie. I never liked the house itself and it's one way to rid

249

myself of Christina's interference.'

'It will give you the money to do up the Dower House,' Tommy added eagerly. 'You can furnish it as you wish and make it into a wonderful home for the boys.'

'Yes, that's true.' Nancy nodded. 'I've thought long and hard, and I know this is the right thing to do. Let's tell Sir Bentley that he can have his theatre in Greystone Park.'

Bertie pulled a face. 'I think my mother is the one who will be the happiest. It must seem like a dream come true.'

Nancy opened the study door. 'I thought I could hear them. They're heading for the drawing room, Bertie.'

Tommy slipped her arm around Nancy's waist. 'I want to see you do this, Nancy. Remember that you are Miss Greystone of Greystone Park.'

'Sometimes I wish I was still Nancy Sunday of Rockwood Castle — life was so much simpler then.'

'It doesn't matter what you call yourself, you are still my Nancy.' Tommy kissed her on the cheek. 'Come on. Let's show Sir Bentley how we do things in Rockwood Castle.'

Bertie reached for the bell pull. 'I'll join you in a minute. Wolfe is usually very quick to answer my call.'

'I can push your chair, Papa,' Tommy said hastily.

Bertie shook his head. 'Thank you, Tommy, but I like to make an entrance. It would take a brave person to take on Wolfe. I think even Sir Bentley, for all his bluster, would hesitate to argue with me when I have my guard wolf at my side.'

Nancy and Tommy left the study and when they entered the drawing room they were still giggling at the thought of Wolfe being used to terrify Sir Bentley.

Felicia turned on Tommy, frowning. 'Why are you smirking, Thomas? We have serious business to discuss.'

'I'm sorry, Grandmama. It was something Nancy said that made me laugh.'

Sir Bentley stood with his back to the fire. 'We need to talk money, Miss Greystone. I understand that you own the property in question.'

'Yes, Sir Bentley. That's true.'

'Wegg, hand Miss Greystone our proposal.' Sir Bentley beckoned to Wegg, who shuffled forward and gave the document to Nancy.

She unfolded the sheet of paper and studied its contents. 'I think I should get my solicitor to look this over before I sign anything, Sir Bentley.'

'Of course you must. I'm glad to see that you have a good business head on those pretty shoulders, Miss Greystone.'

Nancy eyed him coldly. 'I'll go to Exeter tomorrow and talk this over with Mr Mounce.'

'Excellent. I have the architect's design to hand. I've built several theatres in different parts of the country and they are all constructed to this design. However, you may study that and see if the exterior comes up to expectations. I'm sure we can do some minor alterations if required.'

'The interior won't be of interest to Nancy,' Felicia said hastily. 'I, on the other hand, have spent my life in opera houses all over the world. I know exactly how it should be.'

'Wegg, see that Miss Greystone has the plans before she leaves for Exeter in the morning.' Sir Bentley shooed Wegg away. 'As to the auditorium and the

251

stage, I would like Gibson to be present when we discuss it further, Mrs de Marney. He is going to be my theatre manager.'

'But Mr Gibson is my land agent,' Nancy said hastily.

'I'm sure you can find another who is probably better qualified. Talented actors are few and far between, and Gibson has a good head on his shoulders. My theatres have to make money otherwise they will close down very quickly. I don't encourage failure.'

Nancy backed towards the doorway. 'Perhaps you would like to come to dinner tomorrow night, Sir Bentley? We can discuss the ins and outs of the situation better after I have seen my solicitor.'

He acknowledged her suggestion with a nod. 'Of course. I would be delighted to accept.'

'In the meantime I need to speak to Mr Gibson,' Nancy said firmly. 'He'll be going over the entertainment he and the boys have rehearsed for the harvest supper tonight. I don't suppose that will interest you, Sir Bentley.'

'Ah, there you are wrong, young lady. I came from humble beginnings, as I've said before. I will be there to enjoy the celebrations with the rest of the village. They will get used to seeing me around in the near future.'

* * *

Nancy found Nick and the boys in the church hall going through their paces for the show that evening.

'All right, boys.' Nick had to raise his voice in order to make himself heard above their childish babble. 'You may go back to the cottage now. I'll follow along

252

in a minute or two.'

Nancy faced him, curbing her anger with difficulty. 'I think you might have talked it over with me before you accepted Sir Bentley's offer of a position at the theatre, Nick.'

He frowned. 'It was all so quick. I was going to speak to you but you'd gone back to the castle and I had to bring the boys here for a final rehearsal.'

'Even so, you could have kept Sir Bentley waiting for an answer. What am I supposed to do about a land agent if you just walk away?'

'Nancy, you know it won't be like that. The theatre has yet to be built and that will take time. There's no question of me leaving you in the lurch.'

'That's not how it seems to me, but of course I won't stand in your way. You must do what is best for you.'

Nancy was about to walk away but Nick reached out to catch hold of her hand. 'You will probably be married to Freddie by the time the foundations are laid to the theatre. I doubt if there will be a job for me when you are Lady Dorrington.'

'Even so, I trusted you to take care of my estate and yet you are eager to leave at the first opportunity. Maybe you should have kept up with your career on the stage.' Nancy snatched her hand free. She had trusted Nick implicitly and now she felt betrayed. His casual attitude cut all the deeper, reminding her of her past: a person who had been a foundling, an orphan and someone of no consequence. His mention of Freddie had not helped — if she were to be honest with herself she had to admit that she felt she had been abandoned, yet again.

Ignoring Nick's pleas for her to stop and listen,

Nancy left the church hall and walked back to the castle. She glanced over her shoulder once or twice to make sure that he was not following but there was no sign of him. She was beginning to think that Nick had never been serious about helping her to run the estate, and she had merely provided him with an income until something better came along. It was not a comfortable assumption.

That evening Nancy toyed with the idea of staying behind when everyone went to the harvest supper, but with a little persuasion from Tommy she decided that it would seem petty for her to keep away. Tommy drove Hester and Nancy in the chaise and the others followed in a variety of vehicles. It seemed that the whole village had turned out for the occasion and the village hall had been decorated with swags of greenery, baskets of rosy red apples and trugs filled with bright orange carrots and their feathery greenery, as well as turnips, washed and polished so that they gleamed in the light of paper lanterns.

The school hall had been taken over for the harvest supper, and long trestle tables groaned beneath platters of pasties, pies and sticky buns, glistening with sugar. Everyone had donated something to eat, however modest, from a jar of pickled beets, to a baked ham studded with cloves from the castle kitchen, and a gleaming game pie. Bertie and Wolfe had gone out with the shoot and Cook had been working hard, calling on all the maids to help with the preparations.

There was a short service of thanksgiving in the church; the usual musty smell of damp and old hymnals masked by the scent of fruit, vegetables and plaited harvest loaves. Afterwards everyone trooped into the school hall to enjoy the copious amounts of food, all washed down with ale and cider. Then it was back to the church hall for the entertainment. Nick had adapted Mr Dickens' story *A Christmas Carol*, so that the boys could render a much shortened version, for as Nick said in the preamble: 'This is a Christmas story, but the message is the same, whether it is being thankful for a good harvest or showing that kindness and goodwill are more important than actual wealth.'

There was a round of polite applause, but Nancy shot a sideways look at Sir Bentley, who seemed oblivious to any comparison to himself as the richest man present and the old miser, Scrooge. Even Christina seemed a little awed by his presence, and Oscar looked extremely discomfited. Nancy chose to ignore them and concentrate on the performance. Nick himself played Scrooge, with Todd as Bob Cratchit and the boys taking the other parts. Alfie, being the smallest and palest of the boys, played the part of Tiny Tim with heart-rending sweetness and sincerity. Nancy had to hold back tears at the finale and she saw a flutter of hankies in the audience.

There was an enthusiastic round of applause as the performance ended and Sir Bentley rose from his chair, clapping loudly. 'Bravo. Bravo. Well done, Mr Gibson and the cast.' He turned to Wegg, motioning him to stand. 'My amanuensis, Mr Wegg, has something to say.'

Wegg stood up, clearing his throat noisily. 'Ladies and gentlemen, Sir Bentley has authorised me to announce a generous contribution to funds for the village school and the church roof appeal.' He subsided onto his seat and Sir Bentley rose to a thunder of applause.

'I would add that the proposed scheme to build a

255

theatre on the ruins of Greystone Park will go ahead as soon as plans are finalised. This project will bring work and prosperity to the village and will benefit everyone.' He raised his hand to stop another burst of applause. 'And thanks should be given to Miss Nancy Greystone for allowing the theatre to be built on what was once her family home.'

'I object.' Christina rose to her feet, shaking her fist at Nancy, and there was a sudden silence as if everyone in the hall was holding their breath.

'I beg your pardon, ma'am?' Sir Bentley stared at her in amazement. 'You say you object. Who are you, anyway?'

Christina's normally pretty face was a pinched, mean mask with lips drawn back in a snarl. 'I am Christina Greystone Cottingham. I and my sister are the real owners of the Greystone estate. It was left to us by our papa, Sir Michael Cottingham.'

Someone booed and others joined in.

'Sit down, Christina.' A voice from the audience echoed round the hall.

'Who said that?' Christina looked round angrily. 'I will not sit down until I have had my say. The land is mine. I do not want my old home replaced by a cheap playhouse.'

'Madam, it will not be a cheap anything. I have had theatres built all over the country and they are famed for their excellent architecture as well as the performances that are put on regularly.'

'I don't care what you say. I will fight you through the courts if necessary.'

'Then I hope you are very wealthy, madam, because I happen to be one of the most affluent men in England. Your protests and legal costs will be nothing

256

more than a fleabite, so I suggest you sit down and keep silent. I take it the clerical gentleman with the red face who is seated next to you is your husband. Well, shame on you, sir, for allowing this woman to speak out of turn. I will crush any opponent to the cause of bringing education and art to the provinces. Have you anything to say, sir?'

Nancy felt instantly sorry for Oscar, who looked as if he wished the floor would open up and swallow both him and his wife. He rose slowly to his feet. 'I agree with you, Sir Bentley. You won't hear any more of this nonsense from my household.'

'You just want a donation to your church fund,' Christina said savagely. 'What sort of man are you, Oscar Cottingham?'

At this point Patricia rose to her feet. 'Ossie was my friend before you got your talons into him, Christina. Shame on you for dishonouring him in front of the whole village. Sit down and be quiet, and you, Ossie — take her in hand before she ruins your life.'

'How dare you speak about me in that insulting way?' Christina gazed round as if looking for a friendly face, but when she found none, she sank back onto her chair. 'I see I am outnumbered.'

Nancy jumped to her feet. 'I say three cheers for Sir Bentley and his plans for the village. Hip, hip, hooray.'

A scraping of chairs being pushed back on the wooden floorboards preceded the audience rising to their feet to join in.

'Now I suggest if Barnaby Yelland would like to bring his band onto the stage we should begin the dancing. Barnaby . . .' Nancy held out her hands and Barnaby made his way to the stage, followed by Ben Causley and Toby Hannaford, all carrying their instruments. Barnaby tapped the rhythm on the boards with his foot and struck up a jig on his fiddle, accompanied by Ben on his flute and Toby at the piano.

The chairs were pushed to the side and couples took to the floor. Nick made his way to Nancy with an apologetic smile.

'I am truly sorry for the misunderstanding, Nancy. I was wrong in accepting Sir Bentley's offer before speaking to you.'

'We'll leave it at that, Nick.' Nancy turned to find Tommy at her side.

'I'm not much of a dancer, Nancy, but if you'll put up with my ineptitude, might I have this dance?' Tommy's smile lit his eyes as he held out his hand.

Nancy nodded. 'Of course. I'm not very good at the jig, so we'll muddle along together.' She glanced at Nick over her shoulder. 'Well done with the play. You were all magnificent.'

'Nancy, we really need to talk about this.'

'I have nothing more to say. I'm sorry, Nick, but you have made your choice and I will make mine.'

258

18

Patricia decided that she would like a day out in Exeter and she entrusted her baby son, Charlie, to Fletcher's care. Nancy was amazed at the change in Fletcher when she held the baby in her arms. The severe woman suddenly melted into a warm-hearted surrogate aunt, who patently adored the little boy. The rest of the family were sceptical of her ability to look after a small baby, but Patricia had unshakeable faith in her.

'Anyway,' Patricia said as she climbed into the carriage to sit beside Nancy. 'Leo is on hand should there be any problems, but Fletcher would guard Charlie with her life if necessary.'

Nancy smiled. 'I don't doubt it.'

'And I have an excellent wet nurse for him now.' Patricia glanced at Tommy, shaking her head. 'You don't need to know about things like that until you are much older and a married man.'

'You must think I'm an innocent, Aunt Patsy. I wasn't a soldier for long, but I saw a lot of things that I would never have seen had I remained at home. I'm a man of the world now.'

It was Patricia's turn to laugh. 'I'll remember that, Tommy. But enough about me and my delightful son. I am having a day free from motherhood and wifely duties, which is something I thought I would never say.'

'But you are happy, Patsy?' Nancy asked anxiously.

'I am very content with my life, and that's another thing I would never have thought possible. All that striving for fame and fortune is behind me now. I used to think I was like Mama, but now I know that isn't true. I am myself and glad to be so.'

'Are you coming with me to the solicitor's office?'

'If you don't mind, darling, I would like to visit Meggie Brewer. I need a new gown and some blouses, so I thought I would take this opportunity to see her and look at the fashion plates to choose what I want.'

'I'm going to see Mounce with you,' Tommy said firmly.

'I can manage on my own, you know.'

'Of course you can, but I want to be there to hear what he has to say. If you don't mind.'

'Just so long as you know that this is my business, Tommy. I can handle it well enough on my own.'

He laughed. 'I know that, too. I wouldn't dream of interfering.'

'You know me so well.' Nancy leaned over to pat his hand just as the carriage moved forward, throwing her against Tommy with some force.

He held her for a moment longer than strictly necessary. 'Are you all right?'

'Yes, thanks to you.' Nancy scrambled back onto the opposite seat. 'I think Gurney might be getting a bit too old to act as coachman. Maybe he should retire.'

'We can't force him to give up the reins, Nancy. He's been with the family for ever. I'll speak to Papa and perhaps we can arrange for him to take up some duties that don't involve so much physical effort.'

It was Patricia's turn to laugh. 'You two sound like an old married couple.'

260

'No, we don't,' Nancy said hotly. 'We're more like brother and sister. I keep telling Tommy that.'

'Have it your way.' Patricia leaned back against the squabs and sighed happily. 'I adore my baby boy, but it is nice to have a few hours all to myself.'

Nancy exchanged amused glances with Tommy and conversation lapsed for a while as Gurney drove along the country lanes at what felt like breakneck speed. Nancy was relieved when they eventually dropped Patricia off at Meggie's house and drove on to the solicitor's office not far from the cathedral.

The meeting went well and Mr Mounce could not find any loopholes in the agreement that might be detrimental to Nancy's ownership of the land itself. He agreed that the rent for the lease was fair and he could see no reason for her to refuse Sir Bentley's offer. Nancy had already made up her mind to do so, but it was a relief to know that everything was legal and above board.

She left the office with Tommy and they were strolling along Cathedral Yard, heading for the place where they had arranged to meet Gurney and Patricia, when Nancy spotted two small children clinging to the body of a woman who was lying in a doorway.

'Walk on, Nancy,' Tommy said, clutching her arm. 'The woman is probably drunk or drugged on opium.'

'Those children can't be more than four or five, Tommy. They're sobbing.'

'It's not our business. You won't get a thank you for interfering.'

Nancy pulled free from him and went down on her knees beside the woman. One look at the woman's grey face was enough. She lifted the small girl first and handed her to Tommy, who held her at arm's length.

'This nipper is filthy, Nancy. She's running with fleas and lice.'

Nancy pulled the small boy from the woman's stiff arms. 'He is the same, but we can't abandon them, Tommy. I'm afraid there's no hope for the mother. We need to summon a police constable.'

Tommy placed the crying child on the pavement beside Nancy, who was cuddling the boy. 'Wait there. I'll get help.' He strode off, returning minutes later with a harassed-looking constable.

'I'm afraid the woman is dead, Constable.'

'Do you know them, miss?'

Nancy shook her head. 'We stopped because the children were distressed.'

The constable leaned over to cover the woman's head with her tattered shawl. 'I know her. She's a common prostitute, if you'll pardon my language, miss.'

'Are these her children?'

'I assume so. Spiky Sue is well known in these parts.'

'Has she a family? Is there someone who can take care of these children?'

'Not that I know of, miss. I'll have them taken to the workhouse.'

'But they've just lost their mother. Surely there is someone who could take them in and care for them?'

Tommy raised Nancy to her feet. 'Let the constable do his duty, Nancy. This isn't our business.'

'"Mankind was my business",' Nancy said thoughtfully. 'That's what Marley's ghost said in *A Christmas Carol* — you watched Nick's version of it at the harvest supper. These children should be our business, Tommy. We can't abandon them to the workhouse.'

'It would be the only sensible thing to do, miss.' The constable gazed at her, frowning. 'They might have been with old Sue, but whether or not she was their mother I couldn't say.'

'Is there any way to find out who their parents were, officer?' Nancy bit her lip. It was painful to see the small children in such a state of distress.

'Their class don't bother with formalities, miss. Like as not, Sue took them on because they was useful when it came to begging. Kind-hearted folks like yourselves would stop and give a few pence to feed little ones. They was her insurance against a lull in business, if you know what I mean.'

'I think we do, officer,' Tommy said hastily. 'What will happen to these children now?'

'I'll see to it, sir. Don't worry yourself about these kids. They're from the streets. They'll survive.'

'I was in an orphanage until I was seven or eight,' Nancy said angrily. 'You were a sweep's boy, Tommy. If Rosie hadn't saved both of us we might have ended up in the workhouse.'

'We can't take them back to the castle in this state, Nancy.'

'Who is responsible for waifs and strays, Constable? What do we do in order to take them to a place of safety?'

'I can't say, miss. If I take them to the police station they'll go straight to the workhouse. Kids like these never have anyone to claim them.'

'That's so sad,' Nancy said tearfully. 'They are flesh and blood like the rest of us and yet no one cares now their mother is gone.'

'I know what you're thinking, Nancy, but we can't take them home.'

Nancy met Tommy's anxious look with a determined smile. 'You're right. We can't take them to

263

Rockwood Castle, but I can look after them in the Dower House.'

'Nancy, that's madness. The place is barely habitable.'

'It's clean now, which is the main thing. The renovations will be done while we live there.' Nancy turned to the constable. 'I will take them to the Dower House, Greystone Park, Rockwood, and if anyone comes forward to claim them I will hand them over, providing I'm assured that they will receive good treatment.'

'Nancy, are you sure about this?' Tommy said urgently.

'I've never been so certain about anything in my whole life.'

'Very well, miss. I'll send for the wagon to collect the body and I'll leave the little ones to you.' The constable strode away as if relieved to be free from the responsibility of the sobbing children.

'We're supposed to be meeting Patsy at the hotel,' Nancy said anxiously. 'I'm sure these poor orphans are starving.'

Tommy eyed them critically. 'You can't take them into a hotel dining room in that state.'

'Leave it to me, Tommy. I'll ask to see the housekeeper. It would be a hard-hearted woman who refused to help these poor little things.'

* * *

Nancy was right. Mrs Cotton, the housekeeper, was sent for, but her wary expression changed dramatically when Nancy explained the situation.

'I have four children of my own, miss — all grown up now — and I have grandchildren about the same age as these two.'

'Could you at least feed them for me, ma'am? I will pay, of course.'

'Come here, my dears. Auntie Cotton will give you something nice to eat and find you something clean to wear.'

'Really, ma'am, I can't put you to that trouble.'

Mrs Cotton smiled. 'It's my half day. I was just off home anyway. I'll take them with me and find some clothes that my grandchildren have grown out of.'

'We're only staying to have luncheon, ma'am,' Nancy said worriedly. 'I really don't want to put you to so much trouble.'

'It's you who are putting yourself out for them, miss. I call that a very worthy thing to do. If only everyone was as kind and caring, the world would be a better place, as my old ma used to say.'

'Well, thank you. I would be very grateful.'

'Don't mention it. I think I've seen these poor little souls being paraded around by a drunken woman who was no better than she should be. She used them to get money to spend on drink. No wonder she passed away like she did.' Mrs Cotton sniffed and took the children by the hand. 'Come along, my little loves. We'll get you cleaned up and fed, and I'll bring you back here in an hour or so.'

Nancy sent a meaningful look to Tommy and he put his hand in his pocket.

'Here you are, ma'am. This will pay for the young ones' food.'

Mrs Cotton took the money with an appreciative grin. 'Ta, sir. You're very kind.' She walked off, taking the children with her.

'I hope she doesn't take them to the market place

and sell them,' Tommy said, laughing.

Nancy slapped him on the wrist. 'Don't say things like that. She's a good, kind woman, who loves children.'

'And here comes Patricia. Let me hear you explain your decision to take two orphans home with us.'

'Shut up, Tommy. It's not funny.'

'It would have been had you presented her with two filthy, flea-ridden waifs and expected her to share the carriage with them.'

Patricia strolled towards them. 'What's going on? You two look very guilty.'

Nancy gave Tommy a gentle shove. 'Don't take any notice of Tommy. He's being really annoying, but I do have something to tell you.'

'All right, but first I would love a glass of sherry wine. I feel like a pin cushion. Meggie has been fitting me for a couple of blouses and a skirt. You can tell me what you've been doing when we're seated at the table. You have booked luncheon, haven't you?'

Tommy backed away. 'I'll do it now. Take a seat in the guests' lounge and I'll be with you in a minute or two.'

Nancy led Patricia to the lounge and waited until a waiter had served Patricia with a glass of sherry. As she sipped the wine, colour rushed back to Patsy's pale cheeks, and she sat back in her chair, eyeing Nancy curiously.

'Well, now you can tell me what you've done.' Patricia listened intently while Nancy explained. She waited until Nancy had finished. 'It's very laudable, but have you given this enough thought? If you take those small children into your home you will become responsible for them.'

'Yes,' Nancy said eagerly. 'Of course.'

'You will have to bring *them* up as well as those boys, although they are a slightly different case. Even so, you will be their mother, to all intents and purposes.'

'Yes, I will. I won't abandon them, Patsy.'

'But you are still unofficially engaged to Freddie Ashton. What will he say? And, more importantly, what will Lord Dorrington say?'

'I hope Freddie will support me.'

'To be honest, my darling, he hasn't been much help to you since his father insisted that you did not see each other for a year.'

'He's just doing what his father wanted.'

'That's my point exactly, Nancy. Don't you think a man in love would put his fiancée first? Does Freddie think more of his inheritance than of you?'

'That's not fair, Patsy.'

'I love you as if you were my little sister, Nancy. You and I have been through a lot together. I don't want to see you ruin your life.'

Nancy was about to argue when Tommy breezed into the lounge. 'Our table is ready and I'm starving, I don't know about you two.'

Patricia downed the last of her drink and stood up. 'I am famished. Lead on.'

★ ★ ★

True to her word, Mrs Cotton returned an hour later just as Nancy, Patricia and Tommy had finished their meal. Nancy was summoned by a waiter and she hurried into the foyer to greet the children, who looked surprisingly clean and tidy in their second-hand clothes, stockings and boots. Mrs Cotton had even

267

found time to wash their hair, and their hands and faces were also shiny clean.

'They had a good scrub down and I doubt if any of the fleas survived my lye soap, but you will want to bath them again when you get them home, miss.'

'They look amazing. Thank you so much, Mrs Cotton.' Nancy held out her hand. 'Come with me, please.' Nancy hesitated. 'I don't even know their names.'

Mrs Cotton smiled. 'This is Jack and his sister is called May. They don't know their surnames, and to be honest I doubt if they have one, not legally anyway. I couldn't get much out of them but maybe you can, in time.'

Nancy went down on her knees and held out her arms. 'Jack and May are lovely names. I'm going to look after you and take you to a nice home in the country. You'll be safe there.'

'I just hope you know what you're doing, Nancy.' Patricia rose from the table. 'I'm ready to go home.'

★ ★ ★

It was late in the afternoon when they arrived back at Rockwood Castle, having dropped Patricia off at her house. Rosalind was in the drawing room, seated by the fire. She stared at the small children with a mixture of pity and dismay when Nancy explained how she had come to bring them here.

'But, Nancy, you can't just collect every waif you find on the street.'

Nancy clutched the children's hands. 'You took me in, Rosie. I'm only doing the same for these poor little orphans.'

'It's quite different. For one thing, you don't know that they were that woman's children. She might have abducted them from a family in order to use them to make money from sympathetic passers-by.'

'The police constable didn't seem to think so.'

Rosalind turned to Tommy. 'Did you agree to this?'

He shrugged. 'Have you tried to stop Nancy from doing what she wishes?'

'We can't take them back,' Nancy protested. 'The constable was going to leave them at the workhouse.'

'There must be families who would take them in,' Rosalind said thoughtfully. 'I'll ring for Jennet. She can take care of them tonight, but tomorrow you must return them to Exeter, Nancy. Put them in the hands of the proper authorities.'

'You don't mean that,' Nancy cried passionately. 'I won't see them placed in the workhouse.'

Rosalind gave the bell pull a sharp tug. 'You have all those boys to care for. Besides which, what will Freddie say when he finds out?'

'He hasn't shown much interest in Nancy's well-being for months,' Tommy said angrily. 'I think the wretched fellow has changed his mind, or else he has had it changed for him.'

'That's not fair, Tommy.' Nancy glared at him. 'Freddie is keeping his word to his father, that's all. Anyway, tomorrow I'm going to ask Mrs Banks and Ivy Lugg to come and live at the Dower House earlier than I planned. They've already agreed in principle and the boys can't wait to move in. I'll take on Connie Tuckett, Bertha's sister, to look after these two little ones. She'll be glad to get away from home, with all those siblings.'

'You have it all worked out,' Tommy said admiringly. 'But what about the redecorating and the renovations?'

'We will just have to live with the mess.' Nancy spoke with more conviction than she was feeling, but the sight of the pale and exhausted little ones went straight to her heart.

Tommy put his arm around her. 'Good for you, Nancy. I'll do whatever I can to help.'

'If you write notes to Mrs Banks, Ivy and Connie, I'll get one of the stable boys to deliver them today,' Rosalind said thoughtfully. 'You will need all the assistance you can get, Nancy. I'll do what I can.'

'So you do think I'm doing the right thing?' Nancy eyed her expectantly.

'It's a wonderful opportunity for these two, but I'm not sure how it will work out for you, Nancy. You are still only nineteen, with the rest of your life before you. I don't want to see you bowed down with responsibilities that are really not yours.'

* * *

Next day Tommy drove Nancy and the children to the Dower House, where Mrs Banks and Ivy had already established themselves in the large old-fashioned kitchen, and the cleaning women were bustling about on the upper two floors, finishing off the work they had begun days earlier. Nancy went straight to the drawing room, where the remaining furniture was hidden beneath Holland covers. She snatched them off, sneezing as dust flew into the air, and she hurried across the bare boards to open the casement windows. A shaft of late October sunlight illuminated the room, with the wallpaper peeling off and scuffed paintwork. What little furniture remained was old and virtually threadbare, but it would do for a start.

Jack and May stood together, holding hands. They had hardly spoken since Nancy brought them to Rockwood Castle and it was obvious that they were both intimidated and awed by their new surroundings. May was clutching a rag doll that Jennet had found abandoned in one of the nursery cupboards at Rockwood, and Jack's fingers were wound tightly around a tin soldier that Rory had given him.

'You should get the boys here as soon as you can,' Tommy said in a low voice. 'Alfie and Teddy are only a couple of years older than Jack. Maybe he and May will feel they're part of a family with the older lads here.'

'Yes, that's exactly what I was thinking. The only problem is that I wasn't too pleased when Nick told me he was leaving to work for Sir Bentley. I don't want him to move in with them.'

'Of course not. That wouldn't be proper. Would you like me to fetch the boys? I imagine Nick can stay on in the cottage. We haven't any use for it at the moment.'

Nancy nodded. 'Would you? That would be wonderful, Tommy. Thank you.'

Tommy headed for the doorway, but he paused. 'Heaven knows I don't want to throw you into Freddie's arms, but your year of keeping apart is more than half over. Why don't you either send for him or go and see him? Find out how he would feel about adopting a family of lost boys and a small girl?'

'I'm not adopting them,' Nancy said hastily. 'At least, nothing legal. I'm simply their unofficial guardian.'

'He still needs to know what you've taken on. You said your last meeting with him was a little fraught. How do you think he will react to all this?' Tommy encompassed the room with a wave of his arms.

'I suppose you're right, but part of me is scared of the outcome. Can you understand that?'

'Perfectly. But, Nancy, all I want is your happiness. Nothing else counts.'

Nancy bit back tears as the door closed on Tommy. She loved Freddie, but she could not imagine life without Tommy.

'Please, miss. Me and May are hungry.'

Nancy stared at the small boy in surprise. It was the first time he had spoken since they found him and his sister clinging to the dead woman. She leaned over, patting him on the cheek.

'Then we'll go to the kitchen and see what Mrs Banks can offer.' She opened the door again and took them through the maze of corridors to the kitchen at the back of the house.

Mrs Banks was clearly enchanted by the two tiny children and her motherly instincts rose to the fore.

'Poor little mites,' she said, shaking her head. 'They look half starved.'

'I'm sure that won't last long now.' Nancy took a small cake from the batch Mrs Banks had just taken out of the oven. She tossed it gently from hand to hand until it was cool enough to break into two pieces and gave one to each of the children.

'You'd think they never tasted cake before,' Mrs Banks said in amazement as the food disappeared in seconds. 'Fill two cups with milk, Ivy. We'd better ask Farmer Greep to deliver twice the amount tomorrow.'

'Better make that four times the amount.' Nancy

smiled. 'The boys will be here later. We might as well have a full house. Can you cope with that, Mrs Banks?'

'I'm more than happy to feed up those poor lads. They were all skin and bone when you brought them down from London. I'd better make another batch of cakes and something substantial for their supper.'

'I'm afraid it's going to be quite noisy with the workmen here, Mrs Banks. If you need anything doing to your room just tell me and I'll see that it's done. That goes for you, too, Ivy, and Connie Tuckett, if she decides to live in. I'm going to need all the help I can get.'

'Well, a coat of paint wouldn't go amiss, and the mattress feels a bit lumpy.' Mrs Banks handed a cake to Jack and another one to May.

'Just say what you need, both of you. It won't be instant but we have to make a start somewhere. We'll make this into a lovely home for all of us. Is it all right if I leave the children with you for a while? I need to examine the rooms and make a list of things we need urgently.'

'There'll be sheets, pillowcases and blankets, Miss Greystone. What was left here is threadbare and it'll start getting cold soon.'

'Yes. I'll make a note of that. Let me know what you need in the way of pots and pans and anything else for the kitchen.'

Nancy glanced out of the window and to her surprise she saw Alfie, Teddy and Stanley racing round in the yard, the other boys peering through windows in the outbuildings and the wash house. She went to open the door leading into the cobbled yard and came face to face with Nick.

He snatched off his cap with an apologetic smile.

'I'm sorry, Nancy. We weren't trespassing. It's just that the boys wanted to see more of the house and grounds. They're so excited at the thought of living here.'

'That's all right. Come inside. I want to talk to you anyway.'

He followed her into the kitchen, acknowledging Mrs Banks with a smile. 'Something smells good.'

Mrs Banks stood with arms akimbo. 'I suppose those boys are hungry, as always. Lucky I made a big batch of cakes, although they'll go through them quick enough.'

'That's all right, Mrs Banks. Don't stand any nonsense from them. They will have to behave properly from now on.' Nancy led Nick to the drawing room. 'I sent Tommy to fetch the boys, you must have just missed each other.'

'I'm not trying to escape my responsibilities, Nancy. I'll happily work for you until the theatre is built. I've been feeling guilty for letting you down.'

'There's no need. None of us could have foreseen this state of affairs. It will help considerably if you continue to collect the rents and deal with the tenants. I'm going to have my hands full here.'

'I heard that you'd taken on a couple of orphans.'

'There's nothing private in Rockwood.' Nancy met his anxious gaze with a steady glance. 'I do understand why you want to get back to the theatre. I could see how much it meant to you, even with the small play you put on at the harvest festival.'

'Thank you, Nancy. I'm not sure I deserve such consideration, but you're right. My heart was always in entertaining people, but I hope I've done a good job for you.'

274

She smiled. 'Yes, you have. If there's one thing I've learned from all this it's that you have to seize any chance you get in life. You'll do well at the theatre, but I want preferential treatment when I come to see a performance.'

'I will have a box reserved for you and your family.' He took her hand and raised it to his lips. 'One good thing is that if I am not in your employ I can meet you on more or less equal terms. I can speak about my feelings for you in a way that I cannot now.'

Nancy withdrew her hand gently. 'You know my situation, Nick. I am engaged to Freddie Ashton. Our year of separation will finish in a few months.'

'You can be sure of one thing. I would not leave you for a month, let alone a whole year, were I in his position.'

'Please don't say these things, Nick.'

He backed towards the doorway. 'You know where to find me if you need me.'

Nancy waited until she heard the front door close before going over to the window. She watched Nick's tall figure as he strode off towards the ruins of the old house. Perhaps he had been right. Maybe she should take the initiative, even though it was not the sort of thing that a young lady should do, but everyone seemed to think that Freddie had let her down. There was only one way to find out.

19

It took several weeks to get the Dower House into a reasonable living condition, and Nancy spent a great deal of time in the furniture sale rooms, selecting items that would be useful, hard-wearing and make a comfortable home for herself and the children. Sir Bentley had paid a considerable amount as deposit on the land rental, and work had already started clearing the site for the theatre. Some of the slightly older boys had found part-time employment helping the labourers, and had earned their own money legally for the first time in their young lives. They had all settled in well at the Dower House, continuing their lessons with Miss Collins, and this included Jack, who was bright and outgoing now that he was getting to know them all. However, May was still very shy and Rosalind, having taken a liking to the little girl, invited her to the castle to share lessons with Phoebe. As Louise now taught at the village school, Rosalind had hired a young governess and Nancy took May to the castle each morning, collecting her later in the day. Rosalind was delighted to have a playmate for Phoebe, and May blossomed with all the kindness and attention she received.

The only person who was not entirely happy with the situation was Christina, but her efforts to have the theatre banned by the authorities came to nothing and all she could do was to ignore Nancy pointedly if they happened to pass in their respective carriages.

All this time Nancy was making plans to visit Dorrington Place. She had taken on Flossie Madge, who had started off as a kitchen maid at Rockwood and had been promoted to housemaid, even though the castle was fully staffed. Felicia and Claude now looked like permanent residents and Felicia's maid, Violet Tinker, demanded a room to herself in the servants' quarters, which left Flossie having to share with her elder sisters. Rosalind hated sacking perfectly good servants and Nancy had solved the problem by taking Flossie on as her personal maid.

This was all part of her plan to travel to Dorrington Place, taking her maid as chaperone. So far she had not told anyone, not even Tommy, but with Christmas getting ever closer, Nancy wanted to know where she stood. She still loved Freddie, but a shadow had been cast over their relationship and the memory of their time together was fading like the image on an old daguerreotype. She told no one, and the rest of the family were too busy to take much interest in what Nancy was doing. Felicia and Claude were immersed in plans for the theatre, which Sir Bentley insisted should take up the whole of the site now. He suggested an addition to the stable block, creating a purpose-built hotel to encourage even more theatre-goers from out of town, and Nancy had no objections. Each day they had meetings with the architect and the builders, but Nancy was not interested. She had enough to think about without concerning herself with the details. She was receiving a generous amount of money from Sir Bentley and that was sufficient to feed and clothe the children and run her large household.

One grey and chilly November morning Nancy

left May at the castle as usual, but instead of driving the gig back to the Dower House she went to call on Jones, who had been head groom at Greystone Park ever since she could remember. The rest of the grooms and stable boys had found other positions, but Nancy had kept Jones on to take care of the few horses that remained in the stables. He and his wife lived in a cottage at the rear of the coach house. Nancy had insisted that their home must remain, no matter what plans Sir Bentley had for the stable block. Anyway, they would need the coach house and stables for the guests. It would ensure that the staff who had lost their jobs would be needed once more, and Nancy had this written into the contract.

Jones came hurrying down the wooden steps to join her in the coach house. 'Good morning, Miss Greystone. Do you want your horse saddled for a ride?'

'Not this morning, Jones. But tomorrow I intend to visit Dorrington Place. I will need you to drive me in the brougham.'

'Of course, miss. What time would you like to leave?'

'About this time, after I've left May at the castle. And, Jones, please don't tell anyone. I want to keep this trip a secret. Don't drive up to the Dower House — I'll have the gig anyway and I'll leave it here.'

He nodded. 'I understand.'

'Thank you. My regards to Mrs Jones.' Nancy handed him the reins and set off for the house. Her boots crunched on the frosty grass and her breath curled around her head, evaporating into the morning mist. She had laid her plans carefully so that no one knew where she was heading next day. She knew that Tommy was going to spend the day out hunting with his father and Wolfe, not that Tommy was keen on shooting game, but it was for the table and Bertie could still handle a gun with his old expertise. By the time Tommy realised that she was missing, Nancy would have reached Dorrington Place and might even be on her way home. She was not planning to stay there any longer than necessary. She could only hope that Freddie would be there and not in London, but she knew that he disliked town and only went there when it was absolutely necessary. Mrs Banks and the boys thought Nancy was going to Exeter to see the solicitor. Only Flossie knew differently, but she had been sworn to secrecy.

* * *

Next morning Nancy dressed with even more care than usual. She was excited and yet nervous at the thought of seeing Freddie again. The feeling grew even more intense when Jones drove through the enormous iron gates that kept Dorrington Place apart from the rest of the world. Nancy gazed out of the window at the sparkling blanket of frost beginning to melt in the pale sunlight, and the bare branches of the poplar trees lining the avenue that led to the house. Now nerves took over and Nancy realised that she was trembling as the carriage came to a halt and Jones leaped down to open the door.

'Are you all right, miss?' Flossie asked anxiously.

'Yes, I'm perfectly fine. Just follow me.' Nancy alighted from the carriage and walked briskly to the front entrance, which opened as if by magic.

Pickering's cold grey eyes showed no emotion. 'How may I help you, Miss Greystone?'

'Is Lord Ashton at home, Pickering?' Nancy made

an effort to sound casual but her heart was beating twice as fast as normal.

'If you would care to step inside and wait, I will see.' Pickering ushered her into the grand hall. He cast a critical eye over Flossie and marched off with slow, measured steps.

Nancy gazed round in awe. Somehow she could not imagine herself as mistress of this great house. It was so palatial it made her feel like a very young Nancy Sunday, straight from the orphanage. She took a deep breath. She was Miss Nancy Greystone of Greystone Park, a landowner in her own right, and now lease-holder of a theatre and a hotel. She was a person of consequence.

She did not have long to wait before Pickering returned and led her to a small drawing room over-looking the orangery, which instantly brought back memories of the night when Freddie had proposed. She stepped into the room, leaving Flossie in the long glass-enclosed passageway lined with fragrant orange trees.

Freddie was seated at an ornate desk in the corner of the room. He rose to his feet and came towards her, holding out his hands.

'Nancy, this is a wonderful surprise. What are you doing here?'

'I came to see you, Freddie,' Nancy said lamely. It was obvious, but she was almost at a loss for words. He looked just the same — his smile was warm and welcoming. Why did she feel suddenly shy and uncer-tain what to say next?

'Sit down and I'll send for some refreshment.'

'No, Freddie. Not yet, please.'

He took her hands in his. 'You're cold, Nancy.

Come and sit by the fire. Is something wrong?'

She allowed him to guide her to a chair by the hearth and she sank down into its comforting softness. 'I don't know, Freddie. It's been so long since we last saw each other.'

He pulled up a chair and sat down beside her. 'I know, it has. It wasn't my choosing — you know that.'

'Yes, of course, but it doesn't seem to worry you.'

'I've missed you, Nancy. The year will be over in April and then we can finally be together.'

'So what will happen if your papa still doesn't approve of me? I can't claim to have been a wonderful success as the mistress of Greystone Park. I suppose you heard that it was razed to the ground by fire?'

Freddie stared at her in horror. 'No, I haven't had any news of that sort. How did it happen?'

'That's not really important, but I would have thought you might have been keeping an eye on events in Rockwood and Greystone Park if you were really serious about marrying me.'

'My love, I've b-been v-very b-busy here.' Freddie's stammer had returned and he could not meet her gaze. 'P-Papa has given m-me more responsibility for running the estate.'

'Don't you see that is a ploy to keep us apart, Freddie? Does Dorrington Place mean more to you than I do?'

'N-no, h-how could it? I love you, Nancy.'

'And yet you were happy to leave me struggling to run a grand house on my own, despite the fact that Christina Cottingham did her best to have me evicted and finally succeeded.'

'I didn't know any of th-that, N-Nancy.'

'No, you didn't, because you didn't bother to check

up on me, Freddie. I might have been in the house when the arsonist set it on fire, but luckily I was back at Rockwood Castle. You didn't know that either, did you?'

'Y-you're making it all sound as if your misfortunes were my fault.'

'I'm sorry about that, but can't you see that this was just the case? I didn't want to live on my own in that great house. I didn't want to be separated from you for a whole year, just to please your papa.'

'He had his reasons, N-Nancy, my love.'

'I don't think I am your love, Freddie. Not deep down where it counts. I think the love of your life is Dorrington Place and the land around it. I don't think you could love any woman more than you do the house and land you will inherit one day.'

Freddie held his head in his hands. 'Wh-what can I say to convince y-you otherwise?'

Nancy was about to answer when the door burst open and Lady Letitia Barclay strode into the room. She was dressed for riding, which suited her far better than feminine frills. She came to a sudden halt.

'I'm sorry, I didn't know that you were here, Nancy.'

Nancy rose to her feet. 'I was just leaving.'

'Nancy, this is all a misunderstanding. Letitia and her parents are here as my mother's guests. It's not what you think.'

'I'll wait for you in the stables, Ashton. Don't be long.' Letitia swept from the room, allowing the door to swing shut behind her.

'Ashton? Doesn't she know your name by now, Freddie?'

'This is all wrong, Nancy. Letitia is just a friend. She thinks it's funny to call me Ashton instead of Freddie.

282

It's her little joke.'

'You seem to be on excellent terms these days. I won't intrude any longer.' Nancy made to leave, but Freddie leaped to his feet and caught her by the hand.

'No, you're mistaken. Please stay and we can talk and sort it all out. I'll tell Papa that we've waited long enough and it's time to announce our engagement.'

Nancy hesitated. If Freddie had said that sooner she might have believed him, but Letitia's new confidence and her mastery of the situation had chilled her to the bone. She met Freddie's pleading gaze with a sudden overwhelming feeling of pity. She still loved him but he was weak and easily persuaded, unlike his father, who ruled his family with an iron hand concealed under a façade of bonhomie. Lady Dorrington was little better, and Nancy understood for the first time just what she was up against.

'Freddie, you know it's useless. You will never marry me. Your father will put a stop to it one way or another. You might as well give in and propose to Letitia.'

'But I love you, not Letitia.'

'As I said before, your true love is Dorrington Place and the estate. Letitia will bring her fortune to add to and improve what you have already. I think as long as she has her horses and can ride to hounds she will ask very little of you. I would ask too much.'

Freddie shook his head, his blue eyes filling with tears. 'Please don't say that, N-Nancy. I should have s-stood up to m-my papa in the f-first instance and married you.'

'But you didn't, Freddie.' Nancy took his hands in hers. 'You had a choice. You could have disobeyed your papa and married me. Bertie would have given his permission if Lord Dorrington had not interfered, but you chose to do what your father wanted.'

'But I do love you, Nancy.'

'And I love you, Freddie. But I realise now it's not enough. My family will never match up to what your family expects of a prospective bride.' Nancy reached up and kissed Freddie gently on the lips. 'I'm leaving now. Please don't try to stop me.' She released his hands and turned away.

'Please don't go like this, Nancy. Stay for a while and we can sort things out between us.'

She opened the door. 'It's too late for that, Freddie.'

Nancy walked out into the wide corridor where Flossie was standing awkwardly by one of the tall orange trees.

'We're leaving,' Nancy said briefly.

She hurried on, hoping that Freddie would not follow. She knew he was standing in the doorway, staring after her, but she did not turn her head or stop until she came to the main entrance hall. There was no sign of Pickering and Nancy sent the second footman to order her carriage to be brought round from the stables. It was a nerve-tingling five-minute wait, when at any moment she expected Freddie to make an appearance or, even worse, Lord or Lady Dorrington. Eventually Jones drew the carriage up outside the main entrance and Nancy hurried down the steps, followed by Flossie.

'Home, please, Jones,' Nancy said, breathlessly.

She glanced over her shoulder as she climbed into the carriage and caught a brief glimpse of Freddie gazing out of a window. She did not relent although it caused her more pain than she had thought was possible. If Freddie chose to stand up to his parents he would come and find her, but he had not even asked her where she was living or how she was managing. Freddie, she now realised, lived in a pampered world of his own and it seemed that he was afraid to step outside its protective arms.

'I'm sorry, miss.'

Flossie's voice broke into Nancy's reverie. 'Why, Flossie?'

'I can see that things didn't go well, miss. I don't mean to be impertinent.'

Nancy managed a smile. 'Kindness is always welcome, Flossie. But you're right — things didn't go as I had hoped. Maybe I should have stayed at home and waited.'

'At least now you know where you stand, miss.'

'Were you listening at the door, Flossie?'

'No, miss. As if I would do such a thing. I saw you go into the room all pink and excited, and then you came out all pale and sad. You don't have to be clever to work out that something went amiss.'

'You're right, Flossie. But as you said, I know the truth now, and I will have to go on from there. I really don't want to talk about it.'

'No, miss. Of course not. Ma always said I talk too much.' Flossie sighed and leaned against the squabs, gazing out of the window.

Nancy was left to her thoughts and they were not happy ones. She was torn between feeling sorry for herself and sorry for Freddie. Perhaps she should have given him a second chance, but then the memory of Letitia's confident and somewhat proprietorial attitude came back to her. If she were to be honest with herself she realised now that Lord Dorrington had probably been correct in choosing someone like Letitia. She would bring her vast fortune and land to the marriage and Freddie would not have to worry about having a wife who might be easy prey to opportunists and philanderers. Nancy suspected that Letitia would spend most of her time with her beloved horses and riding to hounds, leaving Freddie free to carry on when Lord Dorrington decided that he would hand the responsibility of his estate over to his son.

★ ★ ★

Tommy was pacing the carriage sweep outside the Dower House when the carriage drew to a halt. He wrenched the door open. 'Where have you been, Nancy? I've been going out of my mind with worry.' He took her hand to help her alight and the warmth of his grasp went straight to her heart. She knew his anger was born out of anxiety and she closed her fingers around his. It felt like a lifeline back to some sort of normality.

'Tommy, I'm so sorry, but I knew you would want to go with me, and this was something I had to do on my own. I thought you were out shooting.'

Flossie scrambled down from the carriage and hurried off in the direction of the servants' entrance.

'I was, but I came back early. Did you go to Dorrington Place?' Tommy's frown deepened.

A cold wind ruffled Nancy's skirts and she shivered. 'Let's go indoors, Tommy. It's too cold to stand out here. I hope you haven't caught a chill.'

'You sound like Hester,' Tommy said with a reluctant smile. 'Yes, we'll go inside and you can tell me what happened. I suppose I should be thankful that you've returned.' He tucked her hand in the crook of his arm.

286

Nancy laughed. 'I didn't run away. I needed to speak to Freddie. I wanted to find out how we stood.'

'Past tense, Nancy? I remember that much from lessons at school. Not that I was much good at grammar. What are you saying?'

Nancy led him into the main hall. She came to a halt, listening. 'It's so quiet. Where are the boys?'

'Nick organised a football game between them and some of the village lads. They'll be back soon with enormous appetites. Mrs Banks has been warned.' Tommy opened the drawing-room door. 'Come and sit by the fire and tell me what happened between you and Freddie. I take it you saw him.'

Nancy divested herself of her gloves, bonnet and fur-lined cape. She went to sit in a saggy and slightly battered but still comfortable armchair by the fire. 'We decided to go our separate ways. At least, I did.'

'Freddie didn't like that?'

'I think he's been living in a sort of dream world. I could cope with that, but when Lady Letitia walked into the room, looking immaculate in a very expensive riding habit, I knew that I had lost. Lord Dorrington is determined that Freddie will marry well, even though they don't need the money or the land.'

'But what about Freddie? Or do you think you assumed too much?'

'I think I know him well enough to realise when he's unsure of himself, Tommy. We were close for a while and I loved him, but he will obey his papa no matter what. He wanted me to stay and talk things over, but I knew it was useless. If Freddie really loved me he would never have allowed this state of affairs to exist.'

'I certainly wouldn't,' Tommy said fervently. 'You deserve better, Nancy.'

She gave him a watery smile. 'You would say that.'

'And I mean it, but I won't say any more now. I'll ask Mrs Banks to make you some tea. Have you eaten today?'

Nancy shook her head. 'No, I haven't felt hungry. Oh dear, I nearly forgot. I have to go to the castle to get May.' She half rose from her seat, but Tommy pressed her gently back onto the chair.

'Stop worrying. Rosie is looking after her. When you didn't come to take the child home we both knew something was amiss, so Rosie is going to keep her there for the night. Phoebe and May will have a lovely time together, and you can rest.'

'Thank you both. I don't know what I would do without my adopted family.'

'Adopted nothing. You are as much a part of Rockwood as we are, Nancy. Now stay there and I'll go and see what Mrs Banks has prepared. I'm starving, even if you aren't.'

Tommy left the room without waiting for an answer, leaving Nancy gazing into the orange, scarlet and blue flames as they licked around the hissing and spitting apple logs.

Tommy returned bearing a tray of tea and biscuits. 'Freshly baked,' he said cheerfully. 'Mrs Banks said you were to try some before the locusts returned from the village green. They'll be ravenous but she's thought of that and has mutton stew bubbling away on the range, complete with dumplings.' He set the tray on a small side table and handed a cup and saucer to Nancy.

She smiled. 'You can be quite domesticated when you put your mind to it, Tommy.'

'There are many things I can do that might surprise you.' Tommy took his tea and sat down on the sofa.

'Now, if you feel up to it, tell me exactly what Freddie Ashton said to you. I'd go there and give him a piece of my mind except that I know it would upset you.'

'Yes, there's no need for you to see him, Tommy. He was as upset as I was, but someone had to face the truth. I couldn't go on waiting for him to pluck up the courage to stand up to his father.'

'You did the right thing, Nancy. You have a life here and responsibility for the people who live and work on your land. Lord Dorrington should give you a written apology for doubting that you were worthy of the trust the people put in you.'

'I'm going to concentrate on the children now. I want them to have a good home and an education that will help them to succeed in life. Todd is doing well with Dr Bulmer, and Gus is in the army, safe from Christina's spiteful grasp. The other boys seem to be happy enough where they are working, but I've told them they will always have a home here. The younger ones can make room for them if need be.' Nancy sipped her tea. 'I'm glad I've been able to help the boys. At least I'm doing something useful with my inheritance.'

'More than useful,' Tommy said, nodding. 'But isn't there something you're forgetting, Nancy?'

She met his quizzical gaze with a puzzled frown. 'I don't think so. What is it, Tommy?'

'It's my birthday — I'm nineteen — and Rosie has organised a surprise tea party for me at the castle.'

Nancy threw her arms around his neck. 'Oh! Tommy, I'm so sorry. How awful of me to forget such an important day.'

He gave her a hug. 'Don't worry about it. Just come with me and celebrate.'

'But the boys . . .'

'You know Rosie, she thinks of everything. They've been invited, as well as Todd and the other older lads. Nick will be there, too. Are you still angry with him?'

'No. I understand that the theatre was his life before he came to help me with the estate. I'll find someone else to take over when the building is complete and he takes on the position as theatre manager.'

'I'll wait if you want to change into something more comfortable.'

She kissed him on the cheek. 'You are the best person I know, Tommy. Thank you.'

He drew away, smiling ruefully. 'What are you thanking me for?'

'For being so understanding and not making me feel dreadful about forgetting your birthday. I was so wrapped up in my own affairs that I completely forgot. I'll make it up to you somehow.'

'Just hurry up. I want to get to the castle and pretend to be surprised when Rosie springs the party on me.'

'I'll be ten minutes at the most. Wait for me, Tommy.'

* * *

When Nancy and Tommy walked into the great hall she had to admire his feigned air of astonishment to find the whole family there, including the boys. The only exceptions, as Nancy was quick to notice, were Bertie, Wolfe and Nick, but everyone else was in a party mood and even Hester had a big smile on her face as she handed out iced cakes and glasses of lemonade to the younger members of the family.

Felicia greeted her grandson with a kiss on the cheek, and Claude presented Tommy with a gold half-hunter, which made the other presents seem unremarkable by comparison. Nancy's conscience was bothering her because she did not have a present for Tommy, but she promised herself she would remedy that as soon as she could. In the meantime, Tommy was basking in the affectionate attention of his family and Nancy was delighted for him. After everyone had given him their gifts, Hester sent them all to the dining room, where the table virtually groaned beneath the weight of the food laid out. There were cakes, sandwiches, jellies and even a bowl of rapidly melting ice cream, with a choice of tea or fruit punch to drink. Mrs Jackson had baked Tommy's favourite chocolate cake with chocolate-flavoured icing, the secret of which she kept to herself and refused to give even a hint as to how she had created anything so delicious.

'You must sit at the head of the table, Tommy,' Alex said, smiling. 'You are the important person today.'

Tommy hesitated. 'I can't take Papa's place.' He frowned, gazing around the room. 'Where is he, by the way? Isn't he back yet?'

Rosalind exchanged worried glances with Patricia. 'He should have returned ages ago with Wolfe and Nick.'

Patricia shrugged. 'You know how men are, Rosie. They forget everything when they're after game.'

'Even so, he promised to be here in time for the birthday celebrations.' Rosalind reached out to grasp her husband's hand. 'Perhaps you and Walter ought to go and look for them.'

Walter headed for the door. 'I'll go if Tommy promises to save me a slice of chocolate cake.'

291

He was about to leave the room when Nick burst in, his face ashen and his clothes splattered with blood.

'There's been an accident. Todd, I want you to fetch Dr Bulmer. Alex, we'll need the shooting brake to bring Sir Bertram home.'

'No!' Rosalind's hand flew to cover her mouth. 'What's happened?'

'Sir Bertram was shot accidentally, Mrs Blanchard. He needs help urgently.'

Tommy jumped to his feet. 'Where is he? I'm coming with you.'

Nancy sensed that something dire had happened and she clutched Tommy's arm. 'Better wait here for them to bring your papa home.'

He shook free from her. 'Don't try to stop me, Nancy. I'm coming with you, Nick. We'll bring Pa home.'

★ ★ ★

Dr Bulmer fought tirelessly to save Bertie's life and the whole family stayed up all night, waiting desperately for news. But at dawn the doctor joined them in the drawing room. His face was drawn and pale, making him suddenly an old man. Todd was at his side and it was obvious that the boy had been crying.

'No!' Tommy leaped up from the sofa where he had finally collapsed beside Nancy after pacing the floor for hours. 'No, it can't be true.'

'I'm so sorry,' Dr Bulmer said in a low voice. 'I did everything I could.'

Nancy wrapped her arms around Tommy, holding him close. There were no words to express what she was feeling and Tommy was sobbing as if his heart would break. There was a deathly silence and then Hester rose from her chair by the fire.

'This is a sad day for all of us.'

Rosalind grasped the doctor's hand. 'Thank you so much, Dr Bulmer. I know you will have done everything in your power to save him.'

'My boy, Bertie.' Felicia rose to her feet, swayed and fainted into Claude's arms.

Suddenly everyone started talking in hushed voices, which gradually rose in pitch as they attempted to make their feelings known.

Hester laid her hand on Tommy's shoulder. 'I am so sorry, but you are no longer a child. You are the head of the family now, Tommy. You are Sir Thomas Carey and you must remember your position in life.'

Tommy raised his head from Nancy's shoulder. He wiped his eyes on his sleeve and pulled himself up to a sitting position. 'Papa died alone. I wasn't there to say goodbye.'

Dr Bulmer straightened his crooked cravat. 'Your father passed away peacefully in Wolfe's arms. I can't persuade the man to relinquish his hold. I've never seen anyone so broken.'

Alex turned from the window where he had been gazing out into a wintry dawn. 'Walter and I will go and relieve Wolfe. Come with us, Tommy. We'll say our goodbyes together. Bertie was a great man.'

20

Nancy returned to the Dower House after the funeral and a family gathering to say a final farewell to Bertie at Rockwood Castle. It had been a sombre affair and the funeral itself had been exhausting. Almost the whole village turned out to say goodbye to a much-loved friend and landlord. Nancy's main concern had been for Tommy, but with her support and that of his family he bore up bravely.

Now the house was oddly silent as the boys had been invited to tea at Miss Collins' cottage, no doubt with Miss Moon supervising their every move. May had remained at the castle with Phoebe and was being cared for in the nursery by Jennet, whose love for the children was as strong as ever. Nancy had spent so much time at the castle trying to keep Tommy's spirits up that it was a relief to have a few moments to herself in her own home on this saddest of days.

The Dower House had been transformed from a dilapidated, unloved shell to a comfortable, warm and friendly home for Nancy and the children. The furniture might be an eclectic mix of items bought in sale rooms, some of it well-used, but if drinks were spilled and biscuits crumbled on the upholstery it was not a disaster, and easily remedied.

Nancy took a cup of tea to the drawing room and was about to sit by the fire when she heard hoofbeats on the gravelled carriage sweep. She was not expecting visitors, nor did she wish for company. If she had to listen to any more well-intentioned condolences she felt that her smile would be etched on her face for ever. However, there was certainly someone outside and she went to the window in time to see Freddie dismount from a magnificent Arab stallion. He fastened the reins to an overhanging branch of a tree and strode purposefully towards the front entrance. Nancy glanced at her reflection in one of the wall mirrors and patted a stray hair into place. The young woman wearing her hair smoothed back into a tight bun at the nape of her neck and an uncompromising black mourning dress looked pale and unfamiliar. Nancy pinched her cheeks in an attempt to bring some colour to her face. She waited anxiously, her emotions in a turmoil of uncertainty. After a minute or two a knock on the door preceded Ivy, who entered without waiting for a response. 'Lord Ashton, miss. I asked him to wait but —'

Freddie pushed past her. 'Nancy, I came as soon as I heard the awful news.' He crossed the floor and took both her hands in his. 'I am so sorry. How did it happen?'

Nancy withdrew her hands gently. 'It was a hunting accident, Freddie. A stray shot proved fatal.'

'That's tragic. I know how fond you were of Bertie. He was a good man.'

Nancy glanced over his shoulder to see Ivy hovering in the doorway. 'Bring some refreshment for Lord Ashton, if you please, Ivy.'

Ivy bobbed a curtsey. 'Yes, miss.' Somewhat reluctantly she backed out of the room.

'Do sit down, Freddie. You must have ridden for hours to get here.'

He shrugged off his greatcoat and laid it carefully over the back of a chair, together with his hat and gloves. 'I only heard this morning. I would have attended the funeral had I had more warning.'

Nancy moved away to sit by the fire. 'Thank you, but there was no need. In fact, there was no room. The church was packed and people lined the streets. It was quite humbling, but Bertie was a friend to everyone.'

Freddie took a seat opposite her. 'I passed the ruin of your house on my way here. They've cleared the land already.'

'Yes, they hope to start building the theatre within weeks. Sir Bentley likes to get things done quickly.'

Freddie nodded. 'Yes, so I've heard.'

After a moment's silence, Nancy leaned forward, fixing Freddie with an intense gaze. 'Why did you come here today, Freddie? You could have sent a letter of condolence.'

'I m-made a mistake, Nancy.' Freddie took a deep breath. 'I still love you and I don't want to marry Letitia, no matter what my father says.'

'So what are you saying exactly, Freddie? As I see it, nothing has changed.'

'I'm asking you to marry me, Nancy. I don't care about your background or the fact that you have lost the estate and have taken in all those young criminals. We can find homes for them.'

'I haven't lost the estate, Freddie. The house has gone, but I get a considerable income from the land. I am not a pauper, nor am I prepared to farm out my boys. They are just children who had a difficult start in life and I mean to see that they grow up to be good people and have families of their own.'

'But, N-Nancy, they're not your responsibility.'

'I don't care. I am not shallow and selfish like some people.'

Freddie's blue eyes widened in surprise. 'Are you s-s-saying I'm those things?'

'It seems to me that you've encouraged Letitia to think there's a chance for her, but at the same time you still think I am here just waiting for you to crook your little finger and I'll come running back to you.'

'That's not fair, Nancy. I've had a d-difficult time with Papa, and the estate takes up most of my time.'

'Then there you have it, Freddie. I told you that the land meant more to you than any woman ever could. Go back to Dorrington Place and take up your rightful position. If you are very lucky, Letitia will agree to marry you and produce an heir.'

Freddie rose to his feet. 'Nancy, I am so sorry it has come to this. B-but you are upset. I sh-should have waited until you have had a chance to recover from the shock of losing Bertie.'

'It wouldn't make any difference, Freddie. You left me alone for months. You could have come to see me at any time, but you didn't. I'm not going to keep on repeating this, but you just can't walk in the door and expect to find that nothing has changed.'

Freddie snatched up his outer garments. 'I'll take a room at the inn for tonight. Maybe after you've had a chance to rest and think things over calmly, you'll feel differently.'

'It is too late for you to ride home and your horse needs to rest. I'd offer you a bed here but I have my reputation to think of. You may look down on Greystone Park because it isn't as big and grand as Dorrington Place, but it belongs to me, and I, too, have a position to keep up.'

'I seem to have upset you, Nancy. It's the l-last thing I w-wanted to do. I'll go to the inn and I'll

297

c-call again tomorrow.' Freddie opened the door and almost barged into Ivy, who was carrying a tray of tea and cake. He muttered an apology and his hasty footsteps on the tiled floor echoed off the high ceiling of the entrance hall, followed by the sound of the door opening and closing.

'Shall I leave the tray, miss?' Ivy asked nervously.

'Yes, put it on the table, please. I'll help myself.'

Ivy did as she was bid and hurried from the room, closing the door softly behind her.

Left alone in the silent room Nancy could only wish for the boys to return and fill the house with their noisy chatter. She remained sitting by the fire, staring into the flames until the door burst open and Alfie rushed in, dragging Jack by the hand.

'Miss Nancy, I tried to look after him, but Jack ate too much cake and he's been sick.'

Nancy roused herself from her thoughts and turned to look at Jack, who was pale and tearful.

'It's all right, Alfie. I'll take care of him now, and Connie will put him to bed. He's only little.'

'Miss Moon made us eat a lot of bread and butter afore us got to the cake, but then Jack said he had a bellyache. He was sick on the way home.'

'Well, it was good of Miss Collins and Miss Moon to have you to tea. I'll write them a note tomorrow and you can take it round.'

Alfie pulled a face. 'Maybe Stanley could do it, miss. I told Miss Moon it was her cakes what made Jack ill. They wasn't a patch on what Mrs Banks makes.'

'I'm sure Mrs Banks will be very flattered to hear it, but you're right. I'll send Stanley, or maybe I'll go there myself.' Nancy stood up and took Jack by the hand. 'Come with me, Jack. We'll go to the kitchen and ask Connie to fill a stone bottle with hot water so that you can cuddle up to it in bed. You'll feel better in the morning.'

'Ta, miss.' Jack sniffed and wiped his nose on his sleeve.

Nancy took a hanky from her pocket and handed it to him. Bertie was gone from them and would be sorely missed, but there were young lives to care for and they were her responsibility. She knew she could never quite forgive Freddie for dismissing her boys so casually. Jack clutched her hand, looking up at her trustingly, and she bent down to drop a kiss on his forehead. As she led him out of the room she was met with a wave of sound as the boys erupted through the front door, chattering and laughing, and the whole house came alive again.

* * *

Next morning, having settled the boys with Miss Collins for their lessons, after thanking her profusely for taking care of them during the funeral, Nancy rode over to Patricia's house next to the sawmill. She left her horse with Robbins and, having braved Fletcher at the door, she went into the parlour to find Patricia with little Charlie on her knee and Tommy seated on the sofa.

Tommy leaped to his feet. 'I've just been to the Dower House. You weren't there.'

His indignation made Nancy giggle. 'I took the boys to Miss Collins, and then I came here.'

'Well, it's lovely to see you both,' Patricia said hastily, 'especially after such a sad day yesterday. I often used to argue with Bertie but I will miss him terribly.'

'We all will.' Nancy swallowed hard to prevent herself from crying. 'I wasn't expecting to see you this morning, Tommy. You aren't usually up and about this early.'

'I saw Freddie Ashton at the village pub last evening. What is he doing here, Nancy?'

'What were you doing at the Black Dog is more to the point?'

Tommy sank back on the sofa. 'I took Wolfe there for a glass of ale. The poor fellow doesn't know what to do with himself. He's a broken man.'

Patricia bounced Charlie on her knee as he began to grizzle. 'Wolfe made Bertie his life's work. I don't know what we can do to fill the gap.'

'I don't need him, that's for certain.' Tommy sighed. 'I miss Pa so much it hurts, but I can't manage Wolfe moping around like a lost sheepdog.'

Nancy had a sudden thought. 'He used to share the cottage in the woods with Fletcher at one point, didn't he? They were firm friends. Maybe she can help him now.'

'Somebody must do something,' Tommy said firmly. 'He's driving everyone mad at the castle.'

Patricia reached for the bell and rang it. Fletcher appeared in the doorway before the echo had died away.

'You rang, missis?'

'Yes, Fletcher. Come in, please. We have a problem and we all think you might be able to help, if you are willing.'

Fletcher glanced suspiciously at each of them in turn. 'What's up?'

'It's Wolfe,' Tommy said slowly. 'We don't know how to help him. We're all sad that my father has gone

300

from us, but Wolfe is beyond listening to anything I say to him.'

Fletcher nodded. 'I know, sir. He was devoted to the master.'

'You are his friend,' Nancy added cautiously. 'What would you suggest?'

'He needs something to do that will satisfy him, miss. Wolfe may seem like a hard man but he is at his best when he's taking care of someone.'

'Of course he is.' Patricia ruffled Charlie's golden curls. 'But I don't think he'd make a good nursemaid.'

'What about them boys?' Fletcher stared pointedly at Nancy. 'They need someone with a firm hand. They'll run riot if you don't look out, miss. If you'll pardon me saying so.'

'Of course.' Nancy smiled. 'Why didn't I think of that? There's a room in the servants' quarters that Wolfe could have. Although I love the boys they do need someone to take charge of them when they get rowdy. They're growing up far quicker than I could have imagined.'

'There you are then.' Patricia snapped her fingers. 'A solution that was under our noses. Thank you, Fletcher, and as you thought of it, I suggest you broach the subject to Wolfe.'

'Yes, please do.' Tommy gave her his most persuasive smile. 'He's likely to bite my head off if I say anything, but you know how to handle him.'

'I should say I do.' Fletcher flexed her muscles. 'He won't argue with me, but I'll be gentle with him, poor soul. He's a good man despite his past, but he's not very clever when it comes to thinking things out for himself, if you know what I mean.'

'I think we all do, Fletcher. Thank you.' Patricia

held the baby out to her. 'Will you take Master Charlie for his nap?'

Fletcher's grim features broke into a tender smile as she took the little boy from his mother's arms. 'Come on, young master. We'll go up the wooden hill to counterpane country.'

'That's settled then,' Tommy said smiling. 'But that leaves the question of Ashton. Did he come to see you, Nancy?'

'Yes, he did, but I told him to leave. He can't keep coming and going as he pleases.'

'But he stayed at the pub last night. I heard him book a room.'

'I hope he'll return to Dorrington Place this morning.' Nancy turned to Patricia. 'I'm sure I did the right thing.'

'Did he want anything in particular, or did he just want to commiserate with all of us on our loss?' Patricia met Nancy's anxious gaze with a steady glance.

'He said all the right things, and then he proposed for the second time.'

Tommy leaned forward, scowling. 'He has a nerve. You didn't accept, did you?'

'No, I didn't.'

'And now you're regretting it?' Patricia shook her head. 'Don't weaken, Nancy. I know Freddie is a nice person, but he's dominated by that father of his, and his mother, too. You would never have a life of your own while they are in charge.'

'Yes,' Nancy said sadly. 'I've come to realise that.'

'Do you love him?' Tommy demanded angrily. 'I'll go and set him to rights if he's been turning your head again.'

Nancy rounded on him. 'He didn't turn my head,

302

as you put it. And yes, I do love him, in a way, but not, I think, enough to risk ruining my life by accepting his proposal. To be honest I think Letitia Barclay is far better suited to the sort of life Freddie has to offer, even though it hurts to say so.'

'Then you should leave him in no doubt as to your feelings,' Patricia said firmly. 'Did he say he would call on you again?'

'Yes, he did, but I'm not going to wait around. I'll go to the Black Dog and ask to see him.'

Tommy held up his hand. 'You can't go there on your own. You know women aren't welcome in public houses, and everyone knows you. I'm coming with you.'

'No, Tommy. Thank you, but I must do this for myself.' Nancy rose to her feet. 'I'll go now and hope I can catch him before he sets off for my house.'

'Be firm, darling,' Patricia said, smiling. 'Think of yourself for once, Nancy.'

'Yes,' Tommy added. 'If these last eight months or so prove anything it shows that you can manage perfectly well without Viscount Ashton and his huge fortune.'

'I'll try to remember that.' Nancy picked up her fur-lined cape, which she had laid carefully on the back of a chair, and slipped it on. 'Don't follow me, Tommy. I can handle this myself.'

The pale wintry sun had disappeared behind a bank of heavy cloud and a downpour of sleety rain made Nancy step into the pub porch, where she was almost knocked down by a couple of the men who were supposed to be working on the site of the new theatre. They apologised gruffly, eyeing her up and down as they stepped outside. Clouds of tobacco smoke met her as she entered the taproom and a sudden fall of soot hit the glowing coals, hissing and spitting and sending out a shower of tiny black particles. However, it was a handy diversion and none of the drinkers seemed to notice Nancy as she walked up to the bar and asked to see Freddie.

Ned Causley seemed more interested in the sooty mess on the flagstone floor than answering questions. 'He left half an hour ago, Miss Greystone. Said he was going to hire a chaise, although he didn't say why and it wasn't my business to question him. Hey, you, boy — Frankie — get that cleared up before it gets trodden through to the parlour. My missis will be furious if any gets on the new rug.'

Nancy realised that she was not going to get any more information. She could see that Frankie was too busy sweeping up the fall of soot to spare time to talk to her, and she felt slightly guilty that she had not seen either him or Ben for a few weeks. She slipped out of the pub virtually unnoticed and walked round to the stable where Ben was busy mucking out a stall. He greeted her eagerly but when she asked about Freddie he could only repeat what Ned Causley had said. It seemed that Freddie had been enquiring about hiring a vehicle and had been told that the nearest place he might hire a suitable vehicle was Exeter.

Nancy was puzzled. 'Did he say why he wanted to hire a chaise, Ben?'

'No, miss. But I saw him talking to that Mrs Cottingham after he left here. I had to run an errand for the head groom and I nearly bumped into them as I turned the corner into the high street. She was all dolled up in her Sunday best with a hat covered in great big feathers. She looked like a big bird such as you'd see in the zoological gardens.'

'That's very odd. What on earth would Freddie want with Christina, or rather, what would she want with him?'

'I dunno, miss.' Ben shuffled his feet, avoiding her gaze. 'I'd like to see the young 'uns and the other boys, but I ain't allowed time off.'

'You know you're welcome to come to the Dower House whenever you want, and that goes for Frankie, too.'

'We have to do as our boss says, miss.'

Nancy sighed. This sounded like a job for Wolfe. No one would argue with him when he had his mind set on something. 'Don't worry, Ben. I'll sort it out. You must come to the house for tea on Sunday afternoon. I'll make the arrangements and you won't be prevented from coming.'

'Ta, miss. I don't mind working hard, but I miss the other lads.'

'Of course you do. I promise to make things right, Ben.' Nancy mounted her horse and rode him out of the stable yard. If Freddie had decided to return home to Dorrington Place, that would make life much easier, and if he chose to hire a chaise that was his business. It was probably a coincidence that he was seen passing the time of day with Christina. In fact she could not remember having introduced him to Mrs Oscar Cottingham, but then everyone knew everyone in Rockwood and the surrounding villages. Christina would almost certainly have recognised Freddie and would probably have accosted him to satisfy her curiosity.

Nancy rode back to Greystone Park, stopping for a while to chat to the foreman supervising the final

305

stage of clearing the ruins ready to lay the foundations for the theatre. Sir Bentley had already paid this month's rent on the land with a month in advance, so there was no question of him reneging on the verbal agreement, and the contract was ready for signature by both parties. Nancy felt a frisson of excitement at the thought of the estate coming to life in such a vibrant way. She left and rode on to the Dower House, but to her surprise she recognised one of the old carriages from Greystone Park waiting outside the house. It was one that Christina had taken as her own when she left. Nancy called out to Jones as she rode past the stables and he came hurrying after her to take care of her horse.

'Do you know if Mrs Cottingham is here?' Nancy asked breathlessly.

Jones shook his head. 'No, miss. It's Lord Ashton. He asked me to stable his mount. It isn't a carriage horse.'

'I see. Thank you, Jones.' Nancy dismounted and handed him the reins. She let herself into the house without bothering to summon a servant, and made straight for the drawing room. She flung the door open. 'Freddie. What do you think you're doing?'

He came towards her, holding out his hands. 'I've been such a fool, Nancy. I hardly slept a wink last night for worrying.' He seemed strangely confident, with no hint of a stutter.

'What are you talking about? I thought we settled matters yesterday. And why is there one of Christina's carriages outside?'

'I happened to meet her in the village. It was purely by chance and she asked about you. She seemed very concerned, and when I told her that we'd parted she

306

was adamant that I should try again.'

Nancy laid her cape over the nearest chair. 'Why would Christina care? She hates me for inheriting Greystone Park.'

'She said you two are cousins. Perhaps she's had a change of heart.'

'Never! Not Christina. There is some devious plan behind all this. But you haven't answered my question. Why have you borrowed a carriage?'

'I'm going to take you home to Dorrington Place. I want you to see that my parents have changed their minds about me marrying you. Letitia only wants a larger stable of horses; she doesn't need a husband to make her happy.'

'Oh, and you think if I married you I would be happy?' Nancy peeled off her kid gloves. Her hands were shaking but whether it was with anger or nervousness she did not know.

'I would spend my life trying to make you the happiest woman in the world.'

'It wouldn't work, Freddie. I did love you — quite desperately, in fact — but you abandoned me for months, and when we did meet you weren't at all interested in my problems. All you thought about was your estate business.'

'And for that I am truly sorry. I bitterly regret following my father's instructions so blindly.'

'It's too late for regrets, Freddie. You can take the carriage back to Christina and tell her that I am going nowhere. All she wants is to get me away from Greystone Park. She doesn't care what happens to me, or the boys.'

'I know I said all the wrong things, Nancy. I was a little hasty about the children. What I meant to say

307

was that they should go to good schools. It would make men of them and I would be more than happy to pay the fees.'

'They need a home more than they need schooling, Freddie. Those children have been starved of love and security since birth. They need what they have here — a home where they are cared for and appreciated.'

Freddie gazed at her, seemingly speechless.

'I'm sorry, Freddie, but you need to know how things stand.'

'I can see that I've m-made a t-terrible m-mess of things.'

Nancy watched him walk dejectedly to the door where he came to a halt.

'Could your man take the carriage back to Mrs Cottingham?'

'Yes, of course.'

'I had h-hoped the outcome of my v-visit would be different.'

'Go home, Freddie. Marry Letitia and raise handsome heirs to your combined fortunes.'

He nodded mutely and left the room, closing the door behind him.

Nancy sank down on the sofa, drained of emotion and too exhausted for tears. It would have been so easy to allow him to take her away from all the difficulties that she might face here in Greystone Park, but she was not one to give up easily. She felt as though a small slice of her heart was being taken away with Freddie and would always be his, but their lives had changed and their paths had diverged.

'Goodbye, Freddie,' she whispered.

The door was flung open and Freddie marched

back into the drawing room. 'This isn't good enough, Nancy. Pack a bag — you are coming with me. We'll spend a few days together and try to sort out our problems. I refuse to give up so easily.'

'I can't just leave like that, even if I wanted to. I have responsibilities here, Freddie.' Nancy eyed him warily. She had never seen Freddie so angry.

'There are plenty of people here to look after the orphans. You're just making excuses.'

Nancy was angry now and she turned to face him squarely. 'Go away, Freddie. I won't be bullied into changing my mind.'

Freddie opened his mouth as if to argue, but the door opened and Tommy strode into the room.

'I had a feeling you wouldn't leave without a fuss, Ashton. You'd better go now, or do I have to throw you out?'

Nancy was poised, ready to step between them if they resorted to fisticuffs, but both men backed off, glaring at each other.

'All right,' Freddie said reluctantly. 'I've never forced anyone to do anything they didn't wish to do. I'll go now, but I'll return, Nancy. This isn't the end. I'll win you back if it's the last thing I do.' He left the room and Tommy slammed the door.

'He's gone. Are you all right, Nancy? I won't have that fellow come here and upset you like this.'

Nancy sank down on her chair. 'I'm perfectly all right, Tommy. I could have managed on my own. You didn't have to do that.'

'Maybe not, but he wasn't going to give up easily. I could tell that.'

'He's gone and I doubt if he'll come back.'

'Good riddance, I say.' Tommy took her by the hand.

'He tried to bully you into submission, Nancy. I won't have him do that to you. Come and have luncheon at the castle. You can have a chat with Rosie. She's the sensible one in our family, but I'm sure she'll only repeat what I've just said.'

'If you don't mind, Tommy, I'd rather stay here and spend a little time on my own. I need to think things over carefully.'

'You're not weakening, are you? He's not worth it, Nancy.'

'No, but I need to see Nick about estate matters. I might not have a great house but I still have the tenants to look after. Nick will be working at the theatre when it opens and I'll have to find another land agent.'

'That reminds me: I have to sort out some problems, too. I never thought I'd have to step into Papa's shoes so soon, but I'll do my best.'

Nancy stood up and gave him a quick hug. 'We've both got to learn to stand on our own two feet, Tommy. I'll help you and you can help me.'

He smiled and kissed her on the tip of her nose. 'We'll make a splendid team, as always, Nancy.'

21

Nancy spent the next few days going over the estate business affairs with Nick. It was a relief to know that he was eager to continue working for her until the theatre was up and running and it gave her time to find another land agent. Sir Bentley had already hired a team of expert builders and they had prepared the site and were ready to commence work on the architect's plans. Nancy visited what had once been her home every day, taking an interest in every aspect of the work. She spoke to the foreman and chatted to the workmen, and as her questions were genuine and not in any way critical, they were pleased to keep her informed as to their progress.

Freddie had stayed on for a day or two after their last meeting, but had finally left without trying to contact her again. Nancy could only assume that he had returned to Dorrington Place. She was sad that their relationship had ended in disharmony, but relieved that he had not pressed his suit any further. Sometimes, in the middle of the night when she could not sleep, she regretted her decision to send him away, but in the cold light of morning she knew she had done the right thing. Perhaps Lord Dorrington had been right all along and she was not the right woman to marry Freddie.

It was now early December and winter had come with a vengeance. The serene days of autumn had been washed away by rain and the balmy air replaced by an icy blast from the north. Fingers of frost curled around the carpet of dead leaves that covered the grass, and a cold mist greeted her every morning when she rode about the estate with Nick. Occasionally they met Tommy and his steward, Hodges, facing each other over the invisible line that divided their two estates, which made Nancy and Tommy laugh. Their agents remained aloof, as if seeing the funny side of things might somehow endanger their professional image.

Miss Collins had brought the younger boys up to a reasonable standard of literacy and numeracy, and Louise agreed to take them into her class at the village school. As a precaution against the six- and seven-year-old London boys proving too much for the village youths, Louise asked Miss Moon to supervise playtimes and organise ball games to keep the two factions competing in a friendly manner. It seemed that there was nothing Miss Moon enjoyed more than making the children run, throw, catch and generally enjoy ball games. Everything seemed to be running smoothly. Even Christina kept a brooding silence, a little, Nancy thought, like a volcano that might erupt at any time. She did not imagine for a moment that Christina had said the last word on the theatre, although there seemed to be nothing she could do at this advanced stage in the development. However, Nancy knew Christina well enough to be cautious, but Christmas was not far off and Nancy hoped that the season of goodwill would make Christina more amenable.

★ ★ ★

312

One morning Nancy was putting on her velvet bonnet before leaving the house for a meeting with Nick concerning one of the tenants, who had hit hard times and was too ill to work his land, when to her surprise Ivy announced that the late squire's widow, Glorina Cottingham, was waiting in the entrance hall.

'Show her in, Ivy. I'll see her, although I have an appointment I must keep.' Nancy shrugged on her warm velvet mantle and waited.

Moments later Ivy ushered Glorina into the morning parlour. 'Nancy, so good of you to see me.'

Nancy motioned her to take a seat. 'As you can see, I was just about to go out, but I can spare you a few moments.'

Glorina paced the floor, wringing her hands. 'I've come to warn you, Nancy. I know we haven't seen much of each other recently. I keep very much to myself since the squire's death, and Christina doesn't want me to have anything to do with my grandchildren, which is why I am consigned to the dower house in the manor grounds.' Glorina stopped to look round. 'It's so much smaller than this one. You are more fortunate than I.'

'I'm sorry, but I thought you were about to announce your engagement to Sir Wilfred Madison.'

Glorina shook her head. 'He wasn't the man I thought he was, my dear. I had a lucky escape, but there is someone for me in the not too distant future. It's unclear at the moment, but he will make his appearance quite soon. I see smoke and a burning building, and danger, but I can't make sense of it yet.'

'You tell fortunes. I'm surprised you didn't foresee Jeremiah Stewer's return in your crystal ball.'

'You would think so, wouldn't you? But it's not

always easy to tell what will occur in the future when it comes to oneself.'

'I'm truly sorry for your misfortunes, but is there something you wanted to say to me?' Nancy glanced at the ormolu clock on the mantelshelf.

'Yes, indeed. The reason I came here this morning is that I felt I must warn you that Christina is seeing a London solicitor with a view to putting a stop to building a theatre at Greystone Park.'

'It's not really my concern, Glorina. You should be seeing Sir Bentley about this, although I dare say he already knows.'

'He might, and I hope he does, but it affects you, too. If my daughter-in-law is successful, you will be left with a ruin on your hands and a much depleted income. Not only that, and probably more relevant, is the fact that Christina is preparing to visit Dorrington Place.'

Nancy stared at her aghast. 'Why would she do that?'

'She wants to put a stop to your marriage to Freddie Ashton once and for all. I believe she is going to tell Lord Dorrington that you allowed the estate to go to rack and ruin, and how she has struggled to prevent a theatre being built on the site of her old home.'

'That would not go down well with Freddie's papa.' Nancy eyed her curiously. 'But why are you telling me this? Why would you care what happens to me?'

'You are a good person, Nancy. My sister, Starlina, told me how you went to her for help when Patricia was attempting to emulate her mama with a career in the operatic world.'

'That was a long time ago. I don't think Christina will have much luck in attempting to take on Sir

314

Bentley, who is one of the richest and most powerful businessmen in the country. As to Lord Dorrington, I can't believe she would go that far. Surely she wouldn't leave her husband and children at home just before Christmas, simply to spite me.'

'I hope not, for your sake, Nancy.' Glorina headed for the doorway, her long hennaed curls escaping from the confines of a black straw bonnet. She raised a mittened hand in a wave. 'Goodbye, my dear. Don't say I didn't warn you when everything comes crashing around those pretty shoulders.'

'Just a minute,' Nancy said hastily. 'What do you suggest I do about it? Christina is your daughter-in-law, after all.'

'If you are religious I think you should pray. If not, then cross your fingers and hope that my dear daughter-in-law finds something else to occupy her mind. At the moment she is obsessed with Greystone Park and her loss of inheritance. I can't tell you anything more, other than to be very careful.' Glorina swept out of the room leaving a waft of patchouli, bergamot and vetiver in her wake.

Nancy was inclined to laugh at such dramatics, but Glorina must have been worried to leave the safety of the dower house on the Cottingham estate in order to warn her. Nancy knew there was no love lost between Glorina and her daughter-in-law, but perhaps she ought to warn Sir Bentley, and the best way to do that would be to speak to Nick. She picked up her gloves and reticule and hurried out of the room. As to Christina travelling to Dorrington Place, that was another matter. Nancy was not sure whether to believe that part of the story or not.

Jones had her horse saddled and ready to be ridden

and she mounted from a block placed conveniently close to the front entrance.

'Shall I ride with you, miss?'

'No, thank you, Jones. I'm going to meet Mr Gibson. We've got business to do this morning. I'll be back later this afternoon.'

'Very good, miss.' Jones handed her the reins and she rode off in the direction of the village.

Nick was still living in the cottage in the woods and she waited outside for him to join her.

He gave her a cursory glance. 'You look troubled. What's the matter, Nancy?'

'I had a visit from Glorina Cottingham this morning.'

He untethered his horse and mounted with ease. 'I assume it did not bode well.'

'Not really. She came to tell me that Christina has taken on a London lawyer to challenge Sir Bentley's right to build the theatre on my land. She still thinks that she owns Greystone Park. Nothing, it seems, will dissuade her.'

'She is a clergyman's wife and she has three young children. One would think she had better things to do than to try to get the better of a man like Sir Bentley.'

'I'm afraid Christina will do anything she can to get the estate back. Her papa willed it to her and Sylvia, but Sylvia is married now and living happily in Switzerland. She isn't interested in the estate. It's Christina who is desperate to oust me.'

'What can I do to help, Nancy? I don't know the woman personally, although I've seen her strutting about the village as if she owns it.'

'You see Sir Bentley far more often than I do, and

knowing the type of man he is, I think he would listen to you far more than he would me. Tell him that Christina is not just a silly, jealous woman, she is dangerous and could put the theatre project in jeopardy, let alone the hotel that Sir Bentley also plans.'

'But both will help the community. Can't she see that?'

'Christina sees nothing other than her own point of view. Please make Sir Bentley take the threat seriously. If he ignores it he will be sorry.'

'Don't worry, Nancy. Sir Bentley has the best lawyers in London working for him. But that's not all, is it?'

'Glorina thinks that Christina is planning to visit Dorrington Place to tell Freddie's father what an unsuitable wife I would make his son.'

Nick threw his head back and laughed. 'I'm sorry, Nancy, but that's ridiculous. Surely Lord Dorrington, being a man of the world, will see through her vindictive attack on your good name.'

'Freddie and I are no longer engaged, but that doesn't mean I don't care what his father thinks of me. And I still care what Freddie thinks of me.'

Nick rode alongside her, their horses walking at a sedate pace. 'Why did you end things with Freddie?'

'Lots of small things, Nick, but the main one is that Freddie would send the boys to expensive boarding schools where they would be totally miserable and out of place. I told him that they need to stay with me, in a proper home, and Freddie was horrified by the thought.'

'They are good lads. They deserve nothing less.'

'I knew you'd understand, and you would see that I can't abandon them, not for anyone.'

'Yes, of course. So what will you do about Christina?'

'I'll go to the castle when we've seen Clem Barley and sorted out his problems. I need to speak to Mrs de Marney. I'll warn her that Christina is trying to cause trouble, and if you explain the situation to Sir Bentley, that is about as much as we can do.'

'I'm seeing him this afternoon to look over the final architect's plans. I'll tell him what Mrs Cottingham plans, but that doesn't mean he'll pay any attention to what I have to say.'

'As to Christina — I'll wait and see what she does and then I'll act accordingly.' Nancy urged her horse to a trot. 'Come along, Nick. We're wasting time.'

Clem Barley lived in a tiny cottage on the outskirts of the village. He had been a woodsman, working on the Greystone Park estate since he was a boy, but ill health had made it impossible for him to continue with manual work and he was virtually crippled by arthritis. He lived on his own, his wife having died many years ago and his only daughter lived in Exeter, running a public house with her husband. Nancy and Nick sat in the tiny kitchen listening to Clem's problems, and when he came to the part where he admitted he could not pay the rent, the old man burst into tears.

Nancy laid her hand on his shoulder. 'Clem, don't take on so. You've worked for the estate all your life; I think we owe you rather than you owing us. You may forget the rent. You've earned a retirement free from anxiety.'

Clem sniffed and wiped his eyes on his sleeve. 'Thank you, Miss Nancy. I'm much obliged.'

'How are you managing to look after yourself?' Nick asked, looking round the tiny room with its

318

soot-blackened ceiling and damp walls. 'This doesn't seem like the best accommodation for you.'

Clem looked up, rheumy-eyed and scared. 'You won't throw me out on the street, master?'

'Certainly not.' Nick threw a small log onto the smouldering fire. 'How do you manage for firewood and everyday things like purchasing food?'

'I don't need much, sir. I manage by doing odd jobs for Dr Bulmer, but my back has been bad for weeks now, so I haven't been able to earn much.'

'I think the estate should be paying you a pension for all the years of dedicated service, Clem.' Nancy exchanged worried glances with Nick. 'But I have to be honest. It looks as if you are having difficulty taking care of yourself. Would it be possible for you to go and live with your daughter?'

He shook his head. 'No, miss. She won't have me there. She says she's too busy to look after me, and I want to stay in my own home. I don't want to go into the workhouse, miss.'

'Certainly not. There's no question of that.' Nancy frowned thoughtfully. 'I dare say the older boys could help you, Clem. They could gather wood for you and go to the village shop to purchase what you need.'

'Boys are trouble, miss. They'd be throwing stones at me windows and calling me names.'

'Is that what the village lads do, Clem?' Nick demanded angrily. 'Tell me their names and I'll speak to their fathers.'

'It's only one or two of them, master. The others don't bother me.'

'My boys will treat you with respect,' Nancy said firmly. 'I'll have a talk to them this evening and tomorrow I'll send two of them to do any odd jobs that you

319

find too difficult.'

'You might like to come to the village hall to see us rehearse the play we are going to put on for Christmas, Clem. You and the boys can get to know each other.' Nick rose to his feet, eyeing the empty log basket. 'I'll fetch some wood for the fire. Have you enough food for today, Clem?'

'I got a heel of cheese and some bread, thank you, sir.'

Nancy stood up and opened the only cupboard in the room, but the shelves were bare except for some mouse droppings. 'I'll get Mrs Banks to send you something for your dinner, Clem. And you could do with a woman from the village to give this place a good clean.'

'I ain't much good at that sort of thing,' Clem said apologetically. 'My Beattie used to keep the place neat as a new pin.'

'Don't worry. Everything will all right, Clem.' Nancy gave him a reassuring smile as she left the cottage.

Outside Nick was splitting logs and tossing them into the wicker basket. 'I'll be a while here, Nancy. Then I've got a meeting with Sir Bentley, and after that I'm taking the boys for a run-through of the play.'

'Make sure you warn Sir Bentley about Christina, although I don't think it will bother him greatly.'

'I'll do that, and you'll send one of the boys with food for Clem's supper, is that right?'

'Yes, I'll get Mrs Banks to fill a basket with enough food to keep him going for a day or two. Maybe she can ask one of our cleaning women to take on Clem's cottage at least once a week. He can't go on living in such squalor, and we must give him the pension he deserves.'

320

'I agree. I'll keep a better eye on him in the future, Nancy.'

'I have to leave now, but I'll be at the castle if anyone needs me.' Nancy used the stump of a felled tree as a mounting block and climbed into the saddle. She waved as she rode off, leaving Nick to finish his task.

When she reached the bridge that crossed the River Sawle she reined in at the sight of Wolfe pushing a barrow laden with holly and ivy. It was his dejected look that made her bring her horse to a halt. She had intended to speak to him about moving into the Dower House and this presented an ideal opportunity.

'Good morning, Wolfe. That's lovely berried holly. Is there more to be had? I really should think about decorating the Dower House.'

'Plenty left on the bushes, Miss Nancy.'

Wolfe was about to trudge on but she called him back. 'Just a minute.'

He came to a halt, glaring at her balefully. 'Yes, miss?'

'Is anything wrong? You look out of sorts, Wolfe.'

'Nothing is the same since the master passed away. I'm not really needed at the castle. They keep me on out of charity.'

Nancy shook her head. 'That's nonsense. You are as much part of the fabric of Rockwood Castle as the stone it's made of.'

A faint grin twisted his lips. 'No, miss. That ain't true.'

'You know, I could do with someone like you at the Dower House,' Nancy said earnestly. 'The boys need a man around. At the moment my household is all women, but someone like you would be a great help. There are things that I can't teach them and I want them to grow up to be useful members of society. What do you say?'

Wolfe pushed his hair back from his brow. 'I'm not a charity case, miss.'

'Certainly not. You would earn your keep, Wolfe. I can pay you the same as Sir Bertram did — perhaps more, if you prove your worth. You were in the army once; you know how to discipline young minds and teach them respect.'

'I'd have to ask Sir Thomas first.'

Nancy turned her head away so that he did not see her smile. It seemed odd to hear Tommy referred to as Sir Thomas, but Wolfe was right. Tommy was now the head of the household, although Hester still held sway. 'Yes, of course. Speak to him directly and let me know what he says. In the meantime, I would be most grateful if you would show my boys where to pick the best holly. We really should start thinking about Christmas.'

Wolfe grunted. 'Send 'em to me, miss. I'll do the necessary.'

Nancy thought he smiled but she could not be sure because of his luxuriant grey whiskers. She thanked him and rode on, satisfied that she might be able to help the man who had stood by Bertie with unwavering loyalty.

When she reached the castle she left her horse at the stables but was met by Gurney with a glum expression.

'What's the matter, Jim?'

He pulled a face. 'It's not for me to complain, miss. But we've got Lady Pentelow's carriage and horses to stable. To tell the truth, I don't get on with that Corbin, her coachman. I've left Ned to keep an eye

322

on the fellow.'

Nancy was not really surprised to find that they had been invaded again by Lady Pentelow, who always seemed to turn up at family occasions, although she had not bothered to put in an appearance at Bertie's funeral. However, it was not Nancy's problem. Rosie and Alex would have to put up with Lady Pentelow trying to get the upper hand, as far as Hester was concerned. Not that Hester needed anyone to stand up for her — Hester was perfectly capable of putting Lady Pentelow in her place. Life was never dull when the two dowager ladies were at odds with each other.

'I'm sorry, Jim,' Nancy said sympathetically. 'I know Corbin is difficult, but I'm sure that Hudson will keep him under control. It's time you took things easy, anyway. You've worked hard for this family and everyone appreciates you.'

'Thank you for saying this, miss. I don't expect praise for doing my duty, but you're right, my old bones are not up to the job.'

'I didn't say that, Jim. I meant that you have earned a little respite, particularly at Christmas.'

'I have been invited to Christmas dinner with the Coaker family.'

'There you are then. There's always a good side to things.'

His smile faded. 'Not when Mrs Cottingham is concerned, miss. I don't want to speak out of turn but my wife is related to Curtis, Mrs Cottingham's coachman, and he says she's making him drive all the way to Dorrington Place tomorrow. I thought I should tell you.'

'Thank you, Jim. That's very important information. I'm much obliged to you.' Nancy left him to take care of her horse. So Christina was going to carry out her threat. Nancy was not going to let her ruin what little respect Lord Dorrington may have for her. Tommy would understand how she felt, and at this moment she was desperate to talk to him, but first the formalities must be observed and she would have to pay her respects to Lady Pentelow and Aurelia. She acknowledged Jarvis with a vague smile as he ushered her into the great hall.

'Where is everyone, Jarvis?'

'Mrs Blanchard and Sir Thomas are in the drawing room with Mrs Gibbs, but Lady Pentelow has gone to her room. Shall I announce you, Miss Nancy?'

'No, it's all right, Jarvis. I'll give them a surprise.' Nancy made her way to the drawing room where she found Rosalind seated on the sofa with Aurelia, while Hester sat in a comfortable chair with a grim expression on her face. Tommy was standing with his back to the fire. He looked up as she entered the room and his bored look was wiped away by a welcoming smile.

'Nancy, I was going to call on you this morning.'

'Well, there's no need now, as you can see.'

'Aurelia and Lady Pentelow have arrived early,' Rosalind said calmly. 'Isn't that nice?'

'How are you, Aurelia?' Nancy asked politely. 'You look well.'

'I have recovered from my heartbreak,' Aurelia said with a sigh. 'It seems I am never going to find a man who is right for me.'

'Maybe you should stay as you are,' Hester said gloomily. 'Men are nothing but trouble.'

Tommy laughed. 'I hope you don't include me in that generalisation, Hester.'

'You are just a boy. Heaven help us when you

become a man.'

Nancy was quick to see the flicker of embarrassment in Tommy's brown eyes and she moved to his side, taking his hand in hers. 'Leave poor Tommy alone, Hester. He's the best one out of all of us.'

'Stop! You're embarrassing me,' Tommy said, grinning. 'I know my worth, but Hester is afraid I will become arrogant and boorish now I've inherited the title.'

'You are still a little boy to me and always will be.' Hester sniffed and rose from her seat. 'I suppose I'd better have a word with Mrs Jackson. We weren't expecting you until tomorrow at the earliest, Aurelia.'

'I'm sorry, Lady Carey,' Aurelia said, blushing. 'Grandmama asked Corbin to send a telegram at the last inn where we spent the night, but it seems he has forgotten.'

'It really doesn't matter.' Rosalind sent a warning glance in Hester's direction. 'We were prepared for your visit, Aurelia. You know you are always welcome.'

Aurelia sighed. 'Yes, I suppose so. To be honest, I feel like a leaf drifting in the wind with no purpose other than to fall to the ground and lie there abandoned.'

'It seems to me you should join Walter in writing poetry,' Nancy said earnestly. 'Have you thought of writing down your thoughts, Aurelia?'

'Heavens, no! I always struggled with lessons as a child. My governess quite gave up on me.'

'Well, I think you ought to speak to Walter,' Rosalind said firmly. 'You obviously have a talent with words, Aurelia. You might be interested in the theatre when it is built. Mama and Claude are quite wrapped up in their plans.'

Nancy eyed Aurelia thoughtfully. 'I know someone who might be able to explain what they are hoping to achieve. You know Nick Gibson, my land agent, Aurelia? He's going to be the theatre manager when it's built. He put on a wonderful play with my boys at the harvest supper. I think they are going to repeat it in the village hall just before Christmas. Maybe you could help.'

Aurelia brightened visibly. 'That sounds exciting.'

'I'll take you to the village hall this afternoon when the boys come out of school. Nick is going to get them to run through the play. We can sit and watch.'

'That sounds good to me,' Tommy said eagerly. 'I'll come and cheer them on.'

'Haven't you got estate duties to see to?' Hester demanded. 'Your papa worked tirelessly for Rockwood, just remember that.'

'Don't worry, Hester,' Tommy blew her a kiss, 'I saw Hodges first thing this morning and he's doing the rounds. I'll sort my desk out after luncheon and still have time to accompany Aurelia and Nancy to see the play. Does that make you happy?'

Hester huffed and folded her arms across her bosom.

'Tommy, you never cease to amaze me,' Rosalind said, smiling. 'You've taken on so much and you're doing so well.'

'I'm proud of you.' Nancy curled her fingers around his hand. She lowered her voice. 'There's something I need to speak to you about, in private. I need you to do something for me tomorrow.'

22

Nancy did not have a chance to talk to Tommy until they were seated at the back of the village hall. At the castle there had always been someone interrupting them every time they tried to speak privately, and in the end Nancy had given up. But with everything going on in the hall and the boys full of high spirits as they attempted to recreate Nick's version of *A Christmas Carol*, it was possible to snatch a few words without Aurelia hearing. It was obvious that Nick was very pleased to see Aurelia again and Aurelia looked positively cheerful. Nancy had a sudden vision of herself as a successful matchmaker. Aurelia was desperate for a husband and Nick was in need of a wife, even if he did not realise it.

Aurelia sat on the edge of her seat, clapping enthusiastically at the right time, and otherwise obviously enjoying the performance. Nancy was delighted to see the colour returning to Aurelia's previously pale cheeks and a sparkle to her hazel eyes, making her look young and pretty again. Aurelia did not suit widowhood, and Nick seemed delighted to have someone who was taking a genuine interest in his own acting ability as well as the performance of the boys.

'What is so secret you can't mention it in front of anyone?' Tommy asked in a low voice.

'Christina is setting off tomorrow for Dorrington Place. She intends to cause trouble for me.'

'But I thought you and Freddie had decided to part.'

327

'We have, or at least I have. Lord Dorrington was right at the outset. Maybe Freddie and I should have paid attention to what he said.'

'But you were in love with Freddie.'

'I was, and in a way I still am. Which is why I don't want him to think ill of me. Christina is out to make mischief and I can't allow her to do that.'

'I see. So how can I help? Do you want me to go with you?'

'No, I don't think that would be a good idea.' Nancy smiled at him. 'If I turn up with a handsome baronet at my side it might give Lord Dorrington the wrong idea. He would probably believe everything that Christina said about me.'

Tommy laughed, causing Nick to stop in the middle of a speech.

'Sorry,' Tommy said apologetically. 'Please continue.'

Nick frowned but he shrugged off the irritation and plunged back into his speech.

'I simply want you to cover for me, Tommy,' Nancy said in a whisper. 'Everybody knows everything in Rockwood, and I don't want anyone to know what I'm doing.'

'But you can't go alone, Nancy.'

'I thought I'd take Todd with me. I'm going to ask Dr Bulmer to let him have the day off.'

'Why Todd? He's just a boy.'

'He's part of my success story with the boys. He's a shining example of how helping young people to get away from the city streets and a life of crime can change their fortunes for ever. I want Lord Dorrington to see that I am a serious and responsible woman. To add to my air of respectability I will take my maid,

Flossie, so you don't have to worry about me.'

'But I do. It's several hours' drive to Dorrington Place and the weather doesn't look too promising.'

'I intend to leave first thing and I hope to be back by evening. I don't intend to stay long or wear out my welcome, if there is any.'

'How will you tackle Christina? You can hardly challenge her to pistols at dawn or call her a liar to her face.'

Nancy giggled. 'The latter is the more likely of the two. I won't put it as baldly as that but I will challenge everything she says. I can't allow her to blacken my name, Tommy.'

'Of course not. I'd rather come with you, but I'll do as you ask.'

'Shh!' Aurelia said crossly. 'Please stop chattering. I can't hear what the boys are saying.'

Nancy and Tommy exchanged conspiratorial glances.

'Sorry,' Nancy murmured. She struggled to keep a straight face and she could feel Tommy shaking with suppressed laughter. Suddenly it felt as though they were children again, keeping secrets from Hester and the rest of the adults in the family. Tommy reached out to clasp Nancy's hand and she sat in silence for the rest of the rehearsal, comfortable in his presence.

When the rehearsal finished Aurelia was keen to learn more about the prospective theatre and Nick volunteered to take her to the site, which of course she knew from the days when it was the great house, but he was eager to show her the work that had begun on the foundations.

'What will Lady Pentelow say if you go off with Nick unchaperoned?' Nancy asked mischievously.

'We will be accompanied by six young gentlemen,' Nick said, smiling.

'And I am a respectable widow.' Aurelia tossed her head. 'No one would think to question my behaviour.'

'Maybe you could get away with such a thing in Cornwall, but this is Rockwood.' Tommy winked at Nancy. 'We do things differently here.'

'I know you are teasing me,' Aurelia said crossly. 'I am simply going to walk to Nancy's old home and then Nick is going to show me the plans for the theatre and the hotel. It's so exciting. I can't believe it's happening in this quiet village.'

'You go, and never mind what the gossips say.' Nancy dug Tommy in the ribs. 'Ignore Tommy, he's teasing you. Anyway, I have an errand to run.'

'And I have to attend to the papers that I was supposed to read through this morning,' Tommy said hastily. 'I daren't let Hester know that I fibbed. I'd much rather be out and about than sitting in Papa's study going through bills and dull account books.'

'I'll see you again soon, Aurelia.' Nancy headed for the double doors. 'Don't forget what I said about Sir Bentley, Nick.'

He raised his hand in acknowledgement. 'Don't worry on that score, Nancy. I have it in hand.'

Nancy breathed in the cold, crisp air as they stepped outside. It was mid-afternoon but the sun was already low in the sky and the air smelled of smoke with a faint waft of hot bread from the bakery at the back of Hannaford's shop.

'Christmas is coming,' Nancy said thoughtfully. 'I want this to be the best Christmas ever, Tommy, despite the fact that Bertie isn't with us now.'

'Papa would want everyone to be happy. I miss him,

but I know he's up there somewhere, free from pain and hopefully united with my mother. I would have loved to have known her, Nancy.'

She laid her hand on his arm. 'Of course you would. She was obviously a lovely person or Bertie wouldn't have fallen for her, and you might not exist. Now that would be a tragedy.'

'Are you laughing at me, Nancy?'

'No, never. You are wonderful just as you are, Tommy Carey.'

He grinned. 'Sir Tommy Carey, if you please.'

'Well, Sir Tommy, I'm going to see Dr Bulmer about Todd and you'd better not follow me. You said it yourself, the gossips are always spying on what we do or say.'

'All right. I'll do as you wish, but I'm not happy about you travelling to Dorrington Place with only Todd to take care of you.' Tommy held up his hands. 'I take it back unreservedly. You are a power to be reckoned with and I am a mere mortal. I bow to your superior intelligence.'

Nancy slapped him on the wrist. 'Do be quiet, Tommy. Everything is a joke to you.'

His smile faded. 'Not everything, Nancy.'

★ ★ ★

Next morning Nancy, Todd and Flossie set off early. It was still dark and very cold, with a hard frost spiking the grass. Nancy had chosen the barouche for the journey and Flossie had placed a hot coal in a foot warmer to keep the temperature above freezing. Jones was wrapped up in a many-caped greatcoat with a scarlet muffler around his neck.

331

Nancy was about to climb into the vehicle but she hesitated, turning to Jones, who held the door for her. 'You know that Mrs Cottingham is travelling to Dorrington Place today?'

He nodded. 'I do, miss. Curtis was in the Black Dog last evening bragging about how he was going to get there in record time.'

'You didn't tell him that we were going there, too?'

'Of course not. I know better than that. Curtis is a bag of wind. He likes to boast and pretend he's better at handling a carriage and pair than he is. I could beat him hands down.'

'We're just following them, Jones. I don't want Mrs Cottingham to know.'

'I understand, miss.' Jones raised the steps and closed the carriage door before climbing onto the box.

Nancy made herself comfortable, but she was not looking forward to this journey. In fact she was dreading the confrontation between herself, Christina and Lord Dorrington, but it must be done. Christina's spiteful vendetta must be brought to an end one way or another.

Todd leaned back in his seat. 'This is the only way to travel. When I'm a doctor I'll have my own carriage.'

'You will, indeed.' Nancy smiled, momentarily forgetting the purpose of their journey. 'Dr Bulmer speaks very well of you, Todd. You can do whatever you set your mind to.'

'Thanks to you, miss. If you hadn't brought me and the boys down to Devonshire we'd probably be in prison now or starving in the gutter.'

'No, Todd, you are much too clever to have ended up like that, but you are certainly on the right path now. I'm very proud of you.'

Even in the dim light Nancy could see the flush mount on Todd's cheeks.

'Ta, miss. No one ever said that before.'

'You'll hear it again and again if you continue to work hard. Dr Bulmer thinks you would do well.'

'In two years' time the doctor says I should be apprenticed to an apothecary. It's a five-year apprenticeship and I can't practise until I'm twenty-one, but then I can apply for a licence in my own right.'

'You have plenty of time, Todd. How old are you now?'

'Fourteen, miss. Well, nearly fifteen, I think. They only had a rough idea how old I was when I was left in the orphanage. Ma died of cold and hunger shortly after I was born.'

'I'm sorry, Todd. I never thought to ask you what you knew of your family.'

He grinned. 'That's it, miss. I used to imagine my mum and dad when I was younger. I'd see them living in a fine house with a servant and a dog called Jip.'

Nancy reached out to pat his hand. 'You'll have all that in time, Todd. I know you will.'

'I'd like a puppy,' Flossie said mournfully. 'We was never allowed because a dog costs too much to feed.'

'When I get Jip you can stroke him, Flossie.' Todd leaned back in his seat and closed his eyes. 'Jip is a big dog with soft brown eyes and a yellow coat. He sleeps on my bed at night.' A gentle snore demonstrated the fact that Todd had drifted off to sleep.

Nancy covered his knees with one of the woollen travelling rugs she had had the forethought to bring with her. 'Don't wake the poor boy, Flossie. He needs his sleep.'

'Yes, miss.' Flossie curled up and closed her eyes and soon Nancy was the only one who was wide awake.

★ ★ ★

It was broad daylight when Nancy opened her eyes and the carriage had come to a halt outside an inn. Jones opened the door.

'We need to rest the horses for a while, miss. Do you wish to go inside where it's warmer?'

'Yes, it would be good to stretch my legs. I could do with a hot drink, too. Have you made enquiries as to the Cottinghams' carriage?'

'Yes, miss. They left a few minutes ago. We're not far behind. They'll have to stop again later and we'll catch up with them.'

Flossie opened her eyes and stretched. 'Are we there?'

'No, we're stopping at an inn to get something to eat and drink. You may come in with me.' Nancy leaned over to give Todd a gentle shake. 'Wake up, Todd. I'm sure you'd like a nice hot cup of tea or coffee.'

He yawned. 'Was I asleep?'

'We all dozed off.' Nancy allowed Jones to help her alight. 'We'll stop for a while and then we must press on.' She walked into the inn and was greeted by the landlord, who ushered her into a private parlour, where she was joined by Todd and Flossie. Nancy ordered tea and toast for herself but, sensing Todd's disappointment, she sent for bacon and eggs for both of her young companions. She herself was too anxious to do anything other than nibble on a slice of buttered toast.

They had just finished eating when Jones entered

the parlour. His expression was serious.

'What's the matter, Jones?' Nancy eyed him worriedly. 'Are the horses all right?'

'It's not that, miss. I was just checking on them when someone I once knew rode into the stable yard.'

'Who was it? You look as if you've seen a ghost.'

'Not a ghost, miss, but a demon from the past, you might say.'

'You're worrying me, Jones. Who is this person?'

'Jeremiah Stewer, miss. He used to work for Mrs Cottingham until he was caught stealing. She sacked him and he lost his home. His wife and children went into the workhouse because he couldn't get employment. The poor lady passed away, but the children are still there, as far as I know.'

Nancy stared at him in horror. 'He was the person suspected of burning down Greystone Park.'

'That's what I heard, miss. Stewer swore to get even with Mrs Cottingham. I didn't know him well, but I believe him capable of anything.'

'What is he doing here, Jones? Can you find out? I mean, if he is chasing after Mrs Cottingham she might be in real danger.'

'It's possible, miss. I came to tell you that the horses are fed and watered and ready to be off, but I'll see what I can find out before we leave. By the way, it might be better if he doesn't see you. I think he went into the taproom.'

'We'll be very careful.' Nancy turned to Todd and Flossie. 'I've already settled the bill with the landlord. Are you ready to go?'

Nancy led the way down the narrow corridor to the door leading into the stable yard. The sound of loud voices and laughter in the taproom echoed off the walls, but they managed to reach the carriage without meeting anyone. Jones emerged from the pub and crossed the yard to open the carriage door.

'He's boasting about his intentions, miss. Stewer was never the sharpest fellow. He's telling everyone that he's going to get even with someone who did him wrong. I can only think he means Mrs Cottingham.'

'You don't think he would actually do her harm, do you, Jones?'

'That I can't say for certain, miss. But Stewer was always inclined to violence if he was provoked. That's one of the reasons he lost his job.'

Nancy thought for a moment, although there was really no alternative. 'We must catch up with Mrs Cottingham and warn her.'

'We won't be able to do that, miss. Stewer has a good horse, which he probably stole. He has the advantage over us.'

'Nevertheless, I think we must make the effort. Christina is no friend of mine but if that man was prepared to burn the house down with her in it, he must be desperate. We'll leave right away.'

★ ★ ★

Dark, pot-bellied clouds seemed to swallow up the landscape as the horses made a valiant effort to catch up with Christina's carriage, even though Nancy knew it was an impossible task. Stewer was nowhere to be seen, and it was possible he might have cut across country, but the weather was against him. Small flakes of snow rapidly turned into a blizzard, making it difficult to see the road ahead, and soon the surface was like a sheet of glass. Jones slowed the horses to a steady trot, using his years of experience in handling the reins in all conditions. Nancy could only hope that Stewer might find the going too difficult and give up, although she had a feeling that he was driven by an inner rage and desire for revenge. Anyone who chose to set fire to a house, knowing that there were people inside, had to be more than a little unhinged. Stewer must have been waiting for a chance to wreak his revenge on Christina. Nancy shuddered at the thought of what he might do next.

The weather worsened and the horses moved slowly, keeping the heavy vehicle from sliding off the road. It seemed that they were the only people travelling, but they were in the middle of farming country with nowhere to stop and wait out the storm. It was almost as cold inside the barouche as it was outside as the hot coal in the foot warmer had turned to ash, and Flossie's teeth were chattering so loudly that Todd took off his muffler and gave it to her.

'I don't feel the cold,' he said gallantly. 'You take it, Floss.'

She wrapped the woollen scarf around her neck and sighed. 'Thank you, Todd. You are very kind.'

'Do you two know each other?' Nancy looked from one to the other. 'I didn't realise you were friends.'

'Mrs Lloyd is my aunt,' Flossie said hastily. 'I go to tea at the doctor's house on Sundays. That's how I know Todd.'

'Yes, Mrs Lloyd bakes a wonderful fruit cake, and her apple pie is delicious. I never ate so well in my life.' Todd peered out of the window. 'I don't want to worry you, miss, but it looks as if the snow is building up. We might not be able to go much further.'

'If it's bad for us it must be the same for Mrs

Cottingham and for Stewer.' Nancy clutched the seat as the carriage slithered to a halt. 'What's happened?'

Todd opened the door and leaped to the ground. 'It looks like we've caught up with them, miss.'

Nancy climbed down to the ground and her feet sank into several inches of snow where it had drifted against the hedgerow. She peered through the veil of snowflakes and realised with a shock that the carriage ahead had turned over and was hanging precariously over a wooden gate. She could just make out the shape of a man, who was trying to wrench the door open, his efforts hampered by Curtis, with Jones scrambling through the snow to his aid. Before Nancy could stop him, Todd leaped into the fray and everyone was slipping and sliding in a way that might have been comical if Christina's plaintive cries coming from the interior of the carriage had not sent a shiver down Nancy's spine.

'What are you men doing?' Nancy demanded, lifting her skirts above her ankles as she trod carefully through the snow. 'Get her out of there.'

'I'll leave her to freeze to death,' Stewer said angrily. 'She's the reason my wife died and my nippers were taken from me.'

'Leaving Mrs Cottingham to die won't bring your wife back, Stewer.' Nancy moved closer. 'Unharness the horses before they kick the carriage to pieces and damage themselves. We won't get anywhere without them.'

Curtis gave Stewer a shove that sent him sliding off the upturned carriage onto the ground. 'I'll see to the horses, miss. Jones, you deal with this maniac.'

Jones grabbed Stewer by the collar of his greatcoat. 'We're all in danger, Stewer. Forget your grievances

338

for once or we'll all die right here and your children will remain in the workhouse for the rest of their lives.'

'Get me out of here. I think I've broken my leg,' Christina wailed from the interior of the carriage.

'Serves you right, you heartless bitch.' Stewer punched the side of the coach and yelped with pain.

'That's right,' Nancy said crossly. 'Break your hand and you'll be no use to anyone, least of all yourself. Stop arguing and work together to get Mrs Cottingham out of the carriage. If we can right it, we can all move on. If not, we're stuck here until help arrives and that might take hours or even days if the snow doesn't cease.'

Jones grunted. 'You heard what Miss Greystone said, Curtis, and you, too, Stewer. You are not helping your case by behaving like this.'

'I ain't going to clink. They can't prove I set fire to her house.'

'You've just condemned yourself out of your own mouth,' Nancy said sharply. 'Now get on with it. Break the door if you must, but get her out.'

'I don't need your help, Nancy.' Christina's voice broke on a sob.

'Oh, be quiet, you silly woman.' Nancy beckoned to Todd. 'Give them a hand, please. We all need to get to some kind of shelter or we'll freeze to death.' She stood back while the men battled with the damaged door and eventually managed to wrench it open.

Todd leaned into the carriage. 'Can you move, missis?'

'No, you stupid fellow. I told you, I've broken my leg.' Christina's voice sounded plaintive but also impatient.

Nancy climbed onto one of the wheels and leaned

over to look inside. She could see Christina sprawled at an awkward angle on what was now the bottom of the coach. 'I think Todd had better come down and see if he can help you, Christina.'

'I don't want one of your street urchins poking me about.'

'Todd has been working for Dr Bulmer. He is the only one of us with any medical knowledge.'

'I splinted a kid's arm when she fell out of a tree,' Todd said warily. 'I never done a leg.'

'Come now, boy, bones are bones.' Curtis pulled some strips of wood from the shattered undercarriage. 'Take these and tie them round the afflicted limb.'

Flossie had emerged from the carriage and she slipped off her red flannel petticoat. 'This will do if you tear it into bandages, Todd.'

'Thank you, Floss. You've been paying attention when your auntie gives us lectures on what to do in an emergency.'

Flossie giggled. 'Yes, I'd make a good nurse, but that's not for someone like me.'

'I'm dying down here,' Christina called plaintively. 'I might be bleeding to death, for all you know.'

Nancy took the petticoat and began tearing it into strips. 'Here, Todd. Take this and see what you can do. When she's reasonably comfortable Stewer and Jones will have to lift her out.'

'I ain't helping her,' Stewer said bitterly. 'She's a monster.'

'You will do as I say.' Nancy eyed him coldly. 'You aren't in a position to argue. Help Mrs Cottingham and it's possible your sentence might be reduced.'

Todd lowered himself into the carriage. 'I might need a hand. Can you get down here, Flossie?'

'Yes, of course, but you'll need to catch me.'

'Will you please stop discussing everything,' Christina cried furiously. 'Get me out of here before I freeze to death or die from the pain.'

Jones pulled a flask from his pocket and handed it to Flossie. 'It's brandy. Give her a dose of that and maybe she'll shut up.'

Flossie disappeared into the dark interior of the wrecked carriage and there was nothing Nancy could do other than to wait. Christina's angry cries turned into muffled screams and then silence.

Flossie held her arms up to be pulled from the carriage. 'She's fainted. Todd says now's the time to move her.'

Nancy had been pacing up and down, despite the slippery conditions, but it was necessary to keep warm. 'Jones, you'd better go down first. Stewer, you stay outside, ready to help.'

'Why can't her coachman do it?' Stewer demanded.

'He's been trying to catch the horses,' Nancy said sharply. 'If you'd been paying attention you would have seen them gallop into the field the moment he released them.'

Curtis returned, panting. 'I'm sorry, miss. I couldn't catch them. They've taken fright.'

Nancy wrapped her arms around herself, taking a deep breath. 'We're stuck here, Curtis. The road is too narrow to turn our carriage and Mrs Cottingham can't ride. We need to find shelter until the storm passes, and even then the roads will be treacherous.'

'When I was chasing the horses I saw a building down the lane at the side of the field. Maybe it's a farmhouse or the like. We could make a stretcher from the carriage door and carry the mistress. Even if it turns out to be a barn it would be better than nothing.'

'Yes, you're right. And if we unharness my horses we can take them with us and when the storm abates someone can ride for help.'

Jones lifted Flossie from the carriage and set her down on the ground.

'Thanks, Mr Jones.' Flossie turned to Nancy with a worried frown. 'Her leg looks really bad, miss. Todd's done what he can, but she's going to create something terrible when she comes to.'

'Then we must get her out now.' Nancy gave Stewer a push in the right direction. 'You know what you have to do.'

Grumbling beneath his breath, Stewer climbed back onto the carriage, followed by Jones, and they lowered themselves into the interior. Somehow, with Todd's help, they managed to extricate Christina from the wrecked carriage and Curtis helped them to strap her onto the carriage door. In a swirling, blinding blizzard they all struggled to reach the building that Curtis had described. It was hard going and Nancy had lost all the feeling in her feet and hands as they approached what must once have been a grand house. Only half of it remained standing, and the part that was left seemed to have been abandoned.

'It looks like something from a story by Mrs Radcliffe,' Flossie said, shivering dramatically. 'I read *The Mysteries of Udolpho* when I was in bed with scarlet fever. Dr Bulmer let me stay in his spare bedroom so that Auntie could look after me.'

Nancy took a deep breath. 'Well, that was fiction, Flossie. This is a deserted house — at least, it looks as if there is no one at home — and it's shelter. Flossie, never mind the gothic stories, try the front door.'

23

Flossie slipped and slithered her way to the door and lifted the latch. 'It's not locked, miss.'

'Then we have a roof over our heads. The place certainly appears to be deserted. Curtis, I leave you and Stewer to see to the horses when we've found somewhere to lie Mrs Cottingham down.'

'Very well, Miss Greystone.'

Nancy walked past Flossie, who was peering nervously into the gloomy interior. It might be early afternoon, but the storm had made it seem like dusk and the smell of rot and general decay emanated from the deathly quiet building. Nancy stood in the large entrance hall, hoping she looked more confident than she was feeling, although inwardly she was quaking. The floorboards creaked and cobwebs hung from the ceiling. A staircase disappeared into the darkness above the wide expanse of hallway. As her eyes grew accustomed to the gloom, Nancy could see a door to the right, which she opened and found herself in a large room, empty of furniture apart from a sofa and a table. She held the door wide open.

'There's somewhere to lay Mrs Cottingham down in here. Maybe we could light a fire.'

Stewer and Jones carried the makeshift stretcher into the room. Christina had regained consciousness and, with it, the ability to moan, grumble and curse the people who were trying to help her. Stewer had twice threatened to tip her off into the snow, but warnings from Nancy had kept him more or less in order. However, Nancy knew that it was dangerous to push him too far. His hatred for Christina was patently simmering beneath the surface and might erupt at any moment, but Nancy had to keep him calm. They needed to be united against the weather, the cold and the inevitable pangs of hunger they would feel if the snow grew any deeper and they could not reach anywhere to purchase supplies.

She sent Stewer with Jones to catch the horses and find them shelter. Curtis seemed devoted to Christina and obviously had a score to settle with Stewer, so Nancy did her best to keep them apart. When Jones and Stewer had left the room, she sent Curtis to explore the rest of the house and he went off willingly enough. It was a difficult situation for all, and one that might end in a fight if not handled delicately.

Todd had gone back to the carriage and had rescued two of the lamps, which he brought into the room and lit using a Vesta from a packet that Curtis found in his pocket. There was little they could do for Christina other than try to make her comfortable on the rather lumpy sofa, and cover her with rugs also brought from the carriage. However, nothing they did seemed to please her and she continued to complain bitterly in between groans of pain. Nancy felt like telling her that, had she stayed at home with her family, instead of careering about the country bent on making trouble, none of this would have happened. However, she managed to hold her tongue and left the room, taking Flossie with her.

They went in search of fuel, lamp oil or even a few candles. They headed towards the rear of the building and discovered several rooms leading off a long corridor, all of which would have been used for the storage or preparation of food, or simply for keeping brushes, mops and buckets. There was a linen cupboard and what appeared to be a butler's pantry, but no sign of candles or lamp oil. The kitchen was huge, with a very old cast-iron range, which was in desperate need of a clean. The cupboards were bare, although a tall dresser was full of slightly chipped and cracked china that had probably been used in the servants' hall. However, that part of the house seemed to have been destroyed by fire and the doors on that side of the house had been boarded up.

Having exhausted the kitchen, Nancy went outside into the yard and made a foray into the tumbledown outbuildings, which provided a small quantity of coal and a well-stocked log store. She and Flossie filled wicker baskets they had found abandoned in a cupboard and took them back to the room where Todd laid a fire using twists of old newspaper that had been used to plug a broken windowpane.

'I'm thirsty,' Christina moaned. 'Water.'

Flossie placed the basket of coal on the floor next to Todd, who was on his knees in front of the grate. 'I saw a pump in the yard, although it might be frozen. If it is I could scoop up some snow. We can melt it when we get the fire going.'

'Good idea,' Nancy said approvingly. 'I saw a couple of buckets in the cupboard where we found the baskets. Clean snow will be all right.'

Flossie hesitated in the doorway. 'I don't like this house. Can Todd come with me, miss? I'm scared there might be something or someone waiting to jump out at me.'

Todd rose to his feet. 'You are a cowardy custard,' he said, laughing. 'But I will come with you. I want to take a look around myself.'

'Thank you, Todd.' Flossie beamed at him as she left the room with him following close behind.

Nancy went to the window and gazed out. 'The snow is falling thick and fast, Christina. I'm afraid we will be here overnight.'

'I need a doctor. That stupid boy doesn't know what he's doing.'

Nancy walked over to stand by the sofa. She lifted the blankets and examined the rough splint that Todd had made. 'He's done as good a job as any of us could. Better, I'd say. I'm afraid you will just have to try and bear it until we can get help.'

'Where's the water? Is there a cellar here? Maybe the last owner kept a few bottles of wine stashed away. Anything would do to help the pain.'

'Perhaps Curtis will find something,' Nancy said hopefully. 'He's gone upstairs to see what accommodation there is. We will have to make ourselves as comfortable as possible.'

Christina closed her eyes. 'Why don't you do something useful? Or are you too much a lady now to soil your hands by putting coal on the fire?'

Nancy backed away. 'I know your leg must be painful, Christina, but don't take it out on me. You are the one who caused this to happen, so please stop moaning.'

'I didn't cause the carriage to come off the road. I didn't choose to be in agony, lying on a couch with the springs sticking in my back. And I'm hungry. Isn't there a kitchen where you could light a fire and cook something? You were a servant once, weren't you?'

Nancy threw several small lumps of coal on the fire. 'You are a mean and spiteful woman, Christina Cottingham. You should be thankful that we are all trying to do our best in such difficult circumstances.' Nancy left the room without giving Christina a chance to respond and she made her way to the kitchen. Todd and Flossie came in through the scullery, laughing like children as they hefted two buckets brimming with snow. It was obvious from the state of them that they had been throwing snowballs at each other and their cheeks were flushed from the cold. Their happy faces made Nancy feel more cheerful and she smiled.

'Christina has said one thing that made sense. I should try to light the range and we can melt the snow in a pan. Also, if we search the larders we might find some tea or even coffee beans. Flossie, will you do that, and you, Todd, could you fetch some more coal and kindling if you can find any? I'll clear out the grate and see if I can get the fire going in the range.'

Flossie dumped her pail on the floor beside Nancy. 'I'm starving. I wish there was something to eat.'

'I'll see what I can find, miss,' Todd said eagerly. He retraced his steps through the scullery and a cold draught whistled round Nancy's ears as he opened and closed the outside door.

Flossie began searching the cupboards while Nancy rolled up her sleeves and cleared the ashes from the grate. When Todd reappeared with coal, kindling and more logs, Nancy managed to light the fire. The warm glow suffused the kitchen in light, but it also cast moving shadows on the ceiling and walls.

'We won't have to stay the night, will we, miss?' Flossie asked anxiously.

'I'm afraid so, Flossie. We'll just have to make the

best of it.' Nancy picked up a soot-blackened kettle and filled it with snow before setting it down on the hob. 'We'll have hot water even if we haven't any tea.'

Todd had left them again but he returned carrying a wooden trug filled with carrots, a large turnip and some parsnips. 'Look what I found in a shed behind the log store. These were hidden under a pile of straw, and there's more if we need them. I'm no cook but I reckon we could make these into soup.'

Nancy took the trug from him. 'Todd, you are a genius. Look in all the drawers and see if you can find a paring knife, or anything I can use to peel these vegetables. Were there any potatoes?'

'I don't know. It was too dark in the shed to see, but I did spot some oil lamps in the old cow shed. I'll need a hand to bring all the things in before it gets dark. The snow is getting very thick out there.'

Flossie had been sweeping out the larder and she gave a cry of delight. 'I've found a tin with some tea in it.' She sniffed the contents. 'It's a bit old but it will make a brew.'

'There are some rusty knives in the drawer over here,' Todd added. 'We'll eat tonight. That's for certain.'

'Jones and Stewer should be back soon, if they've managed to catch the horses, and if Curtis finds there are beds in the rooms upstairs we might get some sleep.'

'I'm not sleeping on my own,' Flossie said nervously.

'I'd offer to share your bed, but I don't think your auntie would approve.' Todd struck a pose and grinned.

'She most certainly would not.' Nancy tried not to

348

laugh. At nearly fifteen, Todd was a good-looking boy, with a mischievous sense of humour. She handed him the bucket, having emptied the snow into a large stew pan. 'Will you get some more snow, please, Todd?'

'I will, and when Curtis shows his face I'll need his help to bring in more vegetables. At the rate the snow is falling and drifting we might not be able to get out of the door in the morning.' Todd winked at Flossie and sauntered out of the kitchen.

Nancy passed a knife to Flossie, who was blushing furiously. 'Help me with the vegetables and we'll have a hot meal this evening.'

'Yes, miss.'

'And, Flossie, I wouldn't take Todd too seriously if I were you. He's just a boy.'

'I know that, miss. But I do like him.'

Nancy sighed. 'Yes, I think Todd is going to break a few hearts before he gets much older.' She began paring the vegetables and was thankful for the time she had spent in the castle kitchen when she was growing up. Mrs Jackson had taught her the rudiments of cooking and for the first time it was proving useful.

They worked in silence until all the vegetables were prepared, cut into chunks and added to the pan, which was now bubbling merrily on the hob. Todd returned and at the same time Curtis strode into the kitchen.

Todd placed a pail filled with snow on the table. 'Mr Curtis, I need your help. I've found oil lamps and a sack of potatoes in one of the outbuildings, but the storm is getting worse. I was almost blown off my feet.'

Curtis made for the door. 'Come on then, boy. We'll see what we can retrieve.'

'Before you go out there, what is it like upstairs?'

Nancy asked eagerly. 'Are there any beds?'

He nodded. 'Yes, a couple, miss. But it looks as if someone has been sleeping in one of the attic rooms.'

'They aren't still there, are they?'

'There wasn't anyone in the room, that's all I can say.'

Nancy suppressed a shiver. 'Perhaps it was a vagrant who has moved on. Heaven knows, I wouldn't begrudge anyone a bed for the night in this weather.'

'It could be a villain,' Flossie said in a hoarse whisper. 'Or a murderer.'

Todd rolled his eyes. 'Are you coming, Mr Curtis?'

'Don't worry, ladies,' Curtis said, puffing out his chest. 'We'll see that no harm comes to you.' He strutted off, following Todd into the scullery.

'I don't like it, miss.' Flossie shivered dramatically. 'What if there is someone else living in this old house? What if it's a ghost?'

Nancy laughed. 'I don't believe in ghosts, and if there is someone they are probably more frightened of us than we are of them. It's only temporary, Flossie. I expect the weather will clear by morning and we'll be able to get help.'

Flossie clasped her hands together. 'If we get out of here in one piece I promise I will never be rude to Mrs Banks again.'

Nancy could not find a teapot in the dresser but there was a large jug and she used that instead. 'Have a cup of tea, Flossie. There's no milk or sugar but it's hot and it looks like tea. I'll take a cup to Mrs Cottingham.'

Flossie took a mug from the dresser. 'Better watch out in case she throws it at you, miss. I've heard she does that sometimes.'

'Where on earth did you hear such a thing?'

'Servants talk, miss. Naming no names.'

Nancy shrugged and filled a cup with the bitter brew, which she took to the front parlour. She opened the door and froze in horror to see an unkempt figure leaning over Christina, who was gaping at the man, white-faced and open-mouthed with a scream seemingly frozen in her throat.

'Who are you?' Nancy demanded.

The man raised his head. His bushy grey hair, streaked with white, hung down over his face, which was already half-covered in a beard and moustache, and the only discernible features were his pale blue eyes, shining like agates in the lamplight.

'What's the matter with her?' he croaked.

'Get him away from me,' Christina cried hysterically. 'He's a madman.'

Nancy held the steaming cup of tea out to the man. 'Would you like some tea, sir? I'm afraid there's no milk or sugar, but it's nice and hot.'

He peered at her from beneath shaggy brows. 'Where'd you find that?' He lumbered over to her and took the tea, gulping the hot liquid down with a sigh. 'I haven't had a hot drink in ages.'

Christina half raised herself on her elbow. 'Get him out of here, Nancy. He's going to murder us all.'

Nancy met the man's steady gaze and she knew instantly that this was untrue. 'Who are you, sir? You are not a tramp, I can tell by your voice.'

'Circumstances forced me to this way of life, miss. I was once a respected surgeon.'

'He's mad,' Christina said in a low voice. 'Don't let him near me.'

'Are you really a surgeon, sir?' Nancy held his gaze

351

and something in his eyes convinced her that he was telling the truth before he even answered her.

'I was, miss. As you see, I am in straitened circumstances.'

'Is this your house, by any chance?'

'It was a fine home until the mob tried to burn it to the ground. My wife and children left me. I took to drink.'

'I am Nancy Greystone.' Nancy held out her hand. 'Might I know your name, sir?'

'Rowland Madden. Although I've been out of society for so many years I'd almost forgotten my identity.'

'This lady hurt her leg when her carriage overturned. Can you help her?'

Madden shook his head. 'I told you, I don't practise any more.'

'But you could help Mrs Cottingham. Can you at least make her comfortable until we can get her to a hospital?'

'I'll take a look, but I told you I am no longer in the medical profession.'

'I'm sorry, Mr Madden, but I don't believe you,' Nancy said firmly. 'Once a medical man, always a medical man. Please do something to alleviate her pain.'

'What's going on?' Flossie rushed into the room, followed by Todd and Curtis.

'Don't touch the mistress.' Curtis advanced on Rowland, hands clenched into fists.

'Stop, all of you,' Nancy cried angrily. 'This man says he is a surgeon and I'm inclined to believe him. He might be able to help Mrs Cottingham.'

Madden held up his hand. 'Stand back, please.' He lifted the blanket from Christina's leg, ignoring her feeble protests, and very gently he examined the injured limb.

The silence was broken by the door being flung open and Jones rushed into the room, followed by Jeremiah Stewer.

'Who is he?' Jones demanded. 'What's he doing, Miss Greystone?'

'Please be quiet,' Nancy said crossly. 'This gentleman is trying to help Mrs Cottingham.'

Jones stood back, glaring suspiciously at Madden. 'We've caught the horses, miss. They're in the old stables.'

Nancy nodded, but she was concentrating on Madden as he undid the makeshift bandages and took off the splint.

Christina shuddered and gasped with pain. 'Don't touch me.'

Nancy took her hand. 'He's going to help you, Christina. He's a medical man.'

Madden looked up. 'It's a displaced tibial shaft fracture. I need to align the bones before they do any damage to the surrounding veins and tissue. I need some laths and more bandages in order to make a better splint, although whoever did this one did a good job.'

'That was me, sir,' Todd said shyly.

Madden shot him a sideways glance. 'You did well, boy.'

'Will somebody please look for the things the doctor needs?' Nancy grimaced with pain as Christina clutched her hand in a vice-like grip.

Flossie hurried to the window and pulled down what was left of the curtain, which she tore into strips.

'I'll see what I can find.' Jones backed towards the

door. 'Come and help me, Stewer.'

'I'm not doing anything to help her.' Stewer spat the words out venomously.

'In that case you won't get any food tonight,' Nancy said coldly. 'Go with them, please, Mr Curtis. If Stewer gives you any trouble, tie him to a chair so that he can't do anything stupid.'

'Here, who are you to give orders?' Stewer demanded.

'I'm the person who is in charge here.' Nancy met his narrowed gaze with a steady look. 'Challenge it if you like, but you won't eat and you'll spend a cold night sitting upright in a rickety chair.'

Grumbling, Stewer was dragged away with the joint efforts of Jones and Curtis. Todd was about to leave but Madden called him back. 'You stay, boy. You seem to be a useful fellow to have around.'

Todd moved closer. 'I want to be a doctor, sir. But maybe I'd like to be a surgeon, too.'

'It's a hard profession, boy. I lost everything when a very important patient died under the knife. I was accused of murder and sent for trial.'

Christina uttered a faint cry and closed her eyes. 'I'm going to die.'

'No, madam. I can assure you that the procedure I am about to attempt is very simple and straight-forward. You will feel much more comfortable when it's done.'

'Have you any spirits she could sip to ease the pain, Mr Madden?' Nancy asked anxiously. She could see that Christina was in agony as well as being terrified.

Madden pulled a small silver hip flask from some-where beneath his shabby greatcoat. 'It's my last drop of cognac, but she needs it more than I do.' He took out the stopper and held it to Christina's lips.

She drank the fiery liquid, coughing and spluttering, but he made her finish what was in the flask and stood back to wait for it to take effect. Within minutes Christina's head was lolling to one side and she was snoring gently.

Curtis returned with some laths they had found, but he reported that Stewer had grabbed Jones's greatcoat and had bolted out of the front door. Jones gave chase but returned quickly, covered in snow, and apparently fuming.

'Never mind, Stewer,' Nancy said vaguely. 'He won't get far in this weather and he's really not our concern. In fact, I feel safer with him out of the way.'

Madden took the strips of curtain material that Flossie had wound into neat rolls and laid them beside the laths, which he had sorted according to size. He turned to Todd.

'I need you to assist me, boy.'

'Yes, sir. What shall I do?'

'Hold the lady's head and shoulders. Try to keep her from moving. I'm going to align the bones. I'll do it quickly but she will struggle, so don't let her go.'

'What can I do?' Nancy asked anxiously.

'Stand back, please, miss. I need more room.' Madden traced the line of the bone with the tip of his finger. He waited until Todd had stationed himself at Christina's head.

'I must do this, ma'am. You will be all the better for it.'

It was over in a few seconds. An expert movement by Madden aligned the broken bone and he bandaged the leg quickly and expertly, adding a splint to immobilise the lower leg. Nancy glanced anxiously at

Christina, who was unnaturally quiet. She had fainted from the pain. Todd placed a tattered cushion under her head and moved away.

'That was wonderful, mister. I'd like to work with bones.'

Madden smiled. 'It's a useful skill to have, my boy.' He picked up his hip flask and shook it. 'Now I wish I hadn't been so generous. The cellar is empty, and I cannot offer you a glass of wine or anything to eat. It's a long time since any food was prepared in the kitchen.'

Nancy covered Christina with the blankets. 'I'm making vegetable soup, sir. If you would care to join us it would be our honour.'

'I haven't had a hot meal for so long that I can hardly remember the last time.'

'How have you been surviving?' Nancy asked, frowning.

'There is a farm adjacent to my land. I treated the farmer's little daughter when she had diphtheria and the child survived. The farmer's wife has kept me supplied with bread, cheese and milk ever since. All done in secret, of course. I am *persona non grata* in the village.'

'What did he say?' Flossie nudged Todd.

Nancy stepped in quickly. 'Flossie, Mrs Cottingham is coming round. Will you fetch her a cup of tea? Add a little hot water from the kettle if it's getting too cold.'

'Yes, miss.' Flossie hesitated. 'Will you come with me, Todd?'

'Your bogeyman is here, Floss,' Todd said, laughing. 'All due respect, sir. Flossie has a good imagination.'

'I believe the locals put it about that the house is

haunted and, to be honest, I prefer it like that. It keeps the curious away. You are welcome to stay here until the snow clears, but please don't tell anyone about me.' Madden backed away from the sofa. 'I'd better retire to my attic room.'

'Come on, Floss. Let's get the tea.' Todd led her out of the room, closing the door behind them.

'Of course we won't tell anyone about you, if that's what you want,' Nancy said quietly. 'But please stay and eat with us. It's not much, but I would be very interested to hear your story . . . if you feel like telling me, of course.'

Madden glanced round at Curtis and Jones, who both looked away. 'I'm unused to company.'

Christina was coming round and she attempted to sit up. Nancy hurried to her side. 'Stay still, Christina. The doctor has set your broken bone, but you have to keep your weight off it for a while. Isn't that right, Mr Madden?'

He nodded. 'Rest now is the answer, ma'am. If someone can make you a pair of crutches you will be able to get around, but don't put any weight on the afflicted limb yet.'

Christina stared at him as if he were some fearful apparition. 'Who — who are you?'

'It doesn't matter, ma'am. Just forget you ever saw me. I do not exist.' Madden strode out of the room, leaving everyone staring after him.

'He's an odd one,' Jones muttered.

'I dunno how he can live like a hermit in this tumbledown place.' Curtis ventured closer to the sofa. 'Can I do anything for you, madam?'

'Just go away. I don't feel very well. Where's that tea you promised me, Nancy?'

Nancy helped her to a more comfortable position. 'Flossie will bring it in a minute. Then we'll let you get some rest before dinner.'

Christina brightened considerably. 'Do you mean we have food?'

'It's only vegetable soup, but be grateful for that. We're lucky to have anything.' Nancy shooed Curtis and Jones out of the room. 'Go and sit in the kitchen. It's getting nice and warm.'

Having banked up the fire, Nancy left Christina dozing on the sofa while she went to the kitchen to check on the soup. Flossie passed her in the doorway carrying a cup of tea very carefully.

'I think Mrs Cottingham may have gone to sleep, Flossie. Just leave it on the floor by the sofa where she can reach it if she wakes.'

'Yes, miss.' Flossie glanced behind her to see if Todd was following. 'Come on, Todd. I don't like this creepy house and you've got the lantern.'

24

That night Nancy slept by the fire on a mattress that Curtis and Jones had brought down from one of the bedrooms. Flossie lay a few feet away on a palliasse and Christina dozed fitfully on the sofa. Stewer had not returned, which was something of a relief, but Nancy could not help wondering how he would survive in such adverse weather conditions. When she awoke next morning she went to draw back what was left of the curtains, looking out onto a white world with the snow drifting up to the windowsill.

Flossie and Christina were still asleep, although Nancy had heard Christina stirring and groaning in the night. She had felt sorry for her but there had been nothing she could do to help, and eventually Christina had fallen asleep. Nancy slipped on her boots and was about to go to the kitchen when she heard someone pounding on the front door. She left the parlour and stood for a moment in the ice-cold hallway, wondering whether to answer the urgent summons. She was joined by Jones, bleary-eyed with sleep, his hair ruffled and his clothes crumpled, as if he, too, had slept fully dressed.

'Stand back, miss,' Jones said firmly. 'I'll go.'

'Be careful what you say to whoever it is. Don't mention Mr Madden.' Nancy waited anxiously for Jones to wrench open the front door. As he did so a pile of snow fell onto the floor.

'It's a constable, miss,' Jones called over his shoulder.

Nancy hurried to his side. 'Good morning, officer.'

'Are those your vehicles abandoned in the lane, miss?'

'Yes. As you will have seen, there was an accident and we were forced to seek shelter.'

The constable glanced over her shoulder. 'It wouldn't be my choice of somewhere to stay.'

'I hope we aren't trespassing,' Nancy said innocently. 'We really had no choice last evening.'

'I doubt it, miss. The old house has been uninhabited for at least four years. After the court case the owner simply disappeared.'

Nancy could see that the constable was eager to relate the scandal surrounding Madden, but she was in no mood to encourage him. Besides which, an icy blast was sending flurries of powdered snow into the entrance hall.

'Are the roads passable?' Nancy said hastily. 'We need to be on our way.'

'No, miss. Not really. I had great difficulty in getting here on horseback.'

'When the weather allows, would it be possible to have help righting the overturned carriage?' Nancy asked eagerly.

'I'll see to it, miss. It will be done as soon as possible. In the meantime, are you all right?'

'Yes, but we have very little food. Is there a farm we could get to, even allowing for the snowdrifts?'

'There's Baileys' farm. I'm on my way there now to check on the family.' The constable stepped back, but he hesitated. 'By the way, we caught a man trying to break into a cottage last evening. Do you know anyone by the name of Jeremiah Stewer?'

Jones was about to say something, but Nancy held up her hand. 'It's all right, Jones. The man you speak of is the cause of our problems, Constable. I think you'll find that the police in Exeter are looking for him.'

The constable tipped his cap. 'Thank you, miss. I had a feeling about that one. Much obliged to you. I'll be off then.'

'Just a minute, officer,' Jones said urgently. 'If you are going to the farm perhaps I could ride with you. Maybe they will sell me some cheese and eggs, that sort of thing.'

'Have you your horse to hand, mister?'

'I stabled them in a barn last evening.'

'Best fetch a mount then. I'll wait a while, but please hurry. I have rounds to make.'

Nancy stood aside. 'Come in out of the cold, Constable. Jones will be very quick.'

'A few minutes, miss. That's all I can spare.'

Jones hurried off in the direction of the back yard and Nancy went to fetch her reticule, leaving the constable standing awkwardly in the hall. Nancy was quick to note that he seemed ill at ease in the house and he kept glancing towards the staircase as if expecting to see an apparition gliding down the stairs. She could not altogether blame him. Madden had done a good job in making everyone believe his ruined home was haunted. It had given him the privacy he craved and might even have saved his life. She was eager to know the whole story, but was reluctant to probe into matters he obviously wanted to put behind him. She found her reticule and ran to the kitchen, where Todd was poking the embers of the fire. He looked up and smiled.

'I've filled two pails with snow, miss. Who was that at the door? I'd have come but Mr Jones beat me to it.'

'It's a police constable. He's braved the weather to see if we are the owners of the vehicles, and he's going to take Jones to the farm to fetch food for us. Will you give Jones this money and tell him to buy whatever food they have for sale. He's gone to the stables to get a horse.'

Todd replaced the poker in the hod and took the money from her outstretched hand. 'He'll need a saddle. I saw one in the barn when I was searching for kindling.'

'Better tell him, Todd. I don't imagine Jones could ride bareback, especially in these conditions.' Nancy smiled at the image, and Todd was laughing as he left the kitchen.

Flossie and Christina were still asleep, even with all the noise, and Curtis was nowhere to be seen.

Nancy decided to brave the upstairs of the house and pay a call on Madden. It was only polite to let him know that they would have to extend their stay until the carriage was righted and the roads clear enough to make travel possible.

She made her way upstairs to the top floor, creeping past the room where she could hear Curtis snoring loudly. The old house did not seem so creepy in daylight — it just appeared to be sad and neglected. She came to a long corridor in the attic and she knocked on each door until she received an answer. She entered cautiously and found Madden huddled in blankets in front of a desultory fire. The attic room was sparsely furnished with a single bed, a chest and two chairs. A rag rug on the floor was the only splash of colour.

'Mr Madden, I'm sorry to disturb you.'

He peered at her over the folds of the rug. 'What can I do for you, Miss Greystone? Is the patient worse?'

'No, sir. As a matter of fact she's sleeping quite peacefully. I think she was bothered by pain in the night, but she's calm enough now.'

'What can I do for you?'

'Nothing, as it happens. I was wondering if you would like to come downstairs and have a cup of very weak tea.'

'Who was at the door just now?'

'A police constable called to check on us. It seems he realised this was the nearest place to shelter after the accident.'

'You didn't mention me, I hope.'

'No, of course not. He's taken Jones to the farm to purchase some eggs and cheese.'

'They won't say anything. The Baileys have saved my life.'

Nancy hesitated. 'I don't wish to pry, but surely surgery is always a risk. Why did everyone blame you for something you could not prevent?'

Madden heaved a deep sigh. 'She was a young woman, the mother of four boys. I tried to save her and the baby but sadly I could not. Her husband blamed me, and so did the rest of the village. My wife left me and took our children with her. I received death threats and then someone set my house on fire. But for a sudden storm and torrential rain the whole building would have gone up in flames.'

'That's terrible, but why did you stay here? Surely you could move on and practise somewhere else?'

'The family charged me with gross negligence. I appeared in court and although the judge dismissed

363

the case my reputation was ruined. It was a dreadful time, and one I would prefer to forget.'

'But you stay here, anyway.'

'I prefer it this way. Now, if you don't mind, I'd rather be left alone. You are welcome to remain here as long as you like, but please respect my desire for solitude.'

Nancy nodded. 'I am sorry to have intruded, but thank you for confiding in me.' She left him, closing the door softly behind her, and made her way slowly downstairs to the front parlour.

Christina was sitting on the sofa, propped up with pillows taken from the upstairs rooms.

Flossie jumped to her feet. 'Oh, miss. We didn't know where you'd gone. I thought the bogeyman might have got you.'

Nancy laughed. 'Really? Surely you don't believe that nonsense, Flossie? As a matter of fact I went upstairs to find Mr Madden and let him know that we are having to wait here until it's possible for us to leave.'

'He's a strange man,' Christina said wearily. 'But he has made my leg feel much easier. It only hurts if I try to move in certain ways. Anyway, I'm starving. That soup you made last evening wasn't exactly substantial, Nancy.'

'I'm sorry about that, but I used what little we had. However, Jones has ridden to the farm and hopes to bring back supplies, so we should at least have something to eat. I'll make some tea. That will have to do until he returns.' Nancy did not wait to hear what Christina had to say to that. She went to the kitchen where Todd was seated by the range with his feet up on the rail. He gave a guilty start and stood up.

'I'm sorry, miss. I've done all I can. There's water

boiling in the kettle and the snow in the buckets is melting fast.'

'It's all right, Todd. Thank you for doing all that. There's not much we can do until Jones returns. Have you seen Curtis?'

'He's out with the horses, miss. He said he was going to feed them the rest of the carrots.'

'That's quite all right. The poor things need food as much as we do. I'll make some tea and we can at least have a hot drink. Let's hope Jones returns soon because we're all hungry.'

Nancy set about making tea in the old jug, and when it had brewed she took a cup to Christina, expecting the usual string of complaints. However, Christina drank the tea thirstily, saying nothing.

Flossie had stationed herself by the window and she jumped up with a cry. 'There's Mr Jones. He's coming.'

Nancy snatched the empty cup from Christina. 'Let's hope he's brought us something to eat. Anything would be good.'

'I'm fading away,' Christina said weakly. She collapsed onto the pillows, closing her eyes. 'Do hurry up and bring me some food.'

'Come with me, Flossie.' Nancy opened the door. 'We'll soon find out if we're going to eat today.' She glanced over her shoulder. 'And if you complain again you'll get nothing, Christina. It would give my ears a rest if you did fade away. At least you'd be quiet for five minutes.' Nancy headed out of the room and raced to the kitchen.

Jones had tethered the horse to the pump while he brought in a bulging sack and hefted it onto the kitchen table.

'That looks promising,' Todd said eagerly. He untied the sack and tipped the contents onto the table. 'Cheese, eggs, butter and a big loaf.' He picked it up and sniffed ecstatically. 'It's still warm.'

'Nice woman, that farmer's wife,' Jones said casually. 'I told her our problem and she couldn't do enough to help. She even sold me this old coat, seeing as how that villain Stewer took mine. Mind you, she charged plenty, but you said not to worry about the cost.'

Nancy could not recall saying anything of the sort, but the aroma of the warm bread and the sight of a wheel of cheese, as well as a box of eggs cradled in straw, was enough to make her dizzy with anticipation. 'You did well, Jones. Thank you.'

He puffed out his chest. 'There's a gallon can of milk tied to the saddle. I'll go and get it now.' He hesitated by the door and took a tightly wrapped poke out of his pocket. 'And some tea. Mrs Bailey was most helpful, like I said. And there's more.' He produced another poke. 'It's salt. She said we'd need that.'

Nancy clapped her hands. 'I never thought I would be so grateful for simple things like bread and salt, but I could weep for joy.' She fingered the smooth oval eggs thoughtfully. 'But we must ration ourselves because we don't know how long we will be here.'

'What's the weather like, Mr Jones?' Todd asked. 'Is there any sign of a thaw?'

'Not really, son. It's freezing hard but the constable said he'll get some of the farm workers to try and right Mrs Cottingham's carriage.'

Jones opened the scullery door. 'I'll bring the milk in and then I'll take the horse to the stable.'

'Tell Curtis I'm making buttered eggs for breakfast,'

Nancy said cheerfully. 'We'll have one slice of bread each. The rest we'll save for our next meal.'

'I could eat the whole loaf all to myself.' Todd licked his lips.

Nancy cooked the eggs and sliced the bread as thinly as she could, spreading it sparingly with butter. She put some aside for Madden and took it to him with a cup of tea laced with milk. He stared at her as if dumbfounded by a simple act of kindness, and his eyes filled with tears.

'You shouldn't waste your food on me,' he said gruffly.

Nancy was not fooled. She handed him the plate and placed the cup and chipped saucer on a small table in front of him. 'It's the least we can do. But for you allowing us to stay we might have been shivering in a barn, or worse. We're just waiting for the weather to improve a little and for the village men to right the carriage, and we'll be off.'

'I'll come down a little later to check on the patient.'

'Thank you, Mr Madden. She isn't in pain while she's seated on the sofa. I did have to help her to the privy and that was difficult, but she seems much better, especially now she's had some food.'

Madden picked up the plate and ate ravenously. 'I'm sorry,' he said with his mouth full. 'Manners go out of the window when there is something good to eat. I've only eaten raw eggs for the last four years, and I can't say I enjoy them.'

'Why didn't you light the fire in the range? You could have made yourself much more comfortable.' Nancy looked round the bare room and shivered. 'It's freezing up here, too.'

'I didn't want to light a fire. The smoke from the

chimney would have alerted people to my continued presence, but I do put a match to the fire in here at night when it becomes too cold to bear.'

'You know, sir, you cannot continue like this for ever. One day you will become ill and there will be no one to look after you.'

'I will die here alone. So be it.'

Nancy left him to finish his tea. There was no reasoning with him, but she was not one to give up easily. Here was a man who had once contributed his surgical talents to society, and but for a tragic incident, for which he was not responsible, he would be considered a pillar of the community and would be saving lives. She was not about to let him dwindle into nothingness. She went downstairs, pondering the problem with each step.

* * *

Later that morning Nancy was in the kitchen, helping Flossie to prepare the last of the root vegetables to add to the saucepan of boiling water, when Curtis came into the kitchen. He had used the time he had spent in the barn with the horses to make a pair of crutches from two old brooms. 'I found a rusty saw and hacked off the bristles,' he said proudly. 'I covered the straw with material from a pair of old curtains from the coach house. Mrs Cottingham will be able to move about more easily now,' Curtis said proudly. 'I enjoy a bit of carpentry, although this was not very difficult.'

'That's excellent, Curtis,' Nancy said appreciatively. 'Why don't you take them to Mrs Cottingham and show her how to use them?'

'She might think it a liberty, miss.'

Nancy put down the paring knife. 'All right. Come with me, we'll do it together.' She led the way to the front parlour where Christina was sitting on the sofa, scowling.

'When are we getting away from this dreadful old house?' she demanded crossly. 'I want to go home.'

'Really? Have you given up the idea of going to Dorrington Place to make trouble for me?'

Christina shrugged. 'I can hardly go in this state, can I? Perhaps it was not such a good idea in the first place.'

'I never thought I'd hear you admit that you'd made a mistake. An apology would be nice, Christina.'

'I'm not in the mood. I suppose you think it's amusing to see me suffering like this.'

'Not at all.' Nancy turned to Curtis, who was standing back, eyeing his mistress warily. 'Show Mrs Cottingham what you've made for her, please.'

Somewhat reluctantly Curtis stepped forward, holding out the homemade crutches. 'I thought it would help you to get about, ma'am.'

'How am I supposed to walk with those?' Christina curled her lip. 'They look ridiculous.'

Nancy took the crutches from Curtis. 'That was very ungrateful. Curtis has gone to a lot of trouble to help you, Christina. The least you could do is to thank him.'

'Oh, yes. I suppose so. Thank you, Curtis. If we ever get out of here I will try to use them.'

'You did well,' Nancy said as she ushered him out of the room. She lowered her voice. 'Has Jones returned from the farm? I sent him to get more eggs.'

'I don't know, miss. I'll go and find out.'

'It's all right. I've got to finish making the soup anyway.' Nancy followed him to the kitchen and found Jones seated at the table drinking a cup of tea. He rose to his feet.

'I was just having a drink, miss.'

'That's all right, Jones. Did you get some more eggs?'

'Yes, miss. Better still, I heard that Farmer Bailey is taking some of his workers to attempt to get the carriage back on the road.'

'Does that mean we will be able to leave?' Nancy asked eagerly.

'There are signs of a thaw setting in, miss. It's only slight but it might allow us to travel.'

'I want to go home,' Flossie said plaintively. 'I hate this house.'

'Well, it seems as if it might be possible. Curtis, you and Jones had better see if you can help the farmer and his men. If we can leave before noon we stand a chance of getting home before dark.'

'Yes, miss.' Jones downed his tea in one hearty gulp. 'Come on, Curtis. We can walk to the road and see if we can give the men a hand.' He shrugged on his greatcoat.

'I can't say I'll be sorry to leave here.' Curtis grabbed his coat and opened the scullery door. 'We'll be back as soon as we can.'

Nancy picked up a paring knife. 'I think we'd better finish making the soup, Flossie. Just in case this is a false alarm. We might be here for some time yet.'

★ ★ ★

The soup was ready and there was still no sign of Jones and Curtis. Nancy took a bowl of the broth to

370

Christina with some thinly cut bread and butter, but just then Madden entered the parlour.

'I'm sorry if this is an inconvenient time. I just came to see how Mrs Cottingham is getting on.'

Christina glared at him. 'I'm as well as can be expected for a cripple.'

Madden laughed, making both Nancy and Christina stare at him in astonishment.

'I'm sorry,' he said, chuckling. 'But you do exaggerate, my dear woman. You will have pain and discomfort for several months, but at the end of that time you will be back to normal.' He turned to Nancy. 'I can see the road from my attic window. It looks as if the men have righted the carriage. Now your progress all depends on how much damage has been done.'

'I hadn't thought of that,' Nancy said, frowning. 'I imagined it would be ready to travel the moment it was upright, but the underside is damaged and the door will need to be fixed back on.'

'Maybe you'll be lucky and it can be easily repaired.' He turned to go but Nancy barred his way.

'Mr Madden, by now the whole village will know that your house is habitable, and they will be curious. I don't think you'll get much peace after we leave.'

'I'll have to set some mantraps about the place.'

'You don't mean that?' Nancy said, horrified.

'No, it was my clumsy attempt at a joke.'

'Seriously, why don't you put the property up for sale? Move on.'

'Who would purchase a dilapidated building like this? Anyway, my life was here. I am content to stay.'

'I don't see how you can be happy to give up on the world. You could do so much good as a medical man.'

'I'm going to my eyrie, Nancy. Please don't come up again.'

'For goodness' sake, sir, stop wallowing in self-pity.' Christina put her spoon down and glared at him. 'You've probably saved my leg and you've allowed us all to shelter after the accident, but if you persist in making a martyr of yourself no one will care.'

Nancy gasped. 'Christina, that was cruel.'

'No, she's right,' Madden said slowly. 'But it's the way I have chosen to live.'

'Come with us when we leave.' Nancy grasped him by the arm. 'Don't bury yourself here in this sad ruin. You can live with us at the Dower House until you find somewhere for yourself. That's if you don't mind sharing with seven young boys and a bear of a man called Wolfe. And you could pass on some of your knowledge to Todd, I'm sure.'

Madden shook his head. 'You make it sound all too easy.'

A knock on the door preceded Flossie, who burst into the room, followed by the constable.

'Is anything wrong?' Nancy asked anxiously.

'I've come to warn you that the man, Jeremiah Stewer, was in police custody, but he escaped this morning and he's armed. He stole a firearm. While he was being held he was babbling on about getting revenge on a certain lady. We believe that must be you, ma'am.' He eyed Christina nervously.

'Stewer did work for me once. I had to let him go because he was totally untrustworthy. I believe it was he who set my house ablaze.'

'We are doing all we can to find him, ma'am, but now your carriage is back on the road I suggest you leave as soon as possible. We will catch Stewer, but it would be safer for you to go home.'

'I couldn't agree more.' Nancy turned to Madden. 'Would you consider travelling with Mrs Cottingham? I would send Todd with her, but he's just a boy.'

Christina paled visibly. 'Do you think there's a real danger, Constable?'

'Indeed I do, ma'am. The man was raving in his cell. I believe he has completely lost his mind and might do anything.' The constable turned to Madden. 'As to you, sir, word has got round that you are here. I would respectfully suggest that you go with the lady for your own safety as well as hers.'

'Mr Madden, please do as the constable says.' Nancy met Madden's gaze with a beseeching look. 'Please, for all our sakes.'

25

Nancy and Madden were the last to leave the house. He had packed what he needed but his last act shocked Nancy to the core. She wondered why he was carrying a lighted oil lamp, and when he tossed it into the entrance hall she could not repress a scream.

'Mr Madden — what are you doing?'

He stepped outside and closed the door. 'The house is worthless. Everyone believes the place is haunted so no one would want to live here. This is my way of saying goodbye to my old life. Thanks to you, Nancy, I have had the courage to leave and face the future, whatever happens.'

Nancy could hear the hiss and crackle of the flames as they took hold of the dry wood and she backed away. 'We'd better hurry. The horses are harnessed and waiting to be off. It's going to be a difficult journey on such icy roads.'

She picked up her skirts and started off towards the road where the others were waiting with the two carriages. Christina had been carried to her carriage, insisting that all she wanted now was to return home to Cottingham Manor. At least her attempts to blacken Nancy's name in Lord Dorrington's eyes had been thwarted, but she was paying a high price for her malice.

Nancy hesitated as she was about to climb into the barouche. She glanced over her shoulder and saw smoke emanating from the house. The sound of glass shattering confirmed that the entire building would soon be ablaze and beyond redemption. Madden saluted her as he mounted the step into Christina's carriage, and Nancy acknowledged him with a nod of her head. In a way she understood his drastic method of saying farewell to his old life, but the house could have provided a home for someone. However, it was Madden's choice. She took her seat next to Flossie.

Todd leaned over to close the door. 'We'll be home soon. I can't wait to see the boys and tell them everything that has happened to us.' He sat back and closed his eyes.

The journey was slow and the road treacherous, but the horses were well rested and eventually they arrived home. It was dark when Nancy, Todd and Flossie alighted from the carriage outside the Dower House. Madden had accompanied Christina to Cottingham Manor at her request, but in Nancy's opinion it would be a brave man who chose to live with the Cottingham family.

The front door opened and Mrs Banks stood there, holding a lantern high to light their way up the path.

'I wasn't expecting you so soon, ma'am. We all thought you would be living in luxury at Dorrington Place.'

'It's a long story, Mrs Banks. We're cold, tired and very hungry.'

Mrs Banks held the door wide open. 'Come inside, ma'am. I have a beef stew bubbling away on the range. It's not what you've been used to, dining with the nobility, but it's hot and tasty.'

'Mrs Banks, beef stew sounds like heaven,' Nancy said enthusiastically. She turned to Todd. 'You will stay for supper, won't you? The boys will want to see you before you return to Dr Bulmer's house.'

'Yes, please, ma'am. Maybe I could stay tonight as the doctor won't be expecting me. I'll go home in the morning, if that's all right with you.' Todd carried the luggage into the entrance hall.

'Of course it is.' Nancy held her arms out as young Jack raced across the tiled floor to fling himself into her arms.

'We missed you, Miss Nancy.'

She gave him a hug. 'Well, I'm home now and soon it will be Christmas. We'll have a lovely party with a big tree and presents.'

'Can May come, too? I miss her.'

Nancy felt a pang of guilt. Little May was only four, if that, and she was happy in the castle nursery with Phoebe, but she was staying at the castle more often, and if Jack missed his sister it was likely that May missed him, too.

'Of course May will come. You can see her every day, if you wish. I'll take you to the castle tomorrow and you can see her then.'

Todd held his hand out to Jack. 'Come on, young fellow. Show me where to find the boys. I've got such a tale to tell them.'

Flossie picked up a piece of luggage in each hand. 'You'd think they was family, wouldn't you, miss?'

Nancy gave her a stern look. 'They are family, Flossie. They are my family.'

★ ★ ★

Next day, as she had promised, Nancy took Jack to Rockwood Castle. She was greeted warmly by Rosalind.

'Well, Nancy, how did it go at Dorrington Place?

376

Tommy told me that you had gone chasing after Christina. Did you manage to stop her from upsetting the earl?'

'Tommy shouldn't have worried you. I asked him not to tell anyone.'

'Nancy, darling, you know Tommy better than anyone. He was like a caged animal. He simply couldn't keep it to himself. In the end I managed to get the truth from him.'

'We didn't get there, Rosie. The roads were treacherous and Christina's carriage overturned on a country lane.'

'My goodness. How awful. Was she hurt?'

'I'll tell you everything, but this young man would like to see his sister.' Nancy gave Jack a gentle push towards Rosalind. 'Would it be all right for him to go to the nursery?'

Rosalind bent down and smiled at Jack. 'Of course you can, darling. You may come here whenever you wish. The girls will be so happy to see you.' Rosalind beckoned to Bertha, who was about to carry the cases upstairs. 'Will you take Master Jack to the nursery, please, Bertha?'

Bertha managed a somewhat clumsy curtsey, hampered as she was by the heavy luggage. 'Yes, ma'am. Come with me, young sir.'

Jack ran off happily and Nancy watched him as he climbed the stairs behind Bertha. 'I keep forgetting how close he was to his sister. Perhaps they should be together.'

'Most definitely. It hurts to be parted from someone you love.' Tommy emerged from the morning parlour. 'I thought I heard your voice, Nancy. It's good to have you home again.'

Nancy smiled. 'I must admit I always feel at home here.'

'You know how to make that permanent,' Tommy said with a teasing grin.

A loud clatter made them all turn their heads to see the gauntlet had fallen from the suit of armour and lay on the floor, one metal finger pointing in Nancy's direction.

'Sir Denys agrees with me,' Tommy added, laughing. He picked up the gauntlet and fixed it back in place. 'You'll lose your head one day, old chap.' Tommy patted the helmet and the visor closed as if Sir Denys was agreeing with him.

'Leave the old fellow alone, Tommy.' Rosalind took Nancy by the hand. 'Come into the parlour and tell me everything.'

'I'm coming, too.' Tommy grasped Nancy's free hand. 'I hope you told the Dorringtons that you are too good for their family. I want you here, for ever.'

'Do stop teasing her, Tommy.' Rosalind pushed the parlour door open with her free hand. 'I'll send for some coffee and we can sit round the fire and hear Nancy's news.'

Nancy withdrew from their grasp and took a seat on the sofa. Tommy sat down beside her.

'I'm serious, Nancy. I hope you didn't do anything rash.'

'No, Tommy. As a matter of fact I never reached Dorrington Place.'

Rosalind tugged at the bell pull. 'So you said. This sounds very interesting. What happened?'

'I knew I shouldn't have let you go with just Todd to look after you,' Tommy said bitterly. 'Thank goodness you're here safe and sound.'

'Let her speak, Tommy.' Rosalind sank down in her usual chair by the fire. 'Go on, Nancy. Start at the beginning.'

Nancy related the happenings in detail, with Tommy interrupting constantly and Rosalind telling him to be quiet. In the end Nancy reached the conclusion, leaving them both open-mouthed.

'So you brought this disgraced surgeon back to Rockwood?' Rosalind gazed at her in surprise. 'What will he do without a home or an income?'

'I can't say, but he couldn't stay there, and with Stewer on the run it was too dangerous for Christina to travel alone, especially with her leg splinted.'

'I'd like to meet this man,' Tommy said suspiciously. 'He sounds very odd.'

Nancy glared at him. 'You can't say things like that. He's probably saved Christina from becoming a cripple.'

Tommy rose to his feet. 'I want to meet him. It seems to me that Christina has brought her problems down on us. She's brought a mad doctor back to Rockwood and that man Stewer, having escaped from custody, is now on the loose.'

Rosalind motioned him to sit down again. 'Calm down, Tommy. Stewer is after Christina and is best left to the police, but I agree that we should meet the disgraced surgeon. It does sound as if he could do with some friends.'

'He might be a little deranged to have lived like a hermit for so long,' Tommy said bluntly.

'Stop it, Tommy.' Nancy shook her finger at him. 'I can promise you he is quite sane. Just wait until you've met the man.'

Tommy resumed his seat beside her. 'All right, but

he can't live here. He can stay with Christina and Oscar.'

Rosalind laughed. 'Poor man. That would be a worse punishment than prison.'

Nancy looked round at the sound of the door opening, expecting it to be Tilly answering the summons of the bell, but it was Hester who marched into the room.

'Well, miss, are you going to be the next Viscountess Ashton, or did Christina do her worst?'

'Really, Hester, that's a bit harsh,' Rosalind said, sighing. 'Leave poor Nancy alone. She's had a very trying few days.'

'Yes, and she's lucky to be here,' Tommy added mischievously. 'She's been in a haunted house with a mad surgeon and Jeremiah Stewer on the rampage. Nancy never does things by halves.'

Nancy giggled. 'Really, Tommy, you do exaggerate.'

He threw up his hands. 'What exaggeration? I think that puts it in a nutshell. I have to tell you, Hester, that Nancy never got as far as Dorrington Place. The weather took a turn for the worse and then she became involved with the madman.'

'You are a silly boy, Tommy Carey,' Hester said crossly. 'Now, Nancy. I want to hear it from your lips. What is Tommy talking about?'

Rosalind turned to Tilly, who had slipped into the room unnoticed by the others. 'We'll have coffee and cake, if there is any, please, Tilly. It looks as if we are going to be here for quite a while.'

Tilly bobbed a curtsey and hurried from the room.

'Do you know, I'm getting tired of telling this story,' Nancy said, yawning. 'Could we leave it until everyone is here? I might lose my voice if I have to keep repeating it again and again.'

'Good idea.' Tommy stood up and pulled Nancy to her feet. 'Come and look at the Christmas tree we've put up in the drawing room. It's the biggest one we could find and I need your help to decorate it.'

'What about the boys?' Nancy allowed him to lead her from the room. 'They are just children. They would enjoy putting on the baubles and tinsel.'

'So would I. Come on, Nancy. You and I have done this so many times in the past. Let's do it now, for old times' sake.'

'There will be plenty of Christmases, Tommy.'

'But I fear things are going to change. I want to keep them as they are now, Nancy.'

'Nothing will ever be different between the two of us, Tommy.'

'That's what I'm afraid of.' He took her by the hand and led her to the drawing room, where a handsome pine tree stood in the window. On the floor beside it, the familiar wooden boxes containing the Christmas decorations were set side by side. 'Come on, Nancy. The boys are still in school and this may be our last chance to do this as we used to when we were young.'

Nancy laughed. 'All right. But the boys can do the tree in the entrance hall.'

'Agreed.' Tommy plucked a strand of tinsel and twisted it into a circlet, which he placed on Nancy's head. 'I crown you queen of the castle. You've always been the queen of my heart.'

'Stop talking nonsense and let's make the tree beautiful.'

They worked in perfect unison, hanging the glass baubles and draping the sparkling tinsel over the branches. They had just finished and were standing back, admiring their handiwork, when the door opened and Freddie strolled into the room.

'The tree looks splendid,' he said conversationally.

Tommy bristled. 'What are you doing here, Ashton? You are not welcome.'

'I think that's up to N-Nancy.'

Nancy turned to Tommy, laying her hand on his sleeve. 'Will you give us a few minutes on our own, please, Tommy?'

'He'll try to persuade you that he's in earnest, Nancy. Then he'll do what he always does and he'll run away to Dorrington Place and hide.'

'That's not fair,' Nancy protested. 'Please, Tommy. Five minutes is all I ask.'

Freddie stood his ground, saying nothing, and with obvious reluctance, Tommy left the room. 'But I'll be waiting outside if you need me,' he called loudly as he shut the door.

Nancy struggled to keep her feelings in check. She did not know whether to be pleased or angry with Freddie, but somehow she managed to speak calmly. 'Tommy was right. Why are you here, Freddie?'

'It's almost Christmas. I m-miss you, Nancy. I w-wanted to make one last attempt to persuade you t-to hear me out.'

'Freddie, there is no point. I know you are fond of me. You might even love me, in your own way, but your heart belongs elsewhere.'

'I d-don't love L-Letitia.'

Nancy spotted a glass bauble they had missed and she bent down to take it from the box. 'Your parents approve of her and I know that makes a difference to you. I've done my best to do what Lord Dorrington demanded of me, but I know now that I'm not the

sort of person he sees as being suitable for you, Freddie.'

'B-but it's what I w-want that matters.'

Nancy fastened the last decoration to the tree. 'You
want a biddable wife who won't mind playing second best to the huge estate and all it entails. I'm sure
you do love me, in your way, but I realise that's not
enough, Freddie.'

He gazed at her with shoulders hunched and a
downturn of his lips. 'I do love you. You can have
whatever you wish — jewels, fine clothes, a thorough-
bred horse and your own carriage. Anything.'

'Those things don't matter to me. You are asking
me to abandon my boys and everyone here. The sad
part is that I would never be considered part of your
family.'

'That's not true, Nancy.' Freddie's distress was pat-
ent.

'I'm afraid it is because your parents would always
think of me as an outsider and someone unworthy of
you. If we had children, the boys would be taken from
me at an early age and sent to schools where they
were beaten into becoming men. The girls would be
educated just enough to make them a valuable com-
modity on the marriage market.'

'You're wrong. I wouldn't l-let that h-happen.'

'You wouldn't be able to prevent it, Freddie. It's
just the way that your family have always lived.'

'You could b-bring about change.'

She shook her head. 'You've seen what's happened
with Greystone Park. I did my best but in the end
I was the interloper. I might own the land but I'm
happy living in the Dower House with my boys. With
the new theatre and the hotel attached I am glad to

383

give something to the rest of the country to enjoy and appreciate. And, of course, Mrs de Marney will be in her element. She can cast herself in leading roles until she drops from exhaustion.'

'Is there nothing I can say that will change your mind?' Freddie held out his hands, his eyes brimming with tears.

'No, Freddie. You'll thank me in years to come. Marry Letitia and take care of your estate. Become the Earl of Dorrington and fulfil your destiny. I do love you, but not so desperately that I would risk your future happiness and mine.'

Freddie seemed about to argue but at that moment the door burst open and Tommy strode into the room.

'You heard her, old chap. I am sorry for you, but Nancy knows her own mind. I think you should go now.'

Freddie bowed his head. 'I'll give you until the New Year, Nancy. If you have second thoughts you must come to Dorrington Place and we will talk again.'

'There's really nothing to discuss.' Nancy turned away. It hurt her to reject Freddie, but in her heart she knew that they were still poles apart and it was a gap that they might never bridge. She did not want to take that risk and end up making both of them unhappy. Her heart ached both for Freddie and for herself.

'I'll go now,' Freddie said disconsolately.

'Just a minute.' Tommy laid a hand on Freddie's shoulder. 'It's started snowing again; the roads will be very treacherous, as we found out to our cost. Why not stay with us here at the castle for Christmas?'

'Tommy?' Nancy stared at him in disbelief.

'No, I mean it,' Tommy said firmly. 'Ashton has

come all this way to try to win you, but he knows now he's failed. The least we can do is to offer him some hospitality until the weather improves.'

'But he'll be expected at home,' Nancy protested. 'In three days' time it will be Christmas Eve and Lady Letitia will be waiting for him.'

Freddie gave her a wry smile. 'D-do you really c-care, Nancy?'

'You know I do, Freddie. I would like us to be friends, if that were possible.'

'If that's all I can expect, I suppose it will have to do.'

Tommy slapped him on the shoulder. 'Well said, old chap. Come with me and I'll show you round the castle while the servants make a room ready for you.'

'Really, Tommy. You ought to have checked with Hester or Rosie that there's a suitable room available, especially with Lady Pentelow and Aurelia staying here.'

'We've got plenty of room,' Tommy protested. 'I'm trying to do the right thing, Nancy.'

'Don't worry, I'll send for Tilly.' Nancy rang the bell for a servant. 'She'll know exactly what to do. You go off and show Freddie the dungeons or whatever you were planning.'

Tommy blew her a kiss. 'I knew I could rely on you, Nancy.'

She watched them leave the room, chatting to each other as if they were lifelong friends. They were like small boys in the school playground and she shook her head, wondering if men ever really and truly grew up.

Nancy waited until she had spoken to Tilly before going to the parlour to tell Rosalind and Hester that

Tommy had invited another guest for Christmas. Tilly had confirmed that there was a solar in the east tower that might suit Lord Ashton, and although Hester rolled her eyes and sighed, she left the parlour and went below stairs to speak to Cook as well as sending the cleaning woman to the east tower to make the chamber ready for occupation.

'It is snowing hard,' Rosalind said, gazing out of the parlour window. 'But I still don't understand why Tommy invited his rival to stay for Christmas.'

Nancy shrugged. 'I'm not a prize to be won in a raffle. Freddie knows how I feel and I think he's accepted the fact that we aren't suited, much as I love him, and I do.'

'But it wouldn't be enough,' Rosalind finished the sentence for her. 'I understand, but Tommy is another matter. You know he's loved you since he was a little boy. I don't think he will ever change.'

'I can't imagine my life without him,' Nancy said thoughtfully. 'Being with Tommy is like the air that I breathe. Sometimes I feel we are the same person, joined by invisible cords.'

Rosalind smiled gently. 'Life is complicated, my dear. Anyway, I'm going up to the schoolroom. Louise sets lessons for the children and Jennet makes sure they do them, which is working out rather well. Dolly is a bright child, even if I say so myself. Rory can do well if he concentrates, although he is so like Alex that all he wants to do is to play soldiers or ride the pony we bought him for his birthday.'

'I hope you don't mind Jack coming every day. He misses his sister so much.'

'Of course not.' Rosalind rose to her feet. 'Jack is a dear child. You've done so well with the other boys,

Nancy. You've saved them from being a bunch of feral street urchins, and you've given them back their childhood. You should be proud of yourself.'

'I don't know about that, Rosie. Nick has played a huge part in their progress, and so has Miss Collins. Now I have Wolfe to instil a little discipline into their routine. Everyone has helped me.'

'I'm glad. It was a brave undertaking and it could have proved to be a terrible mistake.' Rosalind went to open the door. 'And talking about Nick Gibson, I suppose you know that Aurelia has taken one of her fancies to him. They've been inseparable more or less since she arrived. Aurelia says it's because she is enthusiastic about the theatre project, but I know her too well.'

'Where is she now? I haven't seen her since we returned.'

'She'll be with my mother, poring over plans for the interior of the theatre. I wouldn't be surprised if Aurelia suddenly found that she could sing — she can definitely put on an act when it suits her.'

Rosalind led the way to the schoolroom, which was part of the old nursery suite, and a burst of song greeted them as they entered.

Standing on her desk, nine-year-old Dolly Blanchard was singing her heart out. Her childish soprano was as clear and pure as that of a choirboy and her pitch and tone were perfect. She came to a sudden halt, eyeing her mother warily.

'Good morning, Mama.' Dolly smiled sweetly.

'Get down before you fall and hurt yourself,' Rosalind said crossly, but Nancy was quick to hear a note of suppressed laughter in her voice.

'I'm so sorry, ma'am.' Jennet rose from her seat,

clasping her hands together nervously. 'Miss Dolly likes to perform, but we have been doing our lessons.' She cast a sideways glance at Rory, who was lining up a set of lead soldiers on his desk with Jack at his side, looking on enviously.

Seated quietly in a corner, May and Phoebe were playing with two rag dolls, both of which had scarlet woollen hair, which they were endeavouring to plait.

Dolly leaped from the desk, landing neatly on the floor beside her chair. 'Grandmama says I have a good voice. Maybe I can perform on the stage in the new theatre when it's built.'

'Yes, perhaps,' Rosalind said casually. 'But you need to learn your lessons before you can even think about going on the stage. That can come when you are older.'

'We have been working, ma'am.' Jennet gazed anxiously at Rosalind. 'Master Rory is not very keen on learning his times tables.'

'I'm going to be a soldier like Papa and Uncle Bertie,' Rory said firmly.

'Your papa knows his times tables, but if you don't learn them he will think you are a silly boy. You wouldn't want that, would you?'

Rory's bottom lip stuck out and his eyes filled with tears. Nancy had to resist the urge to hug the rebellious six-year-old. She gave Jennet an encouraging smile instead. 'You are doing very well with them. I remember struggling with my nine times table, but I learned it in the end.'

'Try harder, darling,' Rosalind said, ruffling Rory's hair. 'We'll leave you to finish your lessons today and as it's almost Christmas you may have a week without any lessons at all. That will give Jennet a rest, too.'

'Thank you, ma'am.' Jennet smiled and nodded.

'You will be needed below stairs anyway,' Rosalind added. 'We have so many guests it's going to be a very busy festive season. But should the man who treated Christina's injury turn up at our door, please don't invite him to stay, unless he wishes to bivouac in the cellars.'

26

It was still snowing when Tommy drove Nancy home in the chaise later that day. The boys had walked over to help with the Christmas tree in the entrance hall, which they completed with much merriment and a good deal of scolding from Hester, who did not approve of small boys in general. Wolfe had come to collect them in an old sleigh that had been left to rot away in one of the outbuildings at Greystone Park, and which he had resurrected in secret and had brought back to almost as good as new. It was pulled by a pair of sturdy Welsh cobs from the Greystone stables. The boys clambered into it and Wolfe stood on the back plate holding the reins. Nancy clapped her hands and smiled to see the boys' delighted faces and rosy cheeks as they drove off, shouting and urging the horses to go faster as the sleigh bells rang out into the crisp cold air.

Wolfe and the boys had been home for a while before Nancy and Tommy arrived. The mouth-watering aroma of hot spices, citrus peel and cooking sherry greeted Nancy as she said goodbye to Tommy and entered the house. Mrs Banks had obviously been very busy in the kitchen, making mince pies, and had boiled a large ham. The mixture of sweet and savoury smells made Nancy realise how hungry she now felt. She had eaten very little at luncheon, although lack of appetite did not seem to affect either Tommy or Freddie. They appeared to be suddenly on the best of terms and that had made Nancy nervous. However, now she was at home in her comfortable surroundings with the sound of the boys' voices and their laughter ringing in her ears. She went to the parlour and sat by the fire, staring pensively into the flames as they licked around the pine logs, crackling and spitting. The smell of the burning sap filled the small room with a comfortingly familiar fragrance.

She was startled out of her reverie by a knock on the door. Flossie entered, bobbing a curtsey.

'Excuse me, miss, but there's a gentleman to see you. He won't go away no matter what I say to him.'

'Who is it, Flossie?'

'He said his name is Madden. And that you would know him.'

Nancy's heart sank. She should have known that Christina would not want to have him around now that she was safe and at home.

'Show him in, please, Flossie.'

'Yes, miss.' Flossie backed out of the room.

Moments later Madden entered, standing in the doorway with his top hat clutched in his hands. A sprinkling of snow on the shoulders of his greatcoat was melting rapidly. Nancy noticed that his trousers were soaked to knee level, as if he had walked through deep snow.

'I do apologise for intruding, Miss Greystone.'

Nancy rose to her feet. 'Have you walked all the way from Cottingham Manor, sir?'

'Yes. I had no alternative. Mrs Cottingham dispensed with my services and I did not know where else to go. I regret to say I am financially embarrassed until I can get to a bank. I've been withdrawing enough funds to last me for several months at a time, but I need to get to Exeter to make this possible.'

'I see. Well then, you must stay here for tonight at least. I'm sure my maid can find you a place to sleep. In the meantime, please come and sit by the fire. You need to dry your clothes.'

'I can sleep in the stable with the horses. I really don't want to put you to any trouble.'

'You sheltered us when we needed it, Mr Madden. It's the least I can do.' Nancy tugged at the bell pull. 'You'll join us for dinner, of course. My boys will be very interested to meet someone like you. I'm sure you have tales you could tell them.'

Madden shrugged off his coat and hung it over the back of a chair. He pulled a face as he sank into a chair by the fire, and steam billowed off his wet trouser legs.

Nancy waited until Flossie returned and gave her instructions to make up a bed for Madden. 'But first I think a cup of tea with a generous dash of brandy might be a good thing. And please tell Cook there will be one more for dinner tonight.'

Flossie eyed him curiously but she left the room without making any comment.

'Now then,' Nancy said, fixing Madden with a straight look. 'Have you any family you could go to, Mr Madden? As I said, you are welcome to stay here for as long as necessary, but you cannot go back to being a recluse. It's a terrible waste of your talent and expertise.'

A grim smile curved Madden's lips. 'I thought I could renounce the world and live like a hermit, but it seems I was mistaken.'

Nancy eyed him thoughtfully. 'I think I might know someone who can help you, but for the moment just concentrate on getting warm and having a good night's sleep. Hester always says that things will look better in the morning.'

The tea and brandy had a soporific effect and Madden dozed in the chair by the fire while Nancy went to make sure that a room had been made ready for him. She primed the boys and when they sat round the dinner table later that evening Madden proved to be an instant success as a storyteller. He had travelled widely during his professional life and he regaled the children with stories of his experiences in faraway lands. They sat mesmerised by him, and when he came to an end they bombarded him with questions. Wolfe remained unimpressed by their guest but he limited his feelings to glowering looks as he sent the boys to wash and get ready for bed.

★ ★ ★

Next morning Nancy set the boys the task of going out to collect holly and a Christmas tree for the drawing room at the Dower House while she took one of the ponies and rode to Rockwood Castle. It was Felicia she wanted to see and she found her in the small parlour that she and Claude had commandeered for their own use.

'Well, I haven't seen you for a while,' Felicia said, buttering a slice of toast. 'What can I do for you, Nancy?'

'As a matter of fact it isn't about me, Mrs de Marney. You've probably heard about our recent stay in a strange house and the eccentric surgeon who set Christina's broken bone.'

'Yes, Rosalind mentioned something of the sort.'

393

Felicia took a dainty bite of toast.

'Well, Christina has thrown the man out to fend for himself. He's obviously a talented surgeon who has fallen on hard times.'

'I thought he killed someone.'

'A patient died, and although it wasn't his fault, the whole community blamed him for her death. His life was threatened and his house set on fire. He's lived in fear for the past four years and all his talent as a surgeon is being wasted.'

'Well, my dear, that is a sad story indeed, but I don't see what I can do about it.'

'Mr Madden needs help and I was wondering if Sir Bentley might take an interest in him. He uses his money to fund so many charities that I wondered if he could recommend Mr Madden for a position in one of the hospitals he supports.'

'That would be entirely up to Sir Bentley.'

'Yes, of course, but if you could introduce Mr Madden to Sir Bentley at the Christmas party tomorrow you would be helping a good man to get his life back.'

'I suppose it couldn't hurt.' Felicia scooped more butter onto her toast. 'I've been wondering how to make myself known as a philanthropist as well as an operatic phenomenon. In fact, I am considering turning the theatre into a charitable institution, which of course will pay me well as I will be running it. We could help people like Madden who have fallen by the wayside.'

Nancy was not sure that Madden would consider himself quite in that category, but she was not about to disagree with Felicia. 'Yes, it would be a very worthwhile cause.'

'Leave it with me, my dear. I realise now that I

can do anything on which I set my mind. Bring the gentleman to the party tomorrow. It will be a good Christmas for him and for me as well.'

Nancy left the parlour wondering who would benefit most from Felicia's sudden interest in less fortunate people. She suspected that where Felicia was concerned it was she herself who was the most important person in the world.

Nancy was making her way to the drawing room when she met Tommy and Freddie as they emerged from the music room. She came to a halt, staring at them in surprise.

'You two look like lifelong friends. What has brought about such a sudden change?'

Tommy smiled. 'We've come to an understanding, Nancy.'

She eyed them suspiciously. 'What sort of understanding?'

'We both love you, Nancy,' Freddie said earnestly.

Nancy was even more suspicious now. The innocent looks on their faces meant that they had been colluding in something from which she was excluded. 'I'm afraid I haven't time to stand here and indulge in chitchat.' She walked on, intending to see Hester and ask if there was anything she could do for the party, but Tommy caught up with her.

'Freddie spoke the truth, Nancy. We both love you and want you to be happy.'

'I don't want you two vying for my attention.'

'Of course not.' Tommy stroked a stray curl back from her forehead with the tip of his index finger. 'You do love me a little, don't you, Nancy?'

The intense expression in his golden-brown eyes made her heart miss a beat. 'Of course I do.'

'Freddie is a far better catch than I am. You know that.'

Nancy backed away. 'I don't want to talk about it, Tommy. Can we just enjoy the party tomorrow and have a lovely family Christmas with everyone here, including my boys, all of them?'

Tommy laughed. 'Your boys make up a party on their own, and of course they are welcome. I wouldn't have it any other way. We'll even welcome your mad surgeon, if he wishes to attend.'

'Don't worry about Mr Madden. I think I've persuaded Mrs de Marney to take an interest in him and to introduce him to Sir Bentley. These are modern times and the old ways are slowly changing. It's people like Sir Bentley who hold sway in the real world now, not old aristocrats like Lord Dorrington. I learned a lot when I lived in London.'

Freddie had come up behind them unnoticed. 'Is this a private conversation?'

'Nancy is just giving me a lesson in modern politics,' Tommy said, smiling. 'Come with me, Ashton. The snow has eased a little and I'm going to deliver the Christmas gifts to the sick and needy.'

'Doesn't Lambert do that now?' Nancy asked, bewildered.

'He only did it when Papa was alive because it was difficult for Papa to get about. I'm reviving the tradition of the head of the family doing it in person. Do you want to come with us?'

Nancy would have loved to go with them, but she had things to do at the Dower House. She shook her head reluctantly. 'I do, but I need to go and see the older boys and make sure they know they are invited here tomorrow. I'll get them together at the Dower

House first and they can walk here together, if the weather permits.'

She turned to Freddie, frowning. 'Won't they be worried about you at home? Surely you want to be with your family on Christmas Day?'

'I'm a c-coward, Nancy. If I return h-home, Letitia will be there and everyone will expect me to propose. I can use the inclement weather as an excuse.'

'You will have to stand up for yourself one day, Freddie.'

'I-I know, b-but n-not yet. I want to stay for the party. P-perhaps I can learn something from all of you.'

She nodded. 'All right, Freddie, if you are sure, but please don't stay if you're under the impression that I will change my mind.'

'I think I know now,' he said ruefully. 'But we can be friends.'

Nancy reached up and kissed him on the cheek. 'Of course we can. Always the best of friends, Freddie.' She watched him and Tommy walk off together and her heart swelled with love for both of them, although she realised suddenly that her feelings for each of them were very different. She sighed. Nothing was easy.

She went in search of Hester, whose down-to-earth common sense could always be relied upon. There must be plenty of work to do in order to prepare for the Christmas party tomorrow. The whole of the village had been invited for the afternoon celebration to be held in one of the barns, and the family and notables would celebrate with dinner in the evening. The gathering in the barn had been Patricia's idea. It was a break from tradition, but Patricia and Rosalind both agreed that it was time to begin again. They had worked together with Nancy, Jennet and Tilly to make the barn look festive with boughs of holly, paper lanterns and trestle tables covered in gaily coloured cotton cloth. But the Christmas party was not foremost in Nancy's mind as she walked into Hester's parlour.

'What's the matter with you?' Hester demanded, eyeing Nancy suspiciously. 'No, don't tell me — it's those two silly boys who both want to marry you. Better make up your mind which one soon, Nancy, or you'll find yourself an old maid, sitting out the dances with the rest of the matrons and plain girls no man wants to partner.'

Nancy sighed. Hester had an uncanny gift for recognising a problem and getting straight to the point. 'Freddie needs a bride from his own class and Tommy is just a boy.'

'I agree about Freddie, but Tommy is more grown up than you think. That young man has loved you since you were both children. Don't throw that away, Nancy Greystone. Think hard before you reject him. Maybe you were destined to be mistress of Rockwood Castle after all. Perhaps Christina was right in that you didn't belong at Greystone Park.'

'I hadn't thought of it like that,' Nancy said slowly. 'Anyway, I thought you were against anything romantic happening between Tommy and me.'

Hester sniffed. 'Anyone can change their mind. I love that boy as if he were my own, despite what I might say. He's come into his inheritance very young, and to be fair he's coping well with the responsibility, but he needs someone strong at his side.'

'And you think I am that person?'

'That's up to you two. I never interfere.'

'Of course not.' Nancy managed to keep a straight face. Hester had ruled the Carey and Blanchard family for so many years that giving family members her honest opinion came as second nature.

'Well, think about what I just said, but first you can help me to go over the guest list and the final details for tomorrow evening. Louise is making sure the children are taken care of, although Wolfe will have to be responsible for your boys. Alex and Walter are supervising the flaming torches to light the way, although if the snow comes down again and freezes overnight we might find ourselves cut off.'

'I'll do whatever you wish, Hester,' Nancy said vaguely, but her mind was elsewhere. Hester's words had struck home. She knew she would have a lot to think about when she finally went to bed that night. 'Where shall we start?'

★ ★ ★

Nancy left for the castle early next morning. Wolfe and Madden were to bring the boys over later, but Nancy wanted to help the family with the final arrangements. When she arrived she found Patricia and Leo in the barn with Walter and Louise. They were putting the finishing touches to the festive decorations while the servants ferried the food from the castle kitchens. It was only a little warmer in the barn than outside, where the snow had frozen hard overnight and a pale wintry sun reflected off the crystals, turning the world into a winter fairyland. Nancy felt a *frisson* of anticipation race through her veins.

'This is going to be a wonderful party,' Patricia said cheerfully. 'I've booked the musicians to come for the evening entertainment and there will be dancing. In fact, I think I'd prefer to be with the villagers than with the guests in the castle.'

'Knowing you, my love, you will be the life and soul of both parties.' Leo came up behind her and dropped a kiss on her hair. 'I think we're done here. Shall we go back to the castle? I don't want you catching a chill.'

Patricia laughed. 'See how he looks after me. Isn't it wonderful, Nancy?'

'I'm the lucky one,' Leo said gallantly. 'I have a beautiful wife and a healthy son. What more could any man ask for?'

Patricia linked Nancy's hand through the crook of her arm. 'I'm freezing. I could do with a cup of coffee or maybe a tot of something stronger. It is Christmas Eve.'

'I'm coming with you,' Louise added eagerly. 'We can't do any more here.'

'I thought you would be helping to decorate the church for the Christmas services,' Patricia said with a mischievous smile.

'Papa has plenty of eager ladies who are only too pleased to devote their time to keeping the church looking good. He and Mama are coming to the party, which surprised me. They don't usually indulge in such frivolities when it's Easter or Christmas.'

Walter led the way out of the barn. 'Maybe he's going to perform a marriage ceremony for Nancy and Ashton.'

Nancy bent down and scooped up a handful of snow, which she tossed at him. 'Most definitely not, Walter.'

He laughed and strode on towards the castle bailey. Nancy quickened her pace. The sun might be shining but it was still bitterly cold and it was a relief to enter the comparative warmth of the castle entrance hall. She patted Sir Denys on the visor as she went past but one of his gauntlets flew off and landed on the flagstone floor.

'I think he's trying to tell you something, Nancy.' Tommy emerged from the morning parlour. He moved swiftly to retrieve the metal glove and put it back in place. 'What are you saying, Sir Denys?' He leaned closer. 'Ah, he's telling you to listen to what I have to say, Nancy. Sir Denys is on the side of the Careys.'

Nancy laughed. 'You are nonsensical, Tommy.'

'I don't know about that,' Patricia said seriously. 'Sir Denys has a habit of foretelling when anything important is about to happen.'

'Don't listen to them.' Rosalind walked past them, heading towards the drawing room. 'I believe Sir Bentley has arrived. I must do my duty. Come on, Alex, you know Sir Bentley likes to talk to you about your army experiences.'

Alex sighed. 'Yes, my love.' He rolled his eyes. 'The sooner that theatre is built the better. I can't stand that man.' He followed Rosalind to the drawing room.

'Come on, Patsy,' Leo said, taking her by the hand. 'Let's get this over and done with. Your mama exhausts me, and that is saying a lot. I've handled drunken crowds and out-and-out villains in my pub at Puddle Dock, but your mama is a different proposition altogether.'

'Don't be unkind, Leo.' Patricia could not quite keep the laughter from her voice despite her attempt at a frown.

Tommy beckoned to Nancy. 'Can we talk in private?'

'Is anything the matter?'

He took her by the hand and headed for his father's old study. Once inside he closed the door. 'I really need to speak to you without everyone watching and listening.'

'What is it, Tommy?'

'I was thinking that Christmas is a good time to make announcements.'

'What sort of announcements?'

'The best sort — happy things — you know.'

'Not really. What are you talking about?'

'Do you want to marry Freddie?'

'Did he ask you to say that?'

'No, Nancy. I am speaking for myself. Do you want to change your mind and accept Freddie's offer of marriage?'

'He hasn't actually proposed again, Tommy. Where is he, anyway? I haven't seen him this morning.'

'He's doing something for me. Your boys are helping him.'

'Doing what?'

'It's a surprise, but we're getting away from the subject. I want to know how you would answer if Freddie did propose again.'

'My answer would still be the same. I love him but not in the way I used to. Feelings change and the months apart have altered everything. His papa was right.'

'That's all I wanted to know. You know I've always loved you.'

'What are you trying to say, Tommy?'

'I'm trying to find the right words to ask you to be my wife, Nancy. I want to be with you for ever and a day.'

Nancy could see that he was in earnest and she knew suddenly where her future lay. She was about to answer when the door flew open and Hester marched into the room.

'Why are you two hiding away in here? Tommy, you are supposed to be the host. You should go to the drawing room and talk to the guests. Sir Bentley seems put out that you were not around to greet him.'

'We'll go right away,' Nancy said hurriedly. 'We were just discussing the arrangements for the party in the barn.'

'The villagers will sort themselves out. Give them enough food and drink and a bit of music and they're happy. But you, Tommy, are needed elsewhere. Nancy, make him do his duty. I have things to organise.' Hester left the room, creating a cool breeze as the door swung shut behind her.

Tommy sighed. 'One day I will have you all to myself, Nancy.'

She laughed. 'But seemingly not today. We need to meet the guests and chat to them. Anything to keep the peace.' Nancy proffered her hand. 'Come, Sir Thomas, we'd better do our duty.'

'Will you promise to think about what I just said? I was never more serious.' Tommy held the door open and Nancy stepped into the passage that led to the entrance hall.

She came to a halt. 'I know that voice. Tommy, it's Glorina Cottingham. What on earth is she doing here?' Without waiting for him to answer, Nancy walked swiftly to the hall where she saw Glorina arguing with Jarvis.

'I beg your pardon, my lady, but you are not on the guest list.'

Glorina shook her finger at him. 'I am welcome here at any time. Ask Mrs Blanchard.'

'What's the matter, Jarvis?' Nancy hurried towards them.

'Lady Cottingham is not on my list, Miss Nancy.'

One look at Glorina's face was enough to convince Nancy that something important must have driven her here on Christmas Eve, of all days.

'It's all right, Jarvis. I'll take care of this.' Nancy held out her hand. 'Would you like to come with me, my lady? I'll take you to the drawing room.'

Glorina shot a triumphant look at Jarvis, who backed away with his nose in the air. 'Is Mr Madden here, Nancy?'

'Yes, as a matter of fact he's staying with us at the Dower House. I understood that Christina asked him to leave.'

'She did, the silly girl. It's Stewer who is the danger, not Rowland Madden.'

Nancy led her to a quiet spot outside the drawing room. 'Would you like to explain?'

'Rowland Madden is a charming, intelligent man, whose story touched my heart. I don't need a crystal ball to tell me he's a good man, but Jeremiah Stewer is the very opposite.'

'Has he been seen recently?'

'Yes. Our gamekeeper found him lurking in the woods and he chased him off, but Stewer came to the house. He forced his way in through the kitchen and he found Christina on her own in the morning parlour. Not only did he threaten her, but he seems to include Madden in his desire for revenge on the Cottinghams.'

'The police are looking for Stewer, but I don't

404

understand what he has against Mr Madden.'

'In his twisted mind he blames Madden for treating Christina after the accident. He wanted her to suffer.'

'You should have sent for Constable Burton.'

'We did, of course, and he's with Christina now, but I wanted to speak to Rowland in person.'

'Do you really think he's in danger?'

'I know Stewer. He's a nasty, vindictive fellow. He won't be happy until he's created mayhem and misery for the Cottingham family and anyone connected to us.'

'In that case you'd better come into the drawing room with me. We can't allow one man to ruin Christmas for all of us.'

27

Sir Bentley was holding court in the drawing room as if the castle belonged to him, although it seemed strange to see him without his acolytes. Nancy could only assume that he had given them some time off to celebrate Christmas, which was hard to believe. He stood with his back to the fireplace, seemingly impervious to the heat from the flames blazing up the chimney, while he expounded on the advantages of taking culture to the masses. Felicia was seated at his side, gazing up at him with adoring eyes, while Claude scowled at him from a distance.

Alex and Leo had come in from the cold and were drinking mulled wine with Walter and Nick Gibson, leaving Aurelia to gaze at Nick from the far side of the room as she sat dutifully beside her grandmother. Lady Pentelow seemed put out that Sir Bentley had taken over the centre stage, which she was accustomed to claim as her own. Hester took a seat in the corner of the room and Rosalind was left to entertain Rowland Madden. There was no sign of Patricia or Louise, but Nancy guessed they had gone to the nursery to check on the children.

'Rowland.' Glorina ignored everyone else as she crossed the floor to greet him. 'I'm so relieved to find you safe and well.'

Madden took a mouthful of mulled wine and gulped it down. 'I'm delighted to see you, of course, but why should I not be safe, Lady Cottingham?'

'Glorina, please, Rowland. I thought we had gone past formalities earlier this week.'

He raised his eyebrows. 'It was a very pleasant interlude, ma'am, but after you had left, your daughter quite literally turned me out. I was fortunate enough to be given shelter by Miss Greystone.'

Tommy had followed Nancy into the room and he stood behind her. 'What is all this about, Nancy?' he said in a low voice.

'Shh, Tommy. Let Glorina explain.'

'You know all about Stewer, Rowland,' Glorina said patiently. 'Well, he's come back, determined to cause trouble and that includes to you.'

'I'm truly sorry, but what have I got to do with anything?'

'It's simply because you treated Christina when she broke her leg. The man's mind is so twisted that he cannot think straight, which makes him even more dangerous. Christina is well protected at the manor house, especially now we know that Stewer is on the loose, but you, Rowland, have no such defences.'

'My dear lady, I managed well enough on my own when the local people were up in arms and wanted to kill me. I'm grateful for your concern, but you need not worry about me.'

Glorina fluttered her long, dark eyelashes. 'Oh, but I do, sir. And I have a feeling that you will soon be taken under a certain gentleman's wing — a titled and influential gentleman, who is not a thousand miles away from here.'

'Of course,' Rosalind said hastily. 'I was forgetting my manners, Mr Madden. Come with me, if you please. I will introduce you to Sir Bentley, who is fast becoming the patron of Rockwood village.' She led the unprotesting Madden to where Sir Bentley had paused to catch his breath.

Nancy and Tommy stood back, watching Sir Bentley's reactions to Madden, all of which seemed hopeful. Nancy turned to Glorina, who was clasping her hands, her gaze intent upon Madden and Sir Bentley. 'You foresaw this some time ago, didn't you, Glorina? When you came to see me at the Dower House you mentioned a stranger who would come into our midst.'

Glorina dragged her attention from Madden to give Nancy a sly smile. 'I am Romany by birth, Nancy, my dear. I often see things that others do not.'

'And yet you didn't foresee the accident and Christina's injuries.'

'No, my dear. I get flashes of foresight, and then they are gone.' Glorina held Nancy's gaze with a hypnotic stare. 'I foresee happiness for you, Nancy. Well-deserved and true. I hear bells and I see snow, and your heart's desire comes true.'

Nancy struggled with the temptation to giggle, but somehow she managed to keep a straight face. 'Well, it is very snowy outside.'

'Don't mock my ability to see into the future.' Glorina's rouged complexion paled suddenly. 'That man, Stewer. He is not far away and he is intent on doing harm.' Glorina rushed across the room to confront Sir Bentley. 'Sir, your theatre is in danger. There is someone out for revenge on Greystone Park itself.'

Sir Bentley stared at her as if she had gone mad. 'Who is this crazed woman?'

Madden laid his hand on Glorina's arm. 'My dear lady, this is not the time or the place for such histrionics.'

Glorina shook his hand away. 'I am speaking the truth. If you don't believe me, go at once to Greystone Park — you will find the man attempting to destroy the foundations for your theatre.'

Nancy crossed the floor to stand beside Glorina. 'Is it Stewer you see?'

Glorina nodded and collapsed in Madden's arms.

'I think someone should investigate,' Nancy said hastily. 'Just in case.'

Sir Bentley beckoned to Leo, Alex and Walter. 'I am going to Greystone Park, but if this woman is telling lies I will have her burned at the stake — or whatever they do to witches in these parts.'

Alex laughed. 'We don't go that far, Sir Bentley, but Glorina does seem to foretell events. Perhaps we had better go to Greystone Park and make certain Stewer is not creating mayhem.'

'I'll go with you, Alex,' Leo said firmly. 'That fellow needs to be behind bars.'

'And I.' Nick moved to their side while Walter nodded in agreement.

'Then we will all go.' Sir Bentley charged towards the door as if he were a general leading his troops. 'We will return, dear ladies.'

Nancy clutched at Tommy's sleeve as he was about to follow. 'Don't go, Tommy. Stewer is a dangerous man.'

Tommy smiled. 'I survived kidnap and near death from Ewart Blaise when I was a boy. I'm a man now, Nancy. I will protect those I love.' He leaned over and kissed her briefly on the lips.

'I'm coming, t-too,' Freddie said urgently. 'We c-can't allow this m-man to ruin Christmas.'

Nancy was about to follow them but Rosalind held

her back. 'Stay here, Nancy.'

'But Tommy might be in danger.'

'There are plenty of them. Together they will be more than a match for one man, even if he is insane.'

'What's going on?' Lady Pentelow demanded angrily. 'Why have the gentlemen abandoned us? Whatever happened to manners?'

Aurelia rose to her feet. 'Don't worry, Grandmama. They will be back soon, I've no doubt. It's just some trouble at the theatre.'

'Theatre! I don't hold with all those goings-on. Painted women and men who are no better than they should be.'

Felicia marched over to her and stood, arms akimbo. 'Are you including me in that category, Lady Pentelow? Because if you are I am very insulted.'

'You are a show-off, madam. You always have been. Just because you can hit a high note you think you are above everybody.'

Felicia turned to her husband. 'Claude, are you going to allow this woman to speak to me like that?'

Claude made for the doorway. 'I think perhaps I'd better go with Sir Bentley, my dear. After all, should anything happen to him, we would lose everything.'

'Oh, yes. Well hurry then, Claude. Don't waste time standing there.' Felicia shooed him out of the room.

'I'd better tell Cook that luncheon will be delayed,' Hester grunted and marched out of the room.

'I'll go and see if Wolfe has brought the boys from home,' Nancy said hastily. 'I told him to take them straight to the barn, so I want to make sure they are there.'

Rosalind nodded. 'At least they'll be safe from Stewer. I wouldn't put it past him to use the boys as hostages for whatever it is he's after.'

'Who knows?' Nancy sighed. 'I'll go to the barn to make sure they've arrived.' She left the room and snatched her hooded cape from the chair in the entrance hall where she had left it on entering the castle. She wrapped it around her head and shoulders and stepped outside into the cold, much to Jarvis's consternation.

'It's snowing again, Miss Nancy.'

'I won't be long, Jarvis. I'm just making sure the boys are not getting up to any mischief.' She thought she heard Jarvis mutter something about 'dratted boys' beneath his breath but she chose to ignore him.

The ground was slippery and snow was swirling round as if whipped to a frenzy by the cold wind. However, she made it to the barn and found the six younger boys sitting on hay bales, munching meat pies.

'Where did you get those?' Nancy demanded.

Alfie grinned at her. 'Cook gave them to us. We've been helping to bring the food here from the kitchen, so she said this was our wages.'

Nancy sighed with relief. 'You've all done well. Enjoy your pies and later on you may have whatever you want, but only when the rest of the guests have had a chance to eat. I'm going back to the house, so I want you to behave.'

'We will,' Stanley said with an angelic smile.

'Where is Wolfe?'

Alfie swallowed a mouthful of pie. 'He's in the kitchen with Mrs Jackson. She said he looks as if he needs feeding up.'

'She said that Mrs Banks isn't as good in the kitchen as she is,' Stanley added.

'They are both excellent cooks,' Nancy said, smiling. 'The visitors will come soon, if the snow doesn't worsen. If you get too cold you must go to the kitchen. Mrs Jackson will look after you until I get back.'

'Where are you going, miss?' Alfie asked anxiously.

'Just to Greystone Park. I promise I won't be long.' Nancy left them and made her way carefully to the stables where she had left her horse. She was worried about Tommy and she knew she would not rest until she knew that Stewer was recaptured and locked up. He was a threat to her home and those she loved, and she simply could not stay away.

Despite warnings from Pip Hudson that the roads were treacherous, Nancy insisted on riding. Once or twice on the way, when her horse slithered and almost threw her, she wished she had taken Pip's advice, but she managed to stay in the saddle and she reached Greystone Park without mishap. The first person she saw was Tommy who, together with Freddie, was wrestling a man to the ground. Nancy reined her horse in and dismounted, but she was restrained by Leo. He pointed to Constable Burton, who was advancing purposefully on the trio.

Nancy was alarmed. She had never seen Tommy use violence, although she knew that during his time in the army he must have been involved in skirmishes, and Freddie was the most peace-loving person she had ever met. However, it was obvious that they meant business and Stewer was handed over to Constable Burton and his colleague.

Nancy rushed over to Tommy, who had a cut lip and the beginnings of a black eye. Freddie had fared better, but he was brushing the snow off his greatcoat.

'Why was it left to you two?' Nancy demanded

angrily. She glanced around at Leo, Alex, Walter and Nick, who looked rather sheepish, but Sir Bentley waved his hand dismissively.

'Well done, everyone. The two young fellows finished him off, but it was a combined effort that finally did for the villain. I suggest we all repair to the Black Dog for a libation.'

'I rather think we should return to the castle, Sir Bentley,' Alex said firmly. 'The ladies will be anxious, and I want to reassure my wife that there is no danger to anyone now.'

'I agree,' Leo nodded, shaking snow off his clothes. 'I believe a splendid luncheon awaits us, so we should get back as soon as possible.'

'Yes, the fellow didn't manage to do much damage,' Nick added. 'He won't be celebrating Christmas in a good way.'

'What are you doing here, Nancy?' Tommy demanded as the others walked off to untether their horses. 'I thought I told you to stay at home.'

Nancy tossed her head. 'Since when did you start giving me orders, Tommy Carey? I decide what I will and will not do. I was worried about you, and Freddie, too.'

Freddie smiled ruefully. 'It's obvious where your heart really lies, Nancy. I saw it in your face when you realised that Tommy was grappling with the criminal. I know when I'm beaten.'

'Don't say that, Freddie.' Nancy laid her hand on his shoulder. 'You were both very brave. I admire you for going to Tommy's aid. I wish I could love both of you.'

Tommy mopped the blood from his lip on a clean hanky that Freddie handed to him. 'Are you saying you choose me?'

'It's not a competition, Tommy,' Nancy said severely. 'I am not a prize to be won.'

'You want to be wooed?' Tommy put his head on one side, eyeing her thoughtfully. 'I can be romantic.'

Nancy laughed. 'I think it's time we returned to the castle. I'm cold and I'm hungry. Romance doesn't come into it at the moment.' She left them and went to retrieve her horse, which had wandered off. 'Help me up, please, one of you. I don't mind who, but please hurry. I can't feel my fingers or toes.'

* * *

Despite the steady snowfall it seemed that all the able-bodied in the village had made their way to the castle to join in the Christmas Eve celebrations. The family, plus Sir Bentley and Madden, had enjoyed a wonderful luncheon and now they were ready to wait on the servants and guests alike. Rosalind, Patricia and Nancy stood behind the trestle tables filling plates with cold roast beef, sliced ham and pork, garnished with pickled walnuts and other delicacies. Pies, pasties and thick slices of bread, liberally buttered, were disappearing fast, as was the wheel of cheese. The jellies, sherry trifle and mince pies were yet to be sampled, but Nancy had to send warning glances to the boys to keep them from demolishing everything in sight.

When the food was gone Alex, Leo, Nick and Walter stepped in to clear away the tables, and the musicians struck up a lively jig to start off the proceedings. Soon the barn was crowded with couples whirling around the floor, kicking up their heels and clapping in time to the music. Aurelia and Nick led the dancers, and

Nancy was pleased to see that Aurelia looked happy with her attentive partner. Rosalind and Alex were holding each other close as they joined in the dance, as were Patricia and Leo. The barn was filled with laughter and happy faces. It was a result that Nancy could only have dreamed of, but Freddie appeared to be content to stay on the outside, looking on. He stood beside Hester and Lady Pentelow, who sat on chairs brought from the castle, watching the proceedings. Lady Pentelow seemed to be nodding off, but Hester was visibly tapping her toes and even joined in the clapping. Glorina had stayed on and had somehow persuaded Madden to dance with her. Nancy was surprised to see that he appeared to be enjoying himself. Maybe it was Glorina's charms, or perhaps he had supped rather more of the fruit punch than was good for him. Nancy had seen Leo add a flask of brandy to the mixture and it was no surprise that the dancing became even more energetic.

Louise was doing her best to keep her mother occupied, but Nancy was always uncomfortably aware that Mrs Shaw still regarded her as the child they had taken from the orphanage to work in the vicarage. Those early years were best forgotten.

'Why so sad?' Tommy placed his arms around Nancy's waist and whirled her into the waltz.

'I'm not sad. I was just remembering how I first came to Rockwood Castle when Rosie saved me from a life of servitude.'

'And she saved me from Hodges, the chimney sweep,' Tommy added, smiling. 'We were very lucky.'

'Perhaps it was fate,' Nancy said, clutching his hand as they moved in time to the music.

'We were meant to be together, Nancy.'

Tommy held her so close that she felt she was melting into his embrace. The other dancers disappeared into the mist and they were the only couple on the floor.

'Marry me, Nancy,' Tommy whispered in her ear. 'Just say the word. You were destined to be queen of my castle.'

Before Nancy had a chance to respond there was a flourish of a trumpet and the musicians paused, gazing at the barn doors, which had been flung open to allow Felicia and Sir Bentley to make a grand entrance, with Claude hurrying to be at his wife's side.

'Don't stop on my account,' Sir Bentley said graciously. 'Please continue with these rustic revels.' He proffered his arm to Felicia. 'I believe this is a waltz. May I have the honour?'

Claude stepped in before Felicia had a chance to accept. 'I rather think this is my dance, Sir Bentley. I am sure Lady Carey would be delighted to partner you.' He grasped Felicia round the waist and propelled her into the midst of the stunned onlookers. 'Musicians, continue to play, if you please.'

Sir Bentley stood for a moment as if frozen to the spot, but the band continued where they had left off and everyone swung into motion. Sir Bentley was left with little choice and he marched up to Hester, bowing as he asked her to dance.

'Hester wins,' Nancy said in a low voice, suppressing a giggle.

'Good for Claude.' Tommy spun Nancy round with surprising expertise. He met her surprised expression with a smile. 'I learned to dance in the army. The colonel's daughter was very persistent.'

'You mean Cordelia?'

'Yes, I believe she had a fancy for me at one time, but my heart has always belonged to you, Nancy.'

'You really mean that, don't you, Tommy?'

'You know I do. I might have died in Gibraltar if you had not come and dragged me back to the land of the living.'

'That's silly.'

'No. I'm serious. I was about to give in and slip away. But you appeared like an angel and I knew I had to fight to stay alive. I want you to marry me, Nancy.'

'But my boys, Tommy — what will happen to them?'

Tommy led her from the dance to a quieter spot by the door. 'They will be part of our family. I suggest we let them have the Dower House with Wolfe in charge. I'll see that they finish their education, or take apprenticeships when they are old enough. We'll take care of them together.'

'I don't know, Tommy. I do love you, but maybe we ought to wait a while. Do you really want to be tied down so young?'

'My darling Nancy. I grew up a lot during my brief time in the army, and taking on the estate has made me much more responsible. I know what I want and that is to be with you for the rest of my days. Do you trust me?'

She blinked away tears of happiness. 'Of course I do.'

'Will you marry me, Nancy?'

'I don't suppose you will give me a moment's peace until I say yes.'

'You know me so well.' Tommy swept her into his arms and kissed her. 'Let's enjoy the rest of the evening and I'll see you safely home. Tomorrow will be the most wonderful Christmas ever. I have it all planned.'

Nancy glanced out through the partially closed doors. 'It's snowing even harder, Tommy. We might be forced to spend Christmas apart if the roads are impassable.'

'That won't stop me. Nothing will. I am determined to make this Christmas memorable.' He proffered his arm. 'Let's dance and forget the snow. Forget everything other than the fact that we're here together.'

★ ★ ★

Next morning Nancy awakened to a cold white light striking through a gap in the bedroom curtains. She knew only too well what that meant. It had been a difficult journey coming home from the castle last evening as it had been snowing heavily. She leaped out of bed and padded barefoot across the floor to draw the curtains. Below was a scene of wintry whiteness. The snow had ceased but it had drifted before it settled and was obviously quite deep.

A knock on the door preceded Flossie, who entered carrying a cup of hot chocolate.

'Good morning, Flossie. Merry Christmas.'

'Merry Christmas, Miss Nancy.' Flossie placed the cup and saucer on the dressing table, but instead of leaving her mistress to enjoy the hot drink, she went to the clothes press and took out a shimmering white garment that made Nancy stare in surprise.

'Where did that lovely gown come from, Flossie? It's not mine.'

Flossie grinned as she carried the gown and laid it reverently on the bed. 'It is yours, miss. Sir Thomas had it made especially for you. I'm to help you dress when you're ready.'

Nancy went to the bed and fingered the delicate silk chiffon spun with silver thread running through the fine material. 'It's beautiful, but it looks too fine to wear in the morning. It's a ball gown, the like of which I've never seen. Anyway, I'll freeze to death if I wear that.'

'There's more, miss. I've to show you, but I was sworn to secrecy. Mrs Wilder and Mrs Blanchard made me promise not to tell you.'

'Oh, heavens! They're all in it. I'm beginning to suspect a conspiracy.'

Flossie took another garment from the clothes press, and this time it was a crimson velvet cloak with a fur-lined hood. 'You won't feel the cold in this.'

Nancy glanced out of the window. 'I don't think I'll be going anywhere this morning. Have you seen the snow?'

'Yes, miss. It's quite deep.'

Nancy shivered as she sipped the rapidly cooling chocolate. 'I will try the gown on, but I'll wear my tartan linsey-woolsey gown to the castle. I appreciate the gift, but it's not suitable for a day like this.'

Despite Nancy's arguments Flossie was insistent and eventually Nancy agreed to slip the garment over her head. Despite the chill in the room, not quite dispelled by the roaring fire, Nancy had to admit that it was a beautiful gown. She even allowed Flossie to put up her hair and stud the curls with white silk orange blossom.

'I look like a bride,' Nancy said mistily. 'He did

propose last evening.'

'You are a beautiful bride, miss.' Flossie wiped a sentimental tear from her eyes. 'I was to have you ready to leave for the castle at half past nine.'

'Well, I'm afraid that won't be possible. The carriage won't stay on the road, even if it makes it as far as the front door. We'll be staying at home for Christmas unless there is a miracle and a thaw sets in.'

'The boys are waiting in the entrance hall, miss.' Flossie's voice shook with excitement. 'You can't disappoint them. At least allow them to see you looking like a princess.'

Nancy smiled. 'You are a sentimental girl, Flossie.' But she did not want to disappoint her, and Nancy hurried downstairs.

The boys were dressed in their Sunday best and were in the process of putting on their coats and mufflers. They stopped when they saw her and stared open-mouthed.

'You look lovely, miss,' Alfie said admiringly.

'Like an angel,' Stanley added.

Teddy sniffed and was given a hug by Rob, while Joe and Mick raced to open the front door. The jingling of bells made Nancy cross the floor to look over their shoulders. She added to their cries of delight as the old sleigh, now painted bright red and decorated with swags of holly and scarlet ribbons, was drawn by the two Welsh cobs. Pip Hudson stepped down from the rear of the sleigh.

'Here, miss. You'll need this now.' Flossie draped the cloak around Nancy's shoulders and Wolfe appeared, as if from nowhere. He swept Nancy off her feet and carried her to the sleigh, settling her down gently and covering her knees with a woollen rug. He stepped back.

'We'll follow you, Miss Nancy. I'll see that the boys come to no harm.'

Nancy was rendered speechless as Pip urged the horses to a walk and the sleigh slid effortlessly over the hard-frozen snow.

They arrived at the church, where most of the village seemed to have turned out, even on Christmas morning. Alex was waiting for her by the lychgate and he carried her through the snow to the porch, where he set her down on her feet. To Nancy's astonishment, Dolly, Phoebe and May were dressed in pink velvet and they carried little posies of Christmas roses. Rosalind handed Nancy a similar but larger bunch of flowers.

'You didn't think Tommy would let you go, did you, Nancy?' Rosalind said, smiling. 'You look beautiful, by the way.'

'I'm stunned. I wasn't expecting all this,' Nancy said shakily.

Walter stepped forward. 'Will you allow me to give you away, Nancy? Although as I'll be giving you to my nephew, I'm really welcoming you into the family for ever this time.'

'Yes, of course, Walter. Thank you.' Nancy tucked her hand in the crook of his arm and the organist began to play Wagner's 'Wedding March', which had been made popular after Princess Victoria's wedding twenty years before.

'Only the best for you and Tommy,' Walter said in a low voice. 'The boy has been planning this for weeks. Thank goodness you said 'yes'. As Hester would say, best foot forward, Nancy, dear.'

They processed up the aisle and every pew was packed. A sea of smiling faces turned to greet Nancy but they melted into the mist when she spotted Tommy waiting by the altar. He looked incredibly handsome in his wedding attire and not a bit nervous. Standing at his side as best man was Freddie, and the Reverend George Shaw was waiting to perform the marriage ceremony.

Nancy handed her flowers to Dolly, who was taking her chief bridesmaid duties very seriously, and the service began. Somehow Nancy managed to make her responses and they were heartfelt, even though the whole thing had taken on a dreamlike atmosphere.

The register was duly signed and Nancy walked back down the aisle on her husband's arm. When they reached the church doors, Tommy took her in his arms and kissed her to tumultuous applause from those braving the cold outside.

'I am so proud of you, Nancy. I want the whole world to know how wonderful you are, my beautiful snow bride.'